THE ENTROPY OF EVERYTHING:
THE INDESTRUCTIBLES BOOK 3

by
Matthew Phillion

The Entropy of Everything: The Indestructibles Book 3

Lost Continuity Press
P.O. Box 1044
Salem, MA 01970

First Printing: PFP Publishing, July 2015
Second Printing: Lost Continuity Press, November 2018
Printed in the United States of America

ISBN-13:978-0-9979165-7-7
(also available in eBook format)

Front cover design:
Sterling Arts & Design

Praise for *the Indestructibles* series

It's refreshing to have the book's one truly indestructible hero be female... But there's plenty that you haven't seen before... Phillion ramps up the action often enough to keep things moving... in the end, it's the heroes' well-drawn personalities that make *The Indestructibles* fly... And [he] doesn't give the villains short shrift either...It's the rare young superhero fan who won't find him — or herself plowing through *The Indestructibles* in as few sittings as possible — and the rare older fan who won't want to scoop it up as soon as junior finishes."

— Peter Chianca *Gatehouse Media*

* * *

"Three cheers for Solar, Dancer, Fury, Straylight, and Entropy: the five brightest stars in the sky . . .a young woman with Supergirl-like strength and abilities; Kate Miller, who wasn't really a superhero at all; a teenage werewolf; a kid with an alien super symbiote living in his brain; and a girl who could control gravity . . .In other words, the superteam was filled with a disparate mix of monsters and freaks. Or, we suppose, they could simply be called Dr. Strange and the Furious Five . . .[an] indefatigably entertaining novel."

—Eric Searleman - Superheronovels.com

* * *

"Like the first installment, [in *Breakout*] superhero fans of all ages are likely to appreciate the plot's action-packed twists and turns, the pop culture references, the revolving door of special guest heroes and villains and above all the humor, which comes both from well-placed one-liners and the characters' well-drawn personalities... Phillion juggles the multi-pronged plotlines well, even managing to fit in a burgeoning subplot involving the resurgence of the generation of heroes that preceded the current crop. And the action is impeccably choreographed, no small achievement when you don't have panels full of artwork to fall back on . . .But the novel's strength is no doubt its characters: the superheroes of *Breakout* are people first, Spandex-clad adventurers second. Add in the particular depth of Phillion's female characters — heroes and villains both — and you've got a superhero saga that really does deserve to break out"

—Peter Chianca, *Gatehouse Media*

* * *

"Superheroes are famous for being perfectionists. Bruce Wayne, Big Barda, Natasha Romanova, Matt Murdock — they all trained diligently to reach their utmost physical and mental potential. And so it is with Kate Miller too ("The Soloist"). In two excellent novels Miller fought evildoers as a member of a superhero team called the Indestructibles. But she was the only member of her crew who wasn't bit by a spider, hit by lightning, or cursed by Galactus. She had to work hard to be a badass. They called her Dancer because she moved like a ballerina and hit like a mixed martial artists fighter. Now, in a prequel to the first *Indestructibles* novel, we get an insight into Miller's motivation. As it turns out, being a ballerina is excellent training for being a crime-fighting vigilante. You never know when a perfectly executed grande jeté will come in handy. Coda: the author recommends listening to Samuel Barber's "Adagio for Strings" while reading his story.

— Eric Searleman - Superheronovels.com

Acknowledgments

When you're writing a book about time travel, you learn a lot. I learned that writing a book about time travel is incredibly complicated. From figuring out how the mechanics of time travel would work in the world of the Indestructibles to determining just how to write scenes where there are two versions of the same character, *The Entropy of Everything* was easily the most challenging book to write so far.

And for that reason, I need to send a huge thank you to my test readers, Stephanie Buck, Bec Gianotti, Christian Hegg, Colin Carlton, and Jen Howland. While I've said before that having people read the story as I'm writing keeps me motivated, this time, your feedback helped me avoid getting lost or overwhelmed by the complexities of time travel. Thank you for your honesty, and for pointing out where I got turned around or bogged down.

(Additional thanks to Steph for not only being my test reader but being the poor person I rambled my thoughts to as I wrote. I'm sorry for all the hours I basically channeled Entropy Emily and talked your ear off.)

Another thank you goes to Jay Kumar and Christine Geiger for their proofreading and copyediting efforts. Any writer will tell you, it's the copyeditor who saves you from yourself. I needed a lot of saving this time around.

Thanks also to Peter Sarno and PFP Publishing, who published the original *Indestructibles* books and helped give the series its start.

To Sterling Arts & Design, AKA the aforementioned Christian Sterling Hegg—much thanks for the artwork you've provided the past few months, including the cover of this book, the one-shot covers, and of course the posters we use at every comic con. And the funny stuff, too. I really was tempted to use the Photoshopped version of me as Doc Silence as my author photo this time.

To my family and friends—thanks for being so ridiculously supportive. And for being understanding now that I've regressed back to my fifteen-year-old self and spend half my waking hours thinking about superheroes. You know how they say you don't get to pick your family? Well if we could, I'd still pick mine. Every day you prove how lucky I am to have you.

And of course, to you, the readers. You don't get to have a third book in a series if people didn't support the first and second books, and your unerring support—particularly those of you who have gone out of your way to talk about the books online, who have sent messages about your favorite characters, who have stayed in touch after we met at a Comic-Con, who crafted cosplays of the Indestructibles—this book doesn't exist without you.

To the reviewers who took the time to read and discuss the books, to the libraries and brick and mortar bookstores who have invited me to speak, to the organizers who gave me the chance to take place in contests and editors who let me write guest columns weighing in on issues important to our tribe of superhero fans—thank you for everything you've done. Every action you've taken to involve me in your communities has helped keep this series going.

If the first book was an origin story, and the second book was about consequences, this book is about self-exploration. This is where our young superheroes must look into a dark mirror and learn about themselves, and about who they want to become. If I'm honest, I'll admit I learned a lot about myself as I wrote as well. I hope you enjoy this dark journey through time. I'll see you on the other side.

Matthew Phillion
Salem, Massachusetts

For my nephews, Joseph, Nicholas, and Callan,
because this is a story about time travel, and you are the future.

And for Stephanie,
who keeps the present in one piece every single day.

PROLOGUE:
POST-APOCALYPTIC

Somewhere in the future, Jane Hawkins landed in the remnants of a flattened city block, a gray landscape that used to be the City's financial district. Now, dusty moonscape of crumpled buildings and powdered concrete, a desolate wasteland lay where living people once thrived.

Jane, the hero known her entire adult life as Solar, looked up at the overcast sky, glad she'd spent time above the cloud cover soaking in the sun's rays. She heard the enemy's approach, the whine of mechanical parts and heavy clunking of robotic footsteps.

I'm getting too old for this, Jane thought, taking in the ruins of the city she'd dedicated a lifetime defending. After each instance she'd return to discover something new had been destroyed. Her team realized something existed here, in the corpse of the City, some clue that would help them defeat their nemesis. But that enemy seemed to realize this as well and defended the vacant landscape with a ferocity they reserved for nowhere else. It had become bad enough that even Titus' werewolf commandos couldn't come back here for fear of whatever new threat waited for them. Only the powerhouses, like Jane, could explore the City and survive.

Robotic joints whirred, some sort of propulsion engine roared, and the first of the robots appeared. Jane, ever-ready, met the flying machine with a fist engulfed in white-hot flames. One hand melted through the robot's head, tore into its torso. Then, her impossibly strong fingers closed around its wiry guts and ripped them out.

Another robot joined the first, a mottled mash-up of scavenged parts with eyes glowing neon green, and Jane smashed it into pieces using the body of its fallen comrade as a blunt weapon.

"What's happening out there?" Titus' growling voice said into Jane's earpiece.

"They've got robots," Jane said.

"New robots or old ones?"

"Old with new tricks," Jane said. "Nothing I can't handle."

"Get out of there," Titus said. "It's not worth it. We'll try something stealthier next time."

Jane finished off the second robot with her boot, crushing its chassis, and then headed toward one of the last buildings still standing in the district. It had once been home to a huge data storage company. Titus and Neal, the team's sentient Artificial Intelligence program, had come upon information that the power source their enemy utilized to keep so many of their weapons running might still be housed there, possibly containing clues on how to get past their defenses.

"I'm right there, Titus," Jane said. "I'm going in."

Then she heard the footsteps. No simple robotic grinding this time, real footsteps, big ones, the sort that shake the ground. Jane waited, looking into the dusty, sooty distance as a huge silhouette started to coalesce.

"Oh come on," Jane said.

"We're coming in to help you," Titus said.

"No," Jane said. "There's nobody there who can help."

"We'll scramble Straylight."

"Tell Straylight to stay put," Jane said. "I've got this."

Then she saw the massive shadow reach back an arm the length of a city bus and wallop the building, huge mechanical fingers tearing into the structure and driving it into the ground, a child smashing a sand castle in petty rage.

"Now I'm mad," Jane said.

"Tell me that boom wasn't our target," Titus said.

"I'm changing targets," Jane said.

She ran, her boots crunched on the gravel and broken glass

beneath her feet. The robot turned its massive, neon green eyes her way, its mouthless face passive and inexpressive, and raised both arms toward her.

Jane launched from the ground, a human missile, enveloped in radiant light, then let the solar power she'd soaked up all day flow through her. One fist forward, she aimed her flight as she'd done since she was a teenager, making her a living bullet, her other arm remained cocked back, fist clenched. The robot put up a hand to grab her, or to stop her, but Jane tore through it like a marathoner ripping through a finish line, as if the metal were tissue paper, and she continued, shattering the giant mech's head with one swing of her fist.

The hulking monstrosity collapsed to the ground, an almost comical crash, its body stiff as a board. Still airborne, Jane saw another robot on its way. And this one had a mouth sporting teeth like a shark's.

"Titus, I'm going to be a while," Jane said.

CHAPTER 1:
HERE AND NOW

Somewhere in the present, Jane flew low over the dark waters of the Atlantic, scanning the ocean's surface for a shark's fin and hoping she didn't find it.

Billy Case, the hero known as Straylight, flew beside her, having one of the strange multi-tasking conversations only Billy ever had. She could see him chatting with the alien consciousness who shared his body—known colloquially as Dude, though the alien never did appreciate the nickname—while Billy simultaneously taunted his best friend and fellow hero Entropy Emily, who refused to fly within a hundred feet of the water's surface.

"Are you sensing him anywhere?" Billy asked, and Jane knew the question was directed at Dude.

The trio were following up on rumors that a science experiment known as Megalodon had been spotted in the area—and by spotted, Jane thought, that meant, had allegedly attacked a fishing vessel and sank it. Dude could sometimes sense things humans could not, and Billy had hoped that the human-shark hybrid they were tracking might show up on the alien's biological radar.

"Is he picking anything up?" Jane asked.

"Nothing," Billy said. He looked up at Emily, floating far above them and steadfastly refusing to come any closer. "Emily! He's long gone! You can come down now."

"Have either of you ever seen *Jaws*?" Emily yelled. "You always think the shark is gone, but he's not ever really gone! Sometimes he's in 3D!"

"Em, he can't hurt you," Jane said. "If he gets too close just bubble of float him away."

"You say that like it's easy," Emily said.

"Everything is for you," Jane said.

"It's not easy being neon green."

"Come down," Jane said.

"No."

"Come down here or go home."

"Okay, I'll go home."

"I was kidding," Jane said.

"Shark!" Billy yelled.

Emily screamed.

Jane turned, ready to fight.

Billy laughed. "Just kidding. It's a sunfish."

"That's not funny!" Emily yelled.

Billy pointed at a large, squat, pale fish drifting lazily along the surface.

Jane looked at Billy and raised an eyebrow.

"Did you actually know it was a sunfish, or did Dude tell you that?"

"Dude's an alien. Why would he know what a sunfish is?"

"Why would *you* know what a sunfish is?" Jane said.

"Listen, farm girl, I do know things sometimes."

"Did you actually know that or did Dude tell you?" Emily yelled down, not hearing Jane ask the question first.

"I know things sometimes, Emily!" Billy yelled back up at her. "Why do you guys think I'm stupid?"

"You cultivate that myth and you know it," Jane said, watching the sunfish putter along. "I think we missed him."

"Megalodon?" Billy said. "Yeah."

"We need to recruit an aquatic member. Maybe see if Atlantis has anyone we can bring on board."

"I can't tell if you're kidding or not," Billy said. "Is there really an Atlantis?"

Jane shrugged.

"Why is Emily so frightened of sharks?" Jane said.

"Can we go home now? I'm really tired of being this afraid for an extended period of time!" Emily yelled.

Billy glanced at Emily, made a vague and almost obscene hand gesture telling her to wait, and then smirked at Jane.

"She had to be scared of something," Billy said. "We know nothing else seems to faze her. Give her sharks. It's her one thing."

"I'm afraid of a lot more than just one thing," Jane said.

"Me too," Billy said. "Let's go home."

CHAPTER 2:
RAT CATCHERS

Kate Miller, the vigilante known as the Dancer, knocked over a forgotten tin can with the tip of a tungsten-capped boot. It clattered to the ground, sending dozens of multi-legged insects scurrying out of the sludge that used to be cheap soup.

All around her, signs of rough living decayed. The underground lair, illuminated by piles of cheap candles and decorated with newspaper clippings and stolen purses, stank like an animal pen left too long unwashed.

"I can't handle this right now," Titus said behind her. The werewolf had reverted to human form and pulled his signature hooded sweatshirt up over his head.

"*This*," Kate said. "This is too much for you to handle? All the things we've seen and this is what gets to you?"

"You don't have super-senses, Kate," Titus said. "Smell that rancid awfulness going up your nose? Multiply it by a thousand. That's what I've got going on right now."

"You're not in werewolf mode anymore," she pointed out.

"Yeah, because it was like, a million times worse with that muzzle," Titus said. He let out a long, alarming exhale. "Oh, I really don't want to get sick in front of you. I like that you almost respect me."

"Almost," Kate said.

"That's what I said."

Kate tapped the button on her earpiece and spoke.

"Alley Hawk from Dancer," she said. "We're in his lair. He's been gone for a while."

"How can you tell?" the gravelly voice of the older vigilante who had become Kate's friend and mentor asked.

"Titus' nose."

"I'm coming to you," Alley Hawk said. "Hang tight."

"Don't get sick," Kate said. "Alley Hawk is coming."

"Don't embarrass you is what you're really saying," Titus said.

Kate stared at him.

Titus shrugged.

"Kate," Titus said, walking up to one of the stacks of candles burning along the wall of the underground next. Wax had spilled down in lumpy trickles like accidental art.

"What?"

"He can't have been gone for a long time. How long could these candles burn without going out? The Vermin King was here recently," Titus said.

"Your werewolf bodyguard has a good eye for detail," Alley Hawk said, emerging from a shadowy corridor into the light. "He's not coming back though."

"How do you know?" Titus said.

"He never does," Alley Hawk said. "The Vermin King never set up a permanent base when he knew he was being chased."

Kate picked up one of the purses and flipped though the contents. No money or credit cards, but otherwise it was difficult to tell what was missing and what was not. The fact that the Vermin King—a strange, mutated killer who'd been Alley Hawk's greatest enemy his entire career and had escaped from a prison for super-powered criminals during the Indestructibles' own breakout not long ago—had been collecting these purses made him somehow even creepier than his appearance. Why keep them? Souvenirs? Trophies?

Kate tossed one handbag aside then stopped when something caught her eye. A glimmer of candlelight off glass, tucked away in a corner of the Vermin King's temporary hideout.

"Huh," Kate said, picking up the object.

It was a snow globe, delicately crafted, with a base decorated in designs hinting at the *Nutcracker*. Alone in the center of the snow globe, a tiny prima ballerina stood waiting to dance.

Kate shook the globe and snow swirled. A spurt of red kicked up from the bottom of the glass ball as she tipped it, filling the globe with crimson fluid. Suddenly the miniature ballet dancer was surrounded by a viscous stream of blood. Kate watched as the red fluid danced around in the water, staining the snowflakes.

"What do you have?" Titus said.

Alley Hawk said nothing, taking the globe from Kate's hands and turning it over and over in his own.

"That's not real blood," he said.

"I know," Kate said. "It's a threat though."

Alley Hawk grunted.

"This was his specialty, back in the old days. Trying to terrorize you enough to distract you."

"So he knows I'm helping you look for him," Kate said.

"We shouldn't be surprised by that," said Alley Hawk. "Does that worry you?"

"Only enough to make me want to make sure I'm ready for him if he comes after me," said Kate.

Alley Hawk nodded.

"Good," he said, placing the globe back on the floor. "We should move on."

Kate closed her eyes.

"Hawk," she said.

The old vigilante paused, waiting for her to continue speaking.

"You know Anachronism Annie is back. Doc's friend," Kate said.

The infamous time traveler had arrived at the Indestructibles base recently, unannounced. Kate had trust issues on a good day; so a woman claiming to move through time set off all her alarms.

"Doc told me," Alley Hawk said.

"What do you think of her?"

"Her nature is to be a good person," Alley Hawk said. "You can trust her motives. But—"

"—But," Titus said. "There's always a 'but.'"

"But she's a time traveler," Alley Hawk said. "Nothing good comes from time travel."

Titus had loosened his grip on his hood and settled for waving his hand in front of his own nose to cut back on the Vermin King's stench.

"I can't imagine what could go wrong with time travel," said Titus.

"So you think what she does is wrong," Kate said.

"It's not her fault," Alley Hawk said. "Annie... she's not a time traveler in the conventional sense. She's a refugee."

"How so?" Kate said.

"She's the better one to explain it, but wherever she's from... it's no longer there to go back to. And time-hopping is what she does. It's who she is."

"But," Kate said.

"But just think about all the things that could go wrong if you go into the past," said Alley Hawk. "Think about all the mistakes you could make if you knew the future."

"Have you ever time traveled, Hawk?" Titus asked.

The old vigilante looked away, eyes narrowed, mouth a tight thin line.

"It's good she's back," Alley Hawk said. "We all thought she was gone forever."

CHAPTER 3:
ANACHRONISM ANNIE

Doc Silence sat across the table from the woman who had once been his best friend. A long time ago, Anachronism Annie said she was going into the future and never coming back, and Doc, by that time used to losing friends, had made his peace with her decision.

Annie was from the future originally anyway. Her specific future was gone, a dead end in the time stream, and she never truly belonged to this world. Disappearing into the unknown was exactly what everyone expected her to do some day.

Which didn't mean Doc hadn't missed her when she was gone.

Annie peered back at Doc through her red sunglasses, almost identical to his own, an old in-joke between the two of them no one else quite understood. Doc wore his red lenses to hide his glowing eyes, the strange deformity from magic gone awry when he was young. Annie, when they first met, asked if he wore rose-tinted lenses to see the world in a better light. When he told her the real story, she got a pair of her own.

The magician and the time traveler, making the world strange together for all those years.

"Why didn't you tell me I was your time-anchor?" Doc said.

Annie had returned to this timeline just hours after Doc himself had been rescued from a different dimension—truly, a scenario as weird as it sounds—pulled back into this world in a rescue attempt by Jane. The first thing Annie did upon seeing him was curse him out

11

for not being here on Earth, because she'd made him her chronological anchor, her method of finding a way back to this timeline among all the others when she returned. An important fact that Annie, who was frequently guilty of not sharing important facts, had neglected to tell him earlier.

Both Annie and Doc had been avoiding this conversation since their return. Doc needed to get the Indestructibles situated after what he later learned had been essentially a jail break, with Jane, Emily, and Billy held in custody by a rogue government agency. And Annie had always needed time to acclimate to a timeline, to adjust her internal clocks correctly.

They'd been avoiding each other, as well. Annie, always hard to read, made only the slightest attempt to mask a guilty appearance every time Doc looked at her, while Doc found himself unexpectedly angry with her. He lost friends constantly, but Annie was the one who left voluntarily, done with this timeline, done with their team, and finally, Doc thought, done with him.

"Of course you were my anchor, Doc," Annie said. "You've been my anchor for everything else. Why wouldn't you be my fix to this timeline?"

"Still," Doc said.

"Still," Annie repeated.

She took her sunglasses off, revealing eyes with irises the same shade of metallic pink as her messy hair. Pink hair, pink eyes, tattoos covering every inch of her arms, her angry, angular build, everything about Annie said back away from her, but they'd been best friends from the moment they met. Billy and Emily reminded Doc of Annie and himself, in several ways. Always together, conversing in a private language no one else really understood.

"Where were you?" Doc asked.

Annie looked at the table, folding her tattooed hands in front of her.

"I kept trying to get home, to this home, Doc," Annie said. "But I couldn't get here, because someone—and by someone I mean you—wasn't here, so I couldn't find my way back to this timeline. I kept bouncing around to different futures. And then I found the last one."

"The one you want to talk to me about," Doc said.

"Yeah," Annie said. "It's a dead future, Doc. A timeline in final decline. A line on the fishbone diagram coming to an end. It's a terminal track. And I want to save it."

"We have rules," Doc said. "Regulations you gave us yourself. We don't get to change the past, we don't get to manipulate the future. You said that. Those are your own rules, Annie."

"We need to save this timeline I found, Doc," Annie said.

She fumbled with her red glasses, crossed and uncrossed her legs under the table.

"Why this one in particular?" Doc asked.

He leaned back in his chair, thinking back to all the reasons Annie gave Doc and their colleagues years ago as to why they should never meddle with the time stream. If you time traveled, you were an observer, never a participant, she said. You can't fix the present; if you change the past, a new timeline is created. The past is immutable. You can't alter the future. It can't be repaired, no matter how hard you tried. If you meddled in the past, you made a new line on the diagram. Nothing else.

Time travel is nothing but trouble, Doc thought. At least his own work, moving between dimensions, had a lasting effect; those other dimensions, like the strange, dreamlike places he and the Lady had wandered through during their banishment last year, were real. They had different rules, different effects, but in the end, they were simply places, like any other place. They existed. If you won a war in the Dreamless Lands, it had a lasting impact.

Time was more complicated than that. Time hated to be changed. Time actively worked against you if you tried to change it. Which was why Annie was so strange, and so hard to understand. Her ability to move through time was unique and dangerous and something she never explained, not even to Doc Silence.

"Doc, the timeline I just came from is dying, and it's our fault," Annie said.

He sat up straighter in his chair.

"How so?"

"That little blue-haired lunatic you recruited?" Annie said. "In this other timeline, someone else found her instead. And they turned her into the most dangerous weapon ever known."

"Emily. We're talking about Emily. The one who earlier today deliberately instigated fights on Internet message boards with strangers. That Emily."

"Doc, you understand she's more powerful than you've let her know," Annie said.

"I'm hoping it'll be a little longer before she's able to figure that out," Doc said. "Who found her? And why didn't I get to her first in this other timeline?"

"Because you're dead."

Doc rubbed his eyes with his thumbs.

"Of course I am," Doc said. "Why wouldn't I be? Do you know who killed... me in this other timeline?"

"We should talk about that later."

"Annie."

"Later."

"Fine," Doc said. "Then will you at least tell me who found her instead? Was it the Children of the Elder Star?"

"They're dead too, Doc," Annie said. "That's what I mean. We're looking at a terminal timeline. And it's our fault. We've got to help them."

Doc studied Annie's face, the lines of worry around her eyes. She looked more tired than he'd ever seen her.

"You got attached, didn't you?" Doc said.

"Doc."

"That was your other rule. Never get attached. You can't stay in another timeline. Don't get emotionally involved."

"Well I was bloody stuck there because of you, you twit," Annie said. "Of course I got attached. Doc, please. Help me help them."

He sighed. It was difficult enough keeping one timeline safe without meddling in another, but if Annie said this was a timeline they needed to help, Doc wasn't sure how to argue with her.

"You and me?"

"And the kids."

14

"You're joking."

"No," Annie said. "We need them."

"Aren't they already there? I know Emily's not an Indestructible there, but the others?"

"Doc, we need them. For more reasons than I can really explain. I have to show you."

Doc rubbed his eyes again, with growing intensity. Time travel was challenging enough for adult heroes. He was confident Jane would be able to handle this request relatively well, but the boys on occasion were still more immature than they let on, and Emily posed a wildcard by just walking out the door in the morning. Finally, Kate would remain a skeptic no matter what happened.

"You're going to have to help me explain it to them," Doc said.

"I've been trying to explain time travel to you for twenty years, Doc Silence," Annie said. "You think I'll be able to teach it to five kids in a crash course?"

CHAPTER 4:
THE GIRL IN THE GLASS BUBBLE

Keaton Bohr never expected to become a zealot.

And yet here, at the end of the world, it seemed the only word appropriate anymore. He'd been called many things in his life: scientist, optimist, dreamer, genius; but never a believer, never a warrior for any cause other than knowledge.

Until he met the White Shadow.

He'd been angry then, disillusioned, a scientist cast aside for unpopular ideas, an idealist screaming to deaf ears. The White Shadow had come to him, found him on a bridge in the City at the end of his rope, thinking about the home he would need to sell, fingers sooty from setting his lab coat on fire in effigy for the corporations who rejected his ideas on clean and alternate energy concepts, and the Shadow had given him purpose.

"I need a man like you," the Shadow said. "I could use someone to help me change the world."

And they certainly did, Keaton the scientist and Shadow the planner, Shadow the avenger, Shadow the former hero.

But this is the end of the world, and it's all our fault, Keaton thought. He had just watched the hero Solar battling his latest weapons, giant mechs like creatures from an old anime. He knew they wouldn't stand up to her, but they were something to keep the hero distracted. And distracting the aging and dwindling Indestructibles had become Keaton's leisure activity these days, when he wasn't doing the bidding of the White Shadow, when he wasn't using their captive to change the face of the world.

When does it all end? Keaton thought. He ran a hand through his thin hair, looked for the cup of instant coffee he'd abandoned earlier, and wondered how their not-so-secret weapon was doing today.

Their secret weapon. We built this future on the back of a little girl, Keaton silently said to himself. And with the things they had created, the monsters and miracles, they'd drawn so many other zealots to their cause. Keaton knew that if any of those fanatics, those blind followers of the White Shadow, knew the doubts he had in his heart, they would kill him.

Or not. He was, after all, the only one who knew how to talk to the girl in glass bubble anymore.

Why not go see her, he thought. He picked up the room-temperature cup of coffee he'd lost and headed downstairs.

The hallways of his lab echoed like a tomb. When they'd first started, there'd been so many other people like him, believers in the White Shadow's cause, people who wanted to change the world by force. They made it easier, those others. Staff and assistants and colleagues, feeding on each other's beliefs and energy. They really did think they could make a better world. There were still followers, but the smart ones—the scientists, the explorers—wandered off, literally and metaphorically. The thinkers had driven themselves to despair. They still had foot soldiers, extremists willing to die for the cause, but men and women of science... the world didn't have many of them left anymore.

Keaton sometimes wondered if they'd been just as enthusiastic about something better how differently things might have turned out. Certainly the thought had occurred to others before him, accounting for some of the attrition as the different scientists began to realize the fruits of their labor were strangling the very world they wanted to change. Many more left after what had become known as the California incident.

There wasn't much disguising the White Shadow's true intentions after the California incident, after all.

Keaton sometimes wondered why he stayed. In part, he thought, it was love. He did love the Shadow, as a friend, as a makeshift family, despite his monstrous decisions. The Shadow had saved Keaton's life after all, had reeled him in from the brink, had given him purpose. The Shadow made Keaton something, and gave him a legacy. A horrific legacy, but, Keaton thought, was it better to be the man who helped end the world, or to simply be nothing at all? The world was on a fast track to self-destruction anyway. All Keaton did was help clear the path for some other species to give it all a try. Let the cats inherit the Earth. The apes had done a lousy job as caretakers.

But the real reason Keaton stayed was locked in the basement laboratory. The girl in the glass bubble.

He remembered first meeting her, when she was just a child, with brightly colored hair and a mouth that never stopped talking. They'd let her keep the hair that color, a way of making her feel human, but after a while the experiments dulled her personality and her spirit, and dying her hair no longer lifted her spirits. Nothing did, really. She rarely spoke anymore, had barely said a word in years, trapped in a bubble the size of a room, the thin geodesic patterns on the glass that harvested her power and turned it into a never-ending supply of energy gleaming in the dark.

Tonight, the girl sat in a chair in the center of the globe where she remained a captive, staring into the darkness beyond her glass room.

Keaton watched her, pity and regret welling up in his gut as it always did. He wanted to set her free, but he knew they'd tampered with her powers too much over the years. They'd done irreparable harm. The dome they kept her in was designed not only to harvest her energy but to keep it in check. The girl had no control over her abilities any longer. To set her free would be like inviting the cosmos to kick Earth into deep space. She was trapped.

And ultimately that was why Keaton stayed. This was his fault, and the girl was his responsibility.

He put an earpiece in allowing him to speak to her through the glass. She didn't turn to look at him as he wandered into view, though her eyes were open, staring off into space.

"How are you today, Emily?" Keaton said, trying to keep his voice cheerful.

She tilted her head in his general direction, but didn't speak. She used to talk with him, to verbally joust with him, to challenge him on scientific theory. Once upon a time, the girl had possessed a great intellect. Another thing wasted in pursuing the Shadow's dream.

And then the girl surprised him.

"They're coming," Emily said, in a voice just above a whisper.

"What's that?" Keaton said, not even attempting to disguise the shock in his voice.

"Don't worry Keaton," Emily said. She smiled, something else Keaton hadn't seen her do in years. "It'll all be over soon."

And the girl closed her eyes, leaned her head back, and drifted off to sleep. Keaton slowly removed his earpiece and backed away.

"Who's coming?" he said, to no one at all.

CHAPTER 5:
MORAL QUANDARIES

Jane sat in a corner booth at a coffee shop where they did *not* carry the Entropy Emi-latte, hoping no one would recognize her, her fiery hair tucked up under a knit hat. Jon Broadstreet, the reporter the local news outlet had assigned as the Indestructibles "expert," sat across from her, typing notes onto an iPad as they chatted. Jane agreed at some point—or maybe someone else arranged it, Jane was never sure—to sit down with Broadstreet every so often to update him on the latest news from the Indestructibles' floating base. It was easier to give controlled interviews than to ignore the press, and Broadstreet was a friendly ear.

Or more than friendly. Emily regularly taunted her that the reporter went easy on them because Broadstreet had a crush on Jane. If that was the case, Jane thought, then the least she could do was be polite during his usually lighthearted interviews. They hadn't had a tough discussion since the incident with the now-ousted new management of the Department, when they'd taken Jane, Billy, and Emily captive. Henry Winter, the hero formerly known as Coldwall and an old teammate of Doc's, had taken over as head of the Department and had done an incredible amount of public relations work to get the heroes and the agency back on the same page. After the dust settled, though, these conversations with Broadstreet had mostly involved updates on the Indestructibles' search for escapees from the Labyrinth prison.

"So other than looking for a missing man-shark hybrid capable of sinking a fishing vessel with his teeth, you're not that busy right now," Broadstreet said, looking up from his tablet to smirk. The reporter was growing a beard and it made him look ridiculous.

"We're trying not to alarm anyone with that information," Jane said, tucking her unnaturally fire-colored hair back up under a wool hat she borrowed from Emily.

"Yeah, good luck with that. Man-shark hybrid. Not alarming at all."

"He's probably just really lonely," Jane said.

"So he's not a super-villain, he just in need of a date," Broadstreet said.

"Couldn't hurt," Jane said, cracking a smile. "He'd be easier to find at the movies."

"Speaking of," Broadstreet said.

"Come on," Jane said, letting out a frustrated laugh.

"The minute you stop laughing when I ask, I'll stop asking," Broadstreet said. "Because I'll know you're actually annoyed. Until then, I'm going to keep asking until I get a 'yes.'"

"So I should practice wearing my annoyed face?" Jane said.

"I'm sure it's terrifying," Broadstreet said, tucking his iPad into a messenger bag. "Really, though? None of you have social lives? You never go out?"

Jane shrugged.

"Fine," Broadstreet said. "You'll tell me all about man-shark, but you won't spill any gossip. I can live with that. Man-shark leads as a headline almost as well as your social lives would. Same time next week?"

"If I'm not off saving the world," Jane said.

"Obviously. Take care, Solar."

"Be good."

Jane watched the reporter head out the front door of the café and put her head down on the table. Why am I the PR person on this team, she thought. I need to delegate. Maybe Doc will help me out.

"One of my old teammates went out with a reporter," Doc Silence said, startling Jane out of her self-pity. The older hero stood over the table, dressed as always in jeans, tee shirt, and his long dark coat. He sat down across from Jane, coffee in hand already.

"I'm not going out with him," Jane said.

"Did I say that?" Doc said. "I'm just making an observation. Heroes and reporters. Long history of dysfunctional . . ."

Jane pulled her hat down over her eyes and leaned back in her seat.

"Have I mentioned how glad I am you're back, Doc?"

"Not nearly enough," Doc said. "I need to run something by you, Jane."

"Run something by me?"

"Yes."

"This is backward," Jane said. "I run things by you. You're Doc."

"You realize who you sound like right now?"

"All right, all right," Jane said. "I'll be the responsible adult. As usual. What's going on?"

"Annie wants us to do something I'm not sure I'm morally okay with."

"Don't tell me she wants us to time travel," Jane said, then took a sip of her cooling coffee.

Doc rubbed the bridge of his nose with his thumb, his eyes scrunched closed.

"She wants us to time travel," Jane said, answering her own question. "One of the first things you taught me was that time travel is bad."

"Exactly."

"In fact, you said that was 'Annie's Rule: Time travel is bad,'" Jane said.

"You see why this is so troubling," Doc said.

Jane stuck her hands up inside her hat and ran her fingers through her hair nervously.

"So did she give you a why?"

"Because," Doc said. "An entire future is dying due to us."

"I don't understand how that's possible," Jane said.

"And now, Jane, you understand the first reason why time travel is bad," Doc said.

CHAPTER 6:
ANACHRONISM ANNIE'S REQUEST

Titus found himself in a part of the Tower he'd never been before. As with much of the Tower's layout, it was hard to figure out if he'd gone left or right, up or down. The building frequently felt as if it adjusted itself to where you wanted to be rather than having a set layout. It occasionally made him dizzy. It also felt as if the structure itself were hiding things.

Like this room, for example. A wide-open space with strangely reflective walls, it seemed to be a museum of some kind, with objects—weapons that didn't seem quite ordinary, gadgets out of a steampunk convention's dreams, photographs of historical figures in places they'd never been—on display behind glass cases or organized like trophies on shelves.

Kate, Emily, and Billy were already there when Titus arrived. Billy and Emily were snooping, picking up objects—that clearly looked like they should not be touched—and guessing their purpose.

"This is definitely a steam-driven back scratcher," Emily said, waving a pitchfork wrapped in copper coils in Billy's general direction.

He responded by blocking her makeshift weapon with a sepia-toned photograph of Theodore Roosevelt in an astronaut suit.

"Hoax or historical cosplay gone wrong? You decide!" he said.

Emily aimed the pitchfork at Billy like a spear.

"Beware, my giant dinglehopper!" she yelled.

"Dinglehopper?" Billy said.

"What, you want a thingamabob instead?"

"Well you do have twenty," Billy said.

"*I want more!*" Emily sang, breaking into a pitch perfect imitation of Ariel from *The Little Mermaid*. She and Billy started harmonizing to "Part of Your World" in startlingly good voices.

"You guys have been practicing this, haven't you?" Titus said.

They both pointed at him in dramatic fashion.

"*Flippin' your fins, you don't get too far. Legs are required for jumping, dancing . . .*" Billy and Emily sang together.

"Don't encourage them," Kate said, sidling up beside Titus and bumping him slightly with her shoulder. "They've been at this a while."

"Are they supposed to be touching those things?" Titus asked.

Kate shrugged.

"Worst that can happen, they disintegrate each other, we no longer have Disney show tunes," she said. "A win-win."

Annie, Doc, and Jane walked in together behind Titus, mid conversation.

"Put the dinglehopper down," Annie said.

"*I'm ready to know what the people know. Ask 'em my questions, and get some answers,*" Emily sang. "So seriously. We going to get some answers? Like why are we here? And is this actually a dinglehopper?"

"It's an electrified trident from another timeline where... never mind, just stop pointing it at people," Annie said.

Emily frowned, but set the trident aside.

Doc gestured to the scattered chairs around the room. Most of the heroes picked a seat. Kate, as usual, chose to pace around the back of the room. Titus didn't join her. She was easier to take when you let her roam, he knew from experience.

"Okay, boss," Billy said. "You got us. What's the story?"

"Annie wants to ask us for a favor," Doc said. "And I said we have to let you decide for yourselves if we go through with it."

"A favor?" Kate said, questioning.

Doc gestured for Annie to speak.

She took a deep breath and took her red-tinted glasses off the same way Doc always did, rubbing her eyes. Instead of Doc's strange glowing eyes, however, her irises were an unnatural shade of pink, but otherwise ordinary. Titus wondered who picked up the affect from whom.

"While this guy," Annie said, gesturing at Doc, "was gallivanting across the astral planes last year, I was trapped. In a future."

"A future? Not *the* future?" Billy said.

"You're a Time Lord?" Emily said.

"I'm a chronomancer," Annie said.

"So you're a Time Lord," Emily said.

"A chronomancer."

"Are you the Doctor?"

"He's the doctor," Annie said, pointing at Doc Silence.

"Who?" Emily said. She turned, beaming at everyone. "You see what I did there? It looks easy but it's really not."

"Emily, please stop," Jane said.

Titus picked up an edge to her voice. Jane was almost as serious as Kate most of the time, but rarely frustrated, and he could sense Emily's usual playfulness was irritating her.

Emily huffed and crossed her arms.

Annie continued. "I'm a time traveler. There aren't many of us. It's more complicated than you'd even imagine," Annie said. "But I ended up stuck in another timeline, one in which something went wrong not long after Doc found most of you. A series of events led to the creation of an alternate timeline. And by the time I found myself there, it was, as I said, terminal—it was a timeline reaching its final stages. A dead branch on the tree."

"How many timelines are there?" Titus said.

Annie smiled.

"We don't know," she said. "It's not an exact science. We don't know how many timelines there are, or what makes an event significant enough to spawn a split in a current timeline. But there are many."

"You told me something about this once, Doc," Jane said. "There are so many worlds. You told me that when you thought you were going to die fighting the Lady."

"I did," Doc said. "There are other realities, other planes, and other timelines. The universe doesn't go in one direction. It's four dimensional."

"Four dimensional?" Billy said. "That' doesn't make any—"

"—You said you wanted to ask us a favor," Kate interrupted from the back of the room.

"I did," Annie said. "I want you to help me save this other timeline."

Doc chimed in.

"This is why we needed to present it to everyone," he said. "Because there are ethics to discuss when interfering with another timeline. We generally thought it was a bad idea to get involved in other timelines before. There are a lot of questions we need to present."

"I like ethics," Emily said. "Ethics are fun. What are we talking about here, hedonistic calculus?"

Jane leaned back in her chair, which creaked when her shoulders pushed against it.

"Last time you started talking ethics, Em, a kid died," she said.

"Yeah, but for the greater good," Emily said.

Billy leaned in, uncharacteristically serious.

Titus wondered what Dude was saying in Billy's ear.

"So would we go back in time? Change their future somehow? Prevent whatever is making it... what did you call it? A terminal timeline?" Billy said.

"Here's where things get weird," Annie said. "Going back in time never actually fixes anything. Believe me, I've tried. If you're successful in making a major change, you risk just creating a new splinter timeline. But once a timeline exists, it exists. You can't go back and alter it."

"That makes absolutely no sense," Billy said.

"This is why it gets strange," Annie said.

"So what are we really doing, then," Jane said. "Going into someone else's future to stop it from, ah, terminating?"

"It's coming up on a terminal event," Annie said. "An event that will cause that timeline to sunset. If we can stop that event from happening, we can, if not make it a better future, at least let the people living there have some sort of future at all."

Kate chimed in next.

"But why this future? You said there are countless timelines. Why fix this one? What's so important about it?"

"When Doc first started teaching me, he said that it was dangerous to mess with other timelines," Jane weighed in. "You're asking us to break a rule you yourself invented."

Annie sighed, her shoulders slumped; her entire frame sagged with exhaustion.

"To be completely truthful?" Annie said. "In part, because I was stuck there, and I came to care about their world, and I don't want to see it end."

"And?" Titus said.

"And because the terminal event is our fault," Annie said. "Our mistakes, this group in this room right now, have led to a world with a dead future. And I feel like we owe it to them to try to save their world."

"Why can't we save it ourselves?" Billy said. "I mean us in the future. We're already there, right? Future us? Why do now us need to go to future us and... I can't believe I'm having this conversation. Am I really having this conversation?"

Annie smiled. It was a smile tinged with such weighty sadness Titus found himself suddenly terrified at what the future did have in store for them all.

"The future Indestructibles need help," Annie said.

"Are we in trouble there?" Jane said.

"It's better if you not know. You'll find out when you get there, but it's never safe to talk about a future that will never happen," Annie said.

"This future can't happen?" Titus said. "You said something happened when we all first came together that changed the timeline. Does that mean this other future is... ?"

"Not something this current timeline can become," Annie said. "I know. It's weird. It makes no sense. You just have to trust me on it."

Kate stopped pacing in the back of the room and squeezed in

between Billy and Titus' chairs to be closer to Annie.

"And if we go, won't that have an impact on our own timeline?" Kate said. "If we go, we effectively leave our own timeline. That has to change things here."

"I can bring you back to the exact moment you left," Annie said. "If I do it right."

"And if we don't die in the future," Billy said.

Everyone stared at him. Emily punched him in the arm.

"What? Someone had to say it."

"You're right. I can't guarantee everyone will come home," Annie said.

"This seems like a really bad precedent," Emily said. "Even us leaving has to have an impact on our own timeline. Everything changes. We change. We're gone. Transfer of energy. Poof. This is a terrible idea."

"And this is why we put it to a vote," Doc said. "You have to decide for yourselves. This is someone else's future. There's no guarantee it will work. There's no guarantee we'll come back. It's incredibly dangerous. But if we succeed, we save an entire timeline from extinction."

"Let's vote, then," Jane said.

"I vote yes," Emily said.

"You just said . . .You just said five seconds ago that it was a terrible idea," Billy said, staring at her incredulously.

"Did you just meet me? Today?" Emily said. "Just because I think something's a bad idea doesn't mean I don't think it'll be totally awesome."

Billy rubbed his face and turned away from Emily.

"I think we should go," he said. "I know it puts our world at risk too, but I can't just... let another world die. It feels like the exact opposite of what we do."

Titus saw both Jane and Doc smile slightly at Billy's phrasing. He knew they both took pride in watching those rare moments when Billy spoke like a hero. Although they were infrequent, Titus knew Billy was always genuine when he did it.

"I think we stay," Kate said. "We have our responsibilities here.

This world is depending on us. If we go, we put everyone here in danger for a future that has already had its chance."

Titus looked at her, trying to hide his own emotions. He understood her logic, but sometimes Kate could be so coldly logical, so ruthlessly efficient that she scared him.

"I understand what you're saying, Kate," Jane said. "And I could almost agree with you. But if something we did wrong doomed an entire timeline... maybe we need to go make it right somehow. Maybe it's our destiny to save them."

"I think you're all crazy," Kate said. She looked at Titus. "Where do you stand on this?"

Titus exhaled long and slowly. He remembered what his mentors among the other werewolves had told him last year. That they were the shaman on the hill. That they were put here to keep the monsters at bay. Did that mean the monsters in some other timeline as well? Or just the monsters in his own small village here? How big was the village he was supposed to protect?

"I think it's our responsibility to go," Titus said. "We have it in our power to help them. If we don't, we're letting a whole world come to an end. I can't bring myself to let that happen."

Titus looked to Kate, but she no longer made eye contact with him. Her attention was focused fully on Doc Silence and Annie now.

"What about you, Doc?" Kate said. "Are you going?"

"I wouldn't leave you to this alone," Doc said. "I wasn't going to make any of you go, but I won't let you go alone. And you can stay, Kate. I know the work you're doing with Alley Hawk is important to you."

Now Kate glanced back at Titus. The expression she shot him caused his stomach to writhe.

"No," Kate said. "If you're going, I'm going. I think you're all insane, but I'm coming."

"So that settles it," Emily said. "Where's the DeLorean?"

"We don't travel in a DeLorean, Emily," Annie said.

"Tardis, then."

"Not a Tardis either."

"No Tardis?" Emily said.

"No Tardis, sorry," Annie said.

"Is it too late to change my vote?" Emily said.

"Em, stop it," Jane said.

"You really don't have to come," Doc said. "It's okay."

"And miss out what you all look like when you're old? No way," Emily said. "I would like the option of revisiting the Tardis situation in the future, though."

CHAPTER 7:
CONTINGENCY PLANS

Henry Winter was bored.

Perhaps bored wasn't the right word. The former billionaire (now broke), former superhero (now not), man known as the armored hero Coldwall, found himself sitting in an empty office in a West Coast outpost of the Department. Ever since the Indestructibles broke him out of the superhuman prison known as the Labyrinth last year, Winter had been running the Department, and that meant a top to bottom housecleaning. The government agency, designed to deal with superhuman threats, had gone off the rails, having been taken over in some areas by outside influences, and so they'd put the former superhero to work fixing their mess.

And compared to flying around in an armored suit, playing Chief Operating Officer for a government agency was one of the most boring things Winter had ever done in his entire life. No, he thought: bored is definitely the right word.

"I almost miss prison," Winter said.

And he hadn't even been there for committing a crime. Locked up as a stolen resource for his technical expertise, Winter hadn't seen the outside world in a decade. He thought flying around the country fixing the Department's problems would allow him to reacclimatize. Instead, he hid in offices to avoid signing paperwork or reviewing personnel information.

"We can put you back in there if you really want," Doc Silence's voice said behind him.

Winter spasmed in surprise, almost falling out of his chair.

"Would you please not... mystically appear in the room without warning me first?" Winter said. "I think I need new pants. Why would you do that?"

"Because it's funny," Doc said, grinning.

The one thing keeping Winter sane in this inane work with the Department was reconnecting with his old superhero colleagues. Not that there were many of them left, but it was good to see Doc again after all these years.

Winter used the cane he still relied on to get around and nudged a wheeled office chair in Doc's direction. He caught it and sat down, leaning back until the chair creaked.

"So is this a social call?" Winter said.

"Nope," Doc said, looking at the ceiling. "The kids and I are going to go on a little errand for Annie."

"I still can't believe Annie's back," Winter said. "I thought she was done with this timeline."

Doc raised an eyebrow.

"I take it this errand has nothing to do with our timeline," Winter said.

"The less anyone not going knows, the better," Doc said.

"Wasn't Annie the one who said we should avoid time traveling at all cost?"

Doc nodded.

"You're going to tell me what this was all about when you return," Winter said.

"If we return," Doc said. "That's why I'm here."

"I don't like ifs," Winter said. "Is it that dangerous?"

"It's time travel, Henry," he said. "It's always dangerous."

Doc slid a manila folder out of his long jacket and handed it to Winter.

He flipped it open.

"What's... you started a super team and you left a demi-god off the roster?"

"Those are the files of the known superhumans I didn't recruit," Doc said. "At the time I only went after kids who had activated their own powers—they were the most at risk, the biggest dangers to themselves, and they needed the most help. And they were already scared. No reason to go telling someone they're the son of a half-forgotten mythological being if they don't know it yet."

"But if you don't come back . . ." Winter said.

"You may want to go find a few myths," Doc said. "Just as a precaution."

Winter shuffled to another random page in the folder.

"You left a half-Atlantean running around out there on her own?"

Doc smirked.

"Long story there," Doc said. "She's not unmonitored."

Winter set the file aside, but kept glancing back at it. His curiosity was on high alert. It was a folder filled with wonder and trouble.

"When are you leaving?" Winter said.

"Tomorrow," he said.

"And you'll return when?"

"Annie says she can bring us back to almost the exact moment we left," Doc said. "You might not even know we're gone."

"Good luck," Winter said.

Doc nodded, then stood up.

"Sam Barren will help, too. We're going to have him stay in the Tower to watch for us. And to make sure the dog doesn't get lonely."

"A dog's living in the Tower," Winter said. "I still can't believe you have a dog living there."

"Different era," Doc said. "Different world."

Doc started to make symbols in the air, preparing a spell that would blink him out of the room as deftly as he arrived. Before he disappeared, Winter stopped him.

"You sure this is a good idea, Doc?" he said.

Silence smiled, that sad half smile whenever he was worried.

Winter had seen it plenty of times over the years.

"We've all broken Annie's rule of time travel at least once, Henry," Doc said. "And came back okay when we were young."

"But we didn't come back the same."

"Nobody ever does," Doc said, before winking out of existence and leaving Winter alone in his office, a folder full of superhumans waiting to be discovered on the desk beside him.

CHAPTER 8:
SECRET IDENTITIES,
OR LACK THEREOF

Billy walked Watson, his—*his*, he frequently reminded anyone who would listen, not *everyone's*—ten pound terrier mutt down one of the long and over-lit corridors in the Tower to meet Sam Barren. Sam, the former Department of What agent who had been their mentor—or, as Emily preferred to call him, their babysitter, while Doc Silence was missing last year—had now volunteered to stay in the Tower to monitor things while they time traveled with Annie. That meant Sam also inherited dog-sitting duty. Whether or not he knew this was part of his job remained to be seen, but Billy figured if he greeted him when he arrived he and Watson might be able to win Sam over.

I still can't believe we're going to time travel, Billy thought. Dude, have you ever time traveled before?

The alien sharing Billy's mind and consciousness didn't answer.

Dude? Billy thought again. Earth to Dude?

What? Dude answered, sounding annoyed.

Were you ignoring me? Billy thought.

When? Dude said.

I just asked you if you had ever time-traveled, Billy thought.

It was entirely possible the alien had traveled through time. Billy was not his first host slash partner. Dude had, under the shared name of Straylight, been acting as half of a superhero duo for more years than he'd ever admitted to Billy. Occasionally the alien said something anachronistic enough that Billy was convinced Dude had occupied an earthling's mind as far back as the Old West.

I was not ignoring you, Dude said.

What were you thinking about then? Billy thought.

Nothing that concerns you, Billy Case, Dude said.

You live in my brain. Everything you think about concerns me, Bill thought. Never mind. Seriously though—have you time traveled?

I have, Dude said. *I can't say I'm looking forward to doing so again.*

Why not? Billy asked.

I am not a fan of paradoxes, Dude said. *Very little good has ever come from stepping outside your own timeline.*

So you're saying I should have voted no, Billy thought.

Again, Dude fell silent.

Seriously, Dude, Billy thought. What are you doing in there, watching TV? Nodding off?

Your shadow approaches, Dude said.

And, as predicted, Entropy Emily came around the corner. She had added a puffy red vest to her usual ensemble of neon green, nuclear fallout symbols, and a scarf reminiscent of the 4th Doctor.

"Where'd you get the life preserver?" Billy asked.

"We're time traveling. We hang out with a guy named Doc. How could I not acquire a Marty McFly vest?" Emily said. "I got you one too. Want it?"

"I'm okay," Billy said.

"You fear the Marty McFly vest, don't you," Emily said. "You think it's too much for you."

"I think it looks like a life preserver."

"You're chicken."

"Nobody calls me chicken," Billy said.

Billy and Emily burst out laughing.

"Where are you taking our dog?" Emily said, picking Watson up and cradling him like a baby. The dog rested his head in the crook of her chin, and Emily swayed back and forth.

"My dog."

"Our dog. We found him together."

"I'm taking him down to meet with Sam in case we never come back from the future and he needs to take care of him," Billy said, walking toward the landing bay where he could hear Sam's ride arriving. "Also, Dude is acting weird."

I'm not acting weird, Dude said.

"Yes you are," Billy said.

"I love when you argue with yourself," Emily said.

* * *

"I said I'd monitor the Tower. I did not say I'd dog-sit," Sam said.

Billy and Emily were plying Sam with ice cream in the kitchen. Emily was stealthily feeding Watson tiny bits of cheese from a block of cheddar and smirking every time Billy tried to stop her with a glare.

"He's not that much work," Billy said. "He's ten pounds."

"I'm an old man," Sam said.

"An old man with a miraculous healing factor," Emily said. "You ain't fooling nobody, Samuel Barren. You have pep in your step."

Sam frowned.

"I suppose you'll expect me to walk him, too," Sam said.

"Look at how short his legs are. He really doesn't go that far," Billy said.

Sam looked back and forth between them, sighing.

"Fine. I'll look after him when you're gone. What does he need, one walk a day?"

"He's on a four-walk per day schedule," Billy said.

"Four!" Sam said. "Who has time for four walks a day?"

"Me?" Billy said.

"Don't you have a secret identity? Some low-paying day job you go to? In the old days the supers all had secret identities," Sam said.

"I don't think I technically do," Billy said.

"I definitely don't," Emily said.

"You have too much time on your hands," Sam said. "We're getting you a job when you get back."

"Doing what?" Billy said.

"Anything," Sam said. He scooped more ice cream into his bowl and rested his elbows on the table. "This is all moot anyway. Not coming back is unacceptable. I expect you all back in one piece before I finish lunch."

"Have you ever time traveled?" Billy asked. "Dude won't tell me anything about when he did."

Sam shook his head.

"Not me, kid," Sam said. "And I'm happier for it. I don't want to know what might have happened. I'm no fan of might-have-been."

"Is anyone?" Emily asked.

Sam smiled at her, a warm grin growing behind his outdated mustache.

"No," Sam said. "I don't think they are."

CHAPTER 9:
INFERNAL MACHINES

Kate Miller arrived alone at the site Anachronism Annie had arranged for the trip. Annie didn't want to try to move all seven of them in an enclosed space because she said time travel could create feedback energy and it didn't make sense to risk it in the Tower, and so she'd configured some sort of contraption in a field just outside the City.

No clouds dotted the blue sky. Spring would be here soon. Kate felt strange being outside in the daylight. It wasn't her natural habitat and hadn't been for a long, long time.

Jane arrived next, wearing her cartoonish uniform. She'd added blue leggings underneath her skirt, Kate noted, so at least she didn't look as much like a cheerleader as she normally had. Jane, of course, turned her face toward the clear sky and let the sun wash over her, her skin glittered like diamonds as she absorbed more solar energy.

"What's with the cape?" Jane asked.

Kate had added a cloak to her uniform, black and utilitarian, which she had wrapped around her shoulders like a cowl.

"Storage space," Kate said. "Can't fit everything I wanted to bring on my belt."

Jane nodded.

"Where's Titus?" Jane asked.

"Not here yet," she said. Kate wanted to be annoyed with him for voting yes on this trip, but she was a good judge of character, and if she hadn't wanted to be around an idealist, Kate would never have started spending time with Titus. She just wished on occasion that idealism didn't come across as suicidal altruism.

"You think this is stupid, don't you?" Jane said. She settled down on the grass and stretched her legs, her hair looking more and more like open flame dancing on the light breeze.

"We haven't caught the Vermin King," Kate said. "The shark-man is still out there. This world needs us right now."

"That's why we're coming back," Titus said, walking up to both women carrying his ridiculous, arcane spear.

Kate still struggled with how much he'd changed in the last year. Whatever transpired up in the woods in Canada—and Titus rarely spoke about what happened there in specific terms—had given him a new purpose, and a level of confidence that took them all by surprise. The pouting werewolf they used to know was all but gone.

"Nice cape!" Billy yelled. He was dressed in full costume as well, walking next to Emily, who had added a puffy red vest to her eyesore of a uniform.

Behind them, Doc Silence, Annie, and Sam Barren followed. Barren had Billy's dog with him on a *Star Wars* leash.

"You know what I'm not seeing right now? A police call box," Emily said.

"I'm not going over this with you again, Emily," Annie said.

"I would settle for a phone booth, like Bill and Ted had," Emily said.

"Not happening," Annie said.

"Okay, fine," Emily said. "How about an Ocarina of Time?"

"I don't even know what an Ocarina is—is she always like this?" Annie said.

"Always," Jane said.

"Perpetually," Billy said.

Annie sighed.

"Okay, look. Fine. I don't normally like to go into details, but here's the deal. I am a natural time traveler," Annie said. "Like you can manipulate gravity, I can manipulate time."

"That seems like a lot of responsibility," Emily said. "But also you must never be late for anything. Ever."

"Shut. Up." Annie said.

"That doesn't work," Billy said. "I've tried."

"Just stop," Annie said. "I can move freely through time. There are so many timelines, it's easier to find my way back to one I've been to if I've got an anchor to go back to. Which was why I had trouble getting back here last time, because Doc decided to go on a vacation to the higher planes."

"I didn't know I was your anchor," Doc said. "I really wish you'd stop blaming me for that."

"Anyway," she said. "To move all seven of us, I need a boost." Annie pointed to a small silver box and a ring of cables on the ground. "This device will give a little kick to my powers. It'll help me move you all easier into the future. And before you ask, yes, I have one waiting for me on the other side to get us home. I made sure of that prior to leaving the last time."

"So you just poof us into the future," Billy said. "By what? Thinking?"

"It's not unlike Doc's teleportation spells, actually," Annie said. "I use math rather than magic but it's remarkably similar. So it should feel really familiar."

"Doc's never teleported us before," Jane said.

Annie glared at Doc. "You've never teleported them?"

"You can teleport us?" Emily said.

"It never really came up," Doc said, shrugging. "Sorry. Three of them can fly, Annie. It never seemed necessary."

Annie ran her tattooed hands through her neon pink hair, clearly distraught.

"They're all going to throw up," she said.

"We're all going to what?" Jane said.

Kate felt her stomach churning. Getting sick to her stomach was one of her few legitimate fears. She looked at Emily who shared her horror.

"What? Why? Why would you do that?" Emily said.

"It's just... what people do when they're not used to teleporting. Most people only get sick the first time," Annie said. "Which wouldn't be a problem if—"

"If Doc hadn't been holding out on us with taxi service by teleportation spell," Titus said. He looked over at Kate, concerned. "You okay?"

"I'm fine," Kate said.

"You're sweating."

"I'm fine," Kate said again. She cracked open a pouch on her belt and pulled out a small pill bottle packed with cotton to prevent rattling and pulled out a tablet.

"Now I really don't think you're okay," Titus said.

"Dimenhydrinate," Kate said. "Motion sickness pill."

"Gimme one," Emily said.

Kate frowned at her but gave the blue-haired girl one of the pills.

Annie herded everyone into the ring of cables. She pointed at Titus.

"You should probably leave the Capitoline Spear here," she said.

"The what which where?" Titus said.

"The mystical artifact you're using as a walking stick," she said. "Unique artifacts are risky to transport between timelines. They carry a lot of embedded power with them."

"It's a spear," Titus said.

"It's a two-thousand-year-old magical artifact that has been used to kill at least one demi-god," Annie said. "Again, Doc? You didn't tell him that?"

"He's not planning on killing any gods, are you Titus?" Doc said.

"Not on my itinerary, no," Titus said.

"And it was his peoples' choice to tell him or not. Because the Capitoline Spear really isn't that dangerous, Annie," Doc said.

"And you," Annie said. "Empty your pockets."

Titus handed his spear over to Sam as Doc removed two amulets, a coin the size of the palm of his hand, an intricate knife made of bone, a broken mirror, a necklace made of blue crystal beads, and what appeared to be a glass eyeball, out of his coat pockets.

"Minor magic, Annie," Doc said. "This is just my everyday gear."

"Anything in this pile luck-based or involve teleportation?" Annie asked.

Doc tossed one of the amulets to Sam and then walked the broken mirror over to him as well.

Annie fixed her eyes on Kate next.

"Anything in that bag of tricks you've got wrapped around your shoulder magical or high-tech?"

Kate shook her head.

Annie nodded. "Okay then," she said.

"So do we need to... hold hands or something?" Emily asked.

"No," Annie said.

"Sing Huey Lewis and the News?"

"No."

"Say the alphabet backwards?"

"Someone help," Annie said.

"Come on, Em. Let her concentrate," Jane said.

Emily crossed her arms and pouted, looking all the more ridiculous as her puffy vest rode up under her chin.

"We'll be back, Sam," Doc said.

"Better be," he said. "I'll keep an eye on things."

Annie began to mumble under her breath, eyes closed.

Kate felt suddenly lightheaded, unsure of herself. Her knees buckled slightly. She looked down at her hands, and saw them flickering, going out of focus like a scrambled television set. She turned to Titus, who was watching her with concern. He too flickered in and out like a fading hologram. He nodded at her. In between flickers, he smiled.

And then they were gone.

CHAPTER 10:
THE WHITE SHADOW

Keaton Bohr had come to hate visiting with the White Shadow. Years ago, the masked hero had plucked him out of obscurity, given him a reason to be, provided a usefulness to his work. The White Shadow found Keaton when the scientist had lost all hope in science, when his ideas on energy manipulation and automatons—ideas Keaton had wanted to use to feed the world and make it a better place—had been ignored for so long he was prepared to give everything up.

The White Shadow approached him that night, dressed as always in an impeccable black suit, face wrapped in white silk like a ghost, no eyes or mouth visible, as Keaton leaned on the guardrail of the bridge leading into the City over the river near the Financial District. A light snow fell, and Keaton watched the lights of the City twinkling in the distance, a million lives quietly going about their activities in pointless repetition.

Keaton knew the White Shadow from the news. He'd been around for decades, a mysterious vigilante, solving crimes, a faceless Sherlock Holmes, working from the darkness, a thinking man's superhero. But this character in front of Keaton, regarding him with the blankest of gazes, was smaller than Keaton would have expected. Slighter, the dark suit hanging on the Shadow's frame seemed as if it were tailored to someone else's body, someone bigger, broader of shoulder.

"I understand you want to change the world," the Shadow had

said to him.

Keaton stood, slack-jawed. The voice felt wrong too. But, he supposed, all these masked heroes are different in person. They need to be. Up close, perhaps they're just human beings like anyone else. He stared and didn't answer.

"It's almost as if they don't want things to get better," the White Shadow said, gesturing towards the City.

And that was how it began, twenty years ago. A lifetime. They were friends at first. The White Shadow shared vast plans with Keaton. Ways to make the world a better place. And now, as Keaton walked down into the depths of the massive laboratory they had converted into a base of operations, he had started to become frightened of the Shadow.

Started to? No, Keaton thought. I've been afraid much longer than that.

He found the White Shadow sitting alone in the dark, as always, in a tall-backed chair, watching monitors upon which the most recent battle with Solar were replaying.

"Your robots held up well this time, Keaton," Shadow said.

"Not really," Keaton said. "She tore them apart."

"We can always make more," Shadow said. "Do we know what she was looking for?"

"The same thing she's always looking for, I suspect," he said.

"Well, we'll give her what she wants soon," the White Shadow said. There was a quiet threat in that simple statement.

Keaton's stomach churned with anxiety. "We will?" he said.

"My friend," the White Shadow said. "She's looking for an end to all of this. And we are so close."

The Shadow waved a hand and the monitors clicked off, leaving them both in near darkness, with only the light seeping in from the hallway illuminating them.

"It's almost over," the White Shadow said. "It's finally almost over."

CHAPTER 11:
TO THE FUTURE

The future," Emily said, sneering and looking around at the desiccated landscape surrounding them, "is disgusting."

Billy had to agree.

Of course the future was extra disgusting because most of the Indestructibles had come through their time-traveling experience dizzy and sick to their stomachs. Everyone sat around a few meters away from their arrival point and tried to get their sea legs back. Even Doc looked a little shaken up by it, though he was holding it together better than the others. Apparently, Kate's anti-seasickness pills hadn't done much for her or Emily. Both their faces were dressed in varied shades of green.

I feel fine, though, Billy thought.

That's because I controlled your inner ear sensations to stabilize your equilibrium, Dude said. *You'd actually be faring very poorly if I weren't here to help.*

"I feel fine," Billy said out loud to everyone.

You never miss a chance to be dishonest, do you, Billy Case?

Nope, Billy thought. Never.

Jane wasn't feeling particularly well either by the look of it, but she'd taken a few steps away from the group and turned her face skyward again.

"It's so gray here," she said. "What happened? Nuclear war?"

"War, and lots of it," Annie said. "The people we need to stop systematically declared war on humanity."

"All of it?" Titus asked.

"At first, they seemed to be doing good—they went after the bad guys in the beginning," Annie said. "But when all the bad guys disappeared, they started coming after everyone else."

"What do you mean, came after everyone else?" Kate asked. She adjusted the newly added cape to ensure her arms were completely free.

"They went after power sources. Food supplies. They destroyed highways," Annie said.

"So they did all this?" Titus asked. "Everything smells like smoke and death."

Annie stood up, stretched her legs, and started walking away.

"That's the sad part," Annie said. "They didn't have to do this. They destroyed the things people wanted, and you know what happened?"

"People destroyed each other to get what was left," Jane said.

Annie pointed at her.

"Which I think was exactly what the adversaries were planning," Annie said. "Follow me. We're not far from the safe house where. . ."

Annie started laughing and caught herself.

"Where what?" Billy said.

"Where the Indestructibles have set up a makeshift base," Annie said.

* * *

The base turned out to be an abandoned community college building. Cars littered the parking lot, upturned and blackened by fire. Here, too, everything was gray and covered with dust and grime. Annie walked ahead of the group and stepped through the shattered glass where large double doors once stood.

Titus made a low growling noise and Billy turned.

"What's the matter, Lassie? Timmy fall down a well?" Billy asked.

"There's others here," Titus said. "Like me."

"What's it like going out with a bloodhound?" Emily asked, looking at Kate.

As usual, Kate ignored her, moving ahead to scout, but Doc put a hand on her arm.

"Wait," he said.

Kate glared at him, but listened.

Titus' eyes started to change color, a precursor to transforming into full werewolf mode. They scanned the darker parts of the hall.

"It will never stop freaking me out when you smell things we can't smell," Billy said.

"I'll tell you if I ever stop freaking myself out when it happens," Titus said. "Also, you talking to yourself all the time is way weirder... Annie?"

"There are other werewolves here, yes," Annie said. "But they're on our side."

Titus cocked his head to one side.

"And... someone singing?" he said.

Now they all stopped to listen, walking slowly and quietly behind Annie as she led them deeper into the building.

Billy finally caught up with Titus' superhuman hearing. The faint sound of a woman singing reached his ears, a delicate voice, but pretty, high and folksy. The closer they drew, the clearer the voice became. A melancholy feeling tingled in his chest. The sound of the woman's voice made him feel suddenly very lonely.

"Of all the comrades that e'er I had, they are sorry for my going away," the voice sang. *"And all the sweethearts that e'er I had, they would wish me one more day to stay."*

"That's... awfully pretty," Emily said.

Billy looked at her.

Emily shrugged. "What, you disagree?"

"But since it falls unto my lot, that I should rise and you should not," the singing voice continued, *"I'll gently rise and softly call, good night and joy be with you all."*

Doc had stopped walking entirely. He stood completely still, hands in his pockets and head bowed. Titus' body had relaxed, no longer ready to pounce, a near smile lit his face.

"Who is that?" Billy asked.

Jane pushed her way to the front of the group, gently moving Annie aside with a hand on her shoulder.

"I think that's me," Jane said.

And she ran on without them, into the hallway ahead.

CHAPTER 12:
THE OTHER SIDE OF THE MIRROR

Jane stormed into the next room at a run, coming to an awkward halt just within the doorway as she discovered a woman standing over a body lying on a medical gurney. The woman was dressed in a uniform, all white, except for a black and gold trim across the shoulders like a tribal version of the sun. Her hair was the color of open flame, and flickered the same way, moving with a life of its own, the way fire always does.

She was singing.

"My father sang that song," Jane said, creeping into the room.

The woman stood up to her full height but did not turn around.

"My adopted father," Jane said. "An old Irish pub song. He sang it whenever he had to leave."

"The Parting Glass," the woman said in Jane's own voice.

She turned, and Jane's breath caught in her throat.

This other Jane had her face, but her skin was different, almost glowing with a golden light, as if all the sunlight she gathered up in the twenty years between them stayed with her and illuminated her from within.

"I'm going to glow," Jane said.

And her older self nodded.

"You already do," the older-Jane said and smiled. "This has to be at least as weird for you as it is for me."

"If I ever see anything stranger than this in my entire life, I'll be amazed," Jane said.

"Who did you bring with you?" her future self said. "Annie must be back."

"I am," Annie said, walking in the room, thumbs tucked into her belt loops. "I told you I'd bring help, didn't I?"

Doc strode in next, placing a hand on younger-Jane's shoulder.

Older-Jane's mouth quirked as if she might cry.

"Oh, Doc," she said, holding a hand out to him. "I haven't seen you in so long."

"Looks like you turned out alright without me," he said as older-Jane took his hand in hers.

Titus and Kate came in next.

The elder Jane gasped and put a hand on Titus' face.

"Look at you," she said. "Look at your face. I haven't seen your face in so long."

"Am I... Is there . . ." Titus said.

"It's better if I let him explain," future-Jane said. "You should hear it from him yourself. But you're here. Your older self is in this building."

She turned to Kate, and a shadow of sorrow fell across her eyes.

"I'm dead, aren't I?" Kate said.

"No," older-Jane said. "But again, it's not my story to tell. I'll bring you to her."

Emily strutted in next; the darkness in the elder Jane's face faded.

"Who is this?" she asked.

"Entropy Emily," Emily said. "I'm the leader."

"Is that so," future-Jane said.

"Emily is our secret weapon," Annie said. "She's going to turn this fight around, whether she knows it or not."

"Don't go giving her a swelled head," Billy said, walking into the room last. "She's got a big enough ego as it is."

Older-Jane lost all decorum and rushed to him, throwing her arms around him ferociously. She picked him up off the ground so only his toes touched the floor.

"You were saying something about never seeing anything weirder in your entire life?" Emily said to younger-Jane.

"I take that back," younger-Jane said. "What's happening?"

Her older self had Billy's shoulders in her hands as if to make sure he still existed.

"So this isn't awkward at all," Billy said.

Older-Jane started to talk, but a harsh sob came out instead.

Billy looked at younger-Jane for help, but she just shrugged.

Another uniformed person walked into the room from a separate entrance, a teenaged girl with dark hair wearing what appeared to be a knockoff of Billy's costume. She looked around at everyone, particularly staring at younger-Jane, before turning to address Annie.

"What the heck is happening in here? And why is Solar crying?"

"I'm sorry," the elder Jane said, composing herself. "Straylight, these are... these are the Indestructibles."

"The beta version," Emily said. "Did she just call you Straylight?"

"Did you just call her Straylight?" Billy asked.

"She did. Because I'm Straylight," the girl said. "Who the heck are you?"

"I'm a girl in this timeline?" Billy said.

"You're totally a girl in this timeline!" Emily said.

"He can't be. She's our age now," Titus said. "You're a different Straylight entirely."

"Oh no," Doc said, stepping back a little.

Younger-Jane watched as he melded into the shadows a bit, letting the events unfold as best they could.

"Dude, did you pick someone else in this timeline?" Billy said, clearly talking to the alien in his head.

"Are you talking to the alien right now?" the new girl asked.

"Of course I'm talking to Dude right now!" Billy said.

"I don't even know how this is possible," the new girl said.

"How what is possible?" Billy said.

"I'm guessing all of it," Titus said. He looked at Kate, who had, like Doc, taken a step away from everyone else to simply observe.

Younger-Jane watched as Titus tried to disappear as well, but, in a throwback to his less confident days, mostly looked like he was mortified.

"This is why I didn't want to tell you guys anything," Annie said. "I knew you'd freak out."

"I am not freaking out!" Billy said. "Okay. I'm freaking out!"

"I'm not you!" the new girl said. "Wait, this is the old Straylight?"

Billy stomped his feet.

"Old Straylight? I'm the old Straylight? Did I quit? Tell me I didn't quit. Wait, Dude, did you dump me? For someone younger?"

"Billy," younger-Jane said. "Give it a minute."

"This is so much worse than finding out I'm a hot girl in this other timeline."

"Watch it," the new Straylight said. "Don't be a creep. I didn't realize my predecessor was a creep."

"I'm not a creep. And where am I?" Billy said. "Did I get captured again? Seriously, did they shoot me with the thing that kicks Dude out again? I don't want to do that twice. I hope that doesn't happen a second time."

"You died, Billy," older-Jane said softly.

She grabbed his hand and held it.

Billy stopped fidgeting and stood completely still as she spoke.

"You're gone. You died."

"I'm dead?" Billy said.

"You were so brave," older-Jane said. "You died saving so many people. It was the stupidest, bravest thing I ever saw."

"I'm dead? You're saying I'm dead?"

"You died a hero, Billy Case," older-Jane said.

"I don't care if I died king of Mars, I don't want to be dead!" Billy said.

"Well it's the truth," older-Jane said. "It's so strange to see you here, like this."

"Yeah, it's pretty weird for me too," Billy said.

Older-Jane shook her head, then looked back and forth from her younger self to Billy.

"You aren't together in your timeline, are you?" she said. "I can tell."

Younger-Jane and Billy locked eyes.

"Together?" Billy, Jane, and Emily all said at the same time.

Emily started laughing so hard she had to cling to Doc's jacket for support.

"The future is amazing," she said, wiping tears of laughter from her eyes.

CHAPTER 13:
THE KING OF WOLVES

After the ruckus died down—at least, after everyone but Emily got themselves back under control—Annie suggested they should find this future's Titus next.

Older-Jane looked at Kate and Titus and frowned.

"Annie, you know he's . . ." she started.

"He'll be fine," Annie said. "He'll be okay."

"I can't wait to find out how messed up I am in the future," Titus said, his voice laden with sarcasm. "I'm not dreading this at all."

Older-Jane smiled.

"You're what's holding this world together, Titus Whispering," she said. "You're doing exactly what you were born to do. But it's been rough on you. Just be ready."

Titus looked at Kate, but the Dancer offered no comfort, looking coldly ahead.

"Let's go," she said.

Jessie, the replacement Straylight, gestured for everyone to follow her. She led them down a poorly lit corridor, through an area that looked like it might have once been an atrium, now littered with glass from broken windows. Through another set of doors into a sort of theater—no, Titus realized, an actual theater, but battered and broken, seats scattered around, water damage permeated the walls. One of those tiered classrooms you see in Ivy League schools on TV.

Sitting on the stage, silhouetted by dim backlighting, was the largest werewolf he'd ever seen. Bigger even than Gabriel, the older, elegant warrior who had taught him how to fight when he went looking for his past last year. Massive, gray-furred shoulders, moving up and down with animalistic breathing. As Titus walked further into the room, he knew suddenly that this was not the only werewolf here, there were others, five, maybe six, resting in the shadows as well. The big wolf had a pack here. Some of them even smelled faintly familiar. Titus knew he might be able to identify them if he transformed, but he held back. Better to wait.

The big werewolf slid off the stage, the ground rumbling as his full weight hit the floor. He waved a massive paw to one side, and the lights in the theater rose slightly. Someone in the back had turned them up, clearly.

"Come here, boy," the werewolf said in a thunderous, low growl.

"I hope he doesn't mean me," Billy said.

The wolf pointed one huge talon at Titus.

Titus took a deep breath and walked forward. The werewolf was covered in scars, ravines in his flesh where the fur didn't grow anymore. It was clear from his gait that there was an injury that never healed either, something in his hip or knee that made his step just slightly off-center.

"Was I ever so damned young," the wolf said, and somewhere behind them, younger-Jane gasped.

"You're me," Titus said, and the wolf nodded his massive head.

"I'm you," he said. "And you're me."

The werewolf inhaled deeply.

"You're not afraid," he said. "You've found them then."

"The others? I did," Titus said.

The werewolf nodded again.

"When Annie said she was going back," the werewolf said, jaws struggling to form her name, "I wasn't sure if you'd find them. I went to find the pack when Doc died, because there was no one else to teach me."

"Things weren't so different for me," Titus said, glancing back to where Doc Silence was hanging away from the group. "Different events, but the same reasons."

The older werewolf smiled. It was a nightmarish sight, rows of white teeth in the darkness.

"Then there's some people who will be happy to see you," the old wolf said. "Leto?"

Leto emerged from the darkness like some sort of goddess of death, the ancient female werewolf who had taught Titus so much all those months before. Leto was in full werewolf form as well, that strange, almost jackal-like head cutting an alien silhouette in the darkness. A pale robe draped over her shoulders contrasted with the jet-black of her fur.

Titus almost ran to her, but held himself back. Remain dignified, he thought. For some reason he felt powerfully compelled to impress his future self.

The next werewolf to emerge from the darkness had no such qualms.

"It's like seein' a ghost," Finnigan said, the red-headed werewolf reverting to human form to throw his arms around Titus and pick him up off his feet. "You were never this pretty, Whispering. You were clearly born better-looking in this other timeline."

Older-Titus huffed a quiet laugh, but said nothing.

"You've hardly changed," Titus said, his arm gripping the stout man's arm. "It's been almost twenty years, and you haven't changed."

"Ah, there's some more gray in with the ginger," Finnigan said. "But you know we werewolves and our lifespans. We tend to keep our looks longer than regular folk."

Titus studied Finnigan's face, unsure. The red-haired werewolf frowned.

"Well I guess nobody spoiled that little genetic quirk for you back home, did they," he said. "That's unfortunate."

The grizzled future-Titus studied the group a moment.

"I hope you've done the right thing, Annie, bringing them here," he said. He gestured at Billy. "You."

"Me?"

The older werewolf didn't respond, instead turning to older-Jane from his own timeline.

"Are you okay," he rumbled.

She nodded at the younger Titus and smiled.

"Not even a little bit," she said. "Are you?"

The big wolf looked around the room, searching for something.

"No," he said. "But we'll make do."

"We're here to help," Doc said, finally stepping forward. "From what I understand, this is all my fault."

"Because you died?" the old wolf said. "I'd sooner blame the person who killed you."

"We'll talk about that later," Doc said.

The old wolf nodded.

"We should get you all brought up to speed," he said. The words sounded uncomfortable and strained through his massive jaws. "Jane, did your spy give you any new information?"

"He did," older-Jane said. "At the cost of his own life, but he did. But I think we should replay the whole situation with our new friends first. Maybe they can help us piece it all together."

Titus discerned that his older self was troubled. "What's wrong?" he said, feeling awkward and alien by asking his future self a question so revealing, yet so simple.

The future-Titus leaned forward.

"Is she here with you?" he asked. "Kate? Is she with you?"

"Of course she is," Titus said, before realizing Kate had been completely silent during the exchange. "Where's Kate?"

"Oh no," Annie said.

"She's gone to find herself," Titus said.

"That's not good," Annie said. "Jane?"

"This way," older-Jane said, leading Annie away. Everyone moved to follow, but both she and Annie held up their hands to stop them.

"No," Annie said. "Doc, and both Janes. That's it."

"Not me?" Titus said.

Annie and older-Jane exchanged looks.

"Stay out of sight," Annie said. "Just hang back."

"Why?" Titus asked, turning to the older version of himself for guidance. He found the elder wolf had shuffled back to the stage, hunched over, his back to the group.

"Just trust me," Annie said. "It's for the best."

CHAPTER 14: DANCING

Kate worked her way silently through the darkened hallways of the building, lights flickered as bulbs clung desperately to the last few watts of their lives. She'd seen the look of pity on older-Jane's face. She realized something was wrong, something with her future, and Kate wasn't about to wait idly by until someone else dictated how and when she'd discover it.

She'd find her own destiny. She always had.

Kate knew a dance studio or rehearsal space would be located near the theater where they'd met the scarred and monstrous future version of Titus, and so she began to work in concentric circles outward from there until she found what she was looking for.

She wondered if that was what the future Titus had waiting for him. A monster and a hero, damaged and limping, a pack of others like him hiding in the shadows and waiting for his commands. They had spoken briefly about what Titus learned in his time in Canada and how he was expected to be some sort of leader among the wolves, that he was a Whispering, whatever that word might mean, and that he would have responsibilities to his kind someday. And that those responsibilities would extend to humankind as well.

Responsibilities always come with a terrible cost, Kate thought. The only safe thing to do is to understand your limits, to know exactly where your breaking point is, to ride that razor edge with skill and care.

Where am I? Kate thought. What do I become? Am I monster as

well? Or am I dead and gone, like Billy, my life ended in some poorly planned attempt at exceeding my own abilities?

Kate wondered also what it would take to kill someone like Billy, protected as he was by the alien powers of Straylight. She'd hosted the alien for a while when Billy was incarcerated. She hadn't had a chance to really test the limits of those powers, but she knew how she'd felt, invincible, filled to the brim with power. Those powers would protect you, she thought, but they could also make you reckless, until the day, eventually, everything fails you.

Alien guardian angels and friends both.

She found the studio, lights out, music playing softly from a small, battery-operated radio. A dim glow seeped in through foggy skylights. In the darkness, a woman danced.

There's a language to dance. Some people become fluent in it and speak their emotions through movement—punctuation through the bend of a limb, exclamation via striated muscle. It is a manner of speaking that doesn't always require fluency to comprehend. Kate had seen people who never understood the intricacies of dance break down in tears at the sight of a performance. Though unable to explain why it cracked something deep inside them, why they remained inconsolable, their primal self clearly read the tale the dancer was trying to express.

But if you are a dancer, and if you're lucky, you can read the story in the dance almost like words on a page.

This dancer spun a tragic drama. A broken ballet, bastardized with pieces of modern, aggressive, frustrated, angry steps, feet landing hard and furious on the floor. She focused on working some inner dialogue out, a cry for help, for forgiveness, for a second chance. She moved across the floor like water.

Kate Miller, the vigilante Dancer, does not feel sadness, she often told herself. I don't have time to feel sad. It makes nothing better, it does not bring back the dead, it fixes nothing.

And yet, watching this woman dance, she felt her heart break in two. Kate stifled a sob with her fist, teeth biting into the fabric of a glove.

Why does this dance hurt so much? she thought.

The woman turned and Kate saw her own face, eyes covered with a blindfold, a cruel scar running up her forehead and into her hairline. She untied the blindfold. Sightless eyes looked back at her.

"I can hear you," future-Kate said. "Who are you? Not one of Titus' little puppies."

Kate didn't answer. She simply stared. Her future self was all lean muscle, but frailer, without the fighting strength Kate herself carried in her shoulders and back. This future self really did look like a ballerina, strong but slender, yet showing the effects of the vigilante life in the scar tissue visible on the bare flesh of her arms and chest.

"Now, I know who you are," the sightless woman said.

"Of course you do," Kate said.

"Annie came back," future-Kate said. "I was hoping I'd be smart enough not to come with her, but you came along anyway."

Future-Kate walked toward the far wall, placed her fingertips against it, then followed the edge until she found a water bottle on the floor. She took a long sip.

"We shouldn't have come here," Kate said.

Her future self nodded in agreement.

"We don't deserve the help," she said. "We had our chance. We failed at every turn."

"What happened to you," Kate said. "To us."

The future dancer shook her head.

"Do you ever feel inferior to them?" she said.

"What?" Kate asked.

"To the other Indestructibles," the dancer said. "What a ridiculous name. The Indestructibles. Is that what you're called in your timeline?"

"It is," Kate said.

"The press called us that in this timeline. Named us. Stupid name," future-Kate said. "We're all destructible. We're all breakable. Some more than others."

"What happened to your sight?" Kate said.

"The visual cortex," the future dancer said. "You know where it is?"

"The back of the brain," Kate said.

The old dancer nodded. "Gone in a split second," she said. "We are not indestructible."

Kate heard footsteps.

Anachronism Annie walked into the room slowly, backlit by the strange, warm glow older-Jane cast behind her. Younger-Jane—my Jane, Kate thought—sauntered almost bashfully behind both.

"Everything okay in here?" Annie said.

"Yeah," Kate said, her voice rough.

"You shouldn't have brought them here, Annie," future-Kate said. "Bring them home before it's too late."

Older-Jane gestured for the others to leave.

Annie stepped back, watching younger-Kate.

The future dancer reached out and grabbed her younger self by the arm, pulling her in close.

"You're always right," the woman whispered. "Remember that. Remember your instincts. You will always be right." Then, she let Kate go, and the younger dancer took an unsteady step back.

Younger-Jane tried to help, but Kate shrugged her off. Their older versions were arguing in hushed tones, the future-Kate clearly agitated, her version of Jane trying to calm her.

The younger versions locked eyes for a second, but Kate turned and stormed away, almost crashing into Titus in the hallway, where the young werewolf stood with Doc Silence.

"Kate?" Titus said, softly.

Kate peered back into the dark dance studio, toward the soft sounds of her future self engaged in a pointless debate, and fumed off into the hallway alone, leaving Titus behind.

CHAPTER 15:
THE SECRET HISTORY OF THE WORLD (PART 1)

Jane returned with her older self, Annie, and Titus to the theater where the others were waiting. Titus wanted to go after Kate, Jane knew, but the young werewolf understood better than to try to speak with the Dancer when she was angry, and clearly her experience with her future self had left Kate shaken.

In the theater, Titus' future self, still in full-on werewolf form, sat on the stage like a king presiding over a court. Doc and Emily sat front and center—Doc, like a petulant student, rested on the back of one of the theater's chairs, and Emily mimicked his posture perfectly—while Billy milled about alone in the back of the hall, deep in conversation with Dude.

Jane caught Emily's eye and gestured at Billy with a nod of her chin, but Emily shrugged and made a cartoonishly large gesture with her whole head toward the nearby Jessie, the future's newer Straylight.

Jane sighed quietly at Emily's lack of subtlety and searched for a place to sit down.

"It may be useful if we had a more complete understanding of where things went differently here," Doc said. "We know some of the basics, but maybe if we learn the 'how,' we might be able to help more."

"What are you going to do?" Jessie asked. "Go back in time and fix it?"

Doc shook his head. "Not an option."

"Because you can't, or because you won't?" Jessie said.

Doc turned his attention from the young hero to the older Titus.

"You wouldn't know this, because I was gone before I was able to tell all of you everything in this timeline, but you can't alter the past," Doc said. He shot a defiant stare at Annie, who glared back at him. "And we know that because we've tried and failed before. The past doesn't want to be changed."

"But we can try to alter the present," Annie said. "We can help here."

"I'm not even going to pretend to understand what you're talking about," Jessie said.

"If I had a dollar for every time someone said that to me . . ." Emily said, but Jane shushed her.

Older-Titus shuffled to the edge of the stage and settled down on his haunches.

"Enough," he said. "Where do you want us to begin, Doc? What don't you know?"

"Near as I can tell, things started to go differently when I died," Doc said. Finnigan and Jessie shifted uncomfortably, but Doc waved them off. "This isn't the first time I found out I died early in another timeline. It's okay."

"I hope I never get to the point where I can say that so casually," younger-Titus said.

His older counterpart grunted, quieting the entire room. Then, he looked at the Jane from his timeline. "You should tell. You know the most about what happened," older-Titus said.

Future-Jane nodded. "This is surreal, you know?" she said, looking at Doc. "Losing you was like... well, John Hawkins was my father, but you were pretty close yourself."

Doc smiled.

"I'm glad for that," he said. "But it'll be okay. Just tell me what you can. Do you know who it was? Who killed me?"

"We knew that right away," future-Jane said. "We knew that as soon as it happened. It was Lady Natasha Grey."

Then future-Jane settled in to tell the story.

* * *

Once, in another past:

Doc Silence watched his students training together and felt a quiet pride well up inside.

His four pupils—Jane, Kate, Titus, and Billy—gathered in the massive space within the Tower that was designed for superhumans to test their limits. A few moments earlier the room had rumbled with mock combat and flashed with the light generated by Billy's and Jane's powers. Now, however, the room was filled with laughter. Doc, situated in the observatory above, couldn't make out the exact words, but Titus was ribbing Billy about something; Jane laughed, watching them with a pride not unlike Doc's own, aware that they were finally becoming something closer to heroes. Kate hung back, as she always did, but Doc knew she was present, in the moment, was now a part of the group, not an outsider no matter how much she initially wanted to be.

I assembled a team after all, he thought, smiling. There was something missing, though, another hero or two, someone who would complement the abilities of this small group. But they were becoming friends, and that was the important thing. Doc had often heard that, in situations of violence, friendship and love is a liability, that it's better to have a professional respect for each other that could be relied upon. But when it came to people like those Doc had worked with his entire life, he knew it had to be more personal. You had to love the people you fought beside here. Because the things you would see, the things you would face as a hero, you'd need something more than just respect to make it through. You needed to think with your heart as often as you thought with your head.

These young heroes were becoming a family, he thought. And that would save them in the end. Love doesn't conquer all things, but it is the light at the end of every tunnel.

Doc was shaken from his own thoughts when Tower's artificial intelligence, Neal, chimed in.

"Designation: Doc Silence," the AI's always professional voice said. "There has been an incident you may want to be aware of."

"Bring it up on screen," Doc said, gesturing at a small monitor on his left.

The AI's eyes were everywhere here. He was, in many ways, the Tower itself. Neal understood where Doc wanted to review the information he had to share before Doc himself knew.

The screen lit up, depicting an aerial view using data filters only the Tower had, a sort of satellite imaging designed to sense unique energy signatures. It was how he found heroes like Billy, because their strange abilities appeared and were picked up by the Tower's network. The system informed the heroes ahead of time what type of obstacles they might be facing, be it nuclear, alien, or some other indefinable challenge. As it was in this case.

Doc frowned when he saw the unique patterns indicate a magical attack outside London. Something strange was happening near Elephant and Castle, a tube stop Doc had been to many times. He'd lived nearby for a short time when he was younger.

"Neal, please confirm. That's a magical energy signature, yes?"

"It is, Designation: Doc Silence. It is—"

"I know those spells by sight, it's okay," Doc said, cutting the AI off.

He glanced back down at the young heroes below him, still laughing and joking together. They weren't ready for magic, he knew. It was partially his own fault—he'd never exposed them to the supernatural, and given them no training in how to deal with it or how to defend themselves from it. But even if he had, they wouldn't be ready. There's nothing in this world as dangerous as magic, he thought. And Doc vowed to keep them from it as long as he could.

He touched the intercom and spoke into a small microphone on the console.

"Jane, come up to the observation deck for a moment, would you?" he said.

She looked up at him and saluted playfully.

No, Doc thought. I'll take care of this myself. And when I get back, I'll start teaching them about magic.

He wished very much that conversation would never have to happen. Doc wouldn't wish magic on his worst enemy, let alone these four kids he cared so much about.

Jane's footsteps clanked on the stairwell leading up to the observation area and she loudly clomped her way in.

"They're doing great, aren't they?" Jane said.

She was as much their teacher as Doc was; Jane and Doc had time together to train before he first reached out to the others, time to acclimate her after Jane's powers first manifested themselves. It was a period to prepare her to lead, Doc knew. It had been clear from their first few days together that Jane possessed the instincts of a leader, the right amount of compassion, self-sacrifice and self-confidence, and he had made sure to instill in her the things she'd need to take these less experienced heroes into the field.

"They are," Doc said. "And so are you. You've come a long way, Jane."

She shrugged.

"Only practicing what you taught me," she said. "You look worried. Are we doing something wrong down there?"

He shook his head.

"No," he said.

"So why'd you call me up here?" she asked.

Doc gestured to the monitor. Pulsating lights of whatever was happening at Elephant and Castle Streets continued to flicker.

"I need to investigate something," Doc said. "And just wanted to let you know I'd be gone a few hours, maybe longer."

Jane raised an eyebrow.

"Want backup?" she said. "I think we're ready for some field work."

"No," he said. Doc held up a hand in response to Jane's disappointed expression, "I don't doubt that you're close to getting out into the field, but these events involve magic. I haven't been able to give you anywhere near the tools you require to help with something like this."

"Sounds like you've been neglectful in your duties, Doctor Silence," Jane said.

He chuckled.

"When I get back, I'll start teaching you about magic," Doc said. "But there's a reason I've held off. It's the final exam, not a prep test. Magic is the most dangerous element you'll ever face. I wanted to let you work your way up to it."

"So when you return, we'll talk about getting the team into the field? Maybe stop muggings or something else?"

"How about rescuing a few kittens out of trees?" Doc said.

"Anything if it will get us out of the training room," Jane said.

"It's a promise, then," Doc said. "You'll hold down the fort?"

"You bet," she said. Jane pursed her lips, suddenly serious. "But if you get into any trouble, you'll call? Even if it's just me. I won't put the others in danger."

"I will," he said. Doc put a hand on Jane's shoulder, amazed, as always, by the way the stored solar energy she used to power her abilities radiated a distinct halo-like heat from her. "See you soon."

"Be safe," Jane said.

"I always am," he said.

Doc turned and cast a silent spell that opened a sliver in space. Through the gateway, he saw London's ever-unique skyline.

"I'll be back soon," he said, not realizing that this would be the last time he'd ever see Jane.

* * *

Then:

Doc Silence stepped out of a portal across the street from the garish statue from which Elephant and Castle, a roadway in central London, derived its name. The road involved one of the more frustrating roundabouts he'd ever encountered during his time living here when he was young—he swore the rotary was the work of a demon, but then again, Doc thought, most roundabouts involve dark sorcery if you looked hard enough for it.

Even still, the bright red elephant with a tiny castle on its back brought back memories of his years in London. He learned so much magic here, back in the early days. London hosted a hotbed of practitioners of magic, both light and dark; he'd come here to study, and to make a name for himself, if he could.

But Elephant and Castle was also the home of one of his worst days here in London. Not fighting a demon, not ending a curse, not failing to solve a case or save the day. No, Elephant and Castle was the place where a young Doc engaged in a terrible argument with someone he worried about, someone who had known what he was going to become. She'd watched him going down a dark path—like roundabouts, all paths of magic are dark, even the good ones—and she'd tried to warn him off.

By then though, Doc had already witnessed too much. It was too late to turn back. His eyes had been transformed to burning violet orbs. He perceived things while simply walking down the street that ordinary people never knew existed. He'd killed a vampire in New Orleans, battled an immortal serial killer in Paris.

There would be no ordinary life for him, not then. So they'd had a row in the subway station, and his friend stormed off. They never spoke again. Sometimes, during those forlorn moments when Doc Silence was alone, he'd add up all the people he had lost to magic together with all the lives he'd saved because of it, and he would try to balance the scales. But sorrow weighs more heavily than victory, and Doc—even with the Tower full of young heroes in training—was and had been for a very long time, alone.

Shaking off thoughts of the past, Doc cast a small spell, a little cantrip to let him know where magic existed in the vicinity. A glittering path, like dots on a map, led him down into the subway tunnels below. He followed, scattering those glowing specks like dust in bright sunlight.

Back in the old days, Doc carried a knife with him. The subway could be a rough place. He realized carrying was illegal here, but he also knew the right spells to make officers of the law look another way, or forget his face entirely. He could walk around this city with a claymore strapped to his back and no one would notice unless they were searching for someone just like him. A magician. A troublemaker.

The subway tunnel was strangely empty. Doc paced slowly down the corridor, feeling the wet density of hard magic all around him. Someone had been casting here, casting large. Pulling terrible things to the surface. Someone who knew magic just as well as Doc did. Maybe more.

The lights flickered. He turned around.

Standing in the mouth of the corridor, Lady Natasha Grey, wrapped in an expensive duster, drew her collar up against the chill. Her eyes, like his, glowed with an inner fire, red-gold to his violet, like open flame.

"What are you doing?" Doc said.

The lights went dark again.

Suddenly they weren't in Elephant and Castle station anymore. Light emanated from cracks of the black stone walls like molten lava. Arms of all shapes and sizes jutted out from the wall—disembodied demon arms, scaled or knobbed, skin deep red or jet black or bone white—reached and grasped at him.

"Why you doing this?" Doc said.

He conjured a weapon to his hand, another simple spell, the weight of an enchanted sword filled his grip. One of the monstrous arms grabbed him and he lashed out with the sword, slapping it away with the flat of the blade.

"Natasha?" Doc said.

She simply gazed at him. Her face blank, her expression stone-like.

Doc began to cast a teleportation spell, hoping, if Natasha wouldn't answer him, he could simply walk away and figure out what this all was later. But the weight of a counterspell came crashing down on his own, preventing his escape. He tried another spell, a variation of the first, and felt a finely woven layer of magic holding him back. This hallway had been prepared for him, a perfect trap designed by someone who was aware of Doc's secrets.

Someone who taught him everything he knew.

"I'm sorry, my little doctor," Natasha said. "I really am. But this is simply business."

"You can't do this," he said. Then Doc gestured with the sword at the Lady. "I know we never see eye to eye, Natasha, but you can't mean to . . ."

"We've had a good run, you and I," the Lady said. "We've played our little game long enough. But all good things must come to an end. You were a worthy adversary and a fine student, Doctor Silence. I'm almost sorry to see you go."

The arms that reached for him grew longer, their claws becoming more vicious. Doc gripped the enchanted sword with both hands, beating back the demonic hands. Then he felt something else biting into his skin, not claws, not a monster, but a spell. Something old, and terrible, and powerful, sapping his strength. His heart raced.

"Why?" Doc said, realizing, suddenly, that Natasha had prepared this trap too perfectly, that he did not have the time, or the strength, to counter all the tiers of counterspells she'd set up before he even arrived. This death trap was designed especially for him, and he'd walked right into it.

Stupid wizard, Doc thought. You really thought nothing could stop you. This is your own fault.

The Lady watched as Doc's strength, both physical and magical, drained. He fought viciously as the walls closed in on him. Red-tinted glasses knocked from his face and fell to the ground. They crunched beneath his own foot during his struggle to remain standing.

"I wish things could have been different," the Lady said. She watched a moment longer, then turned and slowly walked away.

Light in the tunnel faded to oblivion, Doc Silence thought of the future he would never see. So this is how it ends, he thought, feeling the darkness wash over him. Gradually his fist unclenched and the enchanted sword slipped from his hands.

I hope I gave them all enough to survive, he thought. I hope I taught Jane well.

And then, nothingness.

* * *

Now:

The group was quiet after future-Jane finished telling her story. Doc appeared unmoved, fingers steepled in front of his face as he listened.

"And that was the last time we saw you," older-Jane said. "We found out a lot of the details later. The Lady covered her tracks."

"And I hadn't been able to prepare you for dealing with her," Doc said. "You had no idea where to look."

Future-Jane nodded.

"Well that was some super-grim stuff," Emily said. "Holy carp. Got any more horrific fairy tales to tell us?"

"More than I'd rather share," older-Jane said.

Younger-Jane put a hand on Doc's shoulder.

"You don't seem at all bothered by this," she said. "You okay?"

Doc smiled.

"Honestly?" he said. "I'm intrigued. I want to know what was offered to her for killing me. There were a lot of years when she was more than capable of doing so."

"Please don't smile when you talk about being dead," younger-Jane said. "It's uncomfortable enough to talk about when you don't look amused."

Emily hopped off her chair and popped the collar on her goofy red vest.

"Me next," she said.

"What?" both Janes said simultaneously. They exchanged alarmed glances.

"Me next. We heard why Doc's not here. I want to know what happened to me," Emily said.

The elder Titus shifted, his vast, muscular bulk causing the stage to creak.

"That's a more difficult story," he said. "Let's feed you first. We'll fill you in during lunch."

A couple of the older werewolf's pack mates led the group out of the theater. Doc, Annie, and, unexpectedly, Leto held back. When the room was nearly empty, Doc watched as Leto transformed, abandoning her Anubis-like werewolf form for a startlingly beautiful human one.

"It's good to see you again, Doctor," she said.

"Nice to see you as well, Leto. I'm glad you're here."

"We did what we had to, these past twenty years," she said. "The last Whispering is doing well."

Doc grunted.

"We all knew Titus was special, even among the Whisperings," he said. "Is there a reason he doesn't change back to his human shape anymore?"

"That's not my story to tell," Leto said.

Annie glanced back towards the corridor she and the Janes had walked down to find Kate earlier.

"I think I have an idea what the reason is," Annie said.

Leto nodded in agreement.

"Not the world you left, is it," the ethereal werewolf said.

"It never is," Doc said. "Never is."

CHAPTER 16:
THE WATCHER

I t's almost over, the White Shadow thought, gazing at monitors and watching the world crumble to dust. It's almost over, and I did this.

It began so innocently, the vigilante reflected. We initiated all this with the best of intentions. No, we started it with murder didn't we, with kidnapping. We set off on the wrong side of good and never crossed the line back onto the other side of right.

But this is what the world deserves, the White Shadow thought.

In the vigilante's lair, old newspaper clippings hung from the wall, dating back more than fifty years. Photos of the Shadow on the front page, shaking the mayor's hand after preventing a terrorist crisis, hand on the shoulder of the police commissioner after stopping a crime spree, wrapped in the arms of relieved citizens when the Shadow solved a major murder.

This is what the White Shadow did for decades. Saved the day. Made the world a better place. Put bad people behind bars, ensured good folks got home safe to their families.

Except, for every newspaper clipping, there were fifty unsolved murders. For every joyous photo, there would be a hundred awful things the Shadow would never be able to prevent. For every reunion with a rescued family member, there was the heartbreak of knowing someone would never go home.

We tried for a little while to make the world a better place, the White Shadow thought. All of us. Fools and angels, throwing our lives away for people who never appreciated it, for those who never deserved it.

That's what broke the Shadow's spirit, twenty years ago. Knowing that all the good intentions in the world amounted to nothing. The world is comprised of scales, the Shadow thought, and they were always tipping in the wrong direction. We don't deserve this world, the Shadow thought. We have never deserved it.

And so twenty years ago the White Shadow resolved to change things in a different way.

They realized the girl was the key to it all. And understood she would need someone to control her. And knew there was only one person who could stop them, one person who had enough understanding of just how powerful the girl really was. And so Doc Silence was eliminated, and Keaton Bohr recruited, and the girl snatched. It should have been so simple.

But now it's almost over, the White Shadow thought. Because it all went too far.

They didn't deserve it, he thought, eyes flitting back and forth between the yellowing pages of newspapers and the grim, gray images of the monitors all around the room.

We gave them peace, and they didn't want it. We provided them safety, and they waged war. And now look at what we've become. A world torn apart, dying on its feet like a decaying and feeble old dog. We destroyed all the evil in the world and yet mankind just kept manufacturing more. No matter how many displays of power, no matter how much destruction the White Shadow's forces wrought—and there were forces, followers, acolytes who believed in implementing peace, who believed that humanity needed to be told what to do in order to become better—no matter how much they did to hammer their message home, perpetual wars still, perpetual fighting.

So they can have this gray old world a little longer, the White Shadow thought. Because I know how it all ends. This is a place that never sought happiness. And it's time to destroy it and allow whatever the universe deemed worthy to follow them have an opportunity to try.

I've got the might to rip this world in half, the White Shadow thought. I've offered them Solomon's choice, and they've chosen wrongly.

CHAPTER 17:
ONCE AND FUTURE
ENTROPY EMILY

Iwant to know about me," Entropy Emily said, her mouth full of something passing for frozen pizza in the area the future Indestructibles were treating as a kind of kitchen and mess hall.

"You're five feet tall, talk too much, and are too smart for your own safety," Billy said.

He looked more than a little worse for wear, clearly not taking the news that his future incarnation had made the ultimate sacrifice long before the younger Indestructibles arrived.

"No seriously," Emily said. "We know you're dead."

"Say it again. Louder. And with even less sensitivity," Billy said.

"And we know Titus has become Conan the Barbarian Werewolf King. And that Jane grows up to be all glowy and hot."

"Really? And that's the detail you focus on? Hot?" younger-Jane said. Their older counterparts were speaking with Doc just out of earshot, though clearly not far enough, because older-Jane turned to look back at them when Emily spoke.

"You're literally on fire," Emily said. "That's pretty hot." She took another bite of pizza but kept talking anyway. "And Doc let the Lady murder him. So it's my turn. I want to know what happens to me," Emily said.

"I think I can answer that," Anachronism Annie said, breaking away from the conversation with Doc and the others.

"But you weren't here," Emily said. "I want it from the horse's mouth."

"Annie knows more than we do, actually," future-Jane said. She sat down next to her younger self.

Emily looked back and forth between them and repeated the motion as if unsure where to focus her eyes.

"It's true," Annie said. "I've done some time-digging to try to figure out exactly what happened."

"Well we know what happened. Doc never came to get me," Emily said.

"Yes and no," Annie said. "Near as we can tell, there were two incidents that altered your future. One was, in fact, that Doc wasn't here to monitor when your powers manifested themselves."

"Next comes the 'and' doesn't there?" Emily said.

"Yep," Annie said. "*And*, the other thing that happened was that you got hit by a car."

"I've never been hit by a car," Emily said. "Not for lack of trying. I like jaywalking. It's become kind of my sport."

"How did your powers manifest originally, Emily?" Annie asked, smirking as if she knew the answer already.

"I told you, I'm a fan of jaywalking," Emily said. "A car almost hit me. I bubble of floated them away. Then I bubble of floated a lot of other cars away, then problems happened, then Billy tackled me and got me out of there."

"Yeah," Annie said. "In this timeline, that car hit you."

"Well that doesn't sound even remotely fun," Emily said.

"Fine," Annie said. "Let me tell you what happened."

* * *

Twenty years ago:

Well, Emily thought, lying in a hospital bed with a concussion and a broken leg, maybe jaywalking is overrated.

It happened so fast. I guess that's how you get hit by a car, she thought. If it had happened slower she could have gotten out of the way. But she'd darted out across the street, as she had a thousand

76

times before, only this time her usual luck hadn't accompanied her. Boom. Crash. Emily street pizza.

It could've been worse, she thought, I could've been road kill. Instead, I'm sitting here waiting for my mom to come yell at me for running into traffic again. And I can only imagine what will happen if she finds out what outfit I was wearing when I got run over.

She never thought she'd be so happy to be dressed in a hospital johnnie.

Emily kept thinking back to the moment of the accident, though. The strangeness. She'd thrown up her arms—apparently, that's what you do when you know you're about to be hit by a car, you panic and raise your arms up in front of you as if that's going to stop the car—and for a moment, a crystal-clear moment, Emily was absolutely sure she could stop the oncoming car. That she could just... make it float away.

But that didn't happen.

One might deem what happened to Emily afterward floating, but at a high rate of speed, with a very sudden stop.

There was something else, too. In the haze of the aftermath, the terrified driver trying to call 911, the police who were first to arrive on scene, the EMTs stabilizing her, somewhere in there, Emily thought, I swear I saw someone wearing a mask. A white mask, covered his face, leaving it blank. He—was it a he?—wore a dark suit and an old fedora, a red tie. Don Draper meets a pulp fiction action hero. Simply standing there, casually, content to watch Emily die.

Except I didn't die. Rather, I broke five bones and my head has ached for the past four hours, but I'm not dead.

And then the painkillers they'd given her finally kicked in, and Emily nodded off.

When she woke, everything had changed.

Her mother spoke quickly to someone just beyond Emily's line of sight. Emily propped herself up on her elbows, creaky and groggy.

"Mom?" she said, aware that she was about to sound very whiny, and forgetting that she was probably in more trouble than she knew. Her mom had been killing her on the stop-jaywalking thing lately.

And then Emily saw the nurse on the floor.

Something was happening in her room.

"Mom?" she said again, trying to shake the cobwebs out of her head. Her mother pointed at a man in a suit. Emily blinked a few times, and as the man came into focus, she saw he had no face.

"Where's your face?" Emily said, louder than she intended.

Her mother stopped talking. The man with no face turned that blank expression—it was a mask, she knew just like the person she remembered at the scene of the accident, a person in a suit wearing a blank white mask—towards her.

"Leave my daughter alone," Emily's mother said. "You're not him. Not the real one. I knew the real Shadow, you're a fake—"

The man in the suit pushed Emily's mom aside, deliberately knocking her into a chair beside Emily's bed. When her mother tried to get back up, the masked person hit her with the flat of his palm. The strike startled Emily, made the words catch in her throat, yet her mother didn't appear hurt. Stunned, definitely, but not really injured, as if the masked person had wanted to simply subdue her and not put her down.

"You're something special, you know," the masked person said.

The voice was wrong. Too high-pitched. The wrong age. She expected someone from *Mad Men* under there, not this.

"I'm such a special snowflake you don't even know," Emily said, trying to climb out of bed. "And I'm going to show . . ."

The room swam, her belly flip-flopped. Emily bit her lip, trying to fight the nausea, the sour-y sickness of her stomach.

"Listen, Rorschach, why don't you just back off before I... do something I'll regret!" Emily said. She slid her feet to the floor and put up her fists like something she'd seen Rocky Balboa do. Or maybe it was from *I Love Lucy*? She suddenly wasn't sure.

The masked person lifted a hand and, before Emily could fully register what was happening, fired a dart from a small gun. The dart sank into Emily's bony shoulder, and she felt the area around it go numb.

"Sorry, Emily," the mask said. As whatever drugs Emily had been hit with crashed into her system, strange faces began forming in the shadows of the blank face. "But we need you in one piece, and we need to hold off manifesting those powers of yours just a little longer."

"Powers?" Emily said. She tried to sit back on her bed, but slid to the floor instead. "I have powers? Are they pew pew powers, or kablammo powers?"

"Something of each," the masked person said.

Emily felt her consciousness slipping away and she was lifted from the floor and deposited into a wheelchair.

"You don't know it yet," the masked person said. "But you and I are going to change the world."

* * *

Now:

"Remind me to never ask you to read me a bedtime story," Emily said.

"Just telling you what we know," Annie said, shrugging. "Your powers didn't manifest in the same way in this timeline, and someone else got to you first. "

"And the rest of the Get Along Gang never came to get me?" Emily said.

"This was so early on we hadn't discovered Doc's files on other super-powered individuals yet," future-Jane said. "By the time we knew to look for you, you were gone."

Future-Titus shifted again.

Emily found herself incredibly jealous of the way the entire room deferred to him when he simply moved—everyone, future hero and the ones from her own timeline alike, stopped what they were doing to watch the older, scarred wolf when he made a motion. She was about to ask him how he did that but then he started talking.

No one else talked when older-Titus spoke either, Emily thought. I want to learn how to do that, too.

"We did eventually find out you were on the list of people to watch, but it wasn't until our enemy started using your powers as a weapon that we knew how to look for you," older-Titus said.

"And by then, we were looking for ways to stop you, not recruit you," the other werewolf said, the one whom Emily had started thinking of as Lucky Charms.

"Who really took me, then?" Emily said. "Was I recruited by the Emperor? Is it the Cybermen? All things being equal, I'd rather get recruited by the Sith than a race of cyborgs."

"Of course you'd rather join the Dark Side," Billy said.

"I'd rather laugh with the sinners than cry with the saints," Emily said.

"Did you really just quote Billy Joel? Are you suddenly fifty years old?"

"Well there is, in fact, a version of me running around who is almost forty," Emily said. "The same of which cannot be said about you, so—"

"You have to be the meanest person I've ever met," Billy said.

"Watch the hyperbole there, Spud," Emily said.

Jessie and Finnigan exchanged a quizzical look.

"Are we sure she's not actually supposed to be a villain?" Jessie said.

Younger-Titus, always the most mortified person in the room, was holding his head in his hands, rubbing his hair anxiously. "We have this conversation all the time," he said.

"I mean seriously, what's the worst thing I could've done?" Emily said. "I make bubbles of float, it's not like I'm actually a nuclear weapon."

"You destroyed California," future-Jane said.

Silence overtook the room. Everyone stared at older-Jane, and then back at Emily.

"What?" Emily said. "I didn't do it. The other Emily did it. Wait, I destroyed California?"

Future-Jane looked to her younger self, and then to Doc. Both nodded to her in return.

"She can handle it," younger-Jane said.

The elder Jane took a deep breath.

"You know how there was always talk of the wrong earthquake pushing California into the sea? How the San Andreas Fault or something like that might lead to a natural disaster that would tear the geographical area apart?" future-Jane said.

"I think I'm being unfairly accused here," Emily said. "In our timeline there's some kid running around who can make earthquakes we haven't caught yet. Clearly it's his fault."

"No," future-Jane said. "No, we know exactly what happened. One of your gravitational fields appeared and engulfed the entire California coastline years ago. Cars floated away. Buildings unmoored. But we could fix all that. Your powers had been used to cause that kind of destruction before, in New York, in Chicago, but in small areas. A city block maybe, a few square miles."

"I floated the entire state?" Emily said. "Can I be impressed with myself?"

"You didn't float the state, Emily," future-Jane said. "From what we can tell, you put one of your—"

"—Bubbles of float."

"You created one of your bubbles of float around a huge swath of California, and then you... just held it. And you let the rotation of the Earth do the rest."

"I don't get it," Billy said.

"I get it. I understand. Think about when Watson tries to run after a squirrel but you're holding the leash," Emily said. "And he reaches the end of the leash."

"The poor little guy gets jerked backwards," Billy said.

"So she used the weight of the earth to tear California away," younger-Jane said. "That's got to be the most terrifying thing I've ever heard."

"We've had some bad days," Jane's older self said. "We've experienced some terrible things. But that day. We haven't had one like that before or since."

Emily stood silent for a moment, her eyes expanded, her hands played with her functionally useless steampunk goggles. Finally, she said, "I have a request."

"I'm almost afraid to ask," younger-Titus said his head still buried in his hands.

"Can we officially stop saying 'you' when referring to the stuff Evil Emily did? Because, like, separate people," Emily said. "I also think we need a way of telling the Tituses and Janes apart."

"I'm even more afraid to ask," younger-Titus said.

"If you suggest 'Old Jane' I'm going to punch you to the moon," younger-Jane said.

"Okay, I'll think of something else instead," Emily said.

"Solar and Jane," younger-Titus said softly.

"What?" both Janes said, echoing each other.

"We'll call you Solar," he said, pointing to the elder Jane, "and you Jane."

The Janes glanced at each other, nodded in a perfect mirror image, then nodded again at Titus.

"And how will we tell you two apart?" Jane the younger said.

"Whispering," Titus' older self said.

As always, the entire room turned their attention his way.

"By talking softly?" Emily said.

"No," younger-Titus said. "You're the Whispering. That's your title."

"I'm Titus still," the older werewolf said in his rumbling, monstrous voice. "But you can call me Whispering, and we'll call you Titus. I haven't felt like simply Titus in a really long time. You should keep that name."

The two werewolves, young and old, looked at each other with a strange and sorrowful stare, as if they suddenly knew each other's secrets.

"I'm Titus, and you're the Whispering," the younger werewolf said.

"Well, now I'm twice as confused," Emily said, throwing her hands up and walking away.

CHAPTER 18:
TWITTERPATED

After hours of trying to get their bearings in this alternate future passed, the younger Indestructibles had been told to get some rest and were sent off to take their pick of dorm-style rooms scattered throughout the building. Some of the Whispering's pack had taken up residence on one floor, and though they did seem friendly enough, the young heroes settled in elsewhere down the hall.

Jane lay down on a cot and stared at the ceiling, attempting to piece everything together. Nothing about this future was untroubling, but Doc's nonchalance about being dead made her more anxious than she could possibly explain. What did he mean when Doc said this wasn't the first instance that he had learned he'd died? On how many occasions had he traveled through time before?

And then there was the Billy situation. Billy's reaction: now that was how someone should react after finding out they were dead. The poor kid was having a meltdown. She heard him talking to himself through the walls of her room, and she'd even seen him banish Emily, his constant companion, because he wanted to be alone. Or as alone as one could be with an alien living in his brain.

And her reflections didn't even begin to address the fact that they'd been in some kind of romantic relationship, she and Billy. That made no sense to her at all.

"So what do you think about the whole, you and Billy sitting in a tree thing?" Emily said from Jane's doorway, startling her.

Jane sat up and scooted her legs off the cot.

"How long have you been standing there?"

"I've been bubble-of-pacing up and down the hall for a half-hour," Emily said. "I'm waiting for Case to chill out so I can bother him, but he's all twitterpated in there."

"Well, he found out he died," Jane said. "Twitterpated is just the beginning of how he could be feeling."

"You and Billy Case. How about that?" Emily said. She flopped down on the bed beside Jane, making herself right at home, arms flailing above her head.

"Is it weird for you?" Jane said.

"Weird for me? It has nothing to do with me," she said. "You're mourning him. Like, your older you. Solar. Mourning. She's heartbroken."

"I mean is it weird for you now?" Jane said. "I mean you and Billy are... right?"

"We're what?" Emily said.

"Aren't you a thing?" she said.

Emily sat back up, stared at Jane for a second, then started to roar in laughter.

"What. What did I say?" Jane said.

"You think Billy and I are a thing?" Emily said.

"You're attached at the hip. You never go anywhere without each other."

"Jane, Billy's my bro," Emily said. "He's my boy. My best bud."

"Isn't that what couples are?"

"You've never had a boyfriend, have you?"

"Have you?" Jane said.

"No, but I've watched a lot of daytime television," Emily said. "Seriously, you really think Billy and I are a couple?"

"You've just been friends all this time?"

Emily laughed again, this time so hard she choked on her own saliva and caught herself in a coughing fit. She wiped tears from her eyes and put a hand on Jane's shoulder.

"First of all, no, we're not a thing, we have never been a thing," Emily said. "We hang out all the time because we like each other. As human beings."

Jane nodded.

"And also, Billy is so not my type in ways I cannot even get into right now," Emily said. "We'd never be a thing. Not gonna happen."

"You're just friends."

"We're not just friends. I'd commit murder if anyone ever hurt him, don't get me wrong. He's my bro. I'd do anything for him. But the idea of us being a thing is hilarious. We're not even like brother and sister. We're buds. Bert and Ernie are more romantic than us."

"I really hoped we were through with weird conversations today," Jane said.

"Yeah no, we're not done by a long shot," Emily said. "So now that the myth that is Billy and Emily is out of the way... what are you thinking of the whole thing?"

Jane threw her hands up.

"Is it weird that in this timeline I clearly fell in love with Billy and in our timeline, I have absolutely no romantic thoughts even remotely having to do with him?"

"I don't think that's weird at all," Emily said. "I think I'm getting the hang of this timeline thing. Butterfly effect. One little thing changes, everything changes with it."

"I like him," Jane said. "No, I love him, the same way I love you and Titus and Doc and even Kate, you're my family. I'd throw the moon into the sun for any one of you."

"But you don't think of him as someone you'd like to snog."

"So much so that the image seriously just grossed me out a little bit," Jane said.

"Plus you have Broadstreet," Emily said.

"Him either," Jane said. "Em, I just don't think about it at all. It's not important to me. I have more significant things to freak myself out about."

"Not even like, movie stars?"

"I'm not a robot," Jane said. "Can I tell you something serious and not have you make fun of me?"

"I make no promises," Emily said.

"Come on."

"I'll try."

Jane sighed.

"All I do is worry," Jane said. "That's it. I worry. All day. About you guys. About Doc. About the Children of the Elder Star. About catching Megalodon or about if I should have killed Plague or not. I worry about climate change. I worry about my parents, and if I'll be there if they need me when they get older."

"Dude, you should try thinking about boys a little bit, it might help you out."

"Em."

"Or girls. Both. Whatever. That's cool too. Whatever you need to do."

"Em, seriously."

"This is me deflecting because the idea that you're awake at night worrying about all of us is making me sad and I don't want to process it."

"It's okay," Jane said.

"No, it's not," Emily said. "You're a teenager. You shouldn't be... whatever, married to your work."

Jane smiled and put an arm around Emily, who head-butted her shoulder affectionately.

"So you don't think the Billy thing is too weird?" Jane said.

"Oh, completely," Emily said. "But only because I think he's not in your league. He's my best friend and even I think you're too good for him."

"You really are the meanest friend in the world," Jane said.

"It's my job, and you all love me for it," Emily said.

CHAPTER 19:
THE STRAYLIGHTS

A gray dawn rose on the outskirts of the City, and Billy Case was still awake. He hadn't slept all night, and at this point even Dude was annoyed with him.

You realize the only time I rest is when you sleep, the alien said.

Dude, I consider you a combination of my soul mate, my Jiminy Cricket, and my dad, Billy thought. I could really use a little bit of friendly consolation here.

Heroes die, Billy Case, the alien said. *Someday you'll die too. You can only hope that you do so with dignity and grace.*

I'd rather live cowardly forever, Billy thought.

No you wouldn't, Dude said. *I would never have picked you if you wanted that.*

"Tell me you slept last night," the new Straylight, Jessie, said as she walked into Billy's room uninvited. She was young, Billy noted, just a bit older than he had been when Dude first found him, and she swaggered not unlike himself. Dude must prefer people who fake an outward sense of confidence, Billy thought.

"Not even a little bit," Billy said.

"Because you're still freaking out about being dead," Jessie said.

"Everyone keeps acting like I shouldn't be messed up by this," Billy said.

Jessie shrugged in a way Billy found vaguely annoying until he realized he shrugged in a very similar way almost all the time.

"Y'know, everyone talks about you like you were some kind of

87

amazing hero," Jessie said. She leaned against the wall and crossed her arms. "I figured you'd be... cooler. Bigger. Tougher. Not such a wuss."

"Tell you what, you travel through time and find out you died horribly and then we can talk," Billy said.

It's strange, being this close to another host, Dude said.

Stop talking, I'm sparring, Billy said.

Ask her if it's really me she's hosting. I can't tell. My ability to read her Luminae isn't quite right.

What do you mean, not quite right? Billy thought.

I can't explain it. It's a connection we share. It's how we find each other. It doesn't feel normal.

"You don't know if you died horribly. Nobody's told you how you died. Also it's rude to have a conversation with your symbiotic alien in front of a stranger," Jessie said.

"We're hosting the same symbiotic alien. We're practically the same person," Billy said. "How did I die, anyway?"

"You really want to know?" Jessie said.

"'Want' is a bit of a stretch, but I'm curious."

Jessie peered out the doorway into the hall to see if anyone else was around.

"I'm sure I'm breaking some kind of time travel rule by telling you, but who cares," she said. "You died trying to put California back together again."

"Well that sounds absolutely horrible."

"Well, I didn't see it. I was just a kid," Jessie said. "But the way Jane tells it, you tried to fight against the force pulling California into the ocean, hoping to buy people enough time to evacuate. I've seen footage. You lit up the sky like a star."

"Did I look cool?"

Jessie snorted.

"You really aren't very heroic, are you?" Jessie said. "But yeah, a human comet pushing against the coastline as helicopters were falling from the sky trying to get footage of you... it was pretty boss."

"I don't get it," Billy said. "Wouldn't I have just fallen into the ocean? What killed me?"

If she's telling the truth, I did, Dude said.

"Oh, I can't wait to hear this explanation," Billy said.

Jessie shot him a quizzical look.

"Dude says he killed me himself."

I did not say that, Dude said. *Take it back and explain it to her before you frighten her.*

"Dude said I just scared you by saying that," Billy said.

"He's saying the same thing inside my head. Also he says you were an extremely unpleasant young man before you grew up," Jessie said.

"I was. I am," Billy said. "Dude, how'd you kill me?"

The human physiology can only withstand so much of the power my species can share, Dude said. *I am very careful how much I give you access to. Used carefully, I can extend your lifespan and keep you alive. But like an overworked engine, I can burn you out if I'm not careful. If I ever let you use too much of my power, you'd evaporate like parchment in a flame.*

"That is... horrifying," Billy said.

"What?" Jessie said.

"You don't want to know," Billy said.

"I don't believe you," she said.

"So did I save many people? In the end?"

"In the end? I don't know. Probably not," Jessie said. "The other force, the thing tearing the earth apart, was too powerful. There was only so much you could do. But people remembered that, y'know? They remembered the man who burned away trying to save them. Straylight, the boy who became a star."

"I always wanted to be a star," Billy said. "Just more, like, movie star, not an exploding cosmic anomaly."

"It's not a bad way to go," Jessie said. "And anyway, a few hours later, I hear this weird voice talking in my head, and it's your alien, telling me he needs a new hero. And I said, hey, maybe I'll be brave enough to do something that stupid someday."

"Sorry I let you down," Billy said. "I know I'm not what most people would want in a superhero."

"You're new yet," Jessie said. "Got plenty of time to prove me wrong."

They heard a knock at the door, and Titus, the younger version of the werewolf, let himself in.

"What the hell happened to you?" Titus said, looking at Billy.

"No beauty sleep," he said. "What's up?"

"News from the frontlines," Titus said. "Old me and Solar want us all to meet down in the war room."

"Well then," Billy said. "Let's go be heroes."

CHAPTER 20:
THE SPY

Jane stood in front of a monitor hooked up to what her older self had explained was the remnants of Neal's computer system from the Tower. She was afraid to ask the elder Solar what happened to the Tower and why Neal was now a set of boxes plugged into an improvised power supply, but she figured that was a question for another time.

Finnigan tinkered with the keyboard and cursed. "I never know how to work this bloody thing," he said.

A younger werewolf, a dark-haired male in human form, pushed Finnigan out of the way and tapped away.

The elder Solar paced back and forth in the front of the room, a large classroom that had been arranged as a makeshift communications suite. Whispering, the older Titus, sat calmly in a creaky office chair, still in full-on werewolf form, flanked by Leto, the elegant werewolf who seemed to be his advisor. The others trickled in after that. Kate took up residence in the back of the room, sulking. Emily sat near her, mocking the Dancer's sullen body language. Doc and Annie arrived, speaking in hushed tones. Finally Billy and his future counterpart, Jessie, walked in, followed by the Titus.

"Is everybody here?" Solar said.

"All those who will be," Whispering said, his voice rumbling.

Solar gestured to the monitor.

Jane mimicked Solar's body language, then both women leaned forward on the back of a chair to watch the screen flicker to life.

Jane hardly recognized the face on camera when she saw it. The beard had grown in, lines around his eyes added gravity to his features, but she knew that face.

"Broadstreet," Jane said.

Solar looked at her.

"You know Broadstreet in your timeline?" her older self asked.

Jane nodded.

"He's a reporter," she said. "A friend."

"Well here, he's our man on the inside," Solar said. "He's infiltrated the enemy's organization, pretending to be one of them."

"What do you mean by organization?" Billy asked. "I'm still fuzzy on this. I thought the bad guys were destroying the world. Do they have a great retirement package or something?"

"Someone will always want to join in on destroying the world," Kate said quietly from the back of the room.

Solar nodded.

"Remember, when our enemies started, they were on our side," she said. "They went after the same enemies we did. They were better at it, in many ways. These were the people who destroyed the Children of the Elder Star."

"They portrayed themselves as ruthless heroes," Whispering said. "A lot of people signed on. They had a global presence."

"How can there still be followers now?" Titus said.

"Belief is a hard thing to shake," Leto said softly.

The heroes occupying the room instantly turned their attention to her. Jane wondered if she'd taught Whispering how to do that, or if it was some sort of trait werewolves develop as they grew older. "Many of these men and women dedicated their lives to this cause years ago. It's difficult to admit when you've made a mistake, that you've wasted your life."

"So they just keep trying to see it through to the end?" Billy said.

"Nihilism is easier than admitting you're wrong," Emily said.

Attention spun to her now, but in a completely different tone— not with the reverence everyone showed Leto or Whispering, but rather shock at her response.

"What?" Emily said.

"Nihilism?" Billy said.

"The rejection of all moralism, and the belief that life is meaningless," Emily said. "Seriously, Billy, did you not read any of the books I've given you this year?"

"Regardless of why they're still working with the enemy organization, we have a situation," Solar said. "Jon Broadstreet was able to get a message out to us this morning. Neal has only now been able to decode it. Neal?"

"Designation: Solar. There are two of you present in this room. How would you like me to address you?"

Jane smiled at the tone of Neal's voice. Twenty years into the future and the AI sounded exactly the same.

"It doesn't matter, Neal. Call her Jane for now. But play the video," Solar said.

Broadstreet's image came to life.

"... key information on the leadership of the enemy," Broadstreet said. "... finally got a name for you. Details on their power source. Need you to retrieve the information from the Jupiter dead drop... "

"Pause it," Solar said. She turned to Doc and Jane. "All these years, the leaders of this group have been a mystery to us. We've never seen them in public. They work through envoys who are given only enough information to complete the tasks assigned to them. We know there's a core cadre at the top, but who they are and what their motivations are have been entirely concealed. It's remarkable. Keep playing, Neal."

" ...definitely think they're onto me," Broadstreet said. "I'm stationed... the Waterfront District outpost. Going to try to extricate myself within the next 12 hours, but if you don't hear from me, good luck. Do not send extraction team, not worth the fallout. Please make the dead drop your priority."

"Pause it, Neal," Solar said. "When did we receive this message?"

"Four hours ago," the young werewolf at the monitor said.

"He could already be dead," Jane said.

"Neal, call up the satellite view of the Waterfront District. See if there's been any combat in the past four hours," Solar said.

"We're not going to let him die out there," Jane said.

"We absolutely are not," Solar said.

Whispering stood up slowly, taking command of the room.

"I don't want to sacrifice Broadstreet any more than you do, but he's right. The information at the dead drop takes priority," the older werewolf said. "We can't risk losing that intel."

"You're going to lose it anyway if he's captured, right?" younger-Titus said. "Won't they be able to find out where the drop is?"

Titus' and Jane's older selves exchanged a grim look.

"So these guys who used to be considered heroes torture people?" Billy said. "I'm feeling so much better about every bad decision I've ever made in comparison to this."

"Sentimentality or not, you may have to rescue your insider," Annie said, finally joining the conversation.

Jane noticed that the time traveler steered clear of participating in decision-making if she could, and wondered if Annie did so to avoid having too much influence on the events in the timeline. It would make sense for her to make that her habit, even if in this case it was entirely Annie's fault they were trying to change the course of the timeline at all.

"You've basically doubled your superhero numbers in the past 24 hours, y'know," Emily said. "Mathematically, you could do, like, both. Things. At once. Am I wrong?"

Solar smiled. "You're absolutely right," she said.

"Two teams," Jane said.

"How do you want to do this?" Solar said.

"You're going to want to make a show of rescuing Broadstreet," Kate said.

Kate's voice startled Jane. Dancer had been silent so far. "Even if you fail to rescue him, you want it to look like he's the mission. They may not know about your dead drop, but they probably know you had a man inside their organization. If they think he's got the information you need, they'll not go looking for the drop and devote their forces to stopping your rescue."

"You're a cold one, lass," Finnigan said, sounding halfway between impressed and terrified of Kate.

"She's right," younger and older-Titus said simultaneously. The boy and the scarred werewolf exchanged glances; the older wolf nodded to his younger self to continue. "Send the big guns to rescue Broadstreet, and send a stealth team to get the drop."

"But we don't want to risk running into trouble if they've already found the drop," Whispering said. "We'll want enough heavy hitters to go along in case there's trouble."

"Do we want to risk them finding out you've got body doubles now?" Emily said.

"No," Whispering said. "You're right.... Solar?"

"I'll lead the team to rescue Broadstreet," Solar said.

"And I'll bring in my werewolves for a ground assault," Whispering said. "Put on a show of it."

"I want to go with you on the rescue," Jane said. "I can be more help there."

"And we'll give our secret away if we're both there," Solar said. "You should go with the stealth team to back them up in case they need a big gun to step up."

"Titus and Kate are used to quiet operations," younger-Jane said. "They can lead the drop run."

"Finnigan, go with them as a guide. You know the area," Whispering said. The ginger wolf nodded. "Annie, will you go with them as well?"

"Of course," Annie said.

Billy and Jessie exchanged looks, then shrugged.

Jane found their similar body language more alarming than she expected.

"I'd like to go on the main assault so I can get a feel for what we'll be fighting," Billy said. "Dude tells me that if they're using sensors and the like to monitor us, my energy signature and Jessie's will be almost identical. They won't know until the fight's over that we're different."

"Unless they're using their eyes, is all," Jessie said.

"That works," Solar said. "And Jessie, you know our dead drop system, you'll be a bigger help with the stealth team. But please try to be stealthy this time."

"I'm always stealthy," she said.

"See? We're always stealthy," Billy said.

Jane ran a frustrated hand through her hair.

"What about Emily and Doc?" she said.

"I call assault team!" Emily said.

"You should hang back," Doc chimed in. "Be ready to jump in if either team needs you, but right now, our best secret is that they don't know we have you here. You're our ace."

"Aces do not hang out by themselves at the clubhouse," Emily said petulantly.

"Em," Jane said.

"Fine," Emily said. "But if I see any type of trouble, I'm bubble of floating my butt out there and causing some mayhem."

"And what about you, Doc?" younger-Jane said. "The main attack?"

Doc shook his head.

"I have my own mission," he said. "Lady Natasha's never been dealt with, has she?"

"No," Whispering said. "After you were murdered, she went off the grid. We never had any trouble with her again."

"If I know anything about the Lady, it's that she hates feeling like she's been outdone," Doc said. "The second she knows I'm here there'll be a problem. I'm going to take her out of the game."

Jane stomped her foot.

"You're not going to disappear again!" she said. "I won't allow it. We lost you once; we're not losing you again."

Doc smiled wide and laughed.

"The benefit of that year I was trapped with the Lady in those other dimensions, Jane, is that I've got a much better idea of what she's capable of. And I half-expected her to betray me the entire time. I have all sorts of new ways to deal with her now, especially if she doesn't even know I'm alive. I've devised a better plan this time."

"I think you're lying," Jane said.

"Jane, I lost a year with all of you in one timeline and let myself get killed in another. I'm done toying with Lady Natasha Grey. Trust me on this."

Jane didn't, but she stopped arguing.

Doc visibly relaxed and turned his attention to the future versions of the team.

"Did you happen to save any of my things when you had to leave the Tower?" he said.

"We did," Solar said. "Leto knew more about what your belongings were, so . . ."

"I'll show you what we still have," Leto said.

"Good," Doc said. "Because I'm betting the Lady hasn't become any weaker these past twenty years. I'm going to need a few things to make sure only one of us is knocked out of play this time."

CHAPTER 21:
WIZARDS AND WEREWOLVES

oc Silence walked with Leto through the dust-covered halls of the school, the elegant werewolf led him to a vacant room where she'd stored the magician's effects. He marveled at how unchanged she was. They knew each other long ago, before the Indestructibles, when Doc Silence wandered the world, trying to figure out how it worked and how he might make it better.

Leto seemed to sense Doc's reverie and glanced back over her shoulder. She'd reverted to her human form, her face alien and angular and breathtakingly beautiful in ways Doc could never quite articulate. Leto looked like something from before humans were human, when immortal beings roamed the earth instead.

He felt shabby next to her.

"You're thinking," she said.

"I'm always thinking," Doc said. "Were you able to get your warrior out of Titus? Did you find what you needed in him?"

Leto shrugged one lean, muscled shoulder.

"Did you?" she asked. "You're the one who stole him from us."

"I didn't steal him. I gave him a chance to be a part of the world, instead of apart from it."

"Like yourself. You could have been a shaman on the edge of the village too, if you'd only been able to take a step back from it," Leto said.

"You miss too much there," Doc said. "The shaman on the hill can see the whole countryside, but can't smell it. Can't feel the warmth of humanity on his skin."

"So you took him from us."

"I believed you were all dead, Leto," Doc said. "And you did a fine job of making sure the world thought the same thing."

Leto grinned. A smile like moonlight, soft and bright, but cool. "Perhaps I was curious what a Whispering would become if he lived among humans instead," she said.

"It couldn't have turned out to be too much of a disappointment for you," Doc said. "You're here by his side at the end of the world."

Leto stopped by a doorway, the room dazzled with natural light from the outside.

"Whatever choices we made, we got a hero out of it," she said. "When a hero calls you, you stand by his side."

"We got a lot of heroes from this group," Doc said.

"We did."

Doc entered the room to discover much of his old gear still in one piece. Old travel cases, a large box that looked like a treasure chest from a pirate movie, a violin case that never contained a violin, a hatbox decades old. Doc opened a leather chest, the smell of magic and mothballs flooded his nose. He peeked over his shoulder at Leto.

"It's good to see you again, my friend," Doc said.

Now Leto's smile grew warm.

"What would the world do without wizards and werewolves?" she said.

"And some of us are both," Doc said. "Did you help them pack this stuff? Someone who knew their way around my trinkets had to. Everything worth keeping is still here."

"Titus asked for my help," Leto said. "I didn't want to touch your things, but I thought, better to make sure we know where they are than to have them out in the world."

Doc nodded. He removed a thin, blackened necklace from the case, a ruby vial hanging from it, and draped it over his neck. A leather cuff studded with cloudy gray stones went onto his wrist. He lifted a simple red sash, ran it once across his fingers, then wrapped it around his waist.

"Do you really know how to stop the Lady?" Leto said. "It's been twenty years since your death. She may have become even more powerful than before."

Doc upended a stitched leather pouch into the palm of his hand. A half-dozen rings fell out. He sifted through them, selecting one made of dark metal with reddish wood embedded in the band, another with a dark blue jewel. He put one ring on each hand, then added another to his left hand, a wide silver band cut with runes.

"Here's the thing," Doc said, tucking a dirk with a bone handle into the sash around his waist. "I've always held back with her. I care about her. You know that. I've never considered her my enemy."

"Which no one in the magician community could ever quite understand," Leto said.

"You did though," Doc said.

"Werewolves have complicated relationships. Of course I understood," she said.

"Well, now there's no holding back," Doc said.

"What does that mean?" Leto asked.

"It means I know just as many secrets as Natasha does," Doc said. "And this time, I have no reason not to use them."

CHAPTER 22: THE RESCUE

Billy and Solar waited above the darkened enemy base, watching for Whispering's team to get into position. The idea was for the werewolves to be ready to jump in and pull Broadstreet out of the facility while Billy and Solar made a big show of attacking, hoping that the guards would assume the two fliers were the real rescue team.

From this high up, Billy could see exactly how much destruction had befallen the City. Entire neighborhoods were gone. He tried not to think about what happened to his parents over the years in this timeline.

"Is the whole world like this?" Billy asked.

"Parts of it," Solar said. "Anywhere the people tried to take a stand, though, bad things happened. And worse, the more chaotic things got, the worse folks were to each other in general. People do terrible things during bad times."

"Well that's depressing," Billy said.

And unfortunately true, Dude said. *This isn't unique to this timeline, Billy Case.*

I know, Billy thought.

Don't let it discourage you, Dude said.

How do you stop it from discouraging you? Billy thought. I've only been at this a year or so and I'm already seeing that people are pretty much awful to each other all the time. You've been flying around inside other hosts for lifetimes. Don't you ever feel like it's a waste of time?

Sometimes, Dude said, his tone different from usual, more

conversational, less authoritarian. *But there is always someone who deserves rescuing. There is always some good thing worth doing, despite all the bad.*

And that keeps you going, Billy thought.

Yes, Dude said. *I also have no body, so my activity options are limited.*

Very funny, Dude, Billy thought.

"Talking to your alien?" Solar said, smiling, but not taking her eyes off the base below them.

"We're discussing the foibles of human nature," Billy said.

You didn't even know what foibles were until Emily used the word last week, Dude said. *Don't get cute.*

"Well... humans have a lot of foibles to discuss," Solar said. She gestured at the base. "You ready to roll?"

"Absolutely."

"Be careful," Solar said. "These people are used to dealing with super-powered fighters. They'll be ready for us, even if we should catch them off-guard."

"I'm always careful," Billy said.

You're never careful, Dude muttered.

Their enemies were holed up in a converted bank. Solar had suggested that they selected that particular building because it was more defensible than some of the other neighboring abandoned Waterfront District buildings, and the vaults inside could be used for any number of security purposes, including as a jail cell for Broadstreet—if he were still alive.

Solar and Billy began their attack run, both allowing their brightest powers—hers the yellow-gold of sunlight, his the bluish white energy signature Dude provided—to illuminate.

Solar struck first, crashing through the roof of the bank like a meteor and smashing concrete with a deafening bang. Billy followed, zapping enemy fighters with concussive blasts from his hands.

One of the men raised a weapon that looked like a cross between a rifle and a very big plastic squirt gun. He fired, and Billy instinctually dodged the blast, though he could barely see it—the weapon didn't fire a bullet, or even a laser, but something colorless and shimmering, like hot air flickering off blacktop.

Behind him, the bolt clipped an old telephone pole, knocking it over as if swatted by a giant hand.

"Up!" Solar yelled, and she and Billy launched back into the air, dodging more fire from their enemies.

"What are they firing at us?" Billy yelled.

"Gravity guns," Solar said. "Don't let them hit you. They're not lethal to people like us but—"

Before Solar could finish, Billy took a gravity gun blast to the chest, sending him spinning off into the sky. It felt like getting kicked by a large herd animal, he thought, though the protective shielding Dude's powers provided took the brunt of the blast. Billy caught his breath and flew back, catching up as Solar swooped and swerved to avoid weapon-fire.

From this vantage point, Billy saw Whispering's werewolf fighters climbing swiftly through the gaping hole in the ceiling Solar had created, tossing enemy soldiers aside and smashing their rifles. He witnessed one younger werewolf take a shot to the back and fall over. Alarmed, Billy rocketed down, hit the soldier with a hammering blow of white light, and put his hand on the dazed werewolf. One of the fallen wolf's comrades scooped him up over his shoulder to carry him to safety.

"We can't get the door open," Billy heard someone say. He followed the voices to find a pair of werewolves trying to get into a vault, thwarted by the massive metal door.

"Let me try," Billy said.

The wolves backed away, and Billy grabbed hold of the door's massive handle and pulled, drawing deep on the reserve power Dude gave him. The door creaked, then buckled, and hinges cracked and split. He pulled again and the entire wall started to crumble.

"Kid, Solar needs you outside," another werewolf said.

Billy glanced back at his handiwork and nodded. I might have a career option robbing banks when we get back to our timeline, he thought.

No, you really don't, Dude said, his voice disapproving.

Billy launched back into the sky, leaving the team of werewolves to finish pulling the door open. He saw Solar dodging blasts from a group of enemy fighters, and before they realized he was present,

Billy knocked all three out with concussive shots. He joined Solar in the air where she continued to draw enemy fire.

Airborne again, Billy saw the wolves making a retreat, one carrying the injured werewolf. Whispering himself hauled the prone body of Broadstreet. Billy had never seen Titus running at full speed from the sky before, and watching his friend's future self and his allies tear through the city streets on those powerful monstrous legs amazed him. Inhumanly fast, they leapt over abandoned cars as if they were just pebbles in the road.

Then Billy heard a whooping noise and watched a group of vehicles take off after the pack.

"Hoverbikes?" Billy said.

"Gravity bikes," Solar said. "Running on the same technology the guns do."

"We taking them off Whispering's tail?" Billy said.

"With prejudice," Solar said, dive-bombing toward the street.

Solar flew alongside one of the vehicles and walloped it on the back-end with one flaming fist, sending the flying machine spinning out of control to crash into a vacant building.

Billy joined in, having less luck catching his target, shooting beaming blasts but having each shot dodged by the quick spider-like vehicle. Billy flew in closer, felt Dude kick up the power of their flight, and took aim. Another light strike crashed into the vehicle's rear engine, and the flying machine flipped and smashed into the street.

Solar caught a third, ripping it apart with her bare hands, pulling the pilot out and tossing him almost gently to the ground before pushing the gravity vehicle into the crumbling pavement. Billy swooped under a fourth. The hammering weight of its gravity-based engine push him back and almost knocked him out of the air. Alarmed, he fired with both hands, and the flying cart bounced and spun into the sky, out of control, exploding into the second-story windows of an old brick office building.

Ahead, Billy saw the final gravity bike closing in on the wolves. He tightened his fists and flew faster, hoping to catch up in time. Solar soared next to him, burning so bright he felt the heat of her powers against his skin through his protective force fields. He knew neither of them were going to make it in time. Twin guns dropped from the bottom of the vehicle and took aim at the werewolves.

That's when he saw old Titus Whispering turn around and face the machine.

The scarred version of Titus tossed the prone body to one of the other werewolves, almost casually. The younger wolf caught their ally in his arms like a baby and continued to run at top speed. Whispering changed direction and dashed back at the speeding machine, head on, massive claws gripping the pavement, crackling it like paper.

Whispering leapt into the air, slammed down onto the front of the bike, causing its chassis to drag along the ground with enough friction to spark. The guns ripped free, becoming airborne, useless. Whispering bounded off as the machine flipped entirely, crumpling in the street. The older wolf stomped up to the machine and dragged the pilot out with one huge clawed hand.

Billy, close enough now, heard the gravelly voice of his friend's future self filled with dark anger.

"This is our mercy. Tell your friends," Whispering said.

Billy saw blood start to stain the man's shirt as Whispering held him aloft.

"You tell them I had your heart mere inches from my claws and I let you live."

The pilot's eyes rolled back in his head, and Whispering dropped him like a broken toy on the ground.

Solar landed beside Billy. They both approached Whispering slowly. Even after all these years, Billy noted, nobody's quite sure if he's in control as a werewolf. Amazing.

"How did Broadstreet look?" the elder Solar said.

"We should get home," Whispering said, ignoring her question. Then he turned and bounded after his pack.

"What does that mean?" Billy said.

"You know him," Solar said, a sadness creeping into her voice. "What does it mean when your Titus won't answer a question?"

Billy nodded, a knot in his stomach, and flew full speed back toward the makeshift base.

CHAPTER 23:
THE DROP

Titus had never been to the City's dump before, and it didn't occur to him until the "stealth" team arrived there just how badly it reeked, even at the end of the world. "Nobody warns you that having super-senses means things that smell horrible stink a thousand times worse," he said, mostly to himself.

Kate didn't acknowledge the statement at all, walking on the outskirts of the group looking for trouble. Jessie, the new Straylight, snorted under her breath.

It was Finnigan, of course, who offered sympathy. "I wish I could tell you it gets easier, lad, but it never does," he said instead.

"So stay away from public bathrooms and garbage dumps is what you're telling me," Titus said.

"Among other things," Finnigan said.

Annie, walking beside Jane at the back of the group, hustled to catch up.

"Why the dump?" she asked.

"For the drop?" Finnigan said. "Because it's not far from the Waterfront District where our spy was located. And really, who looks for something in a dump?"

"Did he ever risk getting discovered, though?" Jane said. "Nobody really ever goes to a place like this on purpose either."

"He was good about not being followed," Jessie said. "But who knows? There's probably a trap waiting for us."

"There's always a trap," Titus said with a sigh.

He looked up to see Kate standing in silhouette on top of a pile of rusted cars. Like some sort of guardian statue, silent and motionless, watching the horizon, she pointed.

Titus followed her gesture.

They were looking for a specific car, an old hatchback of a particularly aggressive shade of green that had been designated as the drop point for information from Broadstreet. Titus wished he'd been more involved with the reporter back in their home timeline. Knowing his scent, even in a junkyard, would help him track the location of the car easier. Jessie and Finnigan had some idea where they were going, but the place was enormous and had fallen into even more chaos after fighting began in the City.

"Hey, Finnigan," Titus said, calling the older werewolf over.

"Yeah, kid."

"I have to ask—in the future, do I lose the ability to revert to human form?" he said. "Did something happen? We haven't seen... me... other than as a werewolf so far. It's freaking me out."

"You haven't figured that out yet, lad?" Finnigan said. He looked up to where the Dancer had been standing, but she'd moved on.

Titus frowned.

"Maybe I was hoping for something less dramatic."

Finnigan made a huffing sound, not quite a laugh, and not meant to be humorous.

"The fighting changed you," Finnigan said. "We lost people. Good people, good werewolves. There's been a lot of tragedy the past two decades. Recent years, as we started to lose, there's been even more."

"We haven't seen future-Kate talk to anyone," Titus said.

"That's because future-Kate barely speaks to anyone," Finnigan said. "And it's been a long time since she stopped conversing with your future self."

Titus kicked a hunk of detritus at his feet.

"I think . . ." Finnigan said. "I think at first he was just using it as a disguise. What do you see when you look at him?"

"I see a monster."

"Right. Just a big beast covered in scars. But you and I know how to read emotions in other wolves. Regular people don't. They simply see monsters."

"And so he's wearing the wolf as a mask?" Titus said.

"Yeah. Your girl just stopped talking to anyone, shut the whole world out. And you know by then, after everything we'd lost, he needed her. She was his other half. Something that helped the world make sense."

Titus grimaced and tried to locate the Dancer out among the ruins of the junkyard, but didn't see her anywhere.

"I don't like it," Titus said.

"Why's that?" the older wolf said.

"I'd... like to think I'm better than that. That I wouldn't let having my heart broken make me feel like I had to hide myself behind a monster's mask."

Finnigan grinned widely.

"What?" Titus asked.

"Keep that," he said.

"Keep what?"

"Keep that truth in your heart, Titus," Finnigan said. "Because it is okay to love, and it is okay to feel loss, but don't ever let it consume you. Don't ever let sadness steal you from the world."

"I don't want to lose her," Titus said.

"Of course."

"But I don't want to lose myself either."

"And that's okay," Finnigan said.

Titus started at the red-headed werewolf, then shook his head.

"I miss you, Finnigan. You know I never saw you again, after I left to help my friends."

"Am I dead?"

"No. Not that I know of."

"Then you better think about rectifying that when you get home. I'm sure I'm very disappointed," Finnigan said.

They both laughed, and Titus realized how long it had been since he left the others there in the forest so far north of the border, how he'd not found them yet, and wondered if perhaps he was just meant to never see any of his small pack again. And then Finnigan put a hand gently on his shoulder.

"I'll tell you true, lad, I miss you too," he said. "Hasn't been the same since everything went wrong. Made you a stronger warrior, sure, but... I miss my friend. We were great friends before the sadness buried you."

Titus nodded, put his hands in the pockets of his sweatshirt. He tossed a glance over his shoulder and saw Jane staring at him, eyes wide and haunted. He sometimes forgot she had superhuman hearing that was almost as strong as his own. Had she heard every word? Probably. But it didn't bother him. There was no one other than Jane—not even Kate—Titus knew who could be trusted with a story like this. She simply had no malice in her heart.

Then he caught a look of shock on Jane's face and turned to see Kate running at them at full speed.

"You find it?" Titus said.

"You'll want to see this," Kate said.

The group retraced her path to find the car, in an unmistakable shade of green, waiting for them, untouched. But it was also clear looking at the ground that others had been this way. Varied footprints in the grimy mud hinted that before or after Broadstreet made the drop, another group had visited. Had they already retrieved the data Broadstreet left for them? Or had they set up a ruse long before the reporter had arrived?

"It's got to be a trap," Kate said. "I can't tell how long ago they were here, but someone was looking for the drop."

"Okay," Jane said. "I'll go for the car."

"No," Kate said. You hang back. If it's booby-trapped you need to be ready to defend me."

"Defend you?"

"Everyone else here has powers. I'll go to the car so the rest of you can be prepared to act," Kate said.

"I'll walk with you," Annie said.

"Why?" Kate said.

"Because I can control time, you grumpy little thing," Annie said. "I might be able to buy us a few seconds if we need it."

The time-traveler and the vigilante tried to stare each other down, but finally Kate relented and nodded. They approached the car together. Finnigan and Titus transformed into their werewolf forms without a sound. Nearby, Jane and Jessie started to power up.

Kate popped the trunk.

Nothing happened.

She reached inside while Annie stood watch.

When Kate stood up, she held in her hand a small data drive, not unlike the sort of basic thumb drive Titus was used to seeing. She raised it slowly.

Everyone relaxed.

Then the wreckage on either side of the green car shifted, and, like something out of a science fiction movie, two mechanical spiders the size of delivery vans stood up and grasped for Kate and Annie.

Everything unfolded in a blur of slowed time and explosive violence. The robots, spindle-legged and ugly, erupted in motion. Annie threw out her arms instinctively, and Titus could feel the way she tugged on time, somewhere between an undertow and outright vertigo. Kate hunched into an attack position, but before she could move, Jane burst into the sky, crashing through the heart of one of the robots in a streak of flame and screeching metal.

Titus and Finnigan launched into motion, not moving to attack but rather to grab hold of their two vulnerable companions below the monstrous robots. Titus scooped Kate up in one arm, felt her tense, sensed her fury at not being allowed to fight. I'll apologize later, Titus thought, but she has the data drive, she doesn't get to play hero this time. Finnigan did the same for Annie, both werewolves shielding their allies with their own bodies, knowing their supernatural healing would better be able to take a slash from those long, spidery, clawed legs.

The sky lit up. Titus recognized the unique glow of a Straylight blast, and Jessie was in the air, fighting alongside Jane, the two women dismantling the multi-legged robots easily.

Titus put Kate down only to feel her kick off him, using his now-massive chest as a springboard. He watched as she crashed into the first of a half-dozen armed men, all wearing mottled gray uniforms. Kate lashed out, kicking one in the face, taking the futuristic rifle out of his hand and using it to smash a second man on the neck. Titus joined in, not quite sure how Kate already recognized these men as their enemy but trusting her instinct, and used his supernatural strength to toss the men around like ragdolls. Finnigan was beside him seconds later, and the three made short work of the ambush, leaving the uniformed men battered on the ground.

Kate held one, still conscious, by the shirt.

"How did you know we were coming?" she said.

The man hesitated, then stuttered and stumbled over his own words.

Kate viciously slammed him into the muddy ground.

Jane landed between Kate and Titus and looked up at the sky. "We should get out of here before reinforcements arrive," she said.

"We can take them!" Jessie said. "I want to fight."

Annie waved them off.

"Can and should aren't the same. We got what we came for."

"And trust me," Finnigan said, reverting to his human form. "Sometimes the things they send next are a lot more dangerous than the first round."

CHAPTER 24:
VICTORY AND LOSS

I didn't travel all the way into the future to hang out in a school," Emily said. Leto, was waiting by the front door for their friends and allies to return, so Emily followed her, mostly because Old and Even Meaner Kate was the only other real option for company at that moment and Emily wanted none of that noise.

So they stood in the front foyer of the community college building, Leto gazing at the horizon like she could hear the others coming, or perhaps she possessed a psychic bond or something, Emily couldn't be sure. What she did know was that she was bored and there was a dramatic lack of anything to do here, including ways to get into trouble. No Internet, no TV, nobody to taunt—not for lack of trying, as she'd been pestering Leto for hours—no music, nothing.

"Do you play chess?" Emily asked, finally. She'd reached that point. Chess with strangers. Better than nothing, she supposed.

Leto held up a hand. Emily noticed how long the werewolf's fingers were in her human form. And then, of course, she couldn't stop looking at them. Don't look at her weird long fingers, Emily told herself. Don't do it. Don't stare. Stop. Stop looking.

"So you have very long fingers," Emily blurted out.

"The others are close," Leto said, ignoring her.

The first to return were the information retrieval team, approaching on foot to be inconspicuous. They had clearly encountered trouble based on the burn marks and tears on their costumes, but everyone was walking, and nobody seemed hurt.

"How'd it go?" Emily asked.

"Giant robot spiders," Titus said, flanked by Finnigan and sounding a little winded.

"Robot spiders?" Emily asked.

"Seriously," Jessie, the replacement Billy, said.

Emily liked and hated the new girl at the same time. Nobody should take Billy's place, she thought, but hey, if someone needed to take over as Straylight, Jessie seemed like she might be fun.

"I love giant robot spiders," Emily said. "Why'd you leave me behind? This might be the only time in my entire life I get to see them and you've ruined it."

Jane—our Jane, Emily thought, the younger—brought up the rear and shook her head.

"I have a terrible feeling we're going to see more of those creatures at some point," Jane said. "We handled them okay though."

"Too okay," Finnigan said.

"That fight was over exceedingly fast," Titus agreed. "Have you fought those things before?"

"The robots they use are always different," Jessie said. "We think they've got someone who tinkers with them, because they change after every fight, improve a little bit, get better to take us on."

"And those were not up to the caliber of the last few versions," Finnigan said.

"So what do you think?" Jane asked. "That they were a distraction?"

"We'll know soon enough," Leto said, returning to the front door again. "The others are coming. Something's wrong."

Jane and Jessie bolted out the door immediately, rushing to meet the incoming team.

Emily looked around, then punched Titus in the arm.

"Where's Kate?"

Titus turned to Finnigan, back to Emily, then almost started for the door. He stopped, though, when the others arrived, and realized not everyone was able to walk in under their own power.

Finnigan hustled to help a wounded werewolf, now transformed to human form, carry one of their own in.

"He'll live," the newcomer said about the fallen comrade. "Help me get him to a bed."

Older-Titus walked in next, side by side with Solar, who held another man in her arms. His body, limp and ragged, was covered in old bloodstains. She hurried past Emily, heading toward the room the group used as a medical area.

Titus put a hand on Emily's shoulder.

"I've got to go find Kate. Stay put, keep an eye out," he said.

"You're not the boss of—" she started to say, but Titus left at a full run. "Me."

Billy sauntered in next. He smiled at Emily, his eyes wild and tired.

"Bad things, Em."

"Bad things?"

Billy gestured to where Solar had scampered off.

"I think we're too late," he said. "Did the others get what they needed?"

"They got something," Emily said. "No idea what it is."

"Well, let's hope this was worth it," Billy said.

Their Jane grabbed both Billy and Emily by the arm and pulled them along. "Broadstreet's dying," she said.

CHAPTER 25: SACRIFICE

The room was quiet as their ally lay slowly dying.

Jane watched Solar hold the man's hand. He breathed raggedly. She looked over poor Broadstreet's body, the cuts and burn marks. He'd been tortured extensively. Unspeakable injuries marred his face. Still, he smiled at Solar who was holding his hand.

"Did you get the package?" Broadstreet said, his voice a harsh rasp.

"The others did," Jane heard herself say. "You did well, Jon."

"I just hope . . ."

"It *will* help, Jon. And you're going to be here to see that it does," Solar said.

"No I won't," he said.

Broadstreet smiled. It was pained, but also radiant, a smile of true happiness. Jane felt someone put a hand on her shoulder. Annie. The pink-haired woman gripped the Jane of the past tightly as they both watched the future unfold before them.

"I realize what they did to me, and I know you won't be able to fix it," Broadstreet said. "But I believe you won't let it go to waste. That's why I did all of this for you, Solar. You'll do what needs to be done."

"We don't tolerate pessimism around here," Solar said. "Leto's going to fix you up."

Jane found herself involuntarily walking forward; Annie's grip on her shoulder loosened and fell away. She picked up Broadstreet's other hand, Solar looked on. The flickering light from a swaying, old fixture beamed across his forehead and cheeks. Broadstreet's face was older than the one she remembered, lined with more worries, his beard gray-flecked, making him appear so much older than he was.

"I remember that face," he said softly. "That's the one you wore when I first met you."

"We're going to save this world, Jon," Jane said.

"Now I know I'm dying," Broadstreet said. He tried to force a smile. "You know, once upon a time I was in love with you?"

Jane's eyes flicked to her future self, who was staring right back at her, her mouth a stoic, pale line.

"I didn't know that," Jane said.

Solar patted Broadstreet's arm. "But I did," she said.

"It didn't matter in the end," Broadstreet said. "It was only a little thing. Schoolboy crush. We were young and the world wasn't dying. That isn't why I did this though."

"I know," both Janes said together.

"I just hoped to leave the world better than I found it," Broadstreet said. "Just wanted to help people who could possibly make that happen. That's not a bad life, is it?"

Jane's eyes welled up. You don't know this man, she thought, you don't know this future, you know nothing about him. He's a branch on the tree of the life of a boy you barely know in a timeline you may never return to. He's a stranger.

"That's the best life anyone could strive for," she said, instead.

Jane held this Broadstreet's hand, realizing she'd never even shaken hands with the young man she knew in her own timeline. Human beings can be so stupidly brave when we need to be, she thought. For reasons we never really understand.

"You're a good man, Jon Broadstreet," Jane heard Solar say.

He turned his head to her, the golden goddess Jane would someday become, and he smiled again, as if looking for the last time into the sun.

His fingers loosened in hers, and Jane knew he was gone. She knew, she knew in her heart, that somewhere else, in another time, he would live another life, that this would never happen, but this man now lay dead on a table in front of her, and she felt her heart break just a little, another life she couldn't save, another end that should have been better. And she could see, across the table, the same emotions tearing her future self apart.

Leto saved them. The strange woman gently took Broadstreet's hand away from them both each in turn, placed an old blanket over his body, and clicked off the overhead light. Somehow, in the darkened room, it felt less real.

"I don't want to lose any more friends," Solar said. "I'm so tired of losing friends."

"Then let's see what his life gave us," Jane said.

CHAPTER 26:
NEVER BECOME THAT

Kate found a vantage point across the dust-covered street so that she could watch the community college building in peace. She climbed up barricaded windows to the second story of an old storefront where once upon a time someone had lived over their own convenience store. The windows all smashed now, the food now spoiled or stolen. Kate hunched down near the ledge and listened. She closed her eyes, taking in all the sounds around her, listening for the voices of her allies, listening to the wind.

Kate wondered what it would be like without sight.

She heard Titus coming before she saw him. The boy, for all his predatory abilities when he transformed, was hopelessly clumsy as a human. He couldn't walk softly if his life depended on it but located her easily, though, which he always did. The dangers of being close friends with a tracker. They'll know where you are.

Titus didn't ask if she was okay. He never did that anymore, and Kate understood it was because she never answered, never gave him a verbal insight into her mood or her emotions, and so he'd simply stopped asking and relied on his superhuman senses to detect her mood. Titus admitted as much to her, that he could hear her heartbeat, could determine by the speed of her breathing if she was upset. It would be difficult to lie to him. In some ways it made Kate furious, yet in others, it was comforting to know there was at least one person in the world she shouldn't bother wearing her mask around.

He sat beside her. She tensed, annoyed that he'd intruded upon her sulking. But then she put a hand on his knee, half in greeting and half to simply acknowledge he was truly there.

"We don't fare well in the future, do we?" he said, finally.

"This isn't us," she said. "This isn't our future. It's someone else's."

"I know," Titus said. "Still, I thought we'd do better."

Kate closed her eyes again. Now it was she listening to his breathing, straining to hear his heartbeat. To the way his feet scuffled on the tar of the roof.

"So you can speak when you're in your werewolf form," Kate said, uncharacteristically breaking the silence. "Have you been holding out on us?"

Titus shook his head.

"Finnigan told me I'd be able to eventually, but it's harder than it looks," Titus said. "Not only am I not all there, really—I'm me, but I'm also *him*, you know? But I mean... you try talking when your jaw is stretched out into a snout and full of huge fangs."

"Do you need braces?"

"I need practice," Titus responded quickly. "But I never figured I'd need it. I always know I'll change back."

"But here you don't," Kate said.

"Here I don't. No." He scooted around to look at her. "The future me and the future you stopped talking, and he never changed back. I don't understand it."

Because I broke your heart, you stupid boy, Kate thought.

She didn't say a word, though. Kate was always best when she said nothing.

"Does that bother you?" Titus asked.

"I don't want that kind of power over anyone," Kate said.

Titus nodded, his shoulders loosening. He'd been holding his frame tight, as if afraid, and Kate noticed.

Kate unfastened and then refastened her boots.

Titus played with his sweatshirt absently. He scooped up some fine roof dust and scattered it toward a chimney.

"Don't ever let me end up like that," Kate said finally.

119

Titus cocked his head, questioning.

"Down there. That's a woman who's given up. If I ever give up, just put me out of my misery. Don't leave me there like an indoor cat."

"There's nothing wrong with indoor cats," Titus said.

Kate held his gaze for a moment.

Titus looked away.

"What do you want me to do? Kill you if you ever become blinded or something?"

"I don't know," Kate said, sharper than she intended. "I just don't know. But those are two people who have surrendered. Your future you is still fighting, but he's capitulated. Look at him. Those scars. He's been trying to die for years. And me? She's become too much of a coward to find her own way out."

"I won't put you out of your misery if you give up," Titus said.

"I'm not asking you to. I'm asking you to . . ." Kate paused. "I'm asking you to encourage me to be better than that. If I ever need it."

Titus' mouth quirked into the slightest of smiles. "I can do that."

"And don't let me break your heart that badly. I'm not worth it."

"If you're not worth it, neither am I."

"You sure as hell aren't," Kate said.

They laughed, an honest, real laugh, the sort Kate only revealed at the rarest of moments, and lately, almost never.

"We'll be okay," Titus said, wiping a tear of laughter from his eye. "We've got to see our mistakes before we make them. We know things now."

"We do," Kate said. She peered out into the night, feeling lighter than she had a few moments before. "We know things . . ."

Suddenly the attack at the junkyard sprung back to mind. Knowing things. The enemy had known they were coming. They knew things. They knew they'd come for the hidden data cache.

"Titus. Where's the drive we found?"

"The others are going to open it up, see what Broadstreet uncovered."

"Where is it?"

"It's in the school," Titus said. "Why?"

"They knew we were coming," Kate said. "They expected us to come for it. What if they . . ."

And then they both heard the sound of aircraft flying, and looked up into the night sky.

"We have to get them out of the school," Kate said.

Titus was already transforming though, doubling in size, his scrawny human body changing into a massive beast. They jumped down to street level.

And then the college building was hit with a missile and exploded in a ball of red flames.

CHAPTER 27:
BEHIND THE CURTAIN

Everyone gathered around the unit where Neal now resided, waiting for the AI to decode the message Broadstreet left behind. Ordinarily, this sort of waiting was intolerable to Billy, but for the moment, an opportunity to do nothing was welcome. Across the room, he eyeballed the new version of Straylight, Jessie, conversing with both Janes. Billy found himself wondering if her conversations were anything like the sort he had with Dude on a regular basis. Was the alien different with another host? Did he find her less obnoxious? More?

Before Billy could obsess too much on the question, though, he was reminded, quite bluntly, that Emily also did not like waiting around, and at the moment she was far less tolerant of it.

"Waddup?" Emily said, plopping down next to Billy. "How'd it go with your future not girlfriend?"

"Look, it's weird enough that I know about it at all," Billy said. "Could you not make it weirder by putting it like that?"

"But you ran a mission with her," Emily said. "What was it like, bro? What was it like? Bro. Bro. Bro. Did you talk to her? Tell me. Tell me. Tell me."

This would've been annoying enough on its own, but Emily punctuated each period with a jab to Billy's shoulder. Finally devolving into just punching his arm and saying "bro, bro, bro" over and over and over again.

"Stop the jabbing," he said. "Stop it."

122

But Emily hit him one more time for fun.

"So seriously, how bizarre was it?"

"We're in the future. Everything's strange right now," Billy said.

"But we're really not in the future," Emily said. "Think about it. The future implies that we're somewhere that will eventually happen. No matter what we do here, this is a life that will never take place. This isn't the future. It's just a different 'when.'"

"Have you been reading Neil DeGrasse Tyson again?"

"Igor Novikov, actually," Emily said. "A physicist who developed a theory called the Self Consistency Principle. I think we're proving him right."

"Is this going to make my brain hurt?"

"He thought that the ability to impact the future by changing the past is basically impossible," Emily said. "He thought time always balanced the scales to keep order."

"You're going to try to make me read again, aren't you?" Billy said.

"Shut up. You like when I school you with my brain," Emily said. "So seriously though. I'm obsessed by the you-and-Jane thing. Obsessed."

"Why?"

"Because I thought you were more into girls who are half-robot and I thought Jane was more into anybody that isn't anything like you," Emily said.

"Are you sure you're my friend?" Billy said.

"Your best."

Billy sighed.

"I just think it's ridiculous," he said. "Different timeline. Different people. Different actions. Nothing's the same here."

"Got that right," Emily said.

One of Whispering's people waved everyone over to gather around Neal. The AI lit up, projecting a holographic screen in the air.

"Designation: Solar. I have decrypted Jon Broadstreet's last data drop," Neal said.

"Play," Solar said.

Broadstreet's sweaty and lined face appeared on screen.

"I think I finally got what we're looking for," Broadstreet said in the recording. "All these years, we had no idea who was pulling the strings. No idea. But the longer I'm here the more I'm meeting some old timers, people who joined up with the crusade right at the very beginning. Someone mentioned seeing the boss back in the good old days. Got me thinking, and thinking got me digging. Take a look at this."

The hologram shifted, showing surveillance footage from before the world began to fall apart. A candid shot of a man in a white silk mask, slender in a perfectly tailored dark suit.

"Old shots of someone who appears to be the leader of this outfit from about ten years back, maybe a little longer," Broadstreet said. "No names attached, but I realized, I know this guy. Or at least this costume."

The hologram shifted again. Now an older photo. The white-masked man on the cover of a newspaper. This shifted to live action footage, grainy handheld images of the same person in a suit bounding into the darkness of an alleyway. This morphed into a sort of ID screen, with biographical information and a headshot of the masked suspect.

"This can't be possible," Annie said, interrupting. Solar waved a hand to pause the recording when Annie walked to the front of the room. "This can't be him."

"Well, whoever he is, he's wearing a mask," Emily said. She pulled her scarf up over her face and continued talking in a muffled voice. "I could be Princess Leia right now, see? Hard to tell."

"I know him. I've met him," Annie said. "And there's no way the White Shadow is still in commission, let alone operating on the side that's destroying the world. He's a hero."

"Doesn't look like much of a hero," Jessie said. "Looks like a creep in a mask."

"He is, he was a street-level vigilante, like Dancer," Annie said. "Doc knew him too. I mean really knew him, like they were friends."

"Doc has a great track record on his friends in this timeline," Jane said. "Present company excluded of course. No offense. But I mean, his other 'friend' murdered him."

"The White Shadow, though—Jane, did Doc never tell you about him?" Annie said.

"Wait, not the guy from when Doc was a kid?" Jane said.

"That's him. The White Shadow. He met the President. Was almost on a postage stamp. He's a good person," Annie said.

"People change," Billy offered.

"Not this much," Annie said. "I wish Doc were here. He'd be able to tell you more. The White Shadow was a pacifist. He'd also be well into his nineties by now. The guy wasn't a young man when Doc first arrived on the scene. Rumor had it he'd died!"

"Impersonator?" Billy said.

"Copycat?" Jane said.

"Clone!" Emily said. "Clearly a clone. From a bad batch. That's why he's evil."

Annie waved them all off.

"Solar, let's see what else Broadstreet uncovered."

The AI broadcast was restarted and Neal continued to play Broadstreet's message.

"The White Shadow. Hero of the City. He who guarded the night," Broadstreet said. "One of the City's most influential vigilante superheroes. Never killed, never fired a gun, this guy was impeachable. But he dropped off the map before I was even out of school. Everyone just assumed he'd retired. What would he be doing leading this coalition of forces? Did he get fed up with being one man fighting evil? Is he under mind-control? Is this just someone trading on his name? That's the first piece of the puzzle we need to uncover."

The hologram moved again and now showed a balding man with fair hair and spectacles.

"This is Keaton Bohr," Broadstreet said. "He was easier to track down once I got a look at his face. Controversial scientist. Had all these great ideas for alternate energy consumption, robotics. More. But he's another one who seemed to disappear from existence. Last anyone heard of him he'd been stripped of his credentials under a cloud of questionable activity years ago. But—"

The slide moved again. The man in the white mask standing with

Bohr at a facility of some kind. The photo was years old.

"—Here he is," Broadstreet said. "With the man in the white mask. Who is he? He's certainly intelligent enough to have developed some of the weapons we've encountered, but again, there's little information about what he's been up to in recent years."

A series of schematics scrawled across the screen, too fast for Billy to make sense of them. In the back of his mind, he sensed a quiet thoughtfulness from Dude. You get any of that? Billy thought, directing his question at Dude.

This man could have put your species into deep space, Dude said. *There is significant value in his theories. Gravity propulsion. Faster than light travel. Where did he go wrong, I wonder?*

Maybe he's just crazy, Billy thought.

Don't confuse misguided for crazy, Dude warned.

Way to be ominous, Dude, Billy thought. Jessie gave him a dirty look from across the room. She can tell I'm talking with you, he thought. Is she jealous? Freaked out? What's her problem?

You're not exactly without flaw in your interaction with her, Dude said. *The two of you should talk.*

About what, you? Billy thought.

About what you have in common, Dude said.

"So we've got a scientific genius who wanted to do away with fossil fuel consumption and turn us into a green society working with a guy who, while he should be dead of old age, was a legitimate hero before all this started," Jane said. "And somehow they get together and decide to destroy the world?"

"I don't understand it," Solar said. "You're right. What was the trigger? Where did they turn?"

"Quiet," Whispering said.

It was only when older-Titus spoke that Billy realized his younger version had never returned after racing off to find Kate. Ordinarily Billy would think of ways to tease Titus about wandering away, but for once he was legitimately concerned. Where'd they go?

The older werewolf held up a hand, forcing everyone to be silent.

"There's something—" Whispering said.

And then the room exploded.

CHAPTER 28:
TO END IN FIRE

Well, this isn't going to be fun, Emily thought as the roof collapsed above her in red flames. She wondered if this would be house she'd die in, crushed to death by a ceiling in a community college of the future.

"I never got to read the end of *Game of Thrones*," she said out loud.

And then everything got peculiar.

The flames started to move slower, appearing more like dripping pudding than open flames. Emily saw everything moving in slow motion. Werewolves transforming into their more powerful forms, trying to run from the room; Whispering making a valiant effort to reach the machine where the last remnants of Neal's consciousness remained, the large wolf's body outstretched in a powerful leap; Billy and Jessie's bodies alighting in mirrored blue-white glows as the protective energy Straylight provided began to activate; Jane and Jane, Solar and Solar, both women staring defiantly as the building exploded upon them.

Everything frozen in time, creeping along, it was like watching a movie one frame at a time. And through all this, Emily saw Anachronism Annie strolling toward her as if she had all the time in the world.

Annie put a hand on Emily's shoulder.

"You're going to make one of your bubbles of float," Annie said. "You're going to make it big, and you're going to make it envelope the entire room. You got that?"

Emily tried to speak.

"IIIIIIIIII gggoooooooottt iiittttttttt . . ."

"Okay," Annie said. "I can't hold this forever. Stopping time isn't as easy as it looks. Be ready."

"Wwwwwwhhhhaaatttt aaaboooooouuttttt . . ." Emily attempted to talk again.

"I'm going to stay right next to you, and you're going to save my life. Got it?"

"Yyyyyyeeeeeeeeeeessssssss . . ."

"Here we go," Annie said, and then she crouched down beside Emily and covered her neon-pink hair with her hands.

As if someone hit the play button, the world began moving again. The noise from the explosion was a brutal roar in Emily's ears, but she threw out her hands, envisioning the biggest, strongest bubble of float she could think of. She felt gravity alter and end, springing out from the center of her chest and all around her.

Then the world got weird again. But this time, it got her kind of weird.

Flames flickered and died as the bubble touched them, the freakish gravitational manipulations made combustion impossible within its sphere. Huge chunks of building stopped falling in mid-air and suspended there like balloons of brick and concrete. Whispering hung there as well, mid-jump, all momentum lost as the bubble of float grabbed hold of him.

Billy floated by, unable, within the bubble, to control his own flight path; instead, he just looked at Emily expectantly.

"Seriously, Em?"

"Sorry," she said.

Billy continued to drift past. He shrugged at Jessie as she floated in the opposite direction, cursing.

"What do I do next?" Emily yelled.

"This is about as far as I thought things through," Annie said, holding onto Emily's ankle to prevent her from floating away.

"Okay," Emily said. "Okay, I have an idea. I think I have an idea."

"Whatever you're thinking, don't do it," Billy said, drifting toward the edge of the room, bumping into chunks of building along the way.

"Everybody hold onto something," Emily said.

"This sounds like a terrible plan," Finnigan said, but he grasped a gap in the floor with one clawed hand, and grabbed hold of Leto with his other.

"Everyone ready?" Emily said.

"Do it," Whispering growled. He hung onto the Neal computer with one arm and using his feet and hands to grip the nearest wall that hadn't caved in yet.

"Please don't hold it against me if I mess this up," Emily said.

And then she pushed her bubble of float outward.

Debris from the building flew through the air like meteors, some reignited as they escaped the radius of the bubble. Billy was also among the flying debris, spinning out into the night sky while cursing Emily's name.

"I wasn't ready!" he said, his voice trailing off in the distance.

The area illuminated as Jessie took off at high speed in an attempt to catch him.

"I'm sorry!" Emily yelled. "But to be fair, I did warn everyone. Right?"

"Let's never do this again," Annie said.

The sounds of the aircraft that had struck them grew louder as they returned for another pass.

Jane and Solar looked at each other knowingly and then took off together to intercept.

"Everyone out," Whispering yelled, the scorched Neal-computer tucked under his arm like a crate. He pointed at Finnigan. "Move it. Find Kate. Make sure she's okay."

Finnigan nodded and ran off.

"Grab what you can. The building's compromised," Whispering said. He swore and breathed sharply.

Looking down, Emily saw a shard of metal sticking out of the werewolf's side.

"Dammit," Whispering said.

"Let me help you," Leto said.

"It'll heal," he said.

"Give me the bloody computer, you oaf," Leto said.

Whispering huffed, half-annoyed, half-amused. He looked around the room. "The flyers will have to catch up. Annie, take the wounded to the nearest safe zone. My people are going to grab what we can."

"Where are the other kids? Where's your Titus and Kate?" Annie asked Emily.

"You're asking me like I would know?"

Explosions echoed in the distance while the two Solars went to battle with incoming jets. More engines growled in the air though. More incoming bombers.

"We'll find everyone," Whispering said. "Go!"

Annie grabbed Emily's arm and pulled her along.

Not sure what else to do, Emily just ran beside her, hoping her friends weren't following far behind.

CHAPTER 29:
THE STRAYLIGHT CONNECTION

Billy crashed down in the middle of a desiccated baseball diamond a half-mile from the college. Dude's protective shielding took the brunt of the fall, but the impact rattled him to his bones.

"Oh, Entropy Emily, you and I are going to have words when I get back," he said, lying very still in the middle of the field.

Above him, a familiar glow approached. Jessie formed a figure eight in the sky above and then performed a much better landing beside him. She held out a hand and helped Billy back to his feet.

"Why didn't you get thrown a thousand feet?" Billy said.

"Because I listened when your little buddy told us to 'hang onto something,'" Jessie said. "Are you just not good at this stuff?"

"Listening? No," Billy said. "Not particularly."

"I'll keep that in mind," Jessie said. She hunched down, scanning the sky for approaching enemy jets. "We should get back."

"Back to what?" Billy said. "The building's gone."

"There's a backup meeting location," Jessie said.

"Then we head there," Billy said.

Jessie started walking away.

He hustled to catch up. "Shouldn't we fly?"

"Okay, you're new here, so I'm going to forgive you for asking a stupid question, but do you really want to be a ball of glowing light on someone's radar when they just bombed our base back to dirt?"

"We could take 'em if they came after us," Billy said.

Jessie paused, looked at Billy out of the corner of her eye, and smiled.

"You like fighting?"

"You want the responsible answer I tell people back home, or you want the truth?" Billy said.

"I love fighting," Jessie said. "The Boss is trying to convince me it's a bad habit."

They walked together toward more significant cover, a wooded area left mostly untouched by combat.

"The Boss? Bruce Springsteen is telling you not to enjoy fighting?"

"The Boss. Our alien. The guy who lives in both of our heads."

"Oh. Dude."

"You call him Dude?" Jessie said.

"Yeah. You don't?"

"He must hate being called Dude," Jessie said.

"Like 'The Boss' is better?" Billy said.

"It's better than 'Dude.'"

"I don't know. What do you think, Dude? What would you rather we call you?"

I don't need a name, Dude said. *I'm simply a part of you. Of both of you. What you call me doesn't matter in the end, because I simply am. I'm simply here.*

"Did he get all philosophical in your head too?" Jessie asked.

"Yeah," Billy said.

"I think he's more weirded out by the time travel thing than either of us is," she said.

"I don't know," Billy said. "I'm still not quite okay with being dead here."

"Well, now you know what not to do to avoid getting yourself killed," Jessie said.

Billy thought back to the scientist Emily was trying to talk to him about earlier, the Russian guy. Didn't she say that Igor whatever his name was thought time was unchangeable?

Timelines are unchangeable, Dude said, answering Billy's own thoughts. *But this is another branch in the tree. You can't save yourself here, but what happens to you here is not necessarily the same thing that will happen to you back home.*

"Dude, between you and Emily I understand time travel even less than when I started," Billy said. "This isn't helping."

The brush crunched under their feet as they walked.

Billy found himself strangely at ease around this girl, a kindred spirit, someone like him. There aren't many people like us, Billy thought. I never got to meet the guy before me. Neither did she.

"What I want to know is, if you don't die in your timeline, does that mean I never become Straylight?" Jessie said.

"I don't know. I guess? Not yet?"

"I know you can't change this timeline. I get that. I know that you going home doesn't mean that I'll wake up tomorrow and not have these powers anymore," Jessie said. "But you make me anxious. I keep wondering. What am I like in those other timelines where you survive? Am I just... me?"

"This is weirdly gruesome. I never thought talking about a hypothetical 'when I'm *not* dead' would be morbid, but this is pretty morbid."

"I don't like the idea of just being me," she said. "I think I'd be so bored."

"But you wouldn't know the difference, right?" Billy asked. "If you never met Dude, then you'd never know what you missed out on."

"That's even worse," Jessie said.

Billy grimaced.

"Yeah. Actually it is."

He paused, kicking a rock out of their path. "I lost my powers for a little while a few months back. It was not cool."

"Really?"

"Yeah," Billy said. "There are these guns that... Y'know, the how doesn't matter."

"Yeah it does."

"Fine. There are these guns that were designed to kick Dude out of his host body."

"What happened?" Jessie asked.

"Well, Dude joined up with Kate and helped rescue me from prison—this story gets stranger the more I tell it, doesn't it?"

Jessie stopped walking and hit Billy in the chest.

"He joined up with Dancer?"

"That was pretty much my reaction, too," Billy said.

"How did that turn out?"

I have barely begun to recover, Dude said, his tone completely without irony.

"He's still rattled. She wasn't a great host," Billy said.

"I bet her brain is as welcoming as an icebox," Jessie said. "Wow. I actually feel bad for him."

Billy shrugged, and they both started walking again.

"Yeah, well. Anyway. You're right. It was lonely. I almost lost it myself. You'd think having some privacy in my own head would've been amazing, but . . ."

"No," Jessie said. "It's not privacy anymore. It's . . ."

"Vacancy," Billy said.

"I don't want that," Jessie said. "I like to fight, but you know what I love more?"

"Being a hero?"

"Exactly," Jessie said.

"Well, you know what else I learned when Dude wasn't in my head?" Billy said.

"That walking sucks?"

"That someone like me can be a hero, even without possessing any powers," Billy said.

"But powers help," Jessie said.

They both laughed.

Billy looked at his feet and smiled. "Yeah," he said. "Powers definitely help."

CHAPTER 30:
SOLAR REFLECTION

Jane smashed through the hull of the last of the bombers, sending the pilotless machine plummeting to the earth. In her home timeline, she would have tried to guide its descent to prevent loss of life; but here, in the empty wasteland the City and its outskirts had become, that kind of effort felt pointless.

Solar watched the shells of the other bombers burning on the ground below. She gestured that they both should land, and Jane followed her down to street level.

"Did everyone get out okay?" Jane asked as they touched down.

Solar shrugged helplessly.

"We have to hope for the best," she said. "We've done all we can."

"Why did they bomb us?" Jane said. "Were they hoping to smoke us out? Or actually kill us?"

"We've been fighting this battle a long time," Solar said. "It might just be that this White Shadow has become tired of dealing with us and was hoping to take us out once and for all."

"They had to know you couldn't be killed by a bombing run," Jane said. "Or Straylight."

"They could have wiped the rest of them out with a well-timed attack, though," Solar said. "Even Titus' people can't come back easily from nearly burning to death."

Jane watched the sky for more aircraft, but none arrived.

"How'd you end up sharing leadership with Titus?" Jane asked.

Solar glanced over, curious.

"What's that?"

"You and Titus. Whispering. Older-Titus. You share command. Back home everyone kind of leaves the leadership to me," Jane said.

"Do you like it better that way?"

"Not even a little," Jane said.

"Good," Solar said.

"So did you always share the lead, or did it change?"

Solar lifted her hands in a vague, noncommittal gesture.

"He brought his people on board to fight. I didn't feel right taking command, and I don't think they would've followed me as long as he was there," Solar said. "So for quite a while, I was essentially in charge, but Whispering commanded the werewolf tribe."

"What changed?" Jane asked.

"Everything," Solar said. "Things got very bad. Our friends started dying. And then Billy died, and Kate was blinded, and it felt like it was just Titus and I trying to save the world. So to say we shared leadership isn't exactly accurate. There wasn't a reason to lead. We were just the last two people standing, and we stood there by each other's side as equals."

"It's strange," Jane said. "I feel like I know him the least of all the Indestructibles. Kate pretends to be mysterious, but I understand her. I know her story. Billy and Em are open books, but Titus is . . ."

"His people are mysterious for a reason," Solar said. "They have to be. To protect themselves and to look after their legacy. It's how they're raised."

"Did it bother you to give up part of the lead?" Jane asked.

"Would it bother you?"

"You keep turning this back onto me," Jane said.

"Because it's been so long, I don't remember myself when I was your age," Solar said. "I'm curious. Was I arrogant? Was I jealous?"

"I don't feel arrogant. I don't feel jealous," Jane said. "I don't know. Maybe I am?"

"Everyone always said I was so good as to be boring," Solar said. "And they might be right."

"Emily says I'm boring."

"Boring keeps your friends alive," Solar said. "There's no harm in being boring."

"So you think I'm boring too," Jane said. She caught the look of shock on the older reflection of her own face looking back and laughed. "I'm kidding."

"No, you weren't," Solar said. "And that's how I know we're the same person, you and me. I always wished, before this war started, that I'd lived more. That I'd smiled more. That I worried less."

"Is there anything you could have done to worry less?" Jane asked.

"Have fewer friends," Solar said. "Learned less about the world. Not cared as much."

"I don't think any of those things are possible," Jane said.

"Then no," her older counterpart said, face breaking into a smile. "There isn't anything you can do to worry less. So try instead to worry well."

CHAPTER 31:
ROSE

Keaton Bohr found the White Shadow sitting in a conference chamber alone, watching the bombing of the old community college building on a giant screen. The masked vigilante didn't turn around, but held up a hand absently to acknowledge the scientist's entrance.

"Did bombing them really do any good?" Keaton said, watching the screen as the structure burned.

"More than you'd know," the Shadow said. "Computer, from the beginning. Watch."

The screen cycled back to the start of the attack, artillery shells causing the building to collapse upon itself like crumpling matchsticks. Bohr saw the flames erupt, blasting out from the strike point, then mysteriously, almost fluidly, changed shape and extinguish.

"Notice anything familiar about what just happened?" the Shadow said.

Bohr watched again. Any number of superpowers could snuff out flames easily enough, but there was something strange about what occurred. He amplified the image, looking for some clue in the movement of the flames. Instead, it was the motion of the debris that caught his eye.

"The shrapnel isn't moving right," Keaton said. "It hung in the air too long. Took unnatural trajectories when it did fly away. Something altered how the explosion moved. From the inside. We haven't encountered anything like this before. Except . . ."

"Except in our own labs," the White Shadow said.

The girl in the bubble. She could do things like this. Change gravity's effect on falling objects. Cause alterations in density at the molecular level.

"Keep watching," the Shadow said.

They stared as the building exploded in real time now, flames mostly gone but the structure an obliterated disaster. From the rubble, two streaks of fire launched into the air in pursuit of the mechanized bombing vehicles.

"Is that an echo?" Keaton said. "It looks like Solar's energy signature is doubling on screen." He ordered the computer to focus in on the flyers in a single frame of video. "That's no echo," he corrected himself. "There's two of them."

"A second Solar," the Shadow said.

"Another Gawain mutation?" Keaton said. "It may be time. We have a new human born with the Gawain mutation every few decades. Could she have been training her replacement in secret?"

"I'm not sure," the Shadow said. "But clearly they have more help on their side than they had previously. It's been a long time since we've seen them recruit new powered heroes. Reports from our men on the ground in the Waterfront and at the ambush we left in the junkyard seem to indicate there's more of them than before. It warrants researching."

"I'll look into it," Keaton said.

The screen returned to playing the explosion in real time, and he took in the strange sight of werewolves running out of the destroyed building like rats on a sinking boat. "I'm amazed the werewolves are still fighting the good fight," Keaton said. "It seems ridiculous. Either they're zealots or they just like to go into battle."

"Probably both," the Shadow said. "But regardless of why, they need to be dealt with."

"I can return to my research," Keaton said. "I'm sure there's some way to make an airborne silver powder poison."

"No," the Shadow said. "I want you looking at the end game, devising ways to make use of what's left of our girl in the bubble."

"But if that pack of wolves is on the move . . ."

"They will be dealt with," the White Shadow said.

"How? More of our foot soldiers? I don't doubt the conviction of our men, but they can't handle monsters. They don't have the practice or the manpower."

"I've brought in a specialist," the Shadow he said, tapping a command into the room's telecomm system. "Please come in. I'd like to introduce you to Dr. Bohr."

"Who did you recruit? Mercenaries?" Keaton said.

"Better," the Shadow said. "Professional monster hunters."

The chamber door opened, and a short-haired woman dressed all in black walked in. One eye, hidden behind a patch, was surrounded by old scar tissue. Several knives visible on her belt, she carried herself, Keaton noticed, like someone who had knives hidden out of sight as well. The woman was flanked on either side by masked fighters like herself.

"Keaton, this is Rose," the Shadow said. "Rose, meet my second in command, Keaton Bohr."

"You're the professional monster hunter?" Keaton asked.

Rose smirked. It was a vicious grin, marred by the toughness of the scar tissue on her face.

"For centuries, my people have kept the werewolf population in check," Rose said. "We destroy monsters."

"I don't understand," Keaton said. "Why work with us? What's the point? Money's not worth anything anymore. Power? Promises?"

"Oh, we're much easier than that," Rose said.

"Really?" Keaton said.

"Yes," Rose said. "Money is worthless, but professional pride still counts for something. The end of the world is coming. All we want to do is have a chance to finish the work we started while we still can."

CHAPTER 32:
THE CASTLE IN THE SKY

I took Doc Silence some time to find Lady Natasha Grey in this expiring future.

Most magicians worth the title knew how to cover their tracks, to erase their footprints in the ether. It wasn't difficult to do, but it was a challenge to do it well. Unfortunately for Doc, Natasha was the best in the world at hiding her presence.

Fortunately, though, she had very little competition here. There are precautions you take out of habit, Doc knew, and there were safety measures you took when you discovered your mortal enemies were looking for you. Even the Lady was capable of cutting corners, letting her guard down, if she thought she'd removed all threats to herself in the world.

Eventually, using old magic and mortal detective work, Doc found her trail. He followed her through the astral plane, walking across sand that sparkled like crushed diamonds under a purple sky, watching as the ghosts of dead wizards wandered by searching for bodies they could never return to.

He wondered if he would see himself there, among the dead. Magicians had a way of hanging onto this world, peering through the torn fabric of realities, refusing to believe their lives were truly over.

When he found Natasha's hideaway, he smiled. Always the flair for the melodramatic.

Adrift on a cumulous cloud, slowly meandering across the night sky, Natasha built a castle like something from an old fairy tale. Four tall towers, a gate and drawbridge, and guarded by a pair of gryphons riding on the wind. Castle Grey.

She's always said that she wanted a citadel in the sky, Doc thought. But all the years he knew her, the Lady had insisted it wasn't possible. Not because of the magic—the supernatural power to build a castle in the clouds was not as difficult as one might think—but because she was a nomad, because she kept no home and few friends. The Lady remained a creature of impermanence, and to build a home, to build a castle, was to put down roots and stay.

It seems like she's found her compromise, he mused. A castle that moves with the wind.

Doc returned to his body from the astral plane, gathered his belongings, and reviewed the words to key spells and enchantments he might need. One of these, permanently etched to his body, allowed him to fly. He casually stepped off the ground and drifted a few inches from the floor of the small room he'd used as a way station while searching for Natasha. Then, he carefully crafted a teleportation spell that would take him to the castle in the sky.

A heartbeat later, he hung above the clouds, the earth below not identifiable as any particular place in the world. The Lady chose to moor her castle in a place where she wouldn't be disturbed easily, Doc noticed.

He flew slowly toward the front gate of the castle, and two of the massive gryphons, big as Shire horses, landed to block his way.

Doc held out a hand, an arcane symbol glowed there in greeting. Both gryphons relaxed and then bowed their heads in respect. Odd that Natasha would choose such creatures to guard her palace, Doc thought. She'd always been more inclined to darker beasts, demons and devils. Gryphons were violent and dangerous, but they had, over the millennia, always been more servants of light than of darkness, and Doc had made friends among the surprisingly intelligent creatures. You chose very noble protectors for yourself this time, Doc thought. Perhaps it was because gryphons were, for the most part, honorable monsters, and required less care in handling than demons would. The latter always needed more wrangling, more bribery, and the diligence of a constant eye to ensure they wouldn't betray you.

And given Natasha's arrogance, Doc thought gryphons were particularly humble creatures for her to employ. He figured she at best would have discovered a way to be protected by a dragon. Though dragons were notoriously hard to bargain with as well.

Either way, these guards of the Lady's castle allowed Doc to walk right up to the front entrance and knock.

He waited a moment, listened to the echo of his rapping fist against the huge door. Then, the clangs and creaks as the gateway unlocked from within.

Natasha Grey had answered the door herself. She looked not a moment older than the last time He'd seen her, but Doc knew that her unchanging immortality was a bargain she'd made long ago. He hadn't expected her to age in twenty years. Her hair appeared different, longer. She wore a dark gown, simple and black, that fell all the way to her ankles, ending just above her bare feet.

"So now it's ghosts who come knocking on my door these days," Natasha said.

"I'm not a ghost, Natasha."

"Have you come for revenge, then?" the Lady said. "I'd deserve it, I suppose. Though revenge is not a very Doc Silence thing to do."

"Perhaps we might just need to talk for a bit," Doc said.

He'd expected something different from her, more defensiveness, more rage. But this woman standing before him, who had been, through his entire life, the single most dangerous person he knew, felt harmless. Defeated. And something else.

She seemed lonely.

I can't let my guard down, Doc thought, looking into the burning eyes of his friend, his nemesis. I can't allow her to fool me.

But he knew her. He understood her so well. And the one thing he could do that no other magician, no demon, no wizard or immortal being had ever figured out to do was to know when the Lady was lying. Only he knew her tell. It was the one thing he possessed over her, the one way he could stop her if he had to. Because the Lady Natasha Grey was the patron saint of liars, the goddess of falsehood, and that was how she'd built her empire of magic. How she gained immortality. Through the long con.

And Natasha wasn't trying to lie to him now. He knew it.

"Come inside," the Lady said. "You and I have some catching up to do."

* * *

Natasha led him through a vast antechamber, down a long, elegant corridor to a sitting room right out of a post-Edwardian lord's home. Doc listened, both with his human ears and with spells of detection, to determine if there was anyone else in the castle, but it seemed that the Lady decided to live alone in the sky. Small creatures, air elementals and wood golems, moved busily throughout the home, puttering away, keeping it neat.

She gestured to a rose-colored couch, and Doc sat down, crossing his legs. Natasha chose a chair designed in a garden pattern. Another hand gesture summoned a tray with a kettle and teacups and that set floated in, carried by one of the little air elementals, which then poured for the couple. The full teacups rose from the serving tray and flew delicately to the waiting hands of Doc and Natasha.

"Bergamot tea," Doc said.

"Let it never be said I have no sense of humor," Natasha said. She leaned in. "Where are you from, Doctor? Another plane? Another reality?"

"A different timeline," Doc said.

If she wasn't going to lie to him, he saw no reason to be untruthful with her.

Natasha nodded her head just slightly.

"Your little friend."

"Annie, for some reason, thinks this timeline is worth saving," Doc said. "She came to me for help."

"Because you weren't here in this timeline to ask," the Lady said.

"And I'm told you may have had a little something to do with that," he said.

Natasha smiled and gazed out the nearest window, a high-peaked structure of coiled iron and glass.

"It was just business," the Lady said. "And you and I always knew we'd have to face each other someday. How could we exist the way we did forever?"

"And what way is that?" Doc asked.

"Have we never fought in your timeline?" Natasha said. "Have we never been adversaries?"

"All the time," Doc said. He sipped his tea, tasting hints of citrus, then focused on the raised etching of the teacup beneath his fingertips. She probably made this herself, he thought, impressed with the elegance of her imagination.

"And we've never tried to kill each other," she said.

"We simply don't do that," Doc said. "And we've both done some very irrational things to avoid really hurting each other. I'd like to know what's different here."

"How do we ever know?" Natasha said. "You and I, we've walked the planes. We realize how one little thing can alter an entire reality. That an elder god from a time long since forgotten can sneeze in one instance and suddenly there's a reality where the oceans turn pink and the skies are silver. We've been to places where dreams are dreamt by mortals one night and the next they are born in flesh and walk on the other side of the veil. How can we ever understand why we might fight to the death in one timeline, and simply play chess in another?"

They studied their tea, not making eye contact, not speaking. Outside, clouds drifted idly by.

"Are you here to destroy me then?" the Lady said.

"What?"

"You've been brought here to save this dead little world. You know I killed you once. Have you come to stop me from getting in your way again?"

"I think at first I did," Doc said. "But I can't hurt you. Never been able to hurt you. I love you too much. That's always been the problem."

Natasha's glass dropped from her hand and shattered on the floor.

Doc felt a slight breeze when the little air elemental zipped across the room to clean up the mess.

But Natasha waved the creature away. Instead, she picked up a shard of the porcelain glass with her hands and held it up between two fingers.

"In your timeline," the Lady began, never taking her eyes from the broken teacup. "In your timeline, did you ever reveal as much?"

"Did I ever tell you I loved you?"

"Yes," she said.

Doc nodded gently. "Of course I did. You were my closest friend, for a long while. You taught me most everything I know. Of course I told you I loved you."

Natasha smiled. Not a happy smile, one without warmth, filled with subtext and frustration. She finally dropped the piece of porcelain onto the floor.

"So I knew that?" she said.

"Knew it, yes," Doc said. "But believed it, I'm not sure. I was never convinced you really believed me."

"Because I'm an unlovable monster, you fool," Natasha said. "Do you know how difficult it is to cultivate an armor of unlovable traits? It takes centuries to become a legitimate monster."

"But you were my friend," Doc said.

Natasha stood up, strolled over to the window, watched the clouds continue to roll by aimlessly.

"I never tried to kill you there, in your timeline?"

"No," Doc said.

"I wasn't afraid to kill?"

"Not remotely," Doc said. "You terrified me with your ability to destroy things without remorse. But you always left me standing."

"Why would I destroy you?" Natasha said. "You were the only living being who actually cared about me. Why would I kill the one person who cared if I lived or died?"

Doc joined her by the window. Below them, some European village or another rolled by, blissfully unaware of the castle in the sky hovering above them. The place looked untouched by the war, untouched by time.

"Why wouldn't I have told you?" Doc wondered out loud.

"One sentence," Natasha said. "That's how delicate these worlds are. One sentence can change an entire reality."

"It might not have been that one sentence."

"For me it was," the Lady said. "For me this world hinged on one sentence. And clearly it did for you as well. For us, our worlds divided because of one thing you said to me, just one time."

"They say that the past can't be changed," Doc said. "We can't fix things. But can only splinter off another timeline."

"I know."

"So this place will always exist. Even if we save it, even if we stop the people who want to destroy this timeline, all we'll really do is create one more branch, a branch where things turn out a little better."

"While the other branch withers and dies," Natasha said. "Time is more powerful than all of us."

"It is."

"You'll still try, though?" Natasha said.

"It's why we're here," Doc said. "And it's all we've ever done. We try."

"Well," the lady said, putting a hand lightly on Doc's shoulder. "You'll meet no resistance from me. I'm done toying with this world."

Doc listened to the silence again, the vast and empty echoes of Natasha's castle.

"Thank you," he said, pausing. "Why did you build this place, Natasha?"

She placed her free hand against the windowpane.

"Because I saw it in a dream, once," she said. "And when I had nowhere else to go, I started building my dreams."

He placed a hand on Natasha's shoulder.

"If you succeed, if you save this miserable place, Doctor Silence, please don't leave without saying goodbye," she said.

"I promise," he said.

"I need a better goodbye than the last time," Natasha said, in a voice not much louder than a whisper.

CHAPTER 33:
A CAGE MADE JUST FOR ME

The fallback location was a battered strip mall just outside the City. It had taken all night for the entire gathering of heroes to regroup there, arriving on foot and under cover of darkness.

Whispering's wolves arrived first, bounding their way across the overgrown landscape of the City's dying corpse. Others trickled in after that, Finnigan leading a belligerent future-Kate. Several members of the werewolf tribe hobbled in with fast healing injuries and burns sustained from the bombing.

Younger Kate and Titus arrived early, but Kate didn't feel much like talking, retiring to a dark corner in the veterinary clinic where everyone was huddling and scavenging supplies. Titus shrugged off her silence and she watched him join Emily and Annie who stood next to the machine that housed both Neal's artificial consciousness and the data drive with Broadstreet's stolen information. Neither seemed to be functioning.

"Can I make an ironic joke about their fallback base being a vet clinic?" Emily said.

"No," Titus said.

"Not even a little joke?" Emily said.

"Please don't," Titus said. "You know I don't like it when you pretend you think I'm a dog."

"But the sad faces you make are so funny," Emily said. The blue-haired girl turned her attention to the strange box, not unlike an exposed computer, where the AI who formerly controlled their entire flying Tower headquarters now lived. Emily poked around inside the machine, muttering to herself.

"What are you doing?" Titus said.

"Fixing Neal," Emily said. "Whispering said he was damaged in the explosion. We're having trouble getting Neal talking. And the whole 'playing the data recorder we desperately need' thing isn't working."

"Since when do you know how to fix computers from the future?" Titus said.

Emily stepped back and put her hands on her hips.

"Are you saying I can't fix Neal because I'm a girl?" Emily said.

"I'm saying you're overselling your skills," Titus said.

"Because I'm a girl?"

"Because you're a pathological liar," Titus said.

"I'm a genius, yo. I know things."

"Yes you do," Titus said, his tone becoming frustrated. "But Em, you have never, not once, even pretended to try to fix a computer."

"You're jealous I'm stealing your job," Emily said, smirking. "Now give me my sonic screwdriver and let me get to work."

Titus glanced at Annie, who shrugged right back at him.

"Don't look at me," she said. "I don't know what she's capable of. I certainly can't fix it."

"Titus! I need a hydrospanner and a portal gun," Emily said.

"I don't know what either of those are," Titus said.

"Further proof I know things and you don't," Emily said.

Kate felt a wash of warmth flow over her and looked up to see Jane sitting down next to her. Her own Jane, from the past, the young one who didn't glow all the time. Kate turned away to continue watching girl-genius and werewolf argue over the broken computer.

"How are you holding up?" Jane said.

Kate grunted.

"We haven't talked much since we got here," Jane said.

"We don't talk much in general," Kate said.

Jane nodded in agreement. She looked over to where Solar was speaking with the scarred future version of Titus. They seemed to be discussing something important, emphasized with sharp hand gestures. The elder Jane pointed to another room and Whispering waved his massive, clawed hand in that direction in a dismissive fashion.

"Wonder what they're arguing about?" Jane said.

"Me," Kate said. "Future me. They're talking about her."

Jane turned and looked at Kate too quickly for Kate to avoid eye contact.

"What's wrong?" Jane said.

Kate glared at her.

"What?"

"Why are you asking me what's wrong?" Kate said.

"Because you're the closest thing I have to an actual friend anymore, and you look more upset than you usually are, and I'm worried about you," Jane said.

Again, the glower from Kate. "That's the stupidest thing I've ever heard you say," she said.

"What, worrying about you?"

"That you have no other friends," Kate said. "All you have are friends."

"No," Jane said. "Emily and Billy look to me to lead. Doc's a teacher more than a friend, even though he says we've 'graduated' or whatever. He's still a mentor. Titus and I have never really warmed up to each other. Not necessarily in a bad way, but we just don't talk. You, on the other hand, never need anything from me. You don't need me to save you or lead you. You're just here, and I trust you with my life. And I think that makes you my friend."

"Sometimes you're as weird as Emily," Kate said.

"Maybe," Jane said. "Doesn't make what I'm saying untrue."

Kate shuffled around, changing positions to rest on her sit bones. She looked at Jane uncomfortably.

"I am so disappointed in myself," Kate said, finally.

"What?"

"With my future self," she said. "I'm a failure here. I failed."

Jane scooted around to face Kate directly.

"She was blinded. That doesn't make her a failure."

"It's not that she's without sight," Kate said. "Look at her. Watch her. That's a defeated woman. She gave up striving to be better. She's stopped trying. I can't live like that."

"You won't have to," Jane said. "This isn't our future. We make our own."

"I won't be like that, Jane," Kate said. "I will not let anything ruin me. I need to be better than her."

"You will be," Jane said. "Have you talked to her about it?"

"Talked to myself?" Kate raised an eyebrow.

Jane shook her head in response. "Why would future you be any less guarded than regular you?" she said.

Kate sighed, just the slightly out of character exhalation before catching herself.

"Something else happened," she said. "Losing her sight made it worse, but something else went down before that. I don't care what timeline we're in, I don't quit like this."

"Do you want to know what happened?" Jane said.

Kate's mouth quirked into a nonchalant, sarcastic smirk. "I suppose we'll find out eventually," she said.

Emily's cheers of victory from across the room interrupted them. "Fixed it!" she shouted, flinging a piece of plastic across the room.

"I do not understand what happened," a voice, decidedly feminine and not the customary voice of Neal, chirped out of the computer.

"You didn't fix it, you ripped a piece off!" Titus said. "That's not fixing, that's breaking."

"Is he talking?"

"Pardon me," Neal said. "Something seems to be amiss."

"You made Neal a girl!" Titus said.

"Then not only did I fix it, I improved it!"

"Why do I sound like this?" the AI said.

"It's okay, buddy, we'll get your old voice back," Titus said.

"But only if you decide you don't like this one," Emily said. "I think it suits you just fine."

"What happened?" the computer said.

Jane popped up onto her feet and offered a hand to Kate, who accepted. Together they walked over to the crowd gathered around the well-worn casing where Neal's consciousness lived.

"You got blowed up," Emily said. "Like, ka-boom. Pretty bad."

"Not that bad," Titus said "You took some damage. Girl Wonder over here just contributed some ancillary damage though."

"Clearly, he didn't need that piece," Emily said.

"Why does everything smell like pancakes?" Neal said in the most weirdly bewildered voice Kate had ever heard.

"What?" Emily said.

"See! I told you he needed that piece! Now everything smells like pancakes," Titus said.

"You say that like it's a bad thing!" Emily said. "I wish everything smelled like pancakes. And maybe bacon. Pancakes and bacon, I'd wear that as a perfume."

"Enough, Emily," Jane said, breaking up the argument between the blue-haired girl and the increasingly agitated werewolf.

"Would you, or would you not prefer everything smell like pancakes?" Emily said, pointing dramatically at Jane.

"You're going to have to give me an either/or option there," Jane said absently. "Neal?"

"Yes, Designation: Solar. Query: There are two of you?"

Jane cracked a smile, barely able to refrain from laughing at the sound of Neal's new female voice. "I'm sorry. This isn't funny. Neal, we need a look at the rest of Broadstreet's information. What else did he give us?"

They were joined quickly by Solar.

Kate noticed the two Straylights walking in the front door casually, late to the party.

"Right away, Designation: Solar Two."

"I hope you're okay with being Solar Two," older-Jane said.

"Whatever helps tell us apart," her younger self said.

Schematics came to life on screen, a large sphere furrowed with complex line work. It reminded Kate vaguely of the Epcot Center dome.

Broadstreet's voice started to speak. Kate watched both Janes flinch, just slightly. It was apparent they were not yet done grieving over the man's violent death. She looked around the room and saw the werewolf pack appearing mournful also. Broadstreet must've been a friend to them as well.

This is why we can never get attached to people, Kate thought.

"I was able to locate plans for a power source, a generator of some kind," Broadstreet said. "I don't know exactly what it does or how it works, but maybe some of your people can figure it out. Whatever it is, Bohr's been working on it for years. It seems to be his most important project."

"Hey Nealette, freeze frame there?" Emily said.

"Designation: Who are you? Designation: Strange Girl, please do not call me Nealette."

"Whatever," Emily said. "Hey Jane, can I change my superhero name to Strange Girl?"

"I'd rather you didn't," Jane said.

"Whatever," Emily said. She studied the hologram, intuitively turning it with hand gestures and using her fingers to zoom in. She looked uncharacteristically serious as she took a closer look.

"Are you messing with us right now, or are you actually searching for something?" Titus said.

"Be quiet, Fido," Emily said. "I'm working here."

Titus glanced at Kate.

She motioned with her hands as if to say, let it go.

"This is weird. It's like a Dyson sphere, but different," Emily said.

"A Dyson sphere?" Jane said.

"It was a hypothetical megastructure that would surround an entire star, capturing its power output," Emily said. "The mathematician Freeman Dyson first wrote about it, but he was actually upset that they called it the Dyson sphere. I think he was angry that a theoretical idea would be remembered in his name."

"Why would someone build a structure around a star?" Titus said.

"Dyson's idea was that we'd eventually need to maximize the energy the sun puts out in order for us to survive," Emily said. "Me, I think we'll have some sort of self-inflicted extinction event before that ever happens, but, y'know."

She continued to look at the design, flipping the sphere around with her hands.

"Anyway, it's so theoretical it shows up mostly in science fiction, so I'm surprised you don't know what I'm talking about, Titus," Emily said.

"I actually do know what you're talking about. Have you been stealing books from my room again?" Titus said.

"I knew what you were talking about, too," Billy said, joining in on the conversation.

"You lie, Billy Case," Emily said. "I gave you that Charlie Stross book and it ended up as a paperweight."

"No it didn't," he said. "I used it as a coaster."

"Whatever. It's . . ." Emily trailed off, her hands falling to her sides.

"No comeback?" Billy said.

"Shut up, Billy Case," Emily said. "This isn't a Dyson sphere."

Jane put a hand on Emily's shoulder, eyeing the holographic image, trying to figure out what Emily saw that spooked her.

"What's wrong, Em?" Jane said.

"This isn't a sphere to go around a sun," Emily said. "This sphere's designed to go around someone like me. It's a cage made just for me."

CHAPTER 34:
A BLACK HOLE WHERE MY HEART SHOULD BE

Doc Silence returned just before dawn, divining, through some minor magic, just where his companions had escaped to. The corpse of the college building he'd left them in had filled him with dread, but somehow, he knew, even without magic, that they'd survived.

What he found in the new location was a shocked and shockingly quiet Emily, surrounded by peers trying, all without great effect, to comfort her.

"I'm gone for one day and . . ." Doc said. "What happened?"

Both Janes—older and younger—filled him in on Emily's discovery in Broadstreet's notes, while Annie tried to give him background on the White Shadow's role in the war.

Doc interrupted her. "It can't be the White Shadow. Not the original one," he said.

"Doc, we've seen the footage," Annie said.

"I'm not saying this out of nostalgia, Annie," he said. "I mean factually. He was just a regular man, and he'd be elderly now. Not simply old. Infirmed. And none of this—giant robots, bombing cities, wiping out entire villainous organizations through lethal violence—none of this is his style. It's got to be someone else."

"Is proving he didn't do all this that important to you?" Annie said.

"No, but understanding who our actual enemy is, that matters to me," Doc said. "Blindly believing that in this timeline, a kind man who put his life on the line to make the world a better place turned into a dictator just doesn't cut it for me. I need to know more."

Doc dragged a chair over to Emily and sat across from her. She looked up.

"You really do leave at the most inconvenient times," she said.

"I know. What did you find out?" he said.

"Everybody said I was some kind of weapon here, right?" Emily said.

Doc nodded.

"Oh, big scary Emily. She sank California."

"You did," Jessie said.

Billy glared at her.

"What? I'm just telling her the truth. Girl literally dragged California into the Pacific Ocean," she said

"I'm also fueling the revolution," Emily said. She pointed at the hologram still spinning in front of Neal's computer housing. "That thing is using me as a power source."

"I don't get it," Billy said.

"I love you Billy Case, but you don't get a lot of things," Emily said. She looked at Doc. "You want to explain this?"

"Go ahead, Emily," he said.

"Okay," she said. "You know how I always say I have a black hole where my heart is?"

"I always thought that was a figure of speech," Billy said.

"Sorta kinda, but not really," Emily said. "You guys think I'm nuts, but I've spent a lot of time thinking about my powers the past few years. Where they come from. How they work."

Annie shot Doc a knowing, worried look, raising one pink eyebrow.

Doc tried to wave off her concerns with a tilt of his head.

"My mom could fly," Emily said. "Nobody knew why. They don't know why now. She just could. My mom could defy gravity."

"And you don't defy it, you control it," Jane said.

"It acts funny around me. So when I say I have a black hole in here," Emily said, tapping her chest with her fist, "I don't think I've got a region of spacetime exhibiting such a strong gravitational pull that no particle or electromagnetic radiation can escape it. I just mean I'm where gravity starts to get weird."

"Is anyone actually following this?" Billy said.

"I am," Annie said. "Though I have a feeling we're about to lose at least ninety percent of the room's attention."

"I named myself after the second law of black hole mechanics. This is Hawking stuff. Whether black holes have entropy or not," said Emily. "And I think I'm basically the opposite of Jane."

"And now you lost me," Jane said.

"No, hang on," Emily said. "You're a battery. You're solar-powered. Absorb sunlight and turn it into smash and fire and flying and can say 'look at me, I'm a superhero.'"

"And what? You're a... super-villain?" younger-Jane said.

"I really am trying to make this simple," Emily said. "Doc?"

"You're the genius. I just perform magic," he said. He smiled, strangely proud of his youngest protégé, attempting to explain black hole mechanics to a room packed full of aliens and werewolves.

"Let me try to say this really simply," Emily said.

"Oh no," Billy said.

"Shut up Billy Case or I'll bubble of float you right out that window over there," Emily said. She took a deep breath. "Stephen Hawking. Quantum field theory. Black holes radiate blackbody energy at a constant temperature. That radiation carries away entropy. I... I give up. I generate energy. Jane is a battery, I'm a nuclear reactor. Only I'm not nuclear, literally. I'm just a big weird source of change, and change equals power."

"That sphere that you're talking about, in the hologram," Titus said, nodding. "You're saying that it's designed to... store the energy of your black hole but not the energy that a black hole gives off?"

"Finally someone gets me!" Emily said.

"I really didn't actually understand you," Titus said. "I was just checking to see if I was following."

Emily jumped up and leaped into Titus' arms in a bear hug.

"Close enough, fuzzball! Close enough!"

Annie approached the diagram on screen, inspecting it with a scientist's eye. "So if that rambling discussion of quantum mechanics made any sense at all, what you're saying is our enemies have turned you into their own nuclear reactor," she said.

"And if I'm interpreting the schematics correctly, I'm sitting right inside one of those things," Emily said. She looked at Doc mournfully. "And I probably have been since the day you weren't alive to find me."

Doc pushed his red sunglasses up onto his forehead and rubbed his eyes. When he pulled his hands away, the glasses dropped back down onto the bridge of his nose. He looked around the room.

"What do you think we should do?" Jane said.

Doc fixed his eyes quizzically at her older counterpart. "What do *you* think?" he said.

Both Janes glanced at each other, then the Solar spoke. "I'd like to hear your suggestions," she said.

Doc nodded.

"I'd like to find out more about this White Shadow," Doc said. "Kate?"

"Me?" Kate said

"You and I are going on a field trip," Doc said.

"Why me?" Kate said.

"First, because where we're going will require us to be quite stealthy," Doc said.

"I can be stealthy," Emily said. "I'm practically an assassin."

"And second," Doc said, allowing Emily to ramble on, "I need a detective's eyes. And you've got the instincts of a detective."

Kate stared at Doc, not speaking, but her top lip twisted, almost hinting at approval.

"Where are you going?" Solar said.

"I know where the real White Shadow retired," Doc said. "Kate and I are going to go see if there's any clues left as to what happened to him."

"And the rest of us?" Titus said.

"Most of you should hang tight until we get back," Doc said. "But we do need to learn more about that sphere."

"The Entropy sphere," Emily said.

"Fair enough," he said. "The Entropy sphere. And we know where Keaton Bohr studied and worked. I'd suggest a small team investigate and see if he left any research behind that might help us dismantle that contraption."

"Emily and I'll go," Annie said.

"Take backup," Doc said. "Someone who can keep a low profile."

"I volunteer as tribute," Billy said.

"I'd rather someone who can actually keep a low profile," Doc said.

"And the rest of us?" asked Whispering. He'd been hanging back away from the group, listening the entire time, and had remained silent until now. "We're just going to wait here and do nothing?"

"Give us a few hours," Doc said. "Then we'll take more significant action."

CHAPTER 35:
IT WAS HIS HOME

oc Silence and Kate Miller materialized in a dusty street in the City's Oldtown District. The area, part of the City's original construction, felt in many ways like a throwback to an earlier era, narrow streets lined with brownstone buildings, the sidewalks paved in neglected red brick.

"You okay?" Doc asked.

Kate nodded her head vigorously. She didn't like teleportation at all, but Doc's magic transportation was less disorienting somehow than Annie's time travel methods. When he moved them, Kate felt out of sorts, as if she'd slept through a long car ride and was no longer sure where she was. Annie's abilities left Kate feeling like someone had taken her cells apart and then put her back together again in not quite exactly the same fashion.

Doc walked up the front stairs of one of the brownstones—all of which appeared abandoned in this future, long uninhabited, littered with broken windows and lost hopes—and opened the front door as if he owned it. He looked over his shoulder, and Kate followed him in.

The building's interior smelled of mothballs and the burnt, glue-like odor of drying wallpaper. Sprinkled bits of crushed drywall covered the hallway carpet. Doc led them upstairs to the third floor and stopped in front of a specific apartment.

"The White Shadow's hideout was in a condo?" Kate asked.

Doc shook his head.

"Not his hideout," he said. "His home."

Kate was prepared to kick in the locked door but watched as Doc seemed to have a quiet conversation with the lock and doorknob. The knob turned and the door opened.

"Magic?"

"Remembering the names of things is important," Doc said. "I know the names of locks, and can ask them to open for me. All locked doors want to be released. It's their nature, if you simply ask nicely. Doors are meant to be opened."

"Great. You wait until we're alone to start talking like a weird hippie," Kate said. "I appreciate that."

Doc smirked and walked in.

The condominium was sparse, dark. It clearly had not been updated for many years, with aging wall covering, old but sturdy furniture, blinds and carpets that were out of fashion even before Kate was a little kid.

"Look around, see if you notice anything out of sorts," Doc said.

They wandered separately from room to room. Kate saw shoes lined up neatly by the door, a photo of a dog—so old it had started to fade to sepia tones—aged, careworn khaki trench coats, fedoras on a rack near the front door. The worn carpet felt strange beneath her feet, like moss.

She heard Doc rambling in the kitchen. Not quite talking to himself. He was speaking to something. And not someone, but some *thing*, conversing with empty air, listening for responses. It cast a sad and strange portrait, Doc alone next to the weary and yellowing stove and dishwasher.

Kate discovered more loose pictures that had slipped out of a tattered photograph album, the sort of faux-leather book her mother used to keep. She flipped it open. Newspaper clippings of the White Shadow, wearing his mask, meeting with celebrities and police officers, shaking the hands of kindergartners at a local school. The photos predated Kate's own birth from the looks of it.

It seemed irresponsible to her that he might keep an album of newspaper clippings and thus jeopardize his identity. But then again, who would ever see them? This was a place where a man lived alone.

Nothing hinted at anything more than a solitary bachelor's pad, a place where an aging male carelessly but with profound simplicity made a home for himself.

She opened another album. This one was different because she saw his face. Ordinary features. Maybe even a little homely. Narrow jaw, with graying, receding hair, dark eyebrows, slightly crooked teeth. He smiled often in the photos, as if he, somehow, escaped the inevitable pall of gloom that saving lives often cloaks you with. Because saving lives, Kate thought, meant rescuing them from something, and you can't save a life without seeing that which you needed to liberate that life from.

The darkness is so overwhelming, she thought. But here is a man, living alone in quiet solitude, who went to work every day to make the world better. How could he smile?

Then she flipped the album through to another page and saw why.

Curled up in the White Shadow's arm was a little girl. Jet black hair, the same crooked smile, big eyes. The radiance of youth. The Shadow gazed at the girl with such love, such adoration. Something twinged in Kate's heart like a bending, breaking string of a bowed instrument. Fathers and daughters. Fathers and daughters always broke her heart.

"Doc," Kate said.

He joined her from the kitchen, glancing over her shoulder at the photo album.

"He had a kid," Doc said after a few moments passed.

"Apparently."

"We never knew," he said.

Kate studied the picture again.

"You don't usually have families, do you?" she said.

"Superhumans?" Doc said.

"Yeah."

"We really don't," he said, taking one photo of the Shadow and his daughter from the album and tucking it gently, almost reverently, in a coat pocket.

"Because they're at risk?" Kate asked. "They have to be at risk.

Of retribution by the people we put away."

"There's that, yes," he said. They both continued searching around the condo for additional clues, but stayed close together enough to speak. "And there's the question of time. When do you meet someone? When do you raise a child? There's always someone who needs saving. Always some other battle to fight."

"Did you ever want a family?" Kate asked.

Doc laughed.

"That's a strangely personal question coming from you," he said.

"It's not personal," Kate said. "I want to know the logistics. Did your life get in the way? I know you've cared about people. That you're too soft on the Lady, so I realize there's something there, and you and Annie look at each other like there could have been something between you."

"Annie's a funny case," Doc said, quietly thumbing through a drawer in the dining room. "All she's ever wanted was a home. But I don't think she wants the things that anchor you to a home. She drifts on the winds of time. She's impossible to hold on to."

"Did you? Want a home?"

Doc bowed his head as if pausing to think before answering.

"The things I've seen in this world, Kate," he said. "If I had a family, if I brought a life into it... that's all I'd ever worry about. Every day. Every moment."

"I think there's a part of that in all of us," Kate said.

"Yeah," he said as she retraced his steps into the kitchen. "None of us had families, really. I think we all understood. We could risk our lives easier if we didn't have to worry about coming home."

"Emily's mom was a hero for a little while," Kate said.

"She was. One of the few who got away clean," Doc said. "But she's the exception, and wasn't in our game a long time. I'm happy for her."

Kate opened cabinet doors in the kitchen, thumbed through ancestral silverware adorned with handle designs that appeared to be from the Victorian era.

"Do you know who her father is?" Kate asked.

Doc stared at her.

163

"What?" she said.

"Nothing," he said. "I have my suspicions. And if I'm right, if her father weren't such a... If he'd lived up to his potential, then this world never would had needed to endure what it's been subject to."

"Who do think it is?" Kate said.

"Someone I hope you never meet," Doc said.

A frayed newspaper clipping clinging to the refrigerator door with a magnet from Hawaii caught Kate's eye. She picked it up, studying the text closely.

"Doc?"

He joined Kate in the kitchen.

"I don't know if this helps us, but you're right about one thing," she said, handing it to him.

"It really doesn't give us too many answers, but I'm glad I was right," Doc said. He handed the slip of paper back to her.

The White Shadow's death notice. The obituary never referenced the old man's heroics. Instead, it was a simple note about a simple man dying quietly in his sleep, with a photo that matched the man in the album Kate found alongside it.

"Doc, the time of this notice," Kate said. "The date is just a few days after you found me. The same year. He died in his sleep right around the period you were putting the Indestructibles together."

"We never knew how the White Shadow died," Doc said. "No one ever told us. No one came looking. He just seemed to fade away."

"So what does this mean?"

"It means someone's out there destroying the world while masquerading as my friend," Doc said. "And I've got to know who that person is."

CHAPTER 36:
WELL ENOUGH TO BREAK IT

Entropy Emily and Anachronism Annie drifted out of the sky in a bubble of float, a strange pair of travelers making their way across the night horizon.

Billy insisted on coming as well, but for subtlety and stealth's sake, they hadn't let him fly. Because Emily didn't appreciate his forcing his way onto the "away team," as she called it, she gave him his own bubble of float trailing a hundred meters back. He hung suspended in mid-air, arms folded across his chest, waiting for Emily to place him on the ground.

I could have flown here on my own, Billy thought.

And we would have lit up the sky, Dude said. *This way we arrive unnoticed, without commotion.*

A girl sporting neon blue hair and another with neon pink hair just flew across ten miles of sky, Dude, Billy thought. I wouldn't exactly call it a ninja maneuver.

Billy fell the last six feet, dropping out of the sky at the same time Emily and Annie landed gently on their feet. Emily looked back and laughed.

"Sorry! Forgot about you back there."

"No you didn't," Billy said.

They checked out the low-rise industrial building standing before them, part of a massive, now abandoned, business park just outside the City. An aging and poorly maintained sign, FUTURA INDUSTRIES sprouted from overgrown and yellowed weeds.

"Wonder if Fry worked here?" Emily said.

"Keaton Bohr did," Annie said. "And if we're lucky, we'll be able to find some of his early research."

Annie tried the front door, but it was locked from the inside. Emily took a running start and kicked it.

The door held, knocking Emily onto the ground.

"I'll blast it open," Billy said.

"No," Annie said, pulling a strangely antiquated gun from her hip and firing. Green energy splashed against the lock, and the door creaked open.

"You have a gun?" Billy said.

"More like a... blaster," Annie said.

"It looks like something Jack Sparrow would use," Emily said.

"I'll take that as a compliment," Annie said. "C'mon."

The structure inside appeared as if it had been untouched for years. A few tipped over chairs, a ransacked lobby vending machine; otherwise, the building could have been preserved in a time capsule.

The trio ventured deeper into the bowels of the edifice, past an empty reception area. They encountered a few locked doors that were immediately dispatched by Annie's laser gun.

"So I've been meaning to ask," Emily said. They sauntered past offices with ordinary names printed on faux gold plates, past a sad little kitchen with years-old coffee still sitting in the pot resting on a dead burner. "What do all your tattoos mean?"

Annie smirked, then looked down at her bare arms, at the swirling patterns in infinite colors that traced all across her skin. "They mean a little bit of everything," she said.

"Doc has a lot of tattoos, too," Emily said. "But his do things. They're like, spells."

"Yeah, he has a different kind of ink than I do," Annie said.

"He told Jane and me about them once," Emily said. "Like one enables him to become fireproof, another makes sure he never loses his car keys."

"That second one's a lie," Billy said.

"Not really," Annie said. "I know there's one near his neck that's a mark of memory. It might not be for car keys specifically, but it is for memory."

"I could use one of those. I forget my email password three times a week," Billy said.

They reached a stairwell and elevator. Billy pushed the door to the stairs open and they crept down into the darkness.

"I can light this for us," Billy said.

No, Dude said.

"No," Annie said, simultaneously. "Energy signatures. You're here in case we get into a fight. Let's stay mundane if we can."

She pulled a squat flashlight from her belt and held it aloft.

"Is that a future flashlight?"

"It's a Mag-light," Annie said. "I got it at a department store."

"I was really hoping it was a future flashlight," Billy said.

"To answer your question, no, the tattoos don't signify anything," Annie said. "Or rather, they all mean something to me, but they don't do things like the ones Doc has."

"So they're like your scrapbook or something," Emily said.

Annie smiled. "Sort of," she said. "They do remind me of where I've been and who I am."

"Seems like an awful lot of work to go through when you could just take notes," Emily said.

They arrived at a door labeled "Archives." Annie reached for her laser gun again, but Emily just walked in and Billy followed.

"This isn't intimidating at all," Billy said.

Cardboard boxes lined the rooms. Labeled in red marker, rows and rows of research containers were stacked on retail-style racks.

"We don't have to go through all of it," Emily said, bounding off.

"You really think they'll have anything useful in here?" Billy asked.

Annie shrugged.

"No idea," she said. "But it's worth it, isn't it?"

"Why would they keep hard copies?" Billy said.

"Some of this information is older than you are," Annie said. "Believe it or not, people used to work on paper. They had books, too, made out of dead trees."

"Don't mock," Billy said. "You're from the future. Which means

I'm technically older than you are."

Annie chuckled. Her laugh had a familiar mania to it. Something in the back of his mind tickled, as if he'd heard it long before.

"How do you know I'm from the future?" she said. "I could be from the past."

"You have Jem and the Hologram's hair. No way you're from the past," Billy said.

"I could be from the 1980's."

"Whatever," Billy said. "You find anything, Em?"

"It would help if you got up and pushed," she yelled.

"Are you saying you need help?" Billy said.

"Would he be under Keaton, Bohr, or Doctor?" Emily said.

Annie walked between the stacks to find her.

Billy followed grumpily. "I came along as a bodyguard, not to relearn the Dewey Decimal System," he said.

Relearn indicates you actually knew the Dewey Decimal System at some point, Dude said.

"I was speaking in metaphor," Billy said. "Why you gotta give me a hard time about the little things?"

"Found his stuff," Emily said. She was pulling boxes down off the shelves using bubbles of float. "What do you think we're searching for?"

"Whatever looks interesting," Annie said, kneeling to open one of the crates.

"What was he doing here?" Billy said.

"According to Broadstreet's information, Bohr was a renewable energy expert," Annie said. "It was something he came to later in his career. He started out in robotics."

"Let me guess, he has a bunch of PhDs," Billy said.

"Couple of 'em, yeah," Annie said. "Anyway, he was an employee until he got fired."

"Because he was bad at his job?" Emily said, scanning a box of paper printout reports.

"No. He was too good at it. Figured out a renewable energy source that could replace a lot of our existing technology," Annie said.

"I'm too good at my job," Billy said.

"Standing around looking pretty? You could be better at it," Emily said. "So basically he got terminated for developing something that could put his company out of business."

"Or the company's clients, yeah," Annie said. "If you're in the business of selling something, don't invent the thing that makes the product you're promoting obsolete."

Billy threw his hands up.

"Wait. So this guy gets let go and what, a year later he's working with some kind of super villain and has locked Emily in a cage turning her into a weapon?" he said.

"You'd be amazed the lengths people will go to to get back at a boss they're angry with," Annie said. "Though I honestly believe his original intentions were less nefarious. He hoped to build a better world, he just went about doing it wrong. You finding anything, Emily?"

She waived paperwork in the air.

"He was definitely working on variations of the Dyson sphere concept," she said. "Big brain stuff. Ideas grew out of his ideas."

"Wait a minute," Billy said. "So not only did they run him off, they held onto his work?"

Annie nodded.

"Depending on your contract, intellectual property reverts—"

"—See. This is why I'll never act like an adult," Billy said. "Because adults get screwed over all the time."

Hearing you bluntly state out loud that you never intend to mature is one of the more upsetting things you've ever done, Billy Case, Dude said.

"Big brain stuff?" Annie said. "Is that a technical term?"

"I learned it online, so it must be true," Emily said, smirking. "So if none of this had happened, I could be living a life of quiet desperation like Keaton Bohr? Watching someone take all my dreams and put them in boxes?"

"Happens to a lot of people, Emily," Annie said. "Not everyone gets to fly."

"Well, everyone should get to fly," she said. "Flying shouldn't be limited to a special few."

"How generous of you," Annie said.

"What can I say, I'm a woman of the people," Emily said.

"Are you actually getting anything out of all that paperwork you're looking at?" Billy asked.

Emily smiled, sorting a few piles of paper, and then held up a page with a familiar-looking spherical design sketched onto it. "I'm getting," she said. "Not enough to build one of my own. But I'm definitely understanding it well enough to break it if I have to."

"Good," Annie said. "Because that's exactly what we need you to do."

CHAPTER 37:
AND LET SLIP THE DOGS OF WAR

Designation: Fury. It is really okay," Neal said, in the female voice Emily had accidentally changed his settings to. "There is no need to try so hard to fix it."

"It's fine, Neal," Titus said, sweating and cursing under his breath as he tinkered with the mini-Neal computer they'd brought with them to the new hideout.

It really wasn't just about the voice itself. Yeah, Titus missed the familiar tone of their artificially intelligent friend, but Titus was more interested in fixing the computer because he couldn't determine how Emily had broken it. Returning Neal to his preferred vocalization was really a by-product of Titus' frustration that Emily had basically beaten the computer up until it started working again.

"It really bothers you the little blue-haired girl figured it out before you did, doesn't it?" Jessie said, sitting on the edge of an overturned countertop.

"It doesn't bother me that she solved something before I did, it irks me that I don't know what the hell she actually did," Titus said. "Can't I be intellectually curious?"

"Jealous more likely."

"I'm not jealous. I'm confused," Titus said. "In the meantime, though. Neal, can you find anything else of interest Broadstreet gave us?"

"What should I be looking for, Designation: Fury?"

"Maps, weapon designs, personnel information, something

concrete," Titus said.

"I will do this," the computer said.

"Maps?" Jessie said.

"Yeah," Titus said. "I keep thinking, if Emily's going to figure out how to break the... Entropy sphere, we should try to locate it."

"And who we're going to have to get past in order to break it," Jessie said.

"Yep," Titus said.

Jessie picked up a USB thumb drive and inserted it into the computer so Neal could start taking in data.

"Low tech?" Titus said.

"Kinda," Jessie said. "But you'd be amazed at how slowly personal technology advances when you're fighting for your life."

She returned to her seat and continued watching while Titus explored Neal's computer guts.

"I always wondered why the big guy was so attached to this box," Jessie said. "You don't figure gigantic, scarred-up werewolves care about their computers this much, even if the computer does have a personality."

"Neal and I are friends," Titus said. "I'm assuming future me is—was—friends with him as well before all this happed. I realize it sounds absolutely bizarre, but I think I'm the one who's most comfortable with Neal back home."

"The others sometimes struggled with my otherness," Neal said, startling Titus. He'd forgotten he was talking about Neal as if the computer wasn't right there in front of him. "You always treated me the most like a person."

"Because I know what it's like to be the other," Titus said.

"Also you are not a technophobe," Neal said. "That helps."

"Have I—the other me? Have I been distant, Neal?" Titus asked.

The computer paused, like a human being taking a deep breath.

"You hide behind a mask," Neal said. "I don't think you speak to anyone very much at all, Designation: Fury."

Titus looked at Jessie, who waved her hands vaguely.

"I'm the new girl," she said. "That guy in the other room? He's the only Titus I've ever actually known. But he gets the job done and keeps his people safe. I can't find anything wrong with that."

Titus nodded, then opened another hatch on the computer. He reviewed the data spike Broadstreet had given them. He never had an opportunity to investigate it this closely before. A soft, red light pulsed on the surface.

"Neal, does this light indicate that you're pulling information off the drive?" Titus said.

"I do not know what that light signifies, Designation: Fury," Neal said.

"Could you find out?"

"One moment."

"You worried about something?" Jessie said.

"Blinking red lights. Ever see a blinking red light that meant something good?"

"Stop light?"

Neal chirped in, sounding sheepish.

"Designation: Fury. There appears to be some sort of tracking device attached to the drive," Neal said. "It is not embedded within the software. We missed it during our initial examination."

"We have to get out of here," Titus said.

"Tracking device?" Jessie said.

"Get everyone up," Titus said. "Leto! Finnigan! We need to move, we're being tracked!"

Titus pulled the USB stick out of its port and threw it in the air. Jessie blasted it with a bolt of blue-white light, shattering it.

Leto walked in, her movement eccentrically fast but not hurried.

"What's wrong, Titus?" she asked.

"Broadstreet's portable drive was bugged. We could be looking at another incoming bombing raid," Titus said. "We've got to go."

Finnigan staggered in, helping one of the younger werewolves who had been sent out on patrol to stay on his feet. A teenager named James, he was bleeding badly from a deep slash in his side, his face pale and eyes sunken from blood loss.

"What happened, boy?" Finnigan said, covered in the younger man's blood. "Where's the rest of your patrol?"

"Wiped out," James said.

Finnigan guided the younger werewolf to the floor, laying him gently on his back. Leto rushed to him and examined the wound in his side. Titus caught sight of other injuries, clearly sustained from a fight. They appeared to be knife or sword slashes.

"What do you mean? Where are they? Stay with us, lad," Finnigan said.

"They came out of the dark. . .knew how to fight us. . .silver. . ." James said. Titus watched as the light in the werewolf's eyes flickered and faded. And then he was gone. Older than Titus is now, but only by a few years, a life that wouldn't begin until long into the future. Titus wondered if, because of what they did here, James would never exist at all. If this was his one life, in all the timelines, and if it were now over.

"They can't all be dead," Jessie said.

"Hunters," Leto said. She placed her hand upon the bloody face of James and whispered something in a language Titus didn't understand.

"They can't all be dead," Finnigan said.

"If it's the hunters, they could be. These children never had to fight real hunters before," Leto said.

"There's another patrol out there," Jessie said.

Titus looked at Finnigan. They both jumped to their feet and started running.

"Find Solar. Both of them," Titus said to Jessie. "Tell them we'll need help. Leto—"

"I'll find Whispering," she said. "Go."

Titus transformed, faster than he'd ever done before, tearing his sweatshirt to shreds as he doubled in size. And suddenly he was on the run, the world rushing by, awash in heightened senses, the smell of the blood of his future family in the wind.

* * *

It's been too long, Titus thought, from a quiet place in the back of his mind. I've been caged up too long. Cool night air flowed through his silver fur, every sound, every sight, every scent, a thousand times clearer. This is how to experience the world. The muscles in his shoulders and quads felt fluid and potent as the urban decay around him faded into a blur.

The smell of blood and metal surrounded him, familiar and unfamiliar, the blood of friends he barely knew, of friends he would someday know. He could hear the fighting already, the roars of pain and fury, the whisper of blades sinking into muscle, scraping across bone. His people were dying.

Beside him, he could barely make out the squat shape of a red-furred werewolf tearing along as well, Finnigan in full transformation, baying like a tracking hound, calling their enemies out.

Titus tore into the first of their attackers before the man ever saw him, three hundred pounds of werewolf crashing into a black-clad man, one swipe doing cataclysmic damage to his body. Two more men turned to attack, but Titus, his mind so clear time itself seemed to stop, dispatched both. Their silver swords spun in the air and tumbled like falling leaves.

During moments like this, Titus was never sure if he was in charge or if the beast was. During moments like this it didn't matter. Because, during moments like this, his rage and the beast's were one in the same. This was pure vengeance.

He saw a flash of rusty red as Finnigan dispatched another black-clad warrior. Titus, his momentum carrying him forward effortlessly, left yet another combatant trying to hold his severed guts together with his hands.

More screams of the dying echoed and bellowed. The patrol had been ambushed. These men in black knew the damage they could inflict if they could catch werewolves unaware. He heard a shuffle behind him. Another of the attackers, this one moving with greater caution, approached him, a silver katana in his hand. Titus circled him, his opponent clearly more prepared than the others.

The man lunged, a classic thrust of his sword. Titus felt the silver blade skim along his shoulder, drawing blood, burning in that way that only silver burned, but he let the pain wash over him long enough to force the claws of one his hands up into the man's underarm, tearing apart muscle and tendon. The sword dropped from the man's now useless hand, and Titus sunk the talons of his other hand into the man's neck.

This violence should bother me, Titus believed, cloudy and safe in the far reaches of the werewolf's mind. What I'm doing, the actions I'm taking, should horrify me. But these men are killers and so am I, we're all killers here at the end of the world...

He spied one of the black-clad men standing over the body of another younger werewolf—Titus didn't know his name, had never learned it—but before the man could plunge a sword into his fallen comrade, Titus was upon him, tearing through his opponent's body armor like wrapping paper. Titus didn't check to see if the prone wolf was all right. No time. And nothing he could do to help him if he was bleeding to death. Nothing he could do but keep killing, destroy them all before they hurt any more of his kin.

A furious howl caught his attention, and Titus ran towards it, deeper into the urban sprawl. He discovered his future self set upon from all sides by sword-wielding attackers. Whispering held them off like a martial arts master, spinning a long spear—my spear, Titus thought, the one I left in the past—like a helicopter blade, knocking the attackers back, gutting them, cracking their skulls with the butt-end of the weapon. But there were far too many, and the big, scarred wolf was losing ground.

Titus joined the fray, attacking from behind those who were trying to kill his future self his mind a blur of red anger. Together, Titus old and Titus young fought, howling, roaring. We are monsters, Titus thought. We are beasts. We are fury. We are the Whispering.

But still they were outnumbered. He heard yips and yells of pain, sometimes in the distance, sometimes close. He knew they were coming from his own mouth.

And then Leto arrived.

She was unlike anything Titus had ever seen. Taller, leaner, with close, jet-black fur, Leto looked more like a jackal than a werewolf, the head of Anubis set defiantly on the body of a monster. She moved like a ghost among the men in black, a blur of long limbs and golden claws and sprays of arterial blood. One man desperately tried to run, and Leto gestured to him in a movement Titus had seen Doc

Silence exercise many times, and a bolt of reddish light flashed from her hand, catching the man between the shoulder blades and sending him sprawling to the ground.

Her arrival gave both younger and older-Titus a second wind, a reprieve. Together, they finished the fight in a cloud of claws and fangs and glowing eyes. Together they became murder at its most primal.

And then, as quickly as it started, it was over. The bodies of men and wolves littered the street, splattered blood dripped down walls ten feet high. Finnigan limped in before transforming back into human form. Titus tried to let himself revert back to human shape, but the wolf was too much in control, his blood was too high, he was too close to the edge. Breathe, he thought, breathe and return, let go and come back home...

He caught his future self inspecting him curiously. They stared at each other a moment, and then the elder Titus stormed away, searching for survivors.

Among the carnage, Leto had changed back to human form as well. She pinned one of the men in black, still alive, to the ground. She drove a long, dark-bladed knife into the soft flesh of his shoulder. It was then Titus focused on the patch the man wore on the sleeve of his shirt, a stylized red rose. All the attackers had them.

They can't be *hers*, Titus thought. He felt himself coming back down again, his blood no longer boiling. As the rage melted away, so did the beast, his body slowly returning to its human shape. He caught Leto's voice raging at the survivor.

"We let you live," Leto said, her voice angrier than Titus had ever heard it. She was always as impassive as the moon. "You will return to your mistress, and you'll deliver a message to her from us. You'll tell her she should have stayed among the dead. And she will regret this day."

Finnigan put a hand on Titus' shoulder. Titus turned and slipped an arm under Finnigan's to help the red-headed werewolf stay on his feet.

"Took a knife in the leg, lad," Finnigan said. "Help an old man, would you?"

Together, Finnigan and younger-Titus watched Leto drag the surviving man in black away, effortlessly. They disappeared around a corner.

"I've never seen her fight before," Titus said.

"I hope you never do again," Finnigan said. "Although, it's a specter of terrible beauty."

"How bad did we make out?" Titus said. "Who did we lose?"

"Too many, son," Finnigan said. "This is the sort of day that ends wars."

CHAPTER 38:
THE LIMITS OF GRAVITY

Keaton Bohr checked his readings again, and again. He went for a cup of coffee, paced around the near-empty lab, ignoring his few remaining minions, and returned to his workspace to review the results from scratch.

He hoped he was wrong.

Bohr got up, abandoning his coffee, and went down to visit her. He did this more often than he liked to admit, and never told the White Shadow how many hours he spent talking to the girl in the bubble, waiting for her to answer him back. Maybe he thought the Shadow would be angry with him. Or think Bohr was starting to lose his mind. But in the end, Bohr thought, he didn't tell the Shadow because he wanted these conversations to be private. They were none of the vigilante's business. They were between scientist and subject, between jailer and prisoner.

Between failed father and distant daughter. No, Bohr thought. You just think of her that way, because she's been in your care for so long. Because she's your responsibility, and because all of this is your fault. Everything that went wrong is your fault. And this latest news, this latest data, this tragedy... this is your fault as well.

She was sleeping when he arrived, but she was always sleeping these days. That was part of the problem. If they'd worked harder, if they'd taken better care of her. But they always needed more from her. She could change the world with her powers, but only if they had her on their side, only if they could take that irresistible force and make it functional.

"We didn't make it useful," Bohr said, looking at the girl inside the sphere, old before her time, too thin, purple bags sagging beneath her eyes. The latest readings were quite terrifying.

They never understood her, Bohr thought. Not really. Theories about matter and anti-matter, about Hawking radiation and particles and anti-particles... All we ever did was take advantage of what she was capable of, the scientist thought. All we did was see a tool, an infinite engine, a thing to be exploited to remake the world in our image.

But she was just a little girl when they took her, and they wasted her life.

"And now you'll have your revenge," Bohr thought. "And we'll deserve it. Oh how we'll deserve it."

He put his hand against the sphere, wondering how many days they had left before their own personal event horizon.

"We wanted to save the world, and we've destroyed it in the most spectacular fashion," Bohr said. "I'm so sorry, Emily. I wish there was some way you could know that."

Bohr turned and slowly walked away, heading back up into reality, toward the surface. He strode absently past the eccentric young people who still thought they were on Heaven's side, who truly believed in the White Shadow and his plan.

We're the villains, Bohr found himself thinking. We did so well at first, he reflected. We performed good deeds. Together they eradicated the Children of the Elder Star, wiped them from the Earth and from all memory, a brutal war the Children never stood a chance of winning. They put the Atlantean uprising to rest before the governments of the world even knew it was happening. An alien invasion waiting in the wings, a century in the making, and with the power Emily provided, the White Shadow shut it down.

But that wasn't enough. Without enemies to fight, without someone to go to battle with, they started making their own wars. Enforcing peace, the Shadow called it. Babysitting the planet because the planet couldn't babysit itself. And when heroes rose up to stop them, well naturally, they couldn't be trusted either. You were either for us or against us, and before long, everyone was against us.

And still people flocked to their banner, to fight for a world without conflict. Without realizing that they were rushing to join the conflict just by doing so.

He located the White Shadow in the place he often found his friend, in an apartment replete with aging, splintered wooden chairs and a couch with worn springs, a generation too old to be much use. The Shadow always camped in places where things were slightly old-fashioned, not antiques, not vintage, simply weary and out of time.

Out of time, Bohr thought. Everything is out of time these days.

"We've got a problem, Shadow," Keaton Bohr said. He couldn't tell if the Shadow was awake or asleep, sitting perfectly still on the dusty couch, but the vigilante straightened and turned to him as if he'd been waiting for his arrival.

"The world is full of problems, my friend," the vigilante said. "What's wrong?"

"Emily," Bohr said. "You need to check out the latest readings."

"What is it?" the Shadow said.

"At first I thought she was sick," Bohr said. "We've seen fluctuations in her power output before when she's ill. But I looked deeper, and her output is neither up or down—it's different. She's changing."

"And what's that mean for us?" the White Shadow said, standing up to look Bohr straight in the eyes.

Bohr wondered, as he always did, why his employer insisted on wearing the mask so often. I want to look you in the eye when I tell you this, he thought. I want to see your face when I inform you that we've killed the world.

"The sphere isn't designed to contain the new energy she's giving off. I really can't predict what's going to happen next. Either she's going to release enough radiation to obliterate everything on this entire continent, or she's going to create a spatial vacuum significant enough to destabilize the planet. Shadow, she's going to die, and she'll take all of us with her."

"Didn't we always suspect this might be a possibility?" the Shadow said, far more calmly than Bohr was comfortable with.

"A possibility? We always knew she was dangerous, but Shadow, we're talking about an extinction event. Worse. Worse!" Bohr said. "This will be the end of everything. There won't be any moles to rise up and evolve to inherit the Earth after we're gone. There'll be no Earth. We've got to do something."

"No, we don't," the White Shadow said.

"What?"

"Do you know how to fix it?" the Shadow said.

"No. I need more time. Maybe if I had more time . . ."

"Keaton," the Shadow said, putting a hand on Bohr's arm. "It's okay. Everything will be fine."

"It won't be okay," Bohr said. "You're not listening to me. Why aren't you hearing me?"

"Because this is the outcome we've always wanted," the Shadow said. "We understood people didn't deserve this world. And so, we'll simply take it away from them."

Keaton Bohr nodded incredulously, and took a couple of steps backwards.

The White Shadow returned to the lumpy couch and his somnambulant state.

Bohr turned and walked away, heading for his lab with a growing dread in his heart. He had signed on to this expedition, to this mission—all those years ago—to change the world, not end it. And now, he didn't have a clue how to stop it.

CHAPTER 39:
EVERYONE HAS A JOB TO DO

Emily, Billy, and Annie found their friends miles away from where they left them, at an impromptu base camp in an abandoned apartment complex. Billy had to ask Dude to reach out with his alien senses to locate them because everyone knew that the evacuation of the strip mall hideaway meant something terrible had happened.

After finding so few familiar faces when they arrived, Billy realized the worst had occurred while they were gone.

"What's going on?" Annie said, reaching a hand out to take Leto by the arm as they landed.

"We were ambushed," she said. "The hunters have returned."

"Hunters?" Billy said.

"Predators we thought we drove away a long time ago," Leto said. "Slayers of monsters. Killers of our race."

Billy and Emily exchanged a quick, terrified glance.

"Titus?" Emily said.

"I'm right here," younger-Titus said, looking beat up but whole.

"Fido!" Emily said, throwing her arms around him. "You look like someone dropped you off a building."

"Near enough," Titus said.

Billy extended a hand for him to shake, but the young werewolf pulled him into a hug instead.

"What. Was that?" Emily said.

"Just happy you guys are okay," Titus said. "Any word from Doc and Kate?"

"We're here," Doc said, materializing nearby with Kate in tow. "What the hell happened?"

"Trouble," Titus said. "Don't worry, Jane's patrolling the area with Jessie right now looking for signs we might have been followed. I think we're okay."

"Except we're not," Titus' older counterpart said, stomping toward them. "We lost a third of our people back there."

"We're going to kill them all," Finnigan said. The red-haired werewolf was covered in someone else's blood. "We just lost another one. Amy. The girl from . . ."

"I know who she is," Whispering said. "I know the names of everyone we lost tonight."

Doc rubbed his eyes beneath the red-lensed glasses. "They'll come again," he said. "Do you have a plan?"

"I think so," Whispering said. "Follow me."

* * *

Nearly everyone gathered in one of the larger apartments. A few stragglers were stationed elsewhere in the building, caring for the wounded. Kate waited in the back, as always, observing reactions. Emily looked worked up, almost buzzing with energy, clearly dying to tell someone something she'd learned. Billy spoke with Doc, pleading his case for something. Jane paced, her eyes flicking over to Kate every so often, looking for something Kate couldn't quite figure out.

Titus, strangely, stayed very close to the other werewolves. He carried himself differently than his future self, but there was a familiarity there, a pack mentality or something Kate couldn't quite put her finger on. He appeared visibly shaken by the fight with the hunters. They all did. Kate had a feeling the werewolves hadn't suffered a defeat like this in a long time.

Whispering spoke first. He took the center of the room, his lieutenants remained close by.

"We thought we'd wiped out the hunters years ago," he said, his voice sounding inhuman and echoing coming from that massive wolf's snout. "Clearly they've been waiting for us. Waiting for a time to take us on."

"Leto," Titus said. "I heard you say something about their leader. Their mistress. Were you trying to bait her out?"

Leto nodded softly.

"Their leader is the glue that binds them together," she said. "The hunters have only been a threat as long as Rose is free and in charge."

"Rose," Titus said.

Leto and Whispering suddenly looked at him with greater interest.

"You know her in your timeline?" the Whispering said.

"I do," Titus said. "I thought I killed her last year. I've never been sure."

His eyes darted over to Kate in the shadows as he said this. She remembered that fight between Titus and Rose, the brutality of it. Rose nearly killed him, and Titus had barely escaped with his life before he threw the knife-wielding sociopath into the ocean to drown.

"So if you were calling her out," Titus said. "Is it your hope she'll engage us again directly?"

"That's the plan," Leto said.

"Rose won't send minions to do it this time," Whispering said. "She'll come herself. With her best. We've got to wipe them out completely."

"I want to be there, to help," Titus said.

Whispering glanced towards Doc and Annie.

"They're going to be tracking the entire pack anyway," Annie said. "Better they're all together than if he's off on his own."

"What about the injured?" Jane asked. "Will you try to draw the hunters here, using them as bait?"

"I can help with that," Doc said.

Leto tilted her head at him.

"I know you have a bit of magic, Leto, but I can use an obscura spell on this place the hunters will have trouble seeing through. You can at least leave your injured here for a few days without protection."

"We'll head out away from the rest of the group and get their attention," Whispering said. "We know they've been commissioned to take us on, to thin out the people pursuing the White Shadow. They'll follow us. It's in their nature. It's what hunters do."

"We should try to take her alive," Kate said, suddenly.

Those in the room turned to look at her.

"She dies for what she did to us," Leto said.

"Oh, she can die later," Kate said. "But if you think the White Shadow called on her to hunt you, I've got a feeling she'll know where we can get to the Shadow ourselves."

"I make no guarantees," Whispering said. "If it comes down to her killing more of my people or us killing her first, my decision is easy."

"Let me come along, then," Kate said.

"No," the Whispering said.

"Yes," Titus said instead.

The older werewolf stared at him with furious golden eyes, but the younger didn't flinch. "She's seen Rose fight. Kate can beat anyone she's watched move before."

The big wolf smiled, revealing rows of sharp white teeth. "We'll see," Whispering said, but he stopped arguing.

"What did your team find, Doc?" Solar asked.

Doc looked at Kate as if to ask if she'd like to speak first.

She shook her head.

He stood up. "We discovered an obituary for the original White Shadow," Doc said. "So either the old man faked his death, or there's a very spry ninety-year-old running around right now. To be honest, neither prospect is very appealing, but I think we need to confront him."

"Are you going to yank his mask off Scooby Doo style?" Emily said. "I would have ended this world, if not for you meddling kids."

"And what did you find, Em?" younger-Jane said, cutting Emily's rant off before it could get out of control.

"How to break stuff," Emily said.

"We found preliminary research Bohr performed on this... Entropy sphere Emily keeps calling it," Annie said.

"And I can totes break it," Emily said. "We have to find it, but if we locate it, I am so breaking it."

"Any idea how to find it?" Solar said.

Emily jumped to her feet and started pacing, her hands folded behind her back like a pompous professor.

"It has a unique energy signature. Same reason we don't want flyboy over there flying around," Emily said, pointing at Billy. "That's how we can track it."

"You know how to identify that energy signature?" Solar said.

"I am a genius, yo. Give me a lever and I can move the world," Emily said.

"We need the right kind of satellite interface, something that'll let us scan the area from above," Annie said. "The sphere, and the girl inside it, have got to be close. She's providing power for all the Shadow's tricks, the giant robots and gravity guns. It makes no sense for that engine to be far away."

"What about trying to look for it from below?" Billy said.

Everyone turned to look at him as if he'd just belched at a funeral.

"It's so cute when you brainstorm," Emily said.

"Listen, girl genius, I'm serious," Billy said. "If it's gravity based, won't the sphere be creating some sort of pull or something on the ground around it? Wouldn't there be some kind of... seismantic activity?"

"Seismic activity?" Emily said.

"Seismological activity?" Billy said back to her.

"Seismogorical?" Emily said.

"Semicolon?" Billy said.

"Semiconductor?" Emily said.

"Stop messing with my vocabulary, Emily," Billy said. "I'm serious."

"I'm messing with you because you're right and I'm mad I didn't think of it first, cupcake," Emily said.

"Cupcake?" Jessie said.

"It's a term of endearment," Billy said. "So I'm right?"

Emily looked at Annie, and they nodded together.

"Ten points Gryffindor," Emily said. "Are there any seismometers around here though?"

"The lab over at the Institute for Technology and Math has one," Jessie said.

"How do you even know that?" Billy said.

"He says one thing right and he thinks he's the smartest guy in the room," Emily said. "But seriously, have you been there?"

"My older sister went to school there, before... all this happened," Jessie said. "Don't tell me you know how to work a seismometer."

"I can work it out," Emily said.

"You are so full of garbage sometimes," Billy said.

Emily threw her hands up.

"I can't work under these conditions. You're hampering my genius," she said.

"Okay," Jane said, pulling the two combatants apart. "You're going to the Institute. Anything else you need to shut down this sphere?"

"I need some things," Emily said.

Jane frowned. "I'm afraid to ask," she said.

"They mostly do not involve explosives," Emily said.

"Mostly?" both Janes said simultaneously.

"In their inert form, I mean," Emily said. "Though if you could find a decent artillery shell that would be helpful too."

"Artillery shell," Jane said.

"Unexploded landmine would do as well," Emily said.

"We need you to break it so it doesn't do any more harm, not just blow the thing up, Em," Billy said.

"I got this, yo," Emily said to Billy, then turned to Jane. "But seriously, I'll write down a list. Try not to get the land mine too hot, it might explode."

CHAPTER 40:
THE CAGED BIRD

Sometimes at night, when the scientists thought she was sleeping, Emily tried to remember life before her capture, probing for memories she knew were there somewhere. Of her mother. Her house. But blurred, like bleeding newsprint from papers left out in the rain, they remained vague recollections of a time and place that might as well have never existed. There has just always been this life, this place, this cage.

Though now, it was almost over. She felt her heart swelling, her heart or whatever there was in place of it, the singularity where her heart should be. Will I explode? Emily wondered, listening to the hum of machinery in the shadows. Or will I collapse upon myself? What will happen when my heart of darkness gives way?

Emily remembered the early years. When she first began to float. Drifting around in swells of her own making inside the bubble, the girl who could fly, the girl who never had to touch the ground. The way Keaton Bohr laughed and applauded. Everything he did to encourage her, to help her control her powers, to enable her to become strong.

But they wouldn't let her out. Too dangerous, they'd say, too unsafe. You don't know how to manage your energy. You could destroy the world.

She drowned California in an act of pure petulance. Simply wrapped a bubble of float around the state, digging into the fault line like a human hand peeling an orange, and she allowed the earth's rotation to do the rest. Her captors claimed it was an act of war, a warning shot across bow of the planet, but in truth, it was Emily lashing out, angry and lonely, begging for someone to pay attention to her.

They began to medicate her then.

Soon Emily marked time with little acts of defiance. Knocking planes out of the sky, nudging buildings from their moorings, causing earthquakes in places earthquakes don't ordinarily happen. Armed with the power of a goddess and the coping skills of a child, she picked at the world's scabs. But it became hard to focus, difficult to find random acts of destruction she could sink her teeth into.

The drugs they put into her system had a strange effect. Limiting the reach of her powers, if not the output, making it a challenge to dig her fingers into space and time. She had no idea how old she was, anymore. Maybe I'm a cartoon, she thought. Maybe I'm a comic strip on the page, sitting in a box somewhere, waiting for the artist to finish the story. Maybe I'm Oppenheimer. I have become Death, the destroyer of worlds...

I'm so bored, she thought. So tired of my own company.

When she sat quietly still and listened, she could hear the sunlight touching the world above. She could taste the Earth spinning. She could see the moon's pull, changing the tides, the eternal cosmic dance of it all. Sometimes she sat alone, in her cage, and became entertained by the universe's refrain.

Tonight, though, she heard something else. Another heart in the distance, another being with a black hole where her heart should be, another traveler who never belonged in this world. Their hearts sang the same song of eternity, leading reality around like a dog on a leash.

Who are you? Emily asked the heart in the distance, pulling on her, taunting her, asking her to dance. Are you someone like me? Are you a monster? A goddess? Or, are you just a dream? Am I simply looking in the mirror at a face I no longer recognize?

Are you me?

She heard Keaton Bohr returning, his footsteps familiar as they clanked down the hallway. At first, he wouldn't make eye contact with her, but she could read his body language, could sense his anxiety. He'd been a fixture in her life for as long as she could remember. She knew his moods.

"Keaton," she said. The scientist startled, his whole body shaking. He walked up to the cage.

"You're awake."

"What do you know?" she said.

Bohr hesitated, his shoulders slumping.

"We're all going to die, aren't we?" Emily said.

Bohr studied her, his eyes red-rimmed and shining.

"It's okay," Emily said. "I've known the ending to this story for a long time. It was easy to read the signs."

"It didn't have to be this way," Bohr said.

"Yes it did," Emily said. "It's all in the equations. We picked this path. Or you did. You tried to fix everything. Nothing likes to be fixed. The world prefers to be broken, Keaton Bohr. You can't put a band aid on a burning building and make it better."

"I'm going to stop it," Bohr said. "There's still time."

"There's never enough time for the important things," Emily said. "There's always enough time to squander, though. Don't waste your time wasting time."

"Then what should I be doing?" Bohr said.

Emily smiled. Aware it was no longer a pretty smile, she watched as Bohr nearly recoiled in discomfort.

"You're the only one I would want to say goodbye to," Bohr said.

"Well then," Emily said, again flashing her uncomfortable grin. "If that's the case... are there any TV shows you haven't seen the finale of? Because I'd try to watch those soon."

CHAPTER 41:
SEISMOGRAPHY

Billy visited the Institute of Technology and Mathematics once, when he was younger. Not for anything good. He and a couple of friends broke in one night to look around. They wanted to trash the place, but Billy was more interested in seeing what all those brainy kids were up to. Expecting robots and space ships, he found a lot of petri dishes and refrigeration units, long black tables with sinks embedded in them, empty classrooms. Nothing that remotely resembled the future.

He'd been almost as disappointed then as he was now, walking with Annie, Emily, and Jessie in the darkened hallways. Jessie had taken the lead, for no reason other than she'd once been on a tour of the building. The group looked around for some room where they might have possibly study earthquakes.

The campus was enormous.

"Will you even know what a seismograph looks like if you see it?" Billy asked.

Emily waved him off. "I bet there'll be a sign," she said. "Or a pictogram, indicating the earth is shaking or something."

"An entire timeline is depending on you and you're completely faking it?" Billy said.

"What I lack in actual know-how, I make up for in earnest enthusiasm," Emily said.

Jessie raised a questioning eyebrow at Billy.

"The more she talks," Jessie said, "the more I wonder if we got lucky not having her on our team in this timeline."

"Wait 'til you see me in a combat scenario," Emily said.

"Swooping in at the last minute to save the day after the rest of us get beaten half to death fighting the bad guys?" Billy said.

"Saving my death-defying powers for just when I feel like you need me most," Emily said.

Annie held up a hand and everyone turned their attention to her when she pointed at a sign. "I'm no genius, 'yo,' but I'm guessing the geology department would be where we'd want to look," Annie said.

"You take us to the most interesting places, Em," Billy said.

* * *

It turned out, unsurprisingly, that none of them actually knew how to turn the seismograph on.

"I... I have no idea how this works," Annie said, staring at an aging machine involving a lot of paper and few user-friendly instructions.

"You're from the future," Emily said. "Shouldn't our technology make you feel like you're living among Cro-Magnons?"

"Well, I mean I don't know how to fix a video cassette player either," Annie said. "Just because I'm from a place with advanced technology doesn't mean I know how to repair all the old technology that came before."

"I could kick it a bunch of times," Billy offered.

"Yes," Emily said.

"No," Jessie said, simultaneously.

"You gotta admit, this was a great idea at the time," Emily said.

"I'm not even sure this really is a seismograph," Jessie said. "It could be something else entirely."

"What would help is an instruction manual," Emily said.

"What would help is knowing what we're talking about," Billy said. "Annie, what do we do?"

"Look for the instruction manual?" Annie offered.

"Doc would never say something like that," Billy said. "Doc would offer a solution."

"A half-thought out solution that would leave his friends stranded in another dimension?" Annie said.

"Or himself. But there's rarely a need for an instruction manual in Doc's life," Emily added. "Gotta give him props for that."

"His tattoos are an instruction manual," Annie said, offering no further explanation or detail.

Emily and Annie continued to putter around the room, neither appeared particularly sure of herself. Billy and Jessie hung back, even less useful.

"What if we can't find what we're looking for here?" Jessie asked Billy, her body language nonchalant but her tone indicating worry.

"Try something else? We generally just keep trying something else 'til we find an idea that works," Billy said.

"Maybe the wolves come away with a plan?" Jessie said.

Billy sat down in a swivel chair and spun himself around absently. "Y'know, Em, I really did think you were on the right track with this idea," he said. "Hey, Dude? You know how to work a seismograph?"

I would not even know where to begin, Dude said.

"That's okay," Billy said. "We'll come up with an alternative. Hey Em, does this mean sending Jane after those explosives you asked for is a wild goose chase?"

"You can never have too many explosives in a post-apocalyptic world," Emily said. "Besides, if we can find the cage they're keeping future me in, I can totes break it. I just... y'know, epic fail on finding it."

Billy turned his attention to Jessie.

"Hey, fake Straylight," he said.

"What, deceased Straylight?" Jessie said.

"That's cold," Billy said.

"And you're annoying. What do you want?"

"Serious question," Billy said. "In all these years of fighting the ... other guys, has there ever been a location they seemed particularly aggressive in defending?"

Jessie smiled.

"You mean if there are places they kept us away from, they may

194

be hints as to where they're keeping future-Emily," Jessie said.

"Exactly," Billy said.

Annie chimed in next, pulling up a chair near Billy. "They've fought like hell to deter us from downtown, but I think they just don't want us near locations stocked with more plentiful supplies," Annie said.

"And we know they keep weapons stockpiles near the Waterfront," Jessie said. "That area's always well-fortified."

"So we start looking there," Billy said.

"Easier said than done. But it's not a bad idea, now that we have some clue what they're hiding from us," Annie said.

"So it turns out you're not a complete idiot, huh, Billy Case?" Jessie said.

"I'm not without my charms," Billy said.

All the while, Emily continued to putter and tinker with the seismograph, though from the outside, it looked more like she was trying to break it in the slowest way possible than to activate it.

"Guys, I almost have this—whoa," Emily said.

"You almost have it whoa?" Billy said.

Emily leaned heavily against the nearest tabletop, then slid awkwardly to the floor.

"Whoa," she said.

"You okay?" Billy asked, getting up out of his chair to join Emily in the back of the room.

She latched onto Billy's arm, and he felt her pulling away, floating up involuntarily. His own feet, caught up in Emily's bubble of float, began to lift off the ground as well. Billy grabbed hold of the edge of a table to keep them both rooted to the floor.

"Guys," Emily said.

"What's going on?" Annie said, rushing over.

"I'm going to throw up," Emily said.

"I can't possibly express in words how thrilled I am to hear that," Billy said.

"What's happening?" Jessie said, trying to carefully stay outside the drift of Emily's bubble.

Emily closed her eyes, embracing the bubble and her own lack of control. She took a deep breath, stopped struggling and just allowed herself to float. Like a compass, Emily turned, drawn to a point on the horizon. "Guys, we don't need the seismograph," she said, suddenly looking very alert.

"Were you just messing with us before?" Billy said.

"No," Annie said. "I think I understand what's happening."

Emily and Annie exchanged knowing looks.

"She knows I'm here," Emily said.

"Who?" Jessie asked.

"The other me. She senses an anomaly like herself. She sensed me, and is singing to me," Emily said.

"Singing?" Billy asked.

"The songs of the world," Emily said. "The vibrations of the universe."

"What did you have for breakfast, there, sparky?" Billy said.

Emily waved Billy off dismissively.

"I can find her," Emily said, smiling. "I can tell you where she is. She's pulling me toward her. She's calling her missing pieces home."

"She's calling you?" Billy said.

"She knows there's another singularity here. She can hear me breathing and wants me to follow her home."

"Em," Billy said.

"Billy, I can lead us to her," Emily said. "She wants to be found."

"Well that's not alarming at all," he said.

"It's the end of the world," Emily said, spinning in her own bubble of float. "Nothing here is safe. We just have to go with the flow."

CHAPTER 42:
AN ETERNAL WAR

All of the Whispering's pack who were able to fight joined the expedition out of the City, nearly two-dozen strong, moving stealthily through more abandoned streets to take the battle to a place where they were better equipped. Just outside the city limits a stretch of woodlands, nothing spectacular to look at, acted as a quiet buffer between the metropolis and the surrounding suburbs. Here, Titus knew, the pack would stand on their turf, free from distractions, ready to make their best attempt at survival.

"These are Rose's people," Titus said to Leto as she walked past.

The elegant old werewolf nodded. "She leads them, but she didn't create them," Leto said. "Since mankind became aware of our presence, there have always been hunters. And they've always believed they were doing holy work, protecting humanity from the monsters in the shadows."

"But we're the shaman on the hill," Titus said. "We're here to keep people safe."

"There's at least two problems with that," the toothy, rumbling voice of Whispering said behind him. "The first is that we've often failed. History is littered with the carcasses of werewolves who have become monsters."

"And the second?" Titus asked.

"That theory hinges on the false premise that humanity wants to be protected," Whispering said.

"And they really don't?" Titus said.

"Not often," the enormous werewolf said as he sniffed at the night air. "We should get ready. Try not to die. I'd like to think I still exist in your timeline."

"Try not to die yourself," Titus said, watching the hulking form of his future self trot away.

"He's spoken more since all of you arrived than he has in years," Leto said.

"Because of her," Titus said.

"Because of all of it," Leto said. "He's a priest presiding over the end of the world. He stalks around like a monster, but he's very sad."

"I've always thought I should try to be less sensitive," Titus said.

Leto shook her head. "Being sensitive is what saves you," she said. "Time and time again. It's what keeps you from being a monster."

"I suppose," Titus said. "I fought Rose once. Thought I killed her. Not on purpose."

"Even creatures like us rarely kill intentionally," Leto said.

"Has my future self fought her before?"

"More than once," Leto said.

"Good," Titus said. "Because she's something else."

"If we're lucky, she hasn't brought her protégé," Leto said.

"How will I know if I see the protégé?"

"He'll be bigger than any of the other fighters, and tearing us apart," Leto said.

There was a howl of pain in the distance. First blood drawn. The disciples of Rose had arrived.

"I knew they'd come for us if we moved out," Titus said.

"Go with courage," Leto said.

"You too," Titus said, transforming in one fluid motion into a massive silver werewolf, then charging into the night.

* * *

Roars of the mighty and the screams of the dying filled the forest.

Titus encountered the first hunter and almost maimed himself before realizing his adversary wore a collar of silver spikes to protect his neck. Altering his movements at the last second, Titus turned his claws toward the soft spot just above the collarbone, digging in and drawing blood.

The hunter also wore silver spikes on his knuckles and shoulders. Short and sharp, the silver seemed less a weapon and more a deterrent to prevent Titus from tearing at his throat or getting a good grip on the enemy fighter.

They can't cover their eyes with silver, Titus thought, before testing that theory.

He watched one of the younger werewolves losing ground to another fighter, and sprang out of the darkness to land on the man's back, digging his claws in beneath his shoulder blades. He pushed the hunter onto the ground and abandoned the maimed enemy to be finished off by the other wolf, who nodded at him with a gesture that seemed disconcertingly human from a full-fledged werewolf.

Another werewolf, a middle-aged male whose name Titus never learned, fell to the ground, his throat bleeding. The opponent turned that blade toward Titus next, but the hunter disappeared under a cloud of red fur when Finnigan pounced on him, tearing his armor apart. Finnigan flashed a bloody smile at Titus and together they dug into the fray. A silver-tipped arrow whistled past Titus' shoulder, and before he could react, Finnigan—moving with terrifying speed for such a stout creature—changed directions and engulfed the archer before she could nock a second arrow.

Titus heard another shrieking howl and left Finnigan to finish off the archer. One more hunter dropped from the trees onto his back, and Titus felt the familiar burn of a silver knife scrape along his trapezius. The cut wasn't deep, but the heat of the silver drawing blood sent him into a frenzy. He never saw the hunter's face, mindlessly grabbing the man by the neck and smashing him with all his strength into the very tree the fighter had been hiding in.

He found his future self up against a particularly skilled hunter, a woman with a sword in each hand. Whispering held her off with his spear, matching her blow for blow. Titus could see she was too young to be Rose herself, but she fought with similar precision, and the older Titus treated her as an equal combatant, as much on the defensive as attacking.

Titus caught a flash of silver on the edge of his peripheral vision, and leapt into the air without thinking. Before he even realized what he was doing, he'd caught an arrow mid-flight, the silver head scraping his hand on the meat of his thumb. Titus landed, sparing a quick glance to realize that arrow would have hit his future self square in the chest. He roared and leaped at the archer, driving the arrow itself through the bowman's ribcage and into his heart. He looked back to see his future self winning the fight with the duel-wielding hunter, who'd been driven to one knee, losing speed with her blades. Fear overtook her eyes.

Again, racing into the darkness, Titus tore the hamstring of a hunter who'd been close to defeating another young werewolf, not slowing down, not stopping. The world felt strange and vivid, with the monster, the beast, far more in control than Titus was, his thunderously loud heart pounding in his chest.

He smelled lightning and rain and looked up to see a bolt of light smash into the ground. Running toward the light, he saw three hunters on fire, scorched and raw, with Leto in full werewolf form standing with her arms outstretched, hands awash in glowing blue. She howled, and lightning again struck, this time arcing out of her hand to electrocute an enemy who dared challenge her.

Then Titus heard a familiar voice yowl in pain. Finnigan, crying out like he'd never heard him before. Titus tore off toward the sound.

Finnigan had squared off against a hunter so big he looked part werewolf himself, the human carrying a two-handed sword and hulking like some image from a cartoon. Finnigan bent and hunched over, one claw holding his side, breathed heavily, with teeth bared and eyes shining. The enormous hunter raised his sword to strike a killing blow, and Finnigan tried to leap out of the way, stumbling as he clutched his side.

The sword's blow never landed.

Titus found himself airborne, claws dug into the massive hunter's arms, and pulled him to the ground. The sword fell away, and the hunter punched Titus in the stomach, once, twice, the silver spikes on his fists not quite breaking the skin but burning and bruising like nothing Titus had ever experienced before. The human went for

Titus' eyes, but purely on instinct Titus drove the claws on his thumbs up into the man's armpits, feeling his heart swell as the human screamed in agony. He kicked Titus off of him, sending the young werewolf sprawling.

Titus righted himself, quickly finding his feet, but then the big hunter was on him, swinging that huge sword wildly as blood started to pour out from under his arms. Titus dodged the weapon itself but felt the heavy pommel of the blade smash into his ribs, sending him staggering.

Again going for the softest, unarmored places, Titus latched onto the man's collarbone with both hands, digging his claws into the flesh there. He felt the hunter trying to lift his blade again, but with every movement Titus' dagger-like nails inflicted more and more damage to all the connective tissue the hunter required to swing that ridiculous weapon with any effect. His combatant dropped the sword and moved for his belt, and Titus kicked off, putting some distance between himself and the human before the hunter lashed out with a short silver knife.

They circled each other, gladiators in a fight to the death. Titus drifted further and further away from the surface, running on feral instinct, a thousand years of this eternal war between man and beast culminating in single combat.

The hunter lunged, using size against size, hoping that the gleaming knife would find purchase in Titus' flesh. At the last minute, Titus let go, transforming back into his human form, all but disappearing, half his mass gone in a split second.

He drew Gabriel's long knife, the one he always wore on his belt, the weapon he so often forgot was even there. And lightly, like threading a needle, he drove it up under the hunter's ribcage and into his heart.

The enemy looked at Titus, their faces both young and haunted, and staring in surprise.

"I never . . ." the hunter said, flailing weakly with his silver blade. Titus batted it away with one hand and pulled Gabriel's knife from the man's chest, feeling his warm blood pour over his fingers. He let the big hunter fall to the ground and ran to Finnigan.

"I'm alright boy, I'm alright," The red-headed werewolf said, stuck somewhere between human and wolf forms, still clutching his side. "Jaysus this hurts."

"It's okay, Finnigan, we'll get you patched up, we'll . . ."

Finnigan's breathing was shallow, but his eyes were glowing with life.

"We don't die this easy, lad," Finnigan said. "You've got to—"

Titus felt a booted foot slam into his chest, knocking him to the ground. Gabriel's knife fell from his hand, and he let the monster re-emerge, transforming quickly back into his massive body.

"You killed my boy," the newcomer said. She threw back her hood, revealing the same, one-eyed face Titus had sent sprawling into the Atlantic more than a year before. "He was my heir."

"Heir to the dead," Finnigan said.

Rose smiled. "I've been waiting to kill you for a long time too," she said. She raised a sword, her grip reversed, to drive a stabbing blow into the crippled Finnigan. "I've spent my whole life dedicated to killing you creatures. It's almost a shame to finally be able to wipe you out."

And then a hand appeared from the darkness and stopped her.

"You've spent your whole life training to fight them," Kate said, her smile bright and white in the darkness. "But you've never seen anything like me."

* * *

Titus and Kate remained concerned for each other's safety.

"You're going to face people who were born to murder you," Kate said. "Let me try my hand against them."

"So they can kill you as well?" Titus said.

"We'll see what happens when we push them outside their comfort zone," Kate said. She remembered the dark-clad ninjas on the modified oil rig that night when they'd last fought Rose. She was younger then, less trained, but she'd fought dozens of them, and they'd been less specialized than these newcomers. Titus had defeated Rose herself, a woman who had been trained—better than anyone else alive—to kill his species. But what would happen when she confronted something new?

Kate was dying to find out.

She'd been looking for Rose in the darkness, not engaging any of the other hunters, keeping to the shadows, remaining out of sight. She almost missed her, but spotted the woman's familiar walk seconds before she approached Finnigan's prone body. It felt like Rose was looking for someone in particular. Hoping to settle an old score.

Well, Kate had an old score to settle as well.

Rose pulled her arm free of Kate's grasp, reversing her grip on her sword to ready herself.

Kate didn't give her the time to prepare, though. She let the huntress yank her arm free, then kicked Rose in the kneecap, which sent her staggering back.

Rose lunged with her silver sword. Kate sidestepped it, grabbed hold of Rose's hands with both of her own and drove the sword's point into a nearby tree. The tip of the blade sunk into the wood, and Kate twisted, using her own weight along with Rose's to snap the sword off at the pommel.

The weapon out of the way, the two women began to fight in earnest, throwing punches and blocks, kicks and dodges. Rose landed a solid blow to Kate's chin; Kate countered with a kick to the huntress' midsection, the softer spot between hipbone and ribcage. Rose pulled out a short knife, and Kate caught it in her gloved hand, the palm of which had been reinforced to blunt edged weapons. She pulled the huntress in close and head-butted her, not in the nose but in her one good eye. The skull on skull contact sent a white sliver of pain down the middle of Kate's head, but she stepped back to see Rose disoriented and lashing out blindly, her sight hindered by blood pouring down from where her skin had split above the eyebrow.

"You brawl dirtier than anyone I've ever met, girl," Rose said.

Kate smiled, but said nothing.

"You think I need to see you to fight you?" Rose said.

Kate opened one of the pouches on her belt and poured a handful of table salt into the palm of her hand.

"No, but seeing you flail is so much more fun," Kate said.

Rose turned, arching her arm to throw her knife, but Kate tossed the salt at the same time. The knife soared millimeters from Kate's head as the cloud of salt exploded in Rose's face. The huntress screamed.

"His mother took my eye!" Rose yelled, her voice cracking. "Do you understand that, you little monster!"

Kate walked in closer, and Rose pulled out two more knives, but one fell weakly from her hand. She lashed out with the other, and Kate caught her wrist, pulling Rose's arm behind her back. She pushed the lead huntress into a tree.

"Where is he?" Kate said. She clutched Rose's other wrist and turned, pushing little bones to the breaking point. "Where is the man who sent you."

"Man?" Rose said.

"The White Shadow," Kate said.

"Every single one of you is an idiot," Rose said.

"Tell me what I need to know and maybe you'll live," she said.

Rose laughed, a bitter laugh filled with loathing so deep Kate could barely stomach hearing it.

"Where is *he*?" Rose said

She moved quickly, pulling her knees up and pushing off the tree with both legs. Kate stumbled backward, caught herself, and spun out of the way when Rose grabbed another knife. The knife skimmed the back of her wrist and drew blood. She hissed and took a quick step back, trying to get away from Rose's haphazard knife-swings.

Rose ran forward, losing all decorum. Screams of hatred spewed from her lips. She plunged into the waiting point of her own broken sword, still jutting out from the tree trunk. The silver blade passed with brutal ease through her chest, bursting out the back.

Rose gasped, and then laughed. "We won this war twenty years ago," she said, her fingers clutching at the bare blade in her gut. "This was already over."

"Rose," Kate said.

"What a stupid way to die," Rose said.

And then she was gone.

CHAPTER 43:
IT'S NOT GIVING UP

Jane and Solar landed outside an deserted National Guard depot just beyond the City borders, a ghost town of rusty hardware and abandoned buildings. Jane could envision the remnants of a battle here, where soldiers—real, human heroes, not super-powered kids—once made a stand and failed. It took a moment for Jane to realize she stood in a giant footprint.

"They attacked this place with robots?" Jane said.

"The enemy hit here first," Solar said. "They wanted to stamp out all resistance."

"This is awful," Jane said.

"It gave the citizens of the City enough time to get out, though," Solar said. "We were tied up with another attack along the coast and couldn't respond in time."

"The whole thing just makes no sense," Jane said, taking in the destruction around her. "Why did they want the City so badly?"

Solar walked up to a concrete bunker and started shimmying the lock. The metal frame creaked as she worked the door loose with inhuman strength.

"I don't know," Solar said. "Revenge? If this really is the White Shadow behind everything, maybe he wanted to get back at the place he defended for so long? Maybe there was something about this place that made it easier to control Emily's powers?"

Jane grabbed the other side of the door and together they gave up on trying to open the armored gateway and just ripped it off its hinges.

They walked inside the bunker, both women letting a hand burst into flames to give off light. Firearms, some leftover artillery, a combat vehicle—what remained of the depot's supplies—surrounded them.

"Lotta things that can blow up in here," Jane said.

"Good thing we're both flammable," Solar said.

As they walked through rows of what once had been carefully compiled storage units, Jane found her curiosity growing. Why was all this still here? Where did everyone go?

"Is every place this empty?" she asked. "Who's left out there?"

"There's so many people in hiding," Solar said. "We've done what we can to help, but... On the upside, the enemy seems to ignore people if they're just getting by. They drop a hammer on anyone who takes up arms against them, but the rest? They don't really seem to care."

"Is every city in such terrible shape?"

"The big ones are," Solar said. "New York, London... The worst are the places where they used Emily's powers to cause natural disasters. Flooding, drought. There are so few of us. We did everything we could, but how could we keep up?"

"So you went on the offensive," Jane said.

"We tried to," Solar said. "They had those stupid robots, and they had their even stupider followers—you know people who really thought all this destruction was the right thing to do. And the natural disasters and... It was unremitting. Just relentless tragedy day after day."

They found a couple of high-quality flashlights on one shelf and switched to these less flammable, somewhat prehistoric light sources. We're both close to invulnerable, Jane thought, but if the whole place ignites in an explosion it couldn't possibly do anyone any good.

"I've been thinking," Solar said, her tone suddenly shifting from emotional to stone-cold serious.

Jane stopped and directed the flashlight towards her future counterpart's face.

"About what?"

"If things go badly, I want Annie to bring all of you home. To your own timeline."

Jane shook her head.

"No. We're not quitting. Or abandoning you. We're gonna help."

"That's not what I meant."

"You're asking us to give up," Jane said, overwhelmed by the existential strangeness of being disappointed in herself, peering at her own face in the future.

"It's not quite giving up," Solar said. "It's not fair, what we're asking you. You've done everything you can. You've tried to save our timeline. But maybe it's destiny. Maybe we're just destined to end here like this. And if you don't go back before it's all over, your fate ends here as well."

"And perhaps that's how it's meant to end for us," Jane said.

"I don't believe that," Solar said. "No matter what happens, you'll go back to your timeline better for having been here and trying to help."

Jane raised an eyebrow.

"And how is that?" she said.

"Because you've seen our mistakes," Solar said. "If we can't save this timeline, at least you've come here to see how terrible things can get. You can go home and make sure these things never happen in your own timeline. You can pave the way to a better future."

Jane turned her light away from Solar's face and went through the motions of inspecting the bunker. Was she right? Was that the whole reason they'd come to visit this dark future? To serve as a warning? Maybe they can't stop the White Shadow. Perhaps this really is a dead timeline. Incapable of saving. Undeserving of rescue.

"Has Annie ever told you how many timelines there are?" Jane asked.

Solar let out a hard, barking laugh.

"I don't believe there's a finite number," Solar said. "Or if there is, I don't think Annie knows."

"Then why save this one?" Jane said. "She says it's our fault this timeline is dying."

"It's always our fault," Solar said. "I don't mean you and I, or the

Indestructibles, or... in every timeline, there's a catalyst. There's something important that makes it or breaks it. There's an act of horror or an act of heroism. This is what I know from Annie. That every timeline is changed—and charged—by heroes."

"And we're heroes," Jane said.

"I have some bad news for you," Solar said, putting a hand on Jane's shoulder. "You never escape this fate. For you and me and the millions of other Jane Hawkins out there in this..."

"Multiverse," Jane said. "Emily would call it a multiverse."

"Well then. This multiverse. I don't think we ever get to be an ordinary person, Jane," Solar said. "We are cursed to always be special."

Jane felt a twinge of melancholy in her chest, a longing for something she never knew she wanted.

"It would be nice to think there's a timeline where we're ordinary, isn't it?" Jane said. "Where Jane Hawkins gets to be a kid. Grow up, and fall in love. Drive a boring car, go to college. Have a house with a mortgage. Take her girls to soccer."

"Yeah," Solar said.

Jane spied the glistening in her future self's eyes.

"Maybe there is, somewhere. A Jane who has a chance to be ordinary," Solar said.

"But we're stuck being heroes," Jane said.

"There are worse things to be," Solar said. Together, they shone their flashlights on another door, this one blazoned with an alarming emblem warning that explosives were contained within.

Jane laughed. "I have no idea what Emily thinks she's going to do with these things, but I suppose we should get her a few bombs," she said.

"I wish I had a chance to know her here," Solar said. "She seems like, in the right world, she'd be a wonderful friend."

"No one's perfect," Jane said. "But I'm glad she's mine."

CHAPTER 44:
TELL ME HOW THE WORLD ENDS

Keaton Bohr stormed into the White Shadow's chambers. The image of Emily judging him from behind her glass bubble burned into his mind, he remained hell-bent on a mission. Bohr found the Shadow sitting in the dark once again, as if waiting for him to arrive.

"I can't do this anymore," Bohr said.

The White Shadow sighed. A sigh neither impatient nor frustrated; there was something Zen-like about it. The slow, deliberate, release of air.

"Do what?" the Shadow asked.

"Watch us destroy the world. I can't do this. I have to try to stop it."

"Isn't this what you signed on for, though?" the White Shadow said. "Isn't this what we wanted?"

"I wanted a better world!" Bohr said.

"And we failed," the Shadow said, standing up.

"Oh, we have most certainly failed," Bohr said. "We've ruined everything."

"No," the Shadow said. "We stood up and destroyed the world's supervillains. Things did not get better. And when the supervillains were gone, we toppled corrupt governments. And still things did not get better. We took away the crutches humanity depended on in order to stay complacent and dull. And, did things improve?"

"We turned the planet into a constant battleground," Bohr said.

"Is that what you wanted?"

"What I wanted was a world without suffering!" the Shadow said, speaking so quickly Bohr found himself cut-off mid-thought. "For all bad things to finally come to an end. And you know what I discovered?"

"That there are always more bad things?" Bohr said. "There's no limit to the terrible things in this world?"

The Shadow crossed the room, walked up to a window, and opened a blind. The City, in all its crumbling decay, unfolded before them, a bleak red sunrise slowly crept over the horizon.

"No," the Shadow said. "Not exactly."

Bohr rubbed his eyes. The space felt stifling, as if all oxygen abandoned the room.

"Then what? Why won't you stop? Why did we do all of this?" Bohr said. "Is it because you wanted to tear down the old world to build a better one? Because I have some bad news for you—there won't be a better one. We've made certain of that."

"You know what I hate about heroes?" the Shadow said.

"Don't change the subject," Bohr said. "You can't quit this conversation."

"Heroes are missing something in their heads," the Shadow said. "Some sort of off button. A sliver of reason. They go out every day and they stupidly risk their future, they lay down their lives, they die, and there's nothing, no one, nobody anywhere, who is truly deserving of that kind of ultimate sacrifice."

"What are you talking about?" Bohr said. "I thought that's what we were doing here! We were sacrificing ourselves. We were being the bad guys so that we could lay the groundwork for a better world, not turn it into an ash tray!"

"Heroes are given these wonderful send-offs when they die," the Shadow said. "If they're lucky. If anyone ever knows what type of sacrifices the hero has performed, what type of superhuman feats. And then, a few days, or a few weeks, or a few years later, the world gradually goes back to normal. Nothing's changed. Nothing ever improves."

"So you're doing this because nobody appreciates heroes?" Bohr said.

"And you know what's worse?" the White Shadow said, ignoring Bohr's question. "You know what's truly even worse than not being able to change anything?"

Bohr waited in silence, a growing fury burning an acidic pit in the cauldron of his stomach.

"This world will match you blow for blow. Heroes create villains. Every good act is matched in equal or greater force by something significantly more evil," the Shadow said. "Have you ever noticed that? You'd think, after decades of advancement. Year after year of heroic acts. That we'd develop, evolve. That we would move toward enlightenment. That we'd help create a better world."

Bohr's heart raced now. He wanted to rush across the room, throw his ally and friend out that giant window, and end all of this. But that would do nothing, in the final analysis, he knew. And worse, the Shadow was far from wrong. Bohr thought about the world he knew before. Not only realizing that for each new hero who stood up against the darkness, someone else worse always rose up to stand in his or her way, but how, for a very long time, the whole concept of heroism had become reactive. The world kept getting worse, throwing its heroes at its problems—its wars, its disasters, its famines and nightmares—and there was always something more terrifying waiting in the wings.

"I hate you for saying this out loud," Bohr said. "Did you always think this way?"

The Shadow waved him off with a dismissive gesture.

"When I met you, Keaton, I really thought we could save this place," the Shadow said. "I really did."

"And now?"

"Now I think the problem is us," the Shadow said, turning back to the window and the bloody sunrise. "People. Humanity. We're the problem. We're the monster at the door."

"And your solution is to simply wipe us out?" Bohr said.

"I didn't plan it this way, you know," the Shadow said, a vein of sadness once again creeping into that raspy, soft voice. "I didn't realize this would happen when we took that girl all those years ago. I believed we were doing the right thing."

"When did you know?" Bohr said. "When did you figure out where we were headed?"

"If you ever bothered to step out of your lab, you might have seen it sooner," the Shadow said. "But truly I didn't understand how final this plan had become until you told me about the girl's change of condition. Congratulations, Keaton. Your brilliant machines have doomed the world."

Bohr slammed a fist into the wall. "I'm going to stop this. I am!" he said.

"After all this time, Keaton, do you really think you've landed on the side of angels? It's much too late. Sit back. Enjoy. Watch the world fade into darkness. We've earned this. Front row seats to the apocalypse."

CHAPTER 45:
THIS IS HOW THINGS END

Titus sat next to an unconscious Finnigan in a makeshift hospital room, his friend wrapped in bandages and breathing heavily in his sleep. Finnigan's wounds weren't healing as fast as they should have been. The old myth about silver appeared to be true. If you want to kill a werewolf, use silver.

Leto thought he stood a chance of recovering, with some luck and patience. The wound hadn't been immediately fatal—which is why a silver bullet to the head or heart is always the best way to kill our kind, Titus thought—but it tore up Finnigan's insides. If they could keep him breathing long enough, even wounds from a silver sword could heal.

These days, everyone was short on time.

Whispering walked in and sat down on the foot of the bed, the frame creaked under his weight.

"We were close, in this timeline," Titus said. "You and Finnigan. Me and Finnigan."

"He was one of my best friends," Whispering said. "And my oldest. With Gabriel gone, and Billy, it really was just Finnigan and me for quite a while."

"I didn't stay with them, in my timeline," Titus said. "Leto said if I left I might never return. That the world of men would never allow me to go home again."

Whispering let out a huffing, rumbling laugh.

"She's right," he said, studying his unconscious friend's face. "The world of men will always need you, if you don't watch out. It latches on and can't let go."

"How did you find them again?" Titus said.

"I didn't," Whispering said. "Something always got in my way. But when I needed them, this fine old man came looking for me, and brought the others with him."

"Sounds like Finnigan."

"Truth," Whispering said. "I don't think he ever forgave himself for Gabriel's death. I think he wondered that if they'd stayed on the outskirts, if they kept to themselves, they might have survived in peace. But nobody was going to survive this in peace. There's nowhere safe in this world. It wasn't his fault. If anything it was mine. I dragged them into my war."

"How long were you apart?" Titus said.

"Too long," Finnigan said, his voice rasping and quiet.

Titus placed his hand on the old wolf's shoulder and smiled.

"Hi, lad."

"Hello, old man," Whispering said.

Finnigan sighed. It was a rattling, ugly sound.

"Not dead yet," Finnigan said. "Funny that. I thought I was gone."

"You're too stubborn to die," Whispering said.

"So are you," Finnigan said. He turned his attention to Titus. "You fought like hell, boy."

"I do that sometimes."

"Like a monster," Finnigan said. He glanced back at Whispering. "You would have been jealous of your younger self. Reminding you how fast and strong you used to be."

"I'm still pretty strong," Whispering said.

"Not quite as fast though," Finnigan said. He coughed.

Titus watched Finnigan struggle to stifle the spasms. Pain lanced across his face.

"Neither am I. How many'd we lose?" Finnigan said.

"Too many, but fewer than we expected," Whispering said. "It was a fine plan and good fight."

Leto leaned on the door frame, looked in, and beckoned to Titus and Whispering.

"The others are back," she said.

Whispering stood up, placing a paw on Finnigan's knee.

"I'm glad you're still with us, old friend," he said.

After Whispering left, Finnigan reached up and clutched Titus' wrist in his hand.

Titus turned around in surprise.

"Do me a favor, son," Finnigan said, his voice barely above a whisper.

"Anything," Titus said.

"When you get home," he said. "Don't wait so long. To find your family again."

"What?"

"Life's too short, lad. Even for the likes of us," Finnigan said. "Here, now, you—the other you? Ten years he was lost. That's a decade my friend was gone, because he didn't believe he'd be welcomed home again, and we were too proud to come find him."

"I will," Titus said.

"Good," Finnigan said, lying back down, his eyes growing dim with exhaustion and pain. "Too short, this life. Over in the blink of an eye."

* * *

"We've got some good news and bad news," Annie said in the center of a large open room where everyone had gathered. Jane's stomach tied itself into knots after counting the missing faces among Whispering's pack. They'd sustained heavy casualties in the last two battles. She realized not everyone missing had been killed, that there were rooms nearby where some of those who weren't present lay healing faster than any normal human could, but she read the haunted looks on Titus' face, on Whispering's and Leto's. More ghosts were inhabiting this dying world.

"It was bad, wasn't it?" Jane asked Kate, who sat in silence beside her.

Kate's face, as always, was decorated with fresh scratches and cuts, the perpetual pastiche of hand-to-hand combat. She offered no response and stared straight ahead.

Jane shrugged and turned away.

"I want to go home, Jane," Kate said softly.

Jane turned her eyes back to the Dancer, who still looked blankly forward. "Me too," she said.

"I can't shake the feeling this has all been a mistake," Kate said.

Jane opened her mouth to speak, but was interrupted by Annie.

"Our time's running short," Annie said. "Our expedition to try to find a way to track Emily's future self—the source of a lot of our enemy's weaponry, was unsuccessful, but—"

"—She knows where I am, and so I know where she is. We can find her," Emily said. "That also of course means she can locate us, but I actually don't think that's a problem."

"Which is a chance we're not going to take," Annie said, raising one neon-pink eyebrow at Emily. "Emily can feel her other version pulling her somehow."

"It's so weird," Emily said. "Like when the ocean sucks your feet into the sand. Y'know what I mean? It's not exactly like that, there being no actual sand involved but—"

"Right. Long story short, Em has a pretty good idea where she is," Annie said. She tapped a button on a small remote control in her hand and a GPS map of the City was projected on the wall behind her.

"You gotta be kidding me," Billy said.

"That's what I said!" Emily jumped to her feet and tapped the spot on the map where she'd placed a red mark. "The pull is coming from where our old Tower base used to be."

"It'd make sense," Doc Silence said. "We didn't plant the Tower at that spot by accident. It's a place where the weird triangulates. Strange things happen there."

"So we're going to travel right to the source and see about putting that machine channeling the powers of Emily's future self out of commission," Solar said.

"They'll see us coming," Whispering said, leaning on his spear at the back of the room. "I'd suggest we mount an offensive as a distraction while a smaller team tries to get to this other machine, but my people don't have the numbers now to stand up to the enemy's defenses—especially if they send in some of their giant mechs again."

"We haven't seen them in a while," Solar said. "But Jane and I were scouting earlier and—"

"—We discovered two completed robots. Big ones," Jane chimed in. "They looked ready to go."

"We'll lure them away," Billy said.

"Who's this 'we,' partner," Emily said.

"Jessie and I. Team Straylight," Billy said. "We should be able to take on a couple of giant robots, right?"

Annie implored Solar for feedback.

"Jessie, you've fought with them previously alongside me. What's your take? It required both of us to put them out of commission before," Solar said.

"No, I've needed you to take them out," Jessie said. "You could've done it without me. But we don't want them destroyed right away, right? This is a decoy mission. We hope to lead them away. Billy and I can totally do that much."

"Okay," Solar said. "Retreat if you have to. Call for backup if you need to. Jane or I will come running."

"Flying," Emily said.

Everyone ignored her.

"Why not have one of us go with them? Why risk it?" Jane said.

Annie nodded.

"It's a good point, but you'll be with Emily and me," Annie said. "No matter what, our main priority is putting that machine out of commission. We only get one shot at this."

"If we can demolish it, those robots should both shut down soon after," Solar said. "I'd rather have one of us flying beside the Straylights, but Annie's right."

"And the rest of us?" Titus said.

"We have two jobs to do," Doc said. "Take out what's left of the White Shadow's soldiers—there's still enough remaining to be a problem, and they have the weapons to cause trouble if they learn we've commissioned people to disrupt their power source."

"And the other job?" Titus said.

"We're going to take out the White Shadow," Kate said.

The others in the room turned to her.

"We have to. The Shadow's the mastermind."

"What are we going to do, kill the White Shadow?" Titus said. "I think we're done with murder for this week. I'm not sure about the rest of you."

"That's why I'm coming with you," Doc said. "I've got a feeling I know who's really behind that mask. And, if it's who I think it is, I need to be there."

"Because magic?" Emily said.

"Because history. Let's leave it at that," Doc said.

"I'm coming with you," a voice no one had heard in days said.

A startled Jane almost jumped to her feet.

Beside her, Kate actually did, standing before Jane even realized she'd moved.

A makeshift cane in her hand and a black blindfold tied neatly around her eyes, future-Kate stood in the doorway. Dressed for combat, her uniform was darker and more heavily armored than that of her younger self.

"Are you sure?" Solar said.

"I'm done being helpless," the future-Kate said. "I'm coming. I wasn't asking."

Jane watched as Titus and Whispering traded soundless glances. She looked back towards her own Kate, arms folded across her chest, but otherwise expressing no emotion.

"In case anyone might be wondering, we also have explosives," Emily said. "Tons of them."

"Not wondering, but thanks, Em," Billy said.

"And may I just say—"

"Em, c'mon," Titus said.

"I just want to say one thing," Emily said.

Everyone stopped. Acquiescing, they waited.

"Well? We're letting you talk," Jane said. "What is it?"

"Today we are *canceling the apocalypse!*" Emily said in the worst fake British accent any of them had ever heard.

"I knew we shouldn't have let her speak," Billy said.

CHAPTER 46:
MY LIFE AS A DECOY

Billy and Jessie flew high and very visible above the crumbling skyline, still amazed at the destruction heaped upon the City. Whole neighborhoods had been leveled. Familiar spires in the City's profile had gone missing, knocked out like a mouth full of broken teeth.

I'll never take the City's skyline for granted again, Billy thought.

Yes you will, Dude said. *No offense of course.*

Sometimes you underestimate me, Billy thought. I love this city. I grew up here.

'Grew up' is a debatable term, Dude said.

Billy banked over the browning expanse of park that dominated a couple hundred acres of space in the heart of the City. He watched Jessie spin playfully in the air, the two of them moved with the grace of dolphins riding along the prow of a boat. Billy stared into the distance, looking at the empty space where the Tower once stood, both in this reality and in his own timeline. Like a missing picket in a fence, the address seemed too blank, too incomplete without its faux-skyscraper standing there.

"What does it usually take to draw out the robots?" Billy said into an earpiece the others had given him back at the hideout.

"Depends," Jessie said. "Sometimes they don't bother engaging, other times they can't resist."

"Why create giant robots?" Billy asked. "I mean, there had to be something easier they could have made. Tanks or airplanes or something. This feels silly."

"We never really figured that out," Jessie said. "You're right of course. They're not even the least bit practical. I mean the ones we've fought have been powerhouses, I'm not underestimating their strength, I just . . ."

Emily chirped in over the headset. Her disembodied voice caught him off-guard and startled Billy.

"The correct answer is, if you can build a giant robot, then you build a giant robot," Emily said. "If you can make a giant robot and you don't, you're basically spitting in the face of everything good in this world."

"Emily," Jane's voice chimed in as well. "We need radio—"

"Goo goo?" Emily said.

"Stop it," Jane said.

"Gaga?" Emily said.

"Are you singing Queen right now?" Billy asked.

"Can we please maintain radio silence? We're trying to save the world here," Jane said.

"Look, I'm just trying to lighten the mood. Would you rather I sing the Highlander theme?" Emily said.

"When this is all over, you've got to have Em perform her Freddy Mercury impression," Billy said. "It's pretty epic."

"If we get through this in one piece, I'll remember to ask," Jessie said. "Meanwhile, check out what's up ahead."

Billy followed Jessie's outstretched hand to catch sight of two robots, easily six stories tall, walking slowly toward them. They cut a strange, alien silhouette against the backdrop of the morning sun, broad, angular metal shoulders jutting out as arms, just slightly too long for the bodies they were connected to, swayed with rhythmic patience.

"Y'know, I've wanted to be a lot of things, but the star of my own Robotech movie has never been on that list," Billy said.

One of the robots turned a massive head toward them. The other followed suit. Soon they both plodded their deliberate way.

"Ever fought a giant robot before?" Jessie said.

"Battled robots before. Giant not so much," Billy said. "Fought a giant cyborg mole one time. That was kind of weird."

"Seriously?"

"Yeah," Billy said. "Didn't go so well."

"Where do you find a giant cyborg mole?" Jessie said.

"Pretty much in this same neighborhood. Just hanging out. Eating buildings."

"No kidding."

"Nope," Billy said.

The robots gained speed, their massive metal limbs pistoning into a run. Thunderous, clanging footstep sounds filled and then echoed throughout the vacant city streets around them.

"You nervous?" Jessie asked.

"Are you kidding?" Billy said. "I grew up watching Power Rangers and bad anime."

"You get weirder and weirder the longer I know you," Jessie said.

"Hang on," Billy said, tapping his earpiece. "Emily?"

"Seriously guys. What part of the term 'radio silence' is lost on the two of you," Jane said.

"Whaddup?" Emily said.

"I'm about to fight a giant robot. Are you jealous?" Billy said.

"Are they cool?" Emily said.

"So cool."

"Voltron cool?"

"Cooler than Voltron."

"I hate you so much Billy Case. I hate you most of all."

"Love you too, Em. Be safe," Billy said.

CHAPTER 47:
THE BLIND WOMAN'S GAMBIT

Kate didn't like this setup one bit. Too many variables. They'd scouted the area and determined there was only one defensible, livable building in the immediate vicinity of where Emily had identified the lab. Upon arriving there through one of Doc's teleportation spells, they discovered the guesswork seemed right—the place was boarded up and patrolled by some of the White Shadow's remaining loyalists, armed with the gravity guns that had become the signature weapon of this group. Others carried more traditional firearms as well, and Whispering, in full-on werewolf form, warned them of still more surprises to come.

"The hunters must have left some of their men behind," the older werewolf said. "I can smell the silver."

Their strike team was not a large one, with Whispering determining that his people needed to be kept in reserve in case things went wrong. Titus shared with Kate privately that the pack had suffered too many casualties to offer the kind of threat they needed. Better to hit small than risk losing more friends and allies if it wasn't necessary.

Still, they would come if called. Wolves always could be counted upon.

But that left the break-in of Shadow's hideout to Whispering, Titus, Kate and Doc... and Kate's future self—blind and apparently out of her mind, Kate thought. She struggled to look at her future self, disgusted not so much by the injury to her sight but by the strange desperation that seemed to have enveloped her. I've been broken a long time, Kate thought, but I've never been weak. She feels weak to me.

I need to be better than that.

Two ragtag soldiers strolled by, gravity guns slung lazily at their sides.

Again, Whispering's senses remained the strongest. He heard them talking. "Our Straylights have been spotted," the big werewolf said.

"Time to move," Titus said.

The soldiers turned the corner in front of the building, their backs to the little alcove where Kate and the others hid.

"I've got this," she said, not waiting for anyone to protest.

She ran up behind the two men, her feet silent as she flittered across pavement. Before either heard her, she landed a jumping punch to one, knocking him head-first into the brick wall of the building. The other tried to raise his gun but Kate kicked his hands, knowing just the spot to make his fingers turn numb. He coughed in pain and Kate kicked again, slamming the top of the gun into the man's face. The first man began to stir, she pirouetted into a spin kick, and knocked him out.

Kate looked back to see Titus transforming into a big silver werewolf, a younger, less scarred version of the creature beside him. Both scrambled up the side of the building like apes, and Kate watched them quietly but ferociously dispatch a pair of sentries. Titus nodded to Kate, his big, shaggy wolf's head looking ridiculous when performing such a small, delicate movement.

Doc walked up to the front door of the building, blind Kate following close behind him. He put his fingers on the reinforced metal of the door and traced along the creases for a breaking point or weak spot. "Never mind," he said, sighing. "Why go for subtle when you can . . ."

He took a step back, waved his hands, and the double doors simply became butterflies, an entire flock, colored wings drifting away in stark contrast to the pale gray melancholy of the cityscape.

Future-Kate held out her hands, feeling the butterflies and their silky wings fly through her fingers.

"Every time you do something like that," Younger-Kate said.

"I know. It never gets old," Doc said. He offered her a rare smile. "And I'm the one who casts these spells."

Together, both Kates and Doc walked inside.

The interior had, strangely, been left nearly intact, with old black and white tile floors, and a coiling staircase leading up to apartments on the second landing. This was the type of building that survived after the influx of money to the City, Kate realized, the sort of place that refused to change as the world around it was swallowed up by the future. The wood on the railing and staircase was stained dark, deeply chipped, but loved and cared for. History lived here, she thought.

A gravity gun interrupted her reverie and sent a blast of light at her. Kate bounced back in time to watch the bolt splash off the ground, breaking black and white tiles that had been tread upon for generations. Before she could react, her future self charged up the stairs, following the sound of the gun, moving so aggressively the shooter froze, unable to get off another round. The blind Dancer kicked the rifle out of the man's hands, and then, without hesitation, knocked him off the balcony onto the floor below. The shooter landed with a sickening thud.

Another soldier stepped out, an ordinary gun clasped in his hand. He raised it and fired.

Future-Kate reacted, not quickly enough, yet still in time to turn a sure-fired deadly shot into a slight graze along one shoulder. She charged again, forcing the man to fire wildly, missing her entirely. A kick square in the chest, sent him crashing through the railing to the ground below, to join his compatriot on the floor, now both moaning and broken.

"What are you doing?" Kate asked her future self.

"What I have to," she answered. She touched her shoulder where the bullet grazed her, checking to see her armor held. Kate saw her future self's fingers come away bloody.

"You're going to get yourself killed," Kate said.

"I should have done that a long time ago," her doppelganger

said. "I'm going ahead. Tell him not to follow me."

Kate knew exactly whom she meant.

"Don't be stupid," Kate said.

"I always was an intolerant, judgmental brat," her future self said. "I'll race you to the Shadow, then, little me."

Future-Kate turned and left.

Doc put his hand on younger-Kate's shoulder. "We'll get to the Shadow first," he said. "Don't worry. She's just . . ."

"Being me," Kate said. "I need to be better than that."

"Then be better," Doc said.

CHAPTER 48:
STRANGE PLACES IN TIME

"All my life," Emily said, loudly enough to make Jane uncomfortable. "All my life all I've ever wanted is to fight giant robots. Do you realize how important this is to me?"

"Saving the world isn't important enough for you?" Annie asked.

Jane caught the time-traveler smirking behind those red-lensed glasses. She more than anyone had begun warming to Emily's questionable charms.

"I've saved the world. Couple of times at least," Emily said. "But giant robots? This is a once in a lifetime moment I'm missing out on."

"You have not saved the world multiple times," Jane said.

"Don't argue semantics, hot stuff," Emily said. "I think defeating a sentient hurricane is saving the world."

"Delusional and prone to flights of fancy," Jane said to Solar, while mimicking a doctor jotting down notes and nodding in Emily's direction.

They ought to make the best of it, given where they were, Jane thought. Working their way beneath the City, through stagnant sewers, the four women were looking for a way in to an underground space Annie and Doc had called the Vault. When Jane had questioned him about it, he said it hadn't been used in years. An empty space located below the Tower that his old team, and their predecessors, always had but never really used for long. Sometimes a prison, sometimes a lab, but more often than not, simply a forgotten basement where weird things ended up.

"Does it bother anyone else that they're keeping future-Emily in the bottom of our old base?" Jane asked out loud. "It just... it strains logic for me."

Annie shook her head, laughing just a bit.

"The universe has a sense of humor, Jane," Annie said. "I've been in more timelines than I can remember. Traveled across diverse alternate realities. Places where things are backwards or strange or just completely different. And you know what I've found?"

"That it would be a lot easier if you owned a Tardis?" Emily said.

"No, that when a place is important, it's always important," Annie said. "There are locations in our world where significant things happen. Where the events that change everything always seem to occur. Doc told you, the Tower wasn't built on that spot by accident. The founders understood it was a nexus of the strange."

"So what you're telling us is, if we ever find ourselves in another post-apocalyptic alternate future, the problem is probably in our basement," Emily said.

"That's not exactly what I said, but it is annoyingly close," Annie said. "Metaphorically speaking."

"Where else is like this?" Jane said.

Annie smiled broadly.

"You want a tour of the weird world? Let's get through this first and I'll take you on a road trip," she said.

"I love road trips," Emily said.

She caught Jane frowning.

"What? I'm carry-on sized and also I can make hauling luggage easy. You want me on your road trips. I'm a boon." Emily listed to one side and bumped into the wall of the sewer tunnel, having trouble staying on her feet. She caught Jane staring and sneered. "What? I got something on my face?"

"You're walking weird, Em," Jane said.

"These boots pinch."

"That's not what I meant," she said.

"You feeling okay, Emily?" Solar asked.

"I'm feeling fine. Y'know, I tell Jane she's a mother hen, but you guys are really proving me—"

Emily was caught off mid-sentence by an uncontrollable urge to walk face first into the wall. "What the deuce!" she yelled. "I bit my lip!"

Solar rushed to the wall, moving Emily away from the spot where her face collided with the masonry.

"Just a wall," she said.

"What do you say, Emily? Do you feel like you're being pulled in that direction?" Annie said.

"Nope. I feel perfectly normal," Emily said, walking away, taking a hard ninety degree turn, and smacking face first once again. "How many times am I gonna bite my lip! I hate this wall!"

"So move it out of your way," Jane said.

Emily looked back at her and smiled.

"Like in the prison?"

"In the prison?" Solar said.

"They got arrested a few months back," Annie said.

"We got arrested in your timeline?" Solar said.

"I wouldn't exactly say it was arrested," Jane said. "More like involuntary incarceration."

"So arrested," Solar said.

"Totes arrested," Emily said. "I got a bunch of ugly tattoos and did pushups in my cell."

"We had a couch and a TV in our cell," Jane said.

"But it wasn't high-def," Emily said. "Practically hard time."

"Move the wall, Emily," Jane said.

"You're not the boss of me," Emily said. "I don't know why I have to keep reiterating this to everyone." Nevertheless, Emily held up her hands, forming a bubble of float and enveloping the wall in front of her.

"Gentle, Emily," Jane said.

"You think I'm not going to be gentle moving a wall that might be holding the ceiling up above us?"

"I seem to recall you inventing a variation of the bubble of float called a wall of slam," Jane said.

"Y'know, you incorrectly use something called a wall of slam one time and nobody forgives you for it," Emily said.

"Because the wall of slam directly led to our incarceration, if you remember," she said.

"Whatever. I'm moving this wall out of the way," she said.

"With your mouth?" Annie said.

"*Et tu, Brute?*" Emily said.

"Oh don't try to make me feel bad by quoting Shakespeare," Annie said. "I've met him."

Emily stopped everything and just stared at Annie, slack-jawed.

"Shut. Up." Emily said.

Annie pointed at herself. "Time traveler. Remember?"

"If we survive this, can we make a list of people I'm allowed to meet?" Emily said.

"That's a terrible idea," Jane said.

"You get us through this, Emily, and I'll help you at least see, in person, one historical figure of your choice."

"This is amazing," Emily said. "I am so meeting Simone de Beauvoir."

"I. Wait. What?" Solar said.

Jane just shrugged.

"I can't say I saw that coming, but I don't usually see anything Em says coming anymore," Jane said.

Emily once again prepared herself to move the wall, arms outstretched, crafting a very specifically sized bubble of float.

"Maybe we'll get lucky and Jean-Paul Sartre will be there too," Emily said. "Two for one."

She pulled at the empty air with her hands. The wall moved, sliding and buckling in a perfect sphere. Emily clenched her fists and dragged again, and a section of wall broke free and collapsed, leaving the area around it intact.

"I'm holding you to that," Emily said.

Annie threw her hands up. "A promise is a promise," she said.

"Everyone," Solar said, her voice now tense.

Jane followed her gaze through the makeshift tunnel that Emily just created and spied what her future self was staring at.

"Oh no," she said. "This is so much worse than we imagined."

CHAPTER 49:
A CROWDED SKY

Billy skimmed in next to one of the giant robots, so close he could smell the vapors of mechanical heat escaping from it, like a car that had been running in the hot sun too long. The monstrosity stepped back, faster than seemed possible, yet couldn't pivot quickly enough to take a swing at him.

Billy fired a blast of white energy at the robot's armpit simply to antagonize him.

You are enjoying this too much, Dude said.

I was dispatched here to be a human target, Billy thought. Everybody wants to hurt me when I'm having too much fun.

I will not argue with that, Dude said. *But do not be reckless.*

Billy dodged a gravity-gun blast easily, twisting in the air and swinging back around for a strafing run. He fired a string of bolts from his hands into the robot's face.

And try to remember, because we have discussed this more times than I can count, robots do not have brains, Dude said. *Hitting them in the head is not the same as doing so to a living creature. Their motor functions are usually controlled in the chest.*

I'm shooting a robot in the face with light-beams, and you're asking me to be logical about this? Billy thought. Cut me some slack, Dude.

He risked a glance over at Jessie, who played a similar cat and mouse game with the other robot.

She caught his look and tilted her chin at him. "Change

partners?" she said into her earpiece.

"Why not?" Billy said.

They crossed paths mid-air so fast they almost broke the sound barrier, the atmosphere around them ripping at the molecular level.

Jessie's robot, bulkier than the one Billy had been taunting, wore heavier armor plating, but responded in slower movements. It acted more aggressively, though, as if possessing a shorter temper when dealing with irritants like flying humans, and swatted at Billy with greater frequency and more accuracy.

There's some fight in this one, Billy thought.

It is a robot, Dude said. *They only have as much fight in them as they are programmed to have.*

Tell that to Optimus Prime, Billy said.

Ordinarily the pop references you and Emily throw around are lost on me, but that one I know, Dude said.

Well, he is a classic, Billy thought.

He caught a flash of movement out of the corner of his eye and saw Jessie land on the robot's shoulder and throw a barrage of blasts at the mechanical creature's ear, causing its huge metal arms to flail helplessly, like a grown man trying to swat a bee.

Billy glanced around at the barren landscape of the fallen city, looking at crumbling and forgotten buildings. He got an idea.

"Hey Jessie?"

"What, flyboy?"

"This whole area has been evacuated, right?" Billy asked.

What are you thinking about? Dude said.

Hush, Billy thought. You can read my mind. Figure it out.

"There hasn't been anyone living here in a long time," Jessie said. "Most people got out of the City years ago."

"Good. I've got an idea," Billy said. "Cover me."

"I don't 'cover' you," Jessie said. "Unless you're planning on doing something awesome?"

"Everything I do is awesome," Billy said.

"Fine," Jessie said.

He flew straight up, blasting off like a rocket, turning in a wide arc above both robots as the pair of machines reached out for him clumsily. Swinging back around at full speed, he came roaring back, low to the ground, almost skimming the crumbling pavement.

"You're about to do something really stupid, aren't you?" Jessie said.

"No," Billy said.

Yes, Dude said.

When he came within range, Billy fired with both hands, pouring on a damaging explosion of white light into the back of the leaner robot's knee. Pistons and gyros broke loose, metal split and cracked, and the great lumbering machine began to topple.

"Fall down go boom!" Jessie yelled, laughing.

The robot, its body language almost human in its confusion, fell backward. Arms spinning comically, descent out of control, it collapsed into the broken frame of an old skyscraper. Concrete chunks and metal support materials fell, pounding and cracking its carapace.

"I love my job," Billy said.

Jessie laughed into her headset. "I honestly can't tell if you doing that means you're amazing or a complete and utter jerk for enjoying it so much," she said.

"Can't I be both?"

I would lean toward the latter, Dude said.

"I think you can be both," Jessie said. "What do you want to do about the last one?"

Billy turned his attention to the more heavyset robot, which had begun a lumbering approach toward them.

"Who controls these things, anyway? They don't have pilots," Billy said. "Emily would be so disappointed they don't have pilots. She's always wanted a Gundam of her own."

"We think they have remote pilots somewhere," Jessie said. "Never found them. Just as well, means we can destroy these things without feeling bad."

The heavy robot's shoulder opened and a sizeable cannon projected out and locked in, perched beside its head. Something looked vaguely familiar about the design.

"Head's up, big gun's out now," Billy said. "We should be able to just—"

Then the weapon fired, and Billy knew exactly where he'd seen it before. Red-yellow light tore across the sky, the air humming with alien energy. The last time he saw a weapon that used that kind of ammunition, it tore Dude entirely from his body.

"Look out!" Billy said. "Don't let it hit you!"

He dodged another blast of red-yellow energy, passing so close it twisted his stomach into knots. He could still feel the tearing sensation that he experienced when Dude's powers had been yanked from his very cells.

"I got this. Our shields can take a hit from something that big, don't worry about it," Jessie said.

She hasn't seen one of these weapons before, Billy thought.

We need to destroy it, now, Dude said.

On it, Billy thought.

"Jessie, these aren't ordinary lasers, don't let it touch you!"

"I said I've got this!" she said.

Billy rocketed toward Jessie, trying to reach her in time, but as fast as he was, she buzzed through the sky like a jet fighter, moving too quickly to catch.

One of the red-yellow blasts smashed into her. Billy saw her body in silhouette, black on gold, and then watched as the white-blue essence of her alien powers fell away like an inverted shadow, a glimmer of light.

"Jane! We need backup! Jessie's down, they've got null guns. Jessie's been hit!" Billy screamed into his earpiece, hoping Jane or Solar could hear him. He watched Jessie's limp body fall from the sky. Not dying on my watch, Billy vowed, dodging another red-yellow burst of light and turning up the speed. Need a little help here Dude, he thought, and there it was, an influx of speed, power surging through him when he raced to catch Jessie as she fell.

He grabbed hold of both of her wrists and arced back up into the sky. Got you, he thought, I got you, as he sensed another blast sizzle past his skin. Not again, Billy thought, not again not again not again...

He saw the white light, that had just seconds before been

powering Jessie's flight, flying in a circular pattern a few hundred feet above them.

"What's he doing, Dude?" Billy said out loud.

I believe I am looking for a new temporary host, Dude said. *I don't know why I have not traveled to one of the others until Jessie's cells are able to reabsorb the powers.*

I'm sure either Kate is available, Billy thought, looking for a safe place to put Jessie down.

She stirred in his grasp, then looked up. "What the hell just happened to me?" Jessie said. Her eyes opened wide. "Where is he? Where's my partner? Straylight? Talk to me! Where are you!"

"It'll be okay. You're temporarily—whoa," Billy said, rocking unsteadily as he dodged another blast from the robot's shoulder-mounted cannon. "I gotta put you down. He'll come back, that gun just separates you for a bit."

"Why do you know this?" Jessie yelled. Her voice cracked.

Billy felt awful for her, knowing how strange, how alien, how lonely it was to be alone in your own head after all that time. He found a sturdy building and put Jessie down gently. Her feet gave out, so Billy helped her sit then prepared to fly.

"Don't leave me here," Jessie said. "I—I feel sick."

"It'll pass," Billy said. "Don't—don't panic, I'll be back."

He could hear the robot's rumbling footsteps headed their way.

"I can't stay here, I have to lead him away from you," Billy said. "I'll be back."

"You don't need to—" Jessie said, but Billy was airborne again, doing his best as the ammo from the null gun approached faster and closer.

It's like he's becoming a better marksman, Billy thought.

Robots can learn, Dude said.

Billy chanced another look at the sky where Dude's future self had been hovering. The alien was gone.

"Looks like you went to find another victim," Billy said, and then, out of nowhere, he felt something slam into his body like a kick to the heart. I'm hit, he thought, I'm going to fall, I'm going to die...

Then the power crashed over him like a tidal wave. More

strength than he'd ever possessed, his skin electric with it, every sense hitting him with painful clarity. I can see molecules moving, Billy thought. What happened?

My future self chose the best host it could find, Dude said. *We are no longer alone.*

Soon the memories hit him, and the entire world stopped making sense.

CHAPTER 50:
PHOTO ALBUM
AT THE END OF THE WORLD

In a world full of destruction, the den of the White Shadow felt like a hallowed museum. Family portraits hung on the wall—not just of one family, but many. A shrine preserved, honoring what had been lost, a gallery of strangers guarding darkened hallways, a photo album marking the end of the world.

Titus led the way, both old and young, in full-fledged werewolf forms, a pair of tracking hounds on a hunt. Kate had stopped the older one earlier, as he walked inside, her future self long gone.

"She didn't want to be followed," she'd told the scarred werewolf.

Whispering paused to look at the balcony where Kate's future self had stood moments before and then turned to leave. He gazed at the now empty terrace with a silent, heartbreaking longing.

"She'll do what she will. She always has," Whispering said, and he spoke no more of it.

That definitive reaction, Whispering's silent resignation, haunted younger-Kate as they searched inside the Shadow's lair. At first it appeared undignified and pathetic, a lapdog anxiously waiting for its human to come home when everyone but the dog realized that would never happen. But there were those human eyes, the human eyes she knew and cared about, waiting for an answer that would never arrive from a person Kate herself hoped she'd never become.

In this timeline, Titus becomes a hero and I become a ghost, she thought. What an awful thing to be. Both futures tragic and replete with pain.

Titus, her Titus, pulled her aside within the house of mystery.

"Where did she go?" he asked.

"I don't know," Kate said, avoiding eye contact. Sometimes I swear all I do is avoid looking him in the eye, she thought. I don't know how we're even able to carry on a conversation.

"Where do you think she went?" Titus asked. He leaned forward, in human form now, and Kate found herself thrown off by how delicate his features were, the alien contrast between his elfish human face and the monstrous maw of the werewolf.

"How should I know?" Kate asked, growing impatient.

Titus watched his future self prowl ahead, pushing open a darkened doorway with the blunt end of his spear.

"Because you are her and she is you," Titus said. "They're not us, and yet they are. Where would you go?"

"I'd go to find revenge, or I'd go to die," Kate said.

Titus frowned.

"You wanted the truth. She's looking for redemption, and you can only find redemption two ways."

"There are other ways," Titus said.

Always with the optimism, Kate thought. How is it that we're friends? We're friends because he loves you, she thought to herself. And he comes as close as you've ever gotten to caring deeply about anything in this world. Even in this terrible place, he enkindles hope enough for both of us. The monster hopes, the dancer despairs.

Doc Silence joined them, leaning against a wall painted in burgundy. He took out a tissue and rubbed the smudges from his red-tinted glasses.

"You know who the White Shadow really is, don't you?" Kate said. "You realize who we're up against."

"I don't know for sure," Doc said. Whispering drew closer to listen as well, though Kate knew he could hear every word from two rooms away if he wanted to. "I have an idea."

"Can't you just cast a spell and find out?" Titus asked. "Wave your hands around, say some gobbledygook and have a name appear in fire on the ground in front of you?"

"What kinds of movies have you been watching?" Doc said.

"Accurate ones," Titus said.

Doc smiled one of his sad smiles, the ones that never reach his eyes. "I could find out through magic, yes," he said. "But some things are better to discover for yourself. In person. Through words."

"The Shadow doesn't deserve any words from me," Kate said.

"I don't think the White Shadow's going to be much for talking," Doc said. "But still. If it's who I think it is behind that mask, I've got to at least try."

"Why?" Kate said.

"Why?" Doc responded, raising an eyebrow.

"What's the point talking to this person?" Kate said. "Look at what they did. The destruction. Check out what happened to us. To you. To me."

"He wants to understand what happened," Titus said softly.

Whispering nodded silently, approvingly.

"So he can change things."

Doc ran a hand roughly over his head. "We're not supposed to use what we learn here to change anything," he said.

"But we have no choice," Kate said, a strange, unexpected weight growing in her belly. "We can go back and do nothing, but we'll still be different. Everything that happens tomorrow will be different all because we came here."

Doc didn't answer.

"You knew this would happen, didn't you?" Kate said.

"It's okay," Titus said.

Kate glared at him.

"No. It's okay. It really is. Because everything is just what happens. It's why we can't change the past, Kate. Because there's no past. There are just things that happen, and the infinite ways they can be different."

"Butterflies and 'I love yous,'" Doc said, mostly to himself.

Kate leaned in closer. "What?"

"The tiniest things change the world, every day. And the universe is made up of infinite possibilities. We were different the moment we left," Doc said. "In another timeline, Annie never comes home. In another timeline we turn her down. Somewhere, Jane never rescues me from the other planes and Annie can't find her way back. In another place, I don't have an argument in a subway tunnel and everything changes."

"So why do this?" Kate said.

"Because we're agents of change, and we need to do the best we can," Doc said. He brushed his hands off on his long black coat, looking a thousand years old and a million miles away.

Kate removed her gaze from the tired wizard, too young to seem so old, to the scarred and faceless creature who, in this timeline, her best friend would become. She turned to Titus, but he was lost in his own world, eyes distant, pondering thoughts she was afraid to ask about. She listened to the sound of footsteps coming from deeper in this house of mystery. Kate thought of home.

"Then let's do the best we can," she said, walking past Whispering and down the hall on a mission to change a future.

CHAPTER 51:
THE ENTROPY SPHERE

The lab spread out before them like a bird's nest, a room bound by cords and wires, its high ceilings lit from lanterns far out of sight. Jane and Solar entered first, past and future side-by-side; the metallic smell of electronics stung their noses.

The room, a technophobe's nightmare, was walled by screens. Half-finished and abandoned experimental projects lay careless on tables, their guts exposed to the open air. Rows of computers stood ready but unoccupied, lines of numbers flowed and flickered across their screens in the darkness.

The room hummed with power. The air was just a little too cool, like an air conditioner still buzzing on a cold summer night. Coiled cables pulsed like forgotten creatures at the bottom of the sea.

And in the center of the room, a sphere glowed blue, lit from the inside.

"This place looks like the movie sets of *Star Trek* and *Rent* mated and had a baby," Emily said, sidling up to Jane's side.

"This is it?" Jane asked. "This is where all of this trouble originated?"

Annie entered last, her strange, clockwork laser gun in one hand.

"It looks like the inside of a bomb," she said. "How do you feel, Em?"

Emily rocked on her feet and waved her hands around dismissively.

"I'm fine," she said, but Jane could see a glassiness in her eyes.

240

She wasn't quite right.

"There's our generator," Solar said, pointing at the sphere. "Are we going to put it out of business?"

"Wait," Emily said, walking ahead.

The others followed a few paces behind as Emily approached the glowing cage.

Everything about this room seemed wrong to Jane. It felt dangerous, and chaotic, on the edge of being out of control. Annie was right. It was like being inside the guts of a bomb, and this bomb could explode at any time.

Emily stopped in front of the sphere and put her right hand against the glass. Someone else put her left palm up against the surface from the other side, matching Emily's fingers.

"No," Jane said.

"This can't be," Solar said.

A dark reflection of herself stood face-to-face with Emily. This older Emily was frail, an IV piercing her right arm, her skin shining sallow and papery. She didn't have Emily's trademark neon hair. Instead the tresses that fell down her weary face sported a bland, darker shade.

"No... way," Emily said.

"Hello, me," the girl in the bubble said. "Look at me. So pretty and I never knew. We never know, do we, what we have? Not until it's gone."

"You're me," Emily said. "But you're not."

"I always thought I was smarter," the wasted woman said.

"No," Emily said. "There's something different about you. Different from me."

"I think the words you're looking for are hair and dye, darling," the woman in the bubble said.

"Shush," Emily answered back. "What's the matter with you? You're wrong. All wrong. I can feel it."

"Can't you though?" future-Emily said. "Can you feel the chain reactions? Can you feel a universe collapsing in my sorrows?"

Emily leaned in closer.

"What did they do to you?" she asked.

"There is no perfect machine," the girl in the bubble said. "Everything breaks. Even me."

"They broke something in you, didn't they?" Emily said. "I can sense it. I can tell."

Future-Emily lifted one narrow hand and touched her fingertips to her chest.

"They broke my heart," she said. There were blue veins of sadness in her voice as she spoke. She sounded half-mad, like someone who'd never seen the light of day, the sun. "Isn't that funny? I never thought it would hurt this much. They broke it, and it's bleeding. It's bleeding stars."

"You're going radioactive," Emily said. "You're gonna come apart at the seams. Did they do this on purpose? Why?"

"They didn't know," future-Emily said. "Nobody knew. They thought they had in me the cure for everything. I was the future, kiddo. You will be too."

"No," Emily said. "No, we're going to put you back together again."

Emily stepped back, grabbed Jane by the shoulder, and spun her around.

"They did something to me," she said in a harsh whisper. "To her. The black hole where her heart should be. The singularity. It's dying."

"You're going to have to be more specific for me, Em," Jane said. "What does that mean? What can we do?"

"It means she's either going to collapse or explode. I don't know," Emily said. "Jane, I barely understand my own powers and they went and put her engine back together again all wrong. I'm blind here."

"We all are," a new voice said, stepping out from the shadows. "It's just one life, they told me. What's one life when you can change the world."

The newcomer was a man in a lab coat, his face lined with worry more than age, thin hair turning gray. He stopped by the sphere, and put his hand against the glass palm-first.

"I loved you like a daughter, you know," the man said.

The woman in the cage laughed. "You haven't loved me for a very long time, Doctor Bohr," she said. "Maybe years ago, before I became your very own personal tinker toy. Now you just look at me with pity, like a child longs for a broken plaything."

"You treated her like a tool," Solar said, voice rising in anger.

"Fathers and daughters play catch and have tea parties," Emily said. "They don't turn each other into doomsday weapons."

"You'd be surprised," the man said. "History is littered with abused children."

"Who are you?" Solar said. "What do you want?"

"I wanted to change the world. Make it a better place. Same as you," he said.

"At the cost of the life and freedom of one little girl?" Annie said.

"Hedonistic calculus," Emily said.

Jane looked at her, shaking her head.

"You thought what? Enforce peace by utilizing my powers and you could rule the world?"

"We miscalculated," the man said. "On everything. We—"

Emily lashed out, flinging a hand up in the man's direction.

He went spinning into the air, then smashed against a wall full of computer consoles.

"Bored with you now," Emily said. "Other things to do."

Returning to the woman inside the glass cage, she asked, "How do we get you out of there?"

"Little bird, apparently you're not listening to me," her future self said. "This cage is all that's holding me together anymore. And even with that, I don't have much time left."

Future-Emily paused and tilted her head, pressing up against the glass again.

"What do you suppose really happens when a singularity dies?" she said. "I don't know that we've ever really witnessed it. Maybe it will be as if nothing happened. We'll just become an empty spot in the night sky."

"Okay, so future me is a beat poet. That's okay," Emily said. "I can live with this."

"Em," Jane said. "Maybe she's right. If she's as smart as you are, she understands those machines. She knows what'll happen."

"I'm not giving up," Emily said.

"I'm not asking you to give up. I'm asking you to think straight," Jane said. "Talk with her. Maybe she knows a way."

"I'm not quitting on her," Emily said, steamrolling over Jane's voice. "Because this is what I do. I save the day, Jane. I'm going to save the day."

"Get that scientist," Jane said. "Maybe we can force him to help. He seemed to be aware about what was going to happen."

"He's gone," Annie said, rejoining the conversation. "I appreciate the sentiment of knocking him across the room, but . . ."

"Of course he's not here," Solar said. "That would be too easy. What if we break the machine? Isn't that what we came here to do?"

"No," Emily said, running over to a bank of computers and scanning for some clue on the screens.

"I thought we were going to destroy the cage and that would fix everything," Jane said.

"That was before they damaged her ability to regulate her own powers," Emily said. She slammed an undersized fist down on the table. "We let her out of there, she loses the only thing that stops her from bubble of floating us into the sun or . . ."

"Going boom," future-Emily said. "Maybe we should let me do it. Let me explode. Let's find out what happens. It'll be an experiment."

"No. I . . ." Emily swayed and fell to one knee.

Annie reached Emily first, helping her to stand.

"I need to contain her."

"How?" Annie said.

"With my big brain," Emily said. "Keep looking for something that will help her regulate her powers. I've got to help."

Emily left Annie at the computer hub and held out both hands toward her future self.

Jane felt the room swim and sway as Emily's energy washed over all of them, everything taking a turn for the weird. The cage suddenly became a sphere within a sphere as Emily's bubble of float enveloped it, a faint glimmering hue holding things in place.

"I've got you," Emily said through gritted teeth.

"Not forever, little bird," her future self said.

Emily's hands began to shake.

Jane looked on in awe—it was the first time she'd ever seen Emily show signs of limitation to her powers. Lack of control, certainly, but overpowered? Not once, not ever.

"She's right. I can't do this forever," Emily said.

"Of course I'm right," her future self said. "I'm you, after all. I know exactly what you're capable of."

"Do you want to die, is that it?" Emily yelled. "Is that the finale you're pushing us toward?"

Emily's future self gestured around the inside of her sphere, as if graciously showing them the limitations of her world. "If this was all you knew, wouldn't you?" she said. "But that's not it, not all of it anyway. It really isn't. You know everything I do, you understand how this must end."

"Annie?" Jane yelled.

The time traveler looked baffled and worried, a sheen of sweat beading across her face.

"I don't. I don't," she said. "I'm thinking."

And then things got worse.

"Jane! We need backup! They have null guns! Jessie's been hit!" Billy's voice crackled through their earbuds.

Solar looked to Jane.

"Null guns?" she asked.

"The one weapon Billy can't stop," Jane said, an acidic pit burning in her stomach. "If Jessie's already been hit . . ."

"Go," Emily said.

"Em," Jane said.

"Hurry," Emily said. She beamed a huge, mad smile at Jane, gritting her teeth. "We'll figure this one out. Go save our friend."

"I can't leave you here," Jane said.

"Yes you can. Don't leave him out there by himself. We'll be fine," Emily said. A drop of sweat hung from one eyelash, her whole body shook as she tried to maintain control.

Jane nodded gently, and bent down on one knee. She felt her strength build, felt the earth come loose beneath her. And then she exploded upward, through the ceiling, breaking through into the sky as the sun's rays soaked her skin, recharging. Someone would live through the day, she thought. She just didn't know who would be the one to survive.

CHAPTER 52:
DO NOT GO SOFTLY

"Can't you turn their guns into kites or something?" Kate asked Doc as they hunkered down behind a heavy wooden table. Titus and Whispering had ducked out of sight as well when they found another pocket of resistance, a wild-eyed and manic gang of fighters armed with a variety of firearms and one very powerful, and very loud, gravity gun mounted on a tripod.

The bullets were problematic but could be handled; the gravity gun posed a greater challenge. Titus tried charging it and was left with a rapidly mending broken arm for his efforts. Kate focused on Titus as he hid around a corner in werewolf form, his golden eyes appeared almost comically pathetic as his left arm knit itself back together again.

"Kites?" Doc said.

Kate waved her arms around dramatically.

"Magic. Use magic. Make the bad stuff go away," Kate said.

Doc laughed.

He's laughing at me, Kate thought. Nobody laughs at me. Does he think I'm joking?

"You say that like turning complicated weapons into sticks and paper is easy," Doc said. "If—"

A bullet clipped off the table, peppering them both with broken wood.

"If it were that easy," Doc continued, looking at the bullet hole with annoyance, "I would have delivered peace to the world by now."

The air rumbled, and the gravity gun fired again, knocking out part of the wall Whispering was hiding behind. The scarred wolf emerged from the rubble unhurt. He looked at Kate, then at Doc. He held up the spear he always carried and nodded toward the gravity gun.

"Keep your head down," Doc said, before standing up.

Doc waved his hand in a horizontal arc. A bow of light formed in its wake. Darts of white launched from his fingertips, scattering the enemy fighters as they ducked for cover. Doc dropped back down before anyone could fire a shot, and when he did, Whispering's spear whistled overhead like a crossbow bolt, flying with horrifying precision. Kate stole a look to watch the spear strike the gravity gun, splitting it down the middle. Sparking, popping, and sizzling, the weapon's guts fried.

Titus ventured out next, charging into the still-distracted group of fighters. He knocked the first few senseless with a huge, closed fist. Someone managed to discharge a round with a short, stubby machine gun, and Titus roared in pain before pouncing on the man and dragging him to the ground.

Kate leapt to her feet, taking out several guards from behind as they became distracted by the bleeding and furious werewolf in their midst. Elbows, knees, pressure points, nerve packets. Whispering moved in to chase two runners. Kate watched to see if he'd use lethal force or not, but he brought both men down without drawing blood, at least until their faces scraped along the floor.

Titus reverted to his human form, checking the sealed, pink marks where the bullets struck him. The wounds faded in front of Kate's eyes.

"Who are these idiots?" Titus said.

"No matter the cause, there will always be zealots who rally to it," Whispering said in his low rumble.

"How many more could there possibly be?" Titus said. "Why aren't they outside watching superheroes fight robots? What are they doing in here?"

"Waiting for us," Kate said.

"If the White Shadow isn't aware that some of us have arrived already, then we've really overestimated our enemy," Doc said. "And I don't think we have. So the question remains, will the Shadow stay or bolt?"

Solar's voice crackled through their earpieces.

Kate pressed two fingers against her ear to listen.

"Doc Silence? We need you here," Solar said.

"What's wrong?" he said.

"The situation isn't what we expected. We're having trouble containing things. Hoping magic might help slow events down before they get worse."

"Who's there with you right now," Doc said. "Is everyone okay?"

"Jane went to help Billy and Jessie," Solar said. "Emily and Annie are still with me."

"I'll use Annie as a lock to find my way there. Stay put."

"We aren't going anywhere," Solar said. "Hurry."

Doc looked at Kate.

"You okay with this?" he asked.

"I'm always okay," she said.

Doc took something from his pocket, an old penny, cupped it in his hand and blew on it. He leaned in and whispered something to the coin, as if requesting something personal. He turned it over to Kate.

"Don't lose this. You need me, call me. That'll bring me back here," Doc said.

"We won't need you," Kate said.

"Then use it to get me back when you find the Shadow," Doc said.

"We can handle the White Shadow," Kate said.

"I know. But I need to be there. Promise me."

Kate wrinkled her nose, but acquiesced. "Okay. I'll send for you."

"Good," Doc said.

Kate heard him speak a few words in a language not of this earth, and a doorway of pale blue light opened up.

"Be safe." Then, he stepped into the light and disappeared.

One of the enemy fighters started to regain consciousness, and Kate belligerently kicked him in the head. "Stay down."

"Pretty sure he wasn't getting back up, Kate," Titus said.

Whispering licked his fangs absently like a predator after devouring a big meal. Then his head whipped around, ears pointed straight up.

"What?" Kate said.

"You," Whispering said.

"I can hear her too. Future you is fighting someone nearby," Titus said, beginning to transform back into his werewolf shape. "We need to keep going."

Titus completed his transformation and charged onward, racing on the heels of Whispering. Resigned and frustrated, Kate picked up the pace and ran after them. Though she was getting used to watching the Titus she knew and the man and monster Titus would become, running side by side, it made her uncomfortable. It felt too real.

I really just want to go home, she thought.

CHAPTER 53:
A LIFE UNLIVED

Billy Case soared over the City, his city, his home, a metropolis in watercolors, the late day sun cast hot shards of orange light everywhere he looked. The Tower, still whole, was not the floating starship he remembered drifting unmoored above an urban landscape but remained an integral part of it, a real tower, a shining building in the center of town.

The roar of destruction was all he heard.

He watched, unable to move, as a wave of devastation washed over the City, windows exploded outward, skyscrapers toppled, gas mains exploded beneath concrete roadways. The City fell, and then, as the tsunami splashed Billy, he tumbled as well.

* * *

The wreckage of his family hardware store. Empty, forgotten. Roof torn away. Tools to build lay scattered on the linoleum floor. Who would use them now? There was nothing left to rebuild here. The City had fallen. Others had as well, Chicago, Paris, Tokyo.

A burning raged in his stomach, the pain of loss. Something tugged at the back of his mind, something he wished he'd done, something he wanted to say. Goodbye. Who did he not have a chance to say goodbye to? Am I crying? I feel like I'm crying, he thought, but there are no tears.

A hand placed in his. Warm, like the sun. Thin strong fingers.

Her head on his shoulder. Love. In this life, there was love, and there was loss.

* * *

Everything hurts. Why does everything hurt? He looked around. This was no place on earth, not the earth he knew. Carnage. The black ocean rushing in to fill a vacuum that shouldn't exist. Buildings mixed in with earth and stone like toys tossed in a sandbox. Everything washed away. Remnants of sandcastles after the approach of a rising tide.

His entire body burning. From the inside. His life fading away. His companion leaving. Don't leave me here alone, he thought. I can't stand to be alone.

Solar looking at him. Or was it Jane? One in the same. Her hair glowing brightly like a newly struck match in the wind. The sky above looming like something from a nightmare, black clouds and lightning. The end of the world.

No, not the end of the world, Billy Case thought. Just the end of me.

I hope I did enough with my time here. There was never going to be enough time to do everything. Hope I did enough.

* * *

Holiday dinner on a farm. A burly old man. A kindly old woman. Central casting, Titus called them. Of course they've got a farm.

Dinner with friends. Kate pouting on the porch. Jane speaking with her. Jane glows at night. How did I never know she glows at night? Just a little bit. A firefly. A source of energy, a gleam of hope.

Titus with his hand on Billy's shoulder. My friend. Older. We're all older. Titus sporting a few more scars. His hair turning gray. Not gray, silver, yeah silver, like the moon. This is who we become. The four of us. Why only four? Everything's different here. But it's home, and it feels like home, and I'm safe. Snowing outside. Kate far away, Kate always far away, distant, and there's Jane and the snow melts and falls away from her. I wonder if she knows what it feels like to have snowflakes in her hair. How do you describe that? How can you tell someone how it feels to be caressed by mother nature with the first few cold flurries at the onset of a snowstorm?

Christmas dinner is ready. Jane singing a song no one knows.

* * *

I'm cold. So very cold. Not snow now, ashes, things burning. Buildings. People. He hears Titus' voice in his ear. California is gone. How can an entire state be gone? How does that happen?

Something in his heart. Pride. Not proud of himself. Dude is proud of him. His Jiminy Cricket. *You did well,* the voice says. *You were brave. You did everything asked of you in this life.*

You were a hero.

I'm sorry I have to leave, but this life won't let me stay. I'm sorry, my friend. I'll miss you most of all.

And then he's alone in his head, alone in his heart, and all the pain in the world comes flooding back into him, his last moments, last thoughts. This is where I end. But it's okay. Everything I did in my life pointed to this moment. I was never going to run my father's store. Never going to have an ordinary life. Better to have an extraordinary finish.

Solar's hand in his again. Warm. Always so warm. The light of the sun. She's singing again. I know this song, Billy thought. It's the song she sings when she's saying goodbye.

But since it falls unto my lot, that I should rise and you should not...

This isn't my life, Billy Case thought. It's someone else's. Someone else's death. Not mine. It doesn't belong to me.

"You need to come back to us now," Jane said. She sounded close, and young. "Come back, Billy. You're needed here."

* * *

Billy woke up amid chaos, the world a cacophony of explosions and massive footsteps. Jane flew past him, a streak of flames, holding what looked like an entire streetlight in her hands. She used it like a baseball bat to take a swing at the head of a giant robot that had not been there when he was last conscious.

"Wake up, glow bug, I need you," Jane said.

"It's a robot, the brain is in the chest," Billy said, trying to get his bearings.

Three robots surrounded them, two of which Billy did not remember arriving. All three were damaged as Jane ping-ponged between them, throwing haymakers and using debris as makeshift weapons. He searched for and found the robot with the null-gun mounted on its shoulder.

"It's more cathartic to hit it in the head though," Jane said. "And I really need to hit something in the head."

"How long was I out?" Billy said.

"I don't know—you looked like a ball of light when I got here," Jane said. She'd shifted to using a small car as a blunt weapon. "Are you okay?"

The memories he'd seen—his memories?—gnawed at his stomach.

"I'm fine," Billy said.

"You're glowing," Jane said. "Worse than before. You look like a light bulb."

"Dude? Am I going to blow up?" Billy said, taking evasive action to get out of the way of a giant robot fist. Lights along the side of the null gun indicated it was powering up.

Our power levels have doubled, Dude said. *I am trying to keep control of it. Making you look normal is not high on the priority lists for making sure we do not hurt ourselves.*

"Hurt ourselves?" Billy said.

Let me worry about our safety, Dude said.

And what should I be doing, Billy thought.

I think you should enjoy being twice as powerful as you've ever been and tear these monstrosities apart, Dude said. *I have had quite enough of them.*

Me too, Billy thought.

"Coming in hot, Jane, look out," Billy said.

"You sure that's a good idea?" she said.

Billy got a running start, circling around a city block at incredible speed to generate power. He aimed at the robot with the null gun, which had lost sight of Billy and now had its back facing him.

Will our shields hold? Billy thought.

Absolutely, Dude said.

"Like an arrow through the heart," Billy said.

A fist through newspaper, he tore into the robot's metal armor, striking the mechanical creature with a sonic boom. The robot's chest exploded, its innards spraying out the other side like the guts of a shattered clock. The null gun fired, straight up into the sky, disappearing into the darkness harmlessly, a firework failing to explode.

"Where did these other two come from?" Billy said.

"I don't know," Jane said. "They were here when I arrived. Billy, we gotta finish these off quickly. Emily's in trouble."

A robot tried to catch Jane in its fist. She matched the grab with one of her own, tearing a finger off at the root and stabbing the mech through the palm with it.

"Heads-up," Billy said.

"I don't question glowing alien wrecking balls," Jane said, flying up above the robot and out of reach.

Billy aimed both hands at the mech's chest and tried to fire a controlled burst of energy. He got more than he bargained for, hitting it with a blinding stream of blue-white light. The blast obliterated the robot's upper body, sending its remains tumbling to the ground.

"What was that!" Jane said.

"I'm really hoping it's temporary, because I can see this going so wrong all the time," Billy said.

"Take the last one together?" Jane said.

"Please," Billy answered.

They arced away, creating mirroring elliptical flight patterns. Billy and Jane flew at the robot with their fists poised, her red-gold energy signature beside his blue-white streak. They collided with the robot, throwing simultaneous punches, crushing the machine's armored shell and all but splitting it down the middle.

Billy felt himself begin to shake, like coming down from an adrenaline high. He sensed the power beginning to regulate, starting to feel more normal, but the high was soon replaced by nausea, his head spinning.

"Billy, where's Jessie?" Jane asked.

He pointed down to the rooftop where he'd left her.

"Is she hurt?" Jane said.

"No, she got nulled," Billy said.

"I have to get back to Emily," Jane said.

"I'll come with you."

"Everything is getting weird down there," she said. "I'm afraid of explaining whatever the heck is happening in there to you right now. It's like the whole world is about to explode. Check on Jessie. Make sure she's okay. Try to fix her."

"Jane," Billy said.

She swooped in to fly beside him, waiting.

Have you ever felt the touch of snow flurries in your hair? he wanted to ask.

"Be safe," Billy said instead.

"You too," Jane said, offering him a worried smile. She flew away in a burst of flames.

"Dude?" he said.

Believe me, Billy Case, Dude said. *This is even stranger for me than it is for you.*

"That might be the least reassuring thing you've ever said," Billy sighed.

CHAPTER 54:
WE MAKE THE SAME MISTAKES

Kate recognized the sound of herself in pain. She followed it, not needing to rely on the hyper-senses of Titus and Whispering to guide her to her future self.

The trio burst into a large, open room that had once served as a foyer on the far side of the building. And there, they discovered future-Kate sightlessly fighting a slight figure in a black suit and white featureless mask. The White Shadow.

Smaller than I expected, Kate thought, surprised at the Shadow's lean frame and long, thin limbs. The White Shadow didn't move like a ninety-year-old man, though. Still a fighter, future-Kate was talented and quick, but she battled blind and injured, and the Shadow toyed with her, blocking kicks and punches delivered just a little too slowly, taking advantage of future-Kate's lack of eyesight by moving with almost supernatural silence. Kate's future self landed two good punches, solid shots to her opponent's chest, but the Shadow, almost as if aware of and because of younger-Kate, Titus, and Whispering's arrival, spun to one side, put an arm around future-Kate's neck, and held her tight, expertly holding one arm so the other could brutally push on a packet of nerves below.

Future-Kate roared in pain.

"Look at you," the Shadow said in a voice higher and softer than Kate imagined. "Look at all of you. I didn't expect this."

"Let her go," Whispering said.

"Hush now, chieftain," the Shadow said. "I want to ask a few questions of your younger friends. How does it feel to see yourself beaten?"

"She's not me," Kate said firmly.

"I suppose not. And you'll never be her," the White Shadow said. "Because you're all going to die here."

The future Dancer went limp after The Shadow squeezed her neck again. He placed her gently on the ground.

"She's not dead," Shadow said. "You know, she might have been better than me if she were whole. Or if she had more time. Some of the best fighters in history were sightless. But she let her anger get in the way."

Kate stayed in place in the doorway as Whispering and Titus cautiously moved closer along the edge of the room. The Shadow laughed—again, softer, surprisingly higher—and pulled a small knife out of the inside of a sleeve and rested it gently against future-Kate's neck.

"You werewolves are fast, but neither of you will get here before I slit her throat. I really don't care if you kill me, but I know her life is important to you," the Shadow said.

"What do you want?" younger-Kate asked.

"Me?" the White Shadow said and then paused, head tilted to one side, contemplative, curious.

Thin fingers reached up and dug in under the collar to tug on the silky mask, pulling upward. The White Shadow revealed her face. Hollow cheekbones, huge, dark eyes, a full mouth that probably had been pretty in another lifetime, when it wasn't twisted up with hate. A face that seemed so very familiar.

Who are you? Kate thought. I know who you are. I recognize that face. I've seen you before.

"I want to see all my mistakes through to the end," the White Shadow said. "And little Dancer, I've made more mistakes than you could in a thousand lifetimes of your own."

CHAPTER 55:
DOOMSDAY MACHINE

Jane returned to the lab to find it in a state of absolute destruction.

Pieces of equipment swirling around in the air, cables detached and broken free, waving and bending like weeds in the wind. She batted a computer screen aside and sent it sprawling into nothingness. She looked at Solar, who watched with helpless anticipation.

"I don't know what to do," Solar said.

Emily strained to control the entire room, and Jane saw layers of unreality, like heat emanating from steaming pavement in the summer sun, whirling all around her. Em's blue hair whipped in her face.

"Go to the future, they said!" Emily yelled, mostly to herself. "Save another timeline, they said! We're drastically under-qualified to do this!"

"You're doing fine, Emily!" Jane said.

"Don't you dare lie to me, Jane," Emily responded. "I calculate the odds of succeeding as three thousand seven hundred and twenty to one!"

"See? You're fine, you can still do math," Jane said.

"That was a *Star Wars* quote! This is why I need Billy to be here," Emily said. "He would have given the appropriate response."

She spat strands of her own hair out of her mouth.

"Never tell me the odds," Annie said from her perch along the computers. "Welcome back to the end of the world, Jane."

"Can't you slow things down? Buy us some time?" Jane said.

"I can slow time temporarily, but that just means we'll watch it all fall apart in slow motion," she said. "Me pausing time doesn't mean we'll figure out what to do in the interim."

"Come on, Evie Ethel Garland, anyone who has ever watched an episode of *Out of This World* knows how pausing time works!" Emily said.

"How are you even old enough to have seen a show that old?" Annie said. "Maybe Doc will know what do to."

"Doc does not know what to do," Doc Silence said, stepping through a portal dramatically, his long black coat flapping in the unnatural wind gathering in the lab. He made a series of gestures toward the sphere containing future-Emily, spell-light surrounding his fingertips, and then leapt back as if he'd been struck.

"Dammit!" he said.

"What happened?" Annie said.

Doc rubbed his hands, like he'd been zapped by static shock. "We need time," he said and walked quickly up to the sphere to look inside.

Jane joined him, and together they stared at the older and painfully thin version of Emily inside.

"Who brought the beatnik?" future-Emily said.

Doc stepped up to the glass cage, studying the older Emily's face.

"What the hell did they do to you?" he said, his voice heavy, pained.

"Why do you care?" future-Emily said.

"Why would they do this?" Doc said, almost to himself. "It's like discovering hope, then putting it in a bottle and locking it away."

"Why would you say that?" future-Emily said.

"What does it feel like?" Doc said, his voice soft and gentle. "Does it hurt?"

"Not at all," future-Emily said. "I feel fit to burst."

"Not like you're being yanked within yourself?" he asked.

"No," future-Emily said. "I can feel everything for miles and miles. Like I could put my arms around the world and squeeze."

"I'm in pain!" younger-Emily said. "Why is nobody asking me if I'm in pain? Because I. Am. In. A. Lot. Of. Pain."

Doc leaned in close to future-Emily his face almost touching the sphere.

"You know what's going to happen, don't you?" he said.

"Of course I do. It's my heart they broke," future-Emily said. "I know exactly what happens next."

"Then tell me what we need to do to save you," Doc said.

Future-Emily laughed. It was a bitter, hard laugh, emanating from deep in her throat, raspy from dehydration.

"I don't want you to save me," she said. "You know what this means to me? It means I'll finally be free."

"You can be free," Doc said. "I understand. I won't take that from you."

Future-Emily smiled.

For a moment, Jane thought, she looked just like her younger self, happy, healthy, whole.

"Then take me to the stars," she said. "I've always wondered if I could fly that high."

"So have I," younger-Emily said.

"Then let me find out," future-Emily said.

Doc rolled up his sleeves and began to cast a spell.

Jane put her hand on his wrist. "You can't get her off-planet, even with your magic. But I can," Jane said. "I'll take her, I'll fly her up out of the atmosphere. Maybe that'll give us a chance to survive."

"That is the stupidest plan I've ever heard," younger-Emily said.

"Yes, it is," Solar said, stepping forward. She put a hand on her younger self's shoulder. "This isn't your world to save, Jane. It's mine."

"I won't let you die," Jane said.

"Stop being silly," Solar said. "I'm you. You're me. I'll never die. I'll be right here. I'll always be right here."

"Don't do this," Jane said.

"I'll think of something else," younger-Emily said, an uncharacteristic sense of desperation in her voice. "I can think of something else. I just need more time."

Future-Emily was inches from the inside of the cage, looking out with wide eyes. She darted between younger-Jane and younger-Emily.

"I see it now," she said, smiling the tiniest of smiles and turned her eyes to Solar. "They're us."

"They are," Solar said.

"They're us, and they're friends," future-Emily said.

"We are," Jane said. "I'd do anything for you."

"Another reality. Another timeline. Another chance. Another way," future-Emily said. "The road not taken."

"It's the road taken, for us," younger-Emily said. "We took the road."

Future-Emily almost laughed, a dry, silly grin on her face. "Will you be able to return home, if you live through today?" she said.

"Oh I hope so," younger-Emily said. "I just want to go home so much."

"I think we can," Jane said.

Future-Emily smiled bigger, and for that short, glimmering moment, Jane could see her friend in that withered and sunken face. She possessed, just for a second, Emily's relentless hope.

"I'm ready to go now," future-Emily said.

"Solar," Jane said.

"Let me do this," Solar said to her. "This is my burden, Jane. My world to save. I want you to go back and look after your world. Let me do what I was born to do. This is why I'm here."

Jane nodded. She felt a hand on her shoulder, Doc's fingertips holding on tightly. She put her hand over his.

"I'm sorry," Jane said to Solar.

"Be a better me," Solar said. "I missed so many opportunities. Be the best of us, Jane."

"I'll try."

Solar placed a soft kiss on Jane's forehead, a whisper, something to remember her by. Then looked into the sphere at future-Emily, half-dead, her heart tearing the world apart.

"Are you ready to go, Emily?" Jane's future self asked.

"I am," Emily's future self said. "This was such a hard life."

"I know," Solar said.

"I hope the next one is better."

"That's all we can ask for," Solar said. She punched the sphere, shattering the bluish glass, and stepped inside. Jane watched Solar scoop up future-Emily in her arms as if she didn't weigh a thing.

"Don't look so sad," Solar said to Jane. "This was always how it was meant to end."

And so, smiling, the woman Jane would now never grow up to be leapt into the air, a stranger who should have been one of her best friends cradled in her arms, and together, they disappeared into the night sky.

And everyone waited.

CHAPTER 56:
WE ARE ALL MADE OF STARS

Seconds later, Solar and future-Emily escaped Earth's gravity. They broke free of the planet's atmosphere, a wall of energy billowing forth from Emily's broken heart keeping them safe from harm, making sure they did not burn up while they rose into space.

The air grew cold and thin. Sound gave way to silence. Existence began to feel like a memory. Earth transformed into a work of art behind them, an abstract object emblazoned with color and life floating in a contrasting sea of darkness.

Solar took them past the moon.

Emily smiled. She might have laughed, but the silence of space kept that a secret.

They headed for the sun. Solar felt its radiation wash over her, unfiltered by the Earth's atmosphere. She'd never felt so strong in her life. Never so powerful. This is where I was destined to be, she thought. Here, where the sky meets eternity.

Emily dug her fingers into Solar's arms.

They locked eyes.

And Solar sensed a different kind of energy radiating from this stranger in her arms. It felt like fear, like worry, like regret. It seemed like the end of all things.

Together, they gazed into the sun.

Emily put her head on Solar's shoulder.

And then they were gone.

* * *

Younger-Emily felt two hands grab her shoulders. Before she could yell, she was yanked away, the world turning sideways and upside down. "I'm going to throw up," she said.

"No you're not," Annie said, leaning in over her shoulder. "You're going to watch what happens next."

The world turned red. Everything tinged with blood. The walls around her crumbled, turned to dust, blowing away like desert sand.

"This is so messed up," Emily said.

She really did think she was about to be sick. She couldn't feel the ground beneath her feet. Her stomach, her inner ears, everything that helped her body figure out where it was in that very moment suddenly couldn't. Involuntarily, she reached up and grabbed hold of Annie's tattooed wrist.

"Why are you doing this to me?" Emily cried.

The world melted away. And there was nothing. Just stars, and dust, and emptiness, and silence. Emily watched the moon wander off, unmoored from its place in the sky, toppling like some forgotten toy toward the sun.

The Earth was gone.

"We didn't do it," Emily said. "Holy carp, we failed. We failed. We're done."

"No," Annie said, whispering. "You didn't fail. You saved a world, Entropy Emily. You gave a world a chance to live."

"Then what is this, a planetarium show?" Emily said. The angrier she got, the more nauseous she got. Hold it together, Emily, she thought, puking in space can't be fun...

"I told you," Annie said. "That timelines split. When something happens that changes everything. Timelines break off. They become something new."

"And this is the old one?" Emily said.

"Yes," Annie said. "This is what happened in a timeline where you did fail. This is a timeline where you never showed up at all."

"The world is gone, though," Emily said.

"It is," Annie said. "A terminal timeline. This is the end."

"But did we make the right choice?" Emily said. "Did we make the right decision?"

"Every decision is the right decision somewhere," Annie said. She rested her chin on the top Emily's head affectionately. "I'm proud of you, Entropy Emily."

"Can I tell the others about this?" Emily said.

"You can try," Annie said. "But I think there are times you have to see some things in order to believe."

"You're right," Emily said. She looked up into the heavens, the infinite stars, the unfathomable distance. "Does anything really matter in the end?"

"Everything matters, Emily," Annie said. "Everything matters, and we are all made of stars."

"You might be even weirder than I am," Emily said.

Annie laughed, a soft, sad, timeless laugh.

"I'll take that as the highest of praise," Annie said.

CHAPTER 57:
HEROES AND VILLAINS

"Have you ever pulled a string on a frayed sweater?" the White Shadow asked.

Titus, still in full-fledged werewolf form, hunkered down along the edge of the room. He watched Kate burn holes into the Shadow with her eyes. A sense of familiarity there—does she know her? Titus thought.

Meanwhile on the opposite side of the room, Whispering paced back and forth like a caged animal, dying to get to the prone body of future-Kate.

"At first, you try to just rip it out, right?" the White Shadow said. "But you don't succeed, and you pull more string out of the sweater, and you tug again, and then you try wrapping it around your fingertip to snap it, but that doesn't seem to work either. And in the end, you're left with nothing but disappointment and a ruined sweater."

"There are probably more subtle allegories," Kate said.

Why is she responding? Titus thought. Between the three of us, we've got to be able to get to her, to take her out. Why keep engaging her?

"I know," the Shadow said. "Sometimes though, those worn-out allegories are overused because they make the most sense. They're something we can all understand."

The Shadow stood up, began walking back and forth, twirling her short, sharp knife in her hand. She made a "tsk" noise at Whispering.

Titus glanced over to see Whispering readying another throw with his spear.

"I know you," the Shadow said to Whispering. "I've been watching you a long time. I realize how good you are. But let me assure you, I can pierce your friend here in the throat with a throwing knife long before you can hit me with that spear."

Whispering growled, a smattering of curse words layered underneath it.

"And I'm not afraid to die," the Shadow said. "After all, isn't that what we're all here to do? This is the problem, don't you see?"

"What is?" Kate said.

Titus thought about transforming back to his human form, but it seemed pointless. Stand and talk or be ready to kill, neither seemed sufficient to fix anything at all. He gave up, letting himself relax into his human shape. He wished, not for the first time, he'd gotten better at talking in his werewolf form. He'd been trying, but it never seemed to be the right moment, and he felt ridiculous making conversation with a mouth full of dagger-shaped teeth.

"Of course you don't see it," the Shadow said. "This is why I've done all this. Don't you understand? Look at us. We're standing at the end of the world and all you want to do is kill me. For what? To what end? We're all going to die anyway. But here we are, angry monkeys, throwing rocks at each other while the jungle burns. We're so damned sightless. So predictable."

"We're going to stop you," Kate said. "It's not just us."

"Of course it's not just you. It's never been just you. I'm sure right now you've got friends rushing to try to stop the things we've set into play. But it won't matter. We're at the end of this sweater. And it's already ruined."

Kate opened her mouth to speak, but stopped. She narrowed her eyes.

"I had the best of intentions, you know," the Shadow said. "I'm sure the others told you. When we first started, we put down all the villains. All of them. Or thought we did."

"The Children of the Elder Star," Kate said.

"Yes, them. And the Tinkerers, and the Godhead, and Masters of

Destiny, and every other stupid group of madmen who think they somehow deserve to rule the world," she said. "We went after them with a scalpel, and when a scalpel didn't work, we went after them with a hammer. And you know what happened?"

"You inherited their supervillain ability to monologue?" Titus said, shifting back to human form.

The White Shadow smiled broadly.

"We rid the world of a dozen groups of nasty people, and all that happened after that was even more showed up," the Shadow said. "Some were super-powered. Some were ordinary. Some were terrorist groups, or hate groups, or corporations who weren't violent but simply took advantage of those who couldn't defend themselves. And we went after them, as well."

"You're painting yourselves as quite the heroes," Titus said.

"We were," the White Shadow said. "I don't think your friends would disagree with me, either. Would you, Whispering?"

The scarred werewolf nodded his massive head at her. "We thought you were on our side," he said in his rumbling, toothy voice.

"We were," the Shadow said. "But then governments decided we were playing God, and took exception to what we were doing. And they tried to stop us."

"And they lost," Kate said.

"Which is where your friends came in. Trying to put us in our place. Trying to tell us what we were doing was wrong," the Shadow said.

"But you were wrong," Titus said. "You tried to enforce peace."

"Oh, I know," the Shadow said. "But that wasn't our greatest mistake. Where we truly failed was ever thinking we could make this world a better place at all."

Titus raised an eyebrow, looked at Kate.

Kate made no eye contact, standing on the balls of her feet, ready to pounce.

"You really think this world isn't worth saving?" Titus said.

"I *know* it isn't," the Shadow said. "I know because I tried, and I know because I'm not the first. I've seen good men throw their lives away trying to make this world better, little werewolf, and all they get for it is a broken heart and an early grave. We're not worth trying to save. Don't want to be saved. Can't be saved. And so here we are."

The Shadow paused, a look of serene sadness on her face.

"I failed to do what I hoped I could. I didn't think it would come to this. I never intended it," she said. "Not until I saw where we were headed. And then, I think... I think I realized it was all for the same purpose. We were meant to fail. This was destiny."

"What would your father say about that?" a new voice to the conversation said.

Doc Silence appeared beside Kate as if stepping out of thin air. For the first time, he no longer wore his red-tinted sunglasses. Instead, his eyes were open, blazing with purple-red flames, the literal fire flickering and dancing with anger.

"I know who you are, Sasha," Doc said. "I knew your father. You're not the first White Shadow. And I had planned on coming here to speak with you like a reasonable person. I wanted to save your soul, because your father was my friend, and until five minutes ago I thought you both deserved better."

He pointed a shaking finger at the Shadow and the knife in her hand turned to ash and crumbled to the floor. "But I just saw two people who did not deserve to die give their lives up to try to save this world and I want to know why you did this," Doc said, his whole body shaking with anger. "Tell me everything, Sasha, because right now all I want to do is to wipe you from the face of reality."

CHAPTER 58:
HERE WAS A MAN

Once upon a time, there was a man.

Different stories were told about him. Some were true. Some not. In one of those stories, he was a banker, an ordinary man, who saw a crime in the street and, rather than turn his back and walk away, tied his handkerchief around his face, balled his hands into fists, and stepped in to save the day.

During other instances he was a soldier, returning from the war—any war, the story changes with the passage of time, as all tales do—who came home to discover a world he didn't remember, a place he no longer fit into. And so quietly, anonymously, he continued to be a soldier, to be a force for making the world a safer place, impacting one life at a time.

In still different accounts he was a mob enforcer. A thug, a man of violence, who was asked, on one occasion too many, to be a monster, to hurt those who could not defend themselves, and he turned the tables on his masters. He donned a mask and fought the very mob that created him using violence to thwart violence.

And most often people spoke of a man in a suit, an office drone, who sitting in the park at lunch one day, watching the world pass by, witnessing all the terrible things the world inflicts upon its children, tired and disappointed, stood up, never returned to work, and made his life that of a hero.

In all of these legends, there's the silk mask, the featureless, blank slate upon which anyone could paint their own picture. He could be any race. Any tribe. Perhaps he isn't a he at all, but a woman hiding behind a suit and tie in a period when that was all she needed to hide her identity, before the world moved on.

The White Shadow was the City's first hero, and he came to represent the City's heart, the name you cried out to in the night when you were afraid, a shadowy figure in a black suit and tie who would be there when you needed him, who would save you from the cancerous maladies that gnawed away at the City from the darkness. The White Shadow was everyone. Belonged to everyone. He belonged to us. A tabula rasa, the nameless, faceless blank slate. An elusive ghost in the night. A hero.

A hero.

Are any of the stories true? Maybe. Some. An origin is there somewhere. But the genesis of the White Shadow doesn't seem to matter now.

A man named Jeremy Light died that same morning Doc Silence touched down in a cornfield to retrieve a scared young girl who'd set fire to a barn with her hands. Light died not at the hand of violence but the way men often do—or hope to, in a bed, with his family around him, younger than some, older than others, and very old, very old indeed, for a man who took up arms against a sea of troubles and tried to change the world.

Jeremy Light was a father.

There's a saying among those who become heroes, that having families is a hazard they cannot afford, and this is often true, and it's a rule most cling to. But Jeremy Light, the White Shadow, was a man of hope. He became the Shadow because of this hope, because he believed his actions would make a difference, because he thought the things he did would make a better world, and he wanted children to live in that world. He assumed, unlike his peers, that having a family would make the world all the more worth saving. That having someone to return home to each dawn would allow him to become a better hero.

The White Shadow was a man who had faith in love.

A daughter was born.

One of life's bitter ironies is that the world is often most terrible to those men and women who hold great hope in their hearts. And this cruel twist revealed itself to Jeremy Light in many ways. It took his wife from him too soon, from an ordinary, mundane illness. He was never quite the same after that, after watching the love of his life fade away, fighting a battle of her own, a battle he could do nothing to help her win.

But Light's daughter became his best friend. She kept him afloat in hope. She was his future. His dream. And he wished to leave the world in a pleasant and stable enough state that she would never be required to do what he did, would never need to don a mask and try to fight against the inevitable crush of terrible injustices humans inflict upon one another.

Light fought on the streets for thirty years. His knees gave out first. Then his back fell apart. He could feel the weather changing in those knuckles that had dutifully been used to fight criminals and terrible men. Jeremy Light wore his scars with humble pride, not because of how they looked, but because each one reminded him of another day he tried to save the world.

But soon the hurt became overwhelming, his body failed him, and Jeremy Light found himself an old man, all the while watching the world grow worse instead of better. Watching humanity fail itself every single day.

On his deathbed, he told his daughter that he wished he could have left her a better world.

I tried, he said, with his last few breaths. I wanted to leave this place beautiful for you. I don't know what happened. I don't know why I failed. I tried so hard. I should have given more.

And his daughter shushed him, and brushed his brittle white hair away from his face, and watched the light go out in his eyes. This man. Her hero. Her father. This beacon of hope, to her, to so many.

The world never knew what became of the White Shadow. It was what he'd wanted, his daughter knew. There would be no eloquent obituary in the paper, no hero's funeral, no great unmasking. It was what he desired for her, one last bequest, the gift of anonymity, the gift of being left to live in peace.

But all that his daughter could remembered was that her father died sad and heartbroken by a world that let him down.

And she vowed to change it somehow.

She believed there had to be some sort of reckoning to be paid by a world that broke her father's heart.

CHAPTER 59:
A DAUGHTER'S GIFT

And all I know," the White Shadow said, her voice heavy and low, "Is that this world never deserved him."

Kate sensed Doc's emotions escaping from him. Anger, sadness, pain, guilt. Even horror. She didn't need to look at the way the flames in his eyes danced to see how upset he'd become.

"The Shadow was my friend," Doc said. "I never knew."

"You knew he was disappointed," the White Shadow said. "Knew this world broke his heart."

"He was the most private man I'd ever met," Doc said. "We never found out how he died. Never discovered his real name. Sasha, we didn't know you existed. I mean that. He protected you—even from us."

"Especially from you," the Shadow said. "I think he thought it was his gift to me. The opportunity to be perfectly normal. To be anonymous. The right to be simply a person. To not be like him."

Doc waved his hands around, not in an attempt to cast a spell but as an expression of some sort of frustration he couldn't articulate. "All this though? All of this? He wouldn't have wanted it, Sasha."

"I don't even think he could have imagined it," the Shadow answered. "He thought so small. That was why he was so wonderful, wasn't it? He focused on one life at a time. One rescue. A single act of kindness."

"But why cause all this havoc then?" Doc said. "Why did this devastation have to happen?"

"Your little werewolf said it best," the Shadow said. "I wanted to enforce peace. I reflected on my father's life and I kept seeing a man who pleaded so gently for us to be better. He was much too polite to put his foot down and say 'Dammit. Behave.'"

"Why didn't you come to us?" Doc asked. "We weren't aware of you, but you had to know about us. Had to know who his allies were."

"And you gave up!" the Shadow said. "Quit. All of you. Remember? Ran off to the stars, or hid in your books, or found some way to die so you wouldn't have to be responsible for the world anymore. Even you, hiding in your Tower just sitting there watching. You gave up. Quit on my father's dream. Why would I come looking to you for anything? Why would I expect anyone to care?"

Doc's shoulders slumped.

A raged built up inside Kate, a fury in response to these accusations, but she remembered the day Doc asked her to become the failsafe, the day he told her that she would need to be the one to be prepared to put her own friends down if they ever got out of control. If they ever, like Emily in this apocalyptic timeline, became a weapon and not a hero. She asked him if he had been the failsafe for his own friends, and Doc revealed the truth. They hadn't died. "We gave up," he'd said. They gave up. Here stood a girl who wanted to make a finer world, and the men and women she needed most had quit. And so she'd done it alone.

"You had me killed," Doc said.

"I recognized what you were doing," the Shadow said. "Repeating history. Building a team to perform exactly the way your own had done. And I realized you'd stand in my way. Understood you didn't have the guts to accomplish what needed to be done."

"Are you saying your father didn't have the courage either?" Kate said, interrupting.

The White Shadow's eyes widened, a wordless fury twisting on her lips.

"We're doing what he did," Kate said. She felt Doc's tension, sensed Titus moving in closer. "We're your father's legacy, not you. I'm the heir to the White Shadow. You're simply a megalomaniac who stole your father's name and destroyed his fine legacy. Don't wallow in what you thought he wanted. You did this. And should be ashamed."

"We should be," a new voice said.

"Keaton," the Shadow said, her voice heavy, her throat tight.

"I know I am," the newcomer, this Keaton, said. "We did this, you and me."

"We tried to change the world," the White Shadow said.

"Oh we did," Keaton said.

And Kate noticed his hands weren't empty. He carried one of the gravity guns they'd seen earlier, a bit smaller, silver, like something out of an old sci-fi movie. "Look at how we changed the world. Aren't you proud?"

"Keaton, don't," the Shadow said.

"It's much too late for don't," Keaton said. He threw his hands up in a sad, powerless gesture of resignation. "She's gone, Shadow. Emily's gone. And she almost took the world along with her."

"Keaton, please," the Shadow said.

"I wish you'd witnessed it," he said. "I wish you'd seen them die. Emily and Solar. Our responsibility and our enemy. I stood there, and watched the sky. It was like looking into the eye of God, Shadow. And all I saw looking back at me was every single thing we've done wrong."

"I'm sorry," the White Shadow said.

"Oh how I wish that was enough to fix everything," Keaton said. And then he aimed the gravity gun at the Shadow and pulled the trigger.

Everything suddenly happened at once; Whispering charged, not toward the shooter or the Shadow, but for the fallen body of future-Kate. Titus transformed, plummeting on all fours in the direction of Keaton, his claws squealing when they scraped the floor. Kate rushed to the White Shadow, knowing what she would find, understanding with complete certainty that she had witnessed a killing shot, not quite sure if she hoped to be mistaken or not.

And Doc Silence stood like a statue in the middle of the room, allowing all of it to unfold.

Later, Kate would learn that Doc had given up on changing this timeline, that he realized they'd exercised all the good and harm they could do here. But she couldn't help herself. Couldn't stand idly by. Kate never could.

The loud bang of the gravity gun fired once again.

Kate turned, terrified the shot had been aimed at Titus.

She saw the gun fall weakly from Keaton's lifeless hands, heard the strange metal clatter sound when it fell to the floor. Kate scooped up the White Shadow's body in her arms, saw the woman's neck bent at a terrible angle. She stared into the blank and wide eyes looking back at her, then felt Doc's hand on her shoulder. She let the aging wizard take the White Shadow from her and watched as Doc cradled Sasha in his arms like a child.

"I wish I'd known," she heard Doc Silence say. "If only I'd known."

CHAPTER 60:
I'D WANT YOU THERE

Jane helped Annie climb out of the underground lab; Emily floated behind them lazily. The world above waited eerily quiet. You'd never know someone had just saved the planet a few minutes before. Never know two people died so that everyone else could live.

Annie walked away from Jane, stopped twenty or thirty feet from her, put her hands on her hips, kept her back to everyone else. The pink-haired woman moved a hand to her forehead, as if blocking out the sun, tucked a thumb through a belt loop. Her shoulders shook softly, and Jane thought she might be crying.

"We just saw ourselves die," Emily said out of nowhere.

Jane looked at the mess of Emily's blue hair, her cracked goggles perched on the top of her head. She played with her scarf, running the texture of the fabric under her fingertips.

"We did," Jane said.

"That feels like something that shouldn't be able to happen," Emily said.

"It sure does," Jane said. She sat down on a nearby curb.

Emily joined her. "It doesn't seem real, does it?" she said. "I mean, it feels real enough. I feel like we saw what happened. Like Solar's actually gone. But it's not like they were us. It's almost as if this all happened to someone else."

"I think it did," Jane said softly. "No matter what, we'll never grow up to be those people. They share our faces, our DNA, but we

279

can't be them. Can never be them, even if we wanted to be."

Emily pulled off the puffy orange vest she'd been wearing over her uniform. Frayed, scorched, and battered, it looked more like an abandoned life preserver than a fashion statement. She tossed it on the ground.

"But they had our eyes. Our voices. Our fingerprints and hands. I put my palms up against the glass cage and that other me placed her palm against mine, and Jane, they were exactly the same."

"Can I say something weird?" Jane said.

"That's my job," Emily said. "But you can go ahead and try."

"I liked Solar," Jane said. "I don't really even like myself that much a lot of the time, but this future me, trying to hold the world together with her two hands, I grew fond of her, respected her. Wanted to be around her."

"I hate to disappoint you, Jane, but you're the same as her. If Solar is any indication of who you'll be when you're older, you're not going to change that much."

"She seemed so much braver than I am," Jane said.

"Nope," Emily said, smiling a sad little smile. "She was who you're supposed to be some day. I think you should be proud to know that."

Jane put her hand on the back of Emily's.

"Even if you're just trying to make me feel better, Em, thank you," Jane said. "I'll miss her."

"Then just don't stop being who you are, and you'll be with her every day," Emily said.

"That almost makes me feel better."

"It's easy. I just have to tell the truth," Emily said. "Meanwhile I grow up to become a caged lab rat with a fairly tenuous grasp on reality."

"I'm sorry you had to see that," Jane said.

"That's not what bothered me," Emily said. "Not really. What disturbed me is seeing how much like me she is. And how close I could've come to being locked in a laboratory somewhere. Becoming someone's attempt at a Nobel Prize."

"The one thing this timeline's Emily didn't have that you do is us," Jane said. "We'll make sure that never happens to you."

Emily stretched out her legs in front of her, crossing her big-booted feet at the ankle.

"That's not how I'd like to die, if I have a choice," Emily said. "This hurts my heart."

"It won't happen," Jane said.

"But you know what? If I do have to die tragically like this, I hope you're with me," Emily said.

Jane shook her head, almost laughing. "I don't know if that qualifies as a compliment, Em," she said.

"Why's everything gotta be an insult with me?" Emily said. "I mean if I had to go, it'd be nice if yours was the last face I saw. I'd know I did something right if you were the last person who was with me."

"You all right?"

"Dying really messed me up."

"Me too."

"We gonna be okay?" Emily said.

"I don't know?" Jane said. "To tell the truth, I don't really think so."

"Me either," Emily said.

They sat together in comfortable silence.

Jane wondered where the others were. If they were okay.

"Do you think Annie will be alright?" Emily asked.

"I don't know," Jane said. "She knew everyone here longer. She and Solar were friends."

"She still has us, though," Emily said.

"For what we're worth," Jane said. "'*Before us lies eternity; our souls are love, and a continual farewell.*'"

"Did you just quote William Butler Yeats?" Emily said.

"You have Yeats memorized too?—Of course you have Yeats memorized," Jane said. "And yes. 'Ephemera.'"

"You know Yeats?"

"My dad's favorite poet," Jane said. "Read him all the time."

"The farmer who read Yeats," Emily said.

"Yeah," Jane said.

"*Before us lies eternity,*" Emily repeated.

"*Our souls are love, and a continual farewell,*" Jane said. "I don't know."

Jane watched Annie pacing, rubbing her hair, appearing pained and tired.

Emily hit Jane in the upper arm with a backhanded slap. "Is that Billy?" she said, pointing at a great ball of light in the sky.

"Oh, no. I hope not," Jane said, standing up and dusting off the seat of her pants to find out.

CHAPTER 61:
NO MORE MASKS

Kate found Titus sitting alone on the rubble, knees pulled up to his chest, watching something in the distance. She followed his eyes to see Whispering gently lay future-Kate down on the ground. She stirred, reaching out, and touched the werewolf's face with her fingertips.

"What are you doing?" Kate said.

"Shh, I'm listening," Titus said.

"And I'm supposed to be the creepy one," she said, but sat down beside him anyway. "What are they saying?"

Titus raised an eyebrow.

"You really want me to tell you?" he asked.

"Just kidding. I can read lips," Kate said.

Titus sighed. "Of course you can," he said.

Kate watched her future self place her hands on Whispering's monstrous face. She spoke, not sitting up.

"Where's your real face?" Kate could see her asking.

Whispering's words were difficult to make out.

"He said this is the only face he needs anymore," Titus said.

Kate nodded at him impatiently.

"I want to feel your other face in my hands," future-Kate said. "How long has it been? How long have you looked like this?"

Whispering shook his head. Said something unintelligible.

Kate turned to Titus for a translation.

"He said, 'I missed you so much.'"

Future-Kate whispered something so softly that Titus turned to look at Kate for a translation.

"I'll return to you if you return to me," younger-Kate said.

"What?" Titus asked.

"It's what she said. I'll return to you if you will to me."

And then, for the first time since their arrival, they watched Whispering transform back into his human shape.

This older Titus, hair long and unkempt, had gone completely gray, though his eyes still retained a youthful spark. He had magnificent scars across his face and neck, and, perhaps most surprisingly, he wore a long gray beard.

"The future you looks like an aging hippie rock star," Kate said.

Titus didn't respond.

She glanced up to see the slightest smile start to grow on his face.

"Why are you smiling?" Kate said.

Titus just pointed.

When she looked back, Kate saw her future self holding Whispering by the face, her thumbs caressing his cheekbones, her fingers running through his beard. Kate could decipher her words this time.

"This beard is just awful," future-Kate said.

"I know," Whispering said. "Are you back? Are you here?"

Kate's future counterpart nodded, a rare, delicate smile growing on her face.

"Please come back," Whispering said. "I can't do this on my own. I need your help."

"I'm ready to come home," future-Kate said.

Titus put a hand on the center of Kate's back, between her shoulder blades.

She instinctively tensed, then relaxed.

"No one is worth what he put himself through for her," Kate said.

"Maybe they are," Titus said. "I think maybe everyone is worth it to someone."

"No pedestals, Titus," Kate said.

"I wish you could understand that putting someone on a pedestal really is different from recognizing they are important to you," Titus said.

Kate didn't answer. She looked back at their future selves, though, and saw them pressing their foreheads together, speaking softly to each other, conspirators.

"What we believe doesn't matter anyway," Kate said. "He's going to need her."

Titus looked intently at her.

Kate stared back.

"You're so romantic," he said.

By now, the other survivors started to arrive. Jane and Emily walking ahead of a crestfallen Annie, with no Solar in sight. No future-Emily, either. Kate felt a gnawing in the pit of her stomach that things had gone badly for everyone. Doc sat alone, the collar of his long black coat turned up, reflecting in solitude.

And then there was Billy.

Kate only spotted him because Emily was pointing and yelling. Everyone took notice, though, during Billy's reentry, a blazing white figure awash in a glow of energy and light. He held Jessie, who appeared to be incapable of flying on her own and extremely unhappy about it, in tow. Billy set her down and then landed as the others gathered around. Kate and Titus walked up to him together.

"What did you do to yourself now?" Emily said.

"It's a long story," Billy said.

"No it's not," Jessie said. "Flyboy stole my powers."

"I didn't steal your powers, I temporarily and involuntarily borrowed them," he said.

"We leave you alone for ten minutes and . . ." Emily said. "You're like a superhuman toddler."

"You copped her powers?" Titus asked, shielding his eyes as he got closer to Billy's still shining self.

"No. She got hit with a null gun and the other Dude went to the nearest available host," Billy said.

"And he decided the appropriate thing to do was give you twice the power?" Kate said.

"Would you rather he came to find you? It's not like that hasn't happened before," he said.

"I'm okay without, thanks," Kate said.

Billy glanced around, his blue-white light aura gave him a searchlight effect when he scanned the group. "Anyway, I'm working on a solution," he said.

"You mean Dude is working on a solution," Emily said.

"We're partners, we share credit for things," Billy said. "So where's Solar? I need to talk to her."

"Billy," Emily said.

"Because the strangest thing happened out there," Billy said. "Stuff she needs to know. I understand it sounds weird but—"

"—She's gone, Billy," Jane said, speaking for the first time.

Kate watched Jane fight to remain composed, her eyes shrouded in dark circles, her mouth a hard line, holding back tears.

"She's what?" Billy said softly.

"She's gone," she said. "She and future-Emily. They didn't make it."

"They saved the world," Annie said, joining them, looking even worse than Jane did, as if they'd seen their own graves.

Whispering and future-Kate sauntered in, hands almost touching but never actually grasping.

Kate watched Annie smile the faintest of smiles when she saw Whispering's face.

"I remember that ugly mug," Annie said.

Whispering smiled, but the smile didn't touch his eyes. "She's really gone?" he said.

Emily and Jane nodded together slowly.

Whispering looked at his feet. "She was my friend and ally for a long, long time," he said. "There were moments when I felt like she was my only friend."

"Are you okay, Billy?" Emily said, rushing up to her friend. It seemed like he was about to pass out.

"Yeah," he said, a crestfallen expression lurking behind the glow of his halo. "I just... I learned things I wish she'd known. That's all."

An unspoken moment for the departed passed, a long, drawn out silence. A soft breeze wandered its way through the broken streets of the City. The light, clicking sounds of a rolling Styrofoam coffee cup rumbled. Leaves swirled and then gathered together at the bottom corner of a bent and damaged chain-link fence. The conflicting odors of fire and old city smells permeated the air.

Finally, Annie broke the reverie.

"We should go home," she said.

"You go on ahead," Doc Silence said, looking up at the sky at nothing in particular, his glasses lost and missing, his eyes open flames of purplish light. "There's something I need to do first."

He stepped into the air, taking flight as if he were simply going for a walk, and then he was gone.

CHAPTER 62:
BUTTERFLIES AND I LOVE YOUS

Doc returned to the Lady's castle in the clouds to discover it deserted, its guardians gone, its gates wide open. He walked inside, fearless and ready, wondering what sort of monster could drive Natasha Grey from her home.

He found her sitting alone in the parlor, a planar knife in her hand, like the one he'd used not long ago to send himself and another timeline's version of Natasha to a different plane of existence, to keep her from harming his students.

The knife was so thin and so bright it looked like the blade itself was made of still water.

"So tell me, little Doctor," the Lady said, her voice cold and lilting. "Did you save this world, you and your little merry band?"

"What happened here, Natasha?" Doc said.

She ignored him and continued. "I suppose you must have, if you're still here. You wouldn't be able to see me if you'd failed. You'd be dead again, wouldn't you?"

"Natasha," he repeated.

"Look at you, without your glasses," she said, smiling joylessly. "I always liked you when you didn't hide behind those silly red things. You're a being of great power, Doctor Silence. I never could understand why you refused to act like it. Why you always pretended to be simply ordinary."

"Because we've all got to exist here together, Natasha," Doc said. "What are you doing with that planar knife?"

The Lady looked at the knife as if she'd forgotten she held it in her hand, raising an eyebrow at it, seeming to not understand what its purpose was.

"Is a place really worth saving?" the Lady said, standing up, her feet bare on the stone floor. "I mean isn't there a point when it's not? Like an old dog. Even if you love that dog, even if you love it with all your heart, isn't there a point where it's better to let the thing die rather than let it continue suffering?"

"This world wasn't done yet," he said.

"You would say that," she said. "Forever the optimist. Forever seeing the good in things. Look at you with your demon's blood eyes and your big dark coat. You disappointed me so much, my student. So much."

"No I didn't," Doc said. "Don't lie to me. Not here, not now. Not in this place."

The Lady exhaled, a pained smile on her lips.

"I have lived a life without regret, for more centuries than even you know," Natasha said. "I was here when certain things began. I made myself in this world, and I bound myself to countless other planes, and I can count on one hand the actions I regret."

"Two of my students died," Doc said. "Not mine, not really, not the ones who came with me here from my own timeline. But I saw two of them die, together. And I can't tell, Natasha. I can't tell if this is because of us, or because of someone else's mistakes, or because in this timeline everything is just pain and sadness. I need you to help me understand."

"There's no understanding it, little Doctor," the Lady said. "Haven't we talked about all this before? Maybe we didn't, in your timeline. But it's all . . ."

"Butterflies and I love yous," he said.

"Attempting to understand it will drive you mad, Doc Silence," she said. "Your best bet is to stop trying to fix things and just coast on the consequences of what you see happening all around you."

"And retire to a castle in the clouds," Doc said.

"That too," the Lady said.

"We're going home," he said.

"I know."

"What's going to happen to this place?" Doc asked. "Do you know? Do you have any idea?"

"It won't end," the Lady said. "Not yet anyway. Beyond that, who can tell? Someone will come along and destroy it. You know that's the case as well. It happens in every timeline. Someone selfish appears and ruins everything for everyone. It's only a matter of time."

"And what about you?" he said. "What will happen to you?"

The Lady wagged the planar knife back and forth in her hand.

"I'm leaving," she said.

"Leaving?" Doc repeated.

"There's nothing for me here in this world anymore," the Lady said. "I've overstayed my welcome. I've made every bargain I can. There are no more games to play, and no one to play them with."

"Where will you go?" he said.

"The higher planes, maybe," Natasha said. "Or the lower. I'll grow wings and set myself up as a goddess in the Dreamlands. Or maybe wander the Forgotten Places for a while, lose myself in the Mists of Memory."

Doc rubbed his forehead, studied the half-mad face of his nemesis, his friend. I don't know what to do to help her, he thought. She killed me here, murdered me, but even here, even still, I want to make her better somehow. This is where madness comes from.

The Lady walked up to Doc, adjusted the lapels of his coat with her free hand, looked him in the eyes, her red flames to his violet.

"This world was more interesting with you in it," she said. "I do regret making that no longer so."

With her back towards him, the Lady raised the planar knife, and with a dramatic slashing movement, opened a thin crack in reality. She turned around to look at him one last time.

"Take care of yourself, Doctor," the Lady said. "It's true. I do miss you."

She stepped through the tear in reality and it closed quickly behind her, as if the Lady never existed.

Doc stood alone, listening to the creak and sway of the now-empty castle in the sky. He inspected the desk where Natasha had been sitting when he arrived. Resting on the edge sat a pair of red glasses.

Doc's glasses looked older, a little battered, but he knew for certain they were his. Silence picked up the forgotten sunglasses and put them on. He walked out of the castle in the clouds and took flight. He never looked back.

CHAPTER 63:
BEGINNINGS

What remained of the Indestructibles, both past and future incarnations, gathered and set up shop in what used to be an assisted living facility on the north side of the City. It made sense after all—beds, leftover medical supplies, an emergency generator, all the things they needed to put themselves back together again. Although the facility had been evacuated years before, there were even nonperishable foods left behind as well.

Whispering moved among his surviving people, laughing as they tugged at his long gray beard and teased him about how long it had been since they'd been able to see his face. A pale and weak Finnigan nearly coughed himself sick at the sight of the older wolf. Titus took all of this in from a distance, trying to ascertain how this other version of himself had developed into a leader, a chieftain, a just king. He wondered if this was to be his future as well.

Kate spoke at length with her future self. The two Dancers did not share the details of that conversation, though they both knew that eyes were on them, and ears. Titus caught little snippets as he watched them walk arm in arm out into the overgrown garden behind the facility. Even while conversing they acted like dancers, moving in synch with the other, balanced, elegant, graceful.

Emily and Jane sat together alone, not speaking much.

A pall hung over them, a sense that they'd witnessed their own destruction and survived to tell the tale. It was a companionable silence, and they seemed comforted by each other's presence, but they were both quite clearly alone in their own thoughts. Emily found a box of unspoiled yellow snack cakes stashed in a pantry. She made a joke about Twinkies and the end of the world.

Jane almost laughed.

And that would have to be enough, a slight victory, a smile over junk food being one of the few remaining staples in a place still burdened and heavy with death.

Annie disappeared and then returned several times. She told Jane that she was reviewing the time stream, checking to see if their actions had impacted other timelines, satisfying a curiosity about the state of things. She revealed nothing about what she saw, except to say that things were as quiet as they possibly could be in the time stream. No ripples appearing so far.

Not long after, Doc arrived looking haunted and sad. He joined Jane and Emily in their silence. Emily, unusually affectionate, draped one of Doc's arms over her shoulder and napped. The aging magician looked down at her like a proud father might, a proud father who worries, as all dads do.

Jane eventually joined them, sitting down on his other side, and the three rested together like a family cramped in a small room. The gray light of a battered world filtered in through dusty windows.

And Billy Case glowed.

* * *

We've got to fix this, Billy Case thought.

Billy was trying to keep away from everyone he could at the assisted living facility. Entirely a self-conscious activity, part of him wanted to avoid anyone who might have been confused by his behavior when he found out Solar had died, because he had no interest in trying to explain how he somehow had fragments of the memories of himself from this timeline.

But he also continued to glow like a lantern and felt ridiculous and annoying. People were forced to shade their eyes when he passed.

Agreed, Dude said. *This is too much power. I'm afraid what the long-term effects will be on you. I do not believe a single human body can sustain this level of intensity.*

I just meant I don't want to glow all the time, Billy thought. Are you indicating this might even kill me?

There was an uncomfortably long pause before Dude answered.

Kill might be too aggressive a word, Dude said.

Do you have any plan, at all? Billy thought.

There is one possibility, Dude said. *You may not like it, though.*

"What do you mean I may not like it?" Billy said out loud.

"I don't care if you like it or not, if you can fix both of us, you do it," Jessie said, coming around the corner of the hallway where Billy was hiding.

"Are you following me?" Billy said.

"Yes!" Jessie said. "I'm following you! You stole my alien partner!"

"Dude?"

We did not steal her partner, Dude said. *This is unprecedented.*

"He says this is unprecedented," Billy said.

"I want to talk to him," Jessie said. "Put him on the line or something."

"I can't just put him on the line. This isn't a phone!" Billy said. "Come on, Dude. There's got to be a way you can split yourself back up again, right?"

I really do not think I can, Dude said. *I merged with my alternate timeline self at a core level. We became essentially one being at that moment and I gained most of his sentience. All his strength. You felt the effects. You were impacted also, with memories of your other self.*

Yeah, Billy thought. About that. Why didn't I get memories from the other hosts like that when we merged originally?

You have had glimpses, Dude said. *You have said it yourself, that you have phantom memories from my past partners, from other times in history. In this case those memories were very close to your own brainwaves. They merged cleaner, because they came from an older, but otherwise identical host.*

"I hate that you're having a conversation right now and I can't be a part of it," Jessie said.

"How could you tell?" Billy asked.

Jessie sneered at him.

"You really don't think I can tell when you're having a conversation in your own head? I was you six hours ago!"

"Okay, fine!" Billy said. "Dude, you've got to have a suggestion."

You are not going to like it, Dude said. *But it might be our only option.*

"Whatever we must do, Dude. I'm listening."

I can split off a portion of my powers into a new Luminae, Dude said. *It will not be another me, but it will be nearly as powerful, and have much of my institutional memory. This will let us siphon off some of our excess power, and it will need a host right away—Jessie would be the perfect person for it to join with.*

"That sounds alarmingly like we're going to have a baby," Billy said.

It is completely different, Dude said.

"No, not completely different," Billy said.

"You're pregnant?" Jessie said.

Think of it more like when a single-celled organism splits in two, Dude said. *But much more complicated.*

"That is so not making this sound any better, Dude," Billy said.

Either way, it is the only solution I can think of that will work, Dude said. *You are going to need a third person to assist, just in case.*

"Absolutely not," Billy said.

"Absolutely yes, we're doing this," Jessie said. "What's he saying?"

"He's saying we need a midwife," Billy said, putting his head in his hands.

* * *

In what would become the strangest conversation Billy would ever have in his entire life, he and Dude determined who they would seek out to help. The first thought, of course, was Emily, but best friend or not, there was no way Billy wanted to Emily to know about this before he was mentally prepared to be ridiculed for it. Jane was the most trustworthy, of course, but she was in bad shape and Billy was having trouble looking her in the eyes without picturing snow melting in her hair.

Matthew Phillion

Telling Doc about it felt incredibly awkward, and Kate terrified him by default. Which is why Billy sent Jessie to go get Titus.

"You're going to have a baby?" the werewolf said, laughing so hard he choked on his own spit.

"Seriously, Titus, I asked you to help because I believe you would not make fun of me," Billy said. "If I wanted comments from a peanut gallery I could have asked Emily."

"Okay, okay, I'll stop, momma. Don't worry," Titus said. "I'll be your midwife."

"Seriously man—"

"Kidding," Titus said. "What am I doing?"

Titus, Billy, and Jessie sat in a room toward the back of the facility, just a living area with couches and a dead television.

"I think it's pretty straightforward," Billy said. "You're really just here in case things go weird."

"Should I boil some water?" Titus said.

"I guess I'm gonna have to start calling you Emily," Billy said. "It's not like that. Dude will basically break off a percentage of his energy. It'll become its own Luminae a few minutes later, and then it'll need a host. Jessie's right here, so . . ."

"What are we going to name him?" Jessie said.

"Don't do this to me," Billy said.

They really are relentless, are they not? Dude said.

"I've got no friends, apparently," Billy said.

"Junior," Titus said.

"Little Dude?" Jessie said.

"Look, I'm really glad you guys are having fun with this, but can we get it over with now? I'm sick of being nervous and fluorescent," Billy said.

Can I begin, or will your friends continue to mock us? Dude said.

"Let's get it over with," Billy said.

He stood up, arms at his side, and felt a strange tug in his chest. His limbs got cold, as if he'd been hit with a wave of nervous energy. The room turned very warm, and his head swam. He felt one arm lift and then Titus slip himself under it to support him.

"I got ya, bud," Titus said. "No worries."

296

"Dude, tell me this isn't going to get any weirder," Billy said.

And then a blue-white light appeared in the center of his chest and flew out, hovering a few feet in front of him.

"Hey guys, what's going on up here?" Emily said, appearing in the doorway rubbing her eyes. "Oh my god it's a baby Dude!"

"I hate my life," Billy said. His head spun and Titus held on tighter to keep him on his feet.

The light grew brighter and larger, drifting in mid-air a moment. Then it plunged into Jessie's chest. She gasped, and her whole body lit up for a brief second, her veins gleaming beneath her skin. She started to fall, but Emily threw out her hands and caught her in a bubble of float, easing Jessie's limp body into the closest chair.

"Billy, how dare you not invite me to the birth of your first child!" Emily said.

"I hate every single one of you so much," Billy said.

Titus sat him down in another armchair, and leaned in to look into his eyes. "Well, you're not all the way normal, but you're closer to it," he said.

"What does that mean?" Billy said.

"You're not a glow-stick anymore," Emily said, doing the same for Jessie, brushing the girl's hair out of her face. "You still look a little sparkly but you're a lot better than that human light bulb you'd become."

Billy sighed. Dude, you still in there? He thought.

I would really prefer to not have to do that again anytime soon, Dude said. *It felt like I cut off one of my own limbs.*

Are you okay? Billy thought.

I am whole, Dude said. *I have all my memories, I hope. We are at full power. How is the new Luminae?*

"How you doing, Jessie?" Billy said.

"She's new," Jessie said, smiling. "She's really new. She knows things, but... This is so cool."

"She?" Billy said.

"It's a girl! Can we name her after you?" Emily said. "Wilhelmina! Wilhelmina Case has a great ring to it."

"You know what? I have no idea what really just happened here, and I'm perfectly happy to not understand it," Titus said. "You both feeling okay? Are we good?"

"I think we're good," Billy said. "So now there are apparently two Straylights once again."

Jessie shook her head at him. "I'm not Straylight anymore," she said her voice tinged with sadness. "I think I'm something else."

"Well, you're gonna need a new name, then," Emily said. "Can I pick it?"

"I think I should name myself after Solar somehow," Jessie said. "She was the one who found me after you—after the other Billy Case—died. It just feels right to do something to remember her by."

"Would you call yourself Solar?" Titus said.

"No," Jessie said. "Something new for someone new."

"Sunlight," Emily said. "Sunlight, the heir of Straylight."

"It feels really simple," Jessie said.

"If she's anything like our Jane, your Solar would have loved the simplicity of it," Billy said.

Emily gave him a strange glance, but nodded in agreement.

"I think it fits," Emily said.

"You were the one who suggested it, your vote doesn't count," Billy said.

"I think it stays," Jessie said. "Sunlight. I think this world will need sunlight in the days to come."

"You're so very right," Titus said.

Jessie looked at Billy intensely.

"Tell Straylight... tell your Dude I'll miss him," Jessie said. "I'll miss his voice in my head. But I think we'll be just fine."

I know she will, Dude said in Billy's head. *I found her for a reason. I know she will be so much more than fine. All my partners are heroes in their hearts. All of them.*

CHAPTER 64: HOMECOMING

Jane found Doc hiding in a corner, observing everyone as they tried to return to normal. Kate and Titus speaking with their future counterparts. Emily hounding Billy about something he'd prefer not to talk about. Jessie looking strangely lighthearted, smiling like someone who'd been unburdened by a great weight. Whispering's werewolf pack, attempting to forget, at least for a few minutes, the heavy weight of their losses, the death of so many of their tribe. There was a world to live in now, in the present, Jane thought. The melancholy and grief of those deaths will come later. But for now, these people get to exist, to live on.

Because of us.

"We did a good thing by coming here," she said to Doc.

"You think so?" he said.

Doc had found his red glasses somewhere, or another pair perhaps, and he fell back on hiding the purple flames of his eyes behind them again. He came out different after all these recent experiences. Distant. Aloof. Remorseful. Lonely.

Jane wasn't certain which. Maybe all.

"It wasn't perfect. Wasn't flawless," she said. "But they get to survive another day because of our help."

"And a lot of sacrifices," Annie said, walking up to them, wearing her own red-tinted lenses.

"Yeah," Jane said. "We're never going to be the same after all of this, are we?" she asked.

Annie shook her head. "No one ever goes back the same after time traveling," she said. "It's a professional hazard. Once you know the consequences of what happens in the present, everyone thinks about things differently. It's only natural."

"I'm going to miss them," Jane said. "Is that strange? They're our friends. Just different versions of them. But I feel like they're other people. And I'll miss them."

"Just like time splinters into different paths, so do we," Annie said. "Every decision you make or don't make, that creates a different version of you. The paths taken and not."

"So none of us are unique in the universe?" Jane said.

"Or all of you are," Annie said. "You might have shared a face and a blood type with Solar, but you each had your own unique life to live. There might be more than one Jane Hawkins, there might be more than one Solar, but there's only one you."

"Does it ever stop being weird?" Jane said.

"Not at all," Annie said. She turned to Doc. "I'm going to bring you home, but I'm going to come back here."

He nodded. "They're running really short. They need the help."

"I hope it's okay," Annie said.

"You've always done what you wanted," Doc said. "And usually what you wanted was the right thing to do. I'll miss you, Annie, but you do what you must do. And if you're able, come back to us again."

"You'll be my anchor?" Annie said.

Doc smiled at Jane.

"Maybe you should make two anchors," Doc said. "Just in case."

* * *

They said their goodbyes in a field outside the facility, those who would remain standing by to watch.

Leaving his tribe for the second time, Titus had the most difficult time. He clasped hands with his future self, accepted a gentle, enveloping hug from Leto, let Finnigan, barely able to stand yet, grab him by the head and yell at him.

"You find me, you little rug rat, you promise," Finnigan said.

"I will," Titus said.

"And when you do... you tell me not to take Gabriel for granted," Finnigan said. "Tell me that morose old fool is the best friend I'll ever have, and I'll regret it if I don't treat him as such."

Titus threw a bear hug around the injured wolf, who slapped his back heartily in return.

Kate spoke quietly with her future self. They whispered secrets that no one else could hear. Kate listened more than spoke, as if her future self were casting a spell and she fell under its power.

Jane wondered what mysteries they might have imparted upon each other, what universal truths. She felt the drag, a pull, as if she'd forgotten to do something. She searched around for her own future self, hoping she'd reappear.

"It's pretty weird, isn't it?" Emily said.

Jane hadn't realized Emily was so close.

"It would have been nice to at least say goodbye," Jane said.

"Yes," Emily said. "But you know what I keep thinking? We'll become them some day. Or someone like them. Someone better. We didn't need to say goodbye. We just have to be ready to say hello when we meet them again another day, looking back at us through a mirror."

Jane bit her lip, looked at her hands. "Still not as nice as a goodbye," she said.

"I know," Emily said.

Jessie and Billy walked up to them together, Jessie holding something under one arm. An essence now existed between them, Jane thought, some connection that had to come from sharing the same powers. She wondered if Billy and Kate ever felt connected for the same reason, after she'd held Billy's powers for him during that brief period. Maybe it didn't last long enough. Perhaps Kate was just too independent anyway.

"Jane," Jessie said. "The rest of us... we thought you should have this."

She handed Jane what had been in her hands. Black and white and gold fabric. Her future self's uniform. Brand new, undamaged, the gold sun emblazoned on the chest. "The wolves and I, we weren't sure if you'd want to wear it, or just keep it, but we thought it belonged with you," Jessie said.

Jane pulled Jessie into a hug, and the younger girl accepted, holding her tight.

"I don't know how it could be possible, but I hope this isn't the last I see of all of you," Jessie said. She looked at Billy specifically. "You take good care of Dude."

"He's so low-maintenance. He shouldn't give me any trouble," Billy said. He still looked overpowered, Jane noticed, his eyes giving off just a little too much light, his skin more than hinting at luminescence. "Be good, Jessie."

"You too, Billy Case," Jessie said, stepping back to join Whispering and future-Kate.

Annie finished putting the last touches on her machinery, the gear that would help her bring them all back to where they belonged. Those who would remain behind stayed just beyond the contraption. Small waves were exchanged. Sad expressions.

"I didn't think I'd be this sad to go," Billy said, mostly to himself.

Jane looked over at him to see if he'd just been talking to Dude out loud, but he turned to her and gave her a small, melancholy smile. "Neither did I," she said.

Soon the world faded to white, and they were gone.

* * *

They arrived back in their own timeline in the same field they'd disappeared from. A light rain fell from a gray sky. The world felt very still, and very small.

Then they heard a truck rumbling in the distance.

As a unit, the Indestructibles tensed, waiting to see who approached. A black van pulled up in front of them, and the door on the far side opened.

"You all look like absolute hell," Sam Barren said before anyone could see him. He crossed in front of the van and dropped Watson's leash, letting the little gray dog charge into their midst, diving into Billy's arms.

"My boy," Billy said.

Emily took Watson away from him with force to ensure she would receive dog kisses instead.

"My boy," Emily said, giving Billy a dirty look.

"How long were we gone?" Doc said, turning up the collar on his coat against the rain.

"An hour?" Sam said. "Sky opened up right after you left. Went to get some lunch downtown and then the sensors we set up here alerted me you were back. You ruined my meal."

Doc laughed, and put a hand on Sam's shoulder. "Good to see you again too," he said.

"How long were you really gone?" Sam said. "How much time passed for you?"

"Maybe a week on the other side," Annie said, gathering up her gear. Titus was moving behind her, helping, as Kate looked on frowning.

"See, that's why I hate time travel," Sam said.

"You're preaching to the choir, captain," Emily said. "Also I'm starving."

Sam made a gesture toward the van. "Get in. I'm betting none of you want to fly home," he said.

"Not even a little," Emily said. "To my chariot, Jeeves."

The others headed for the van as well. Jane began to walk with them, but Billy caught her wrist. His hair was plastered to his forehead in the rain. She had trouble looking him in the eyes as they glowed eerily bright in the overcast daylight. "Give me a second," Billy said.

"Not now, Billy," Jane said. "Let's go home."

"No," Billy said. "I feel the memories fading already. They're not going to last. I thought they might be permanent but I don't know if they'll disappear, and I need to tell you."

"Tell me what?" Jane said, suddenly feeling nauseous with worry.

"They're both gone, the versions of us in that timeline, but some of his old memories transferred to me during that last big battle, and I have to tell someone," Billy said. "I can't keep it to myself. It just doesn't feel fair."

"What is it?" Jane said.

"It doesn't matter what happens here," Billy said. "We have our own futures to live. Our own lives to lead. But you need to know. That other Billy, he loved that other Jane so much. I just think you need to realize that. Because they're both gone, and because we're not them, and we'll never be them, but someone needs to understand that. Someone needs to remember that for a little while, they had something true."

"And what about us?" Jane said. "What are we supposed to do with this? What does it mean?"

"I don't think it means anything," Billy said. "It doesn't have to signify anything. It's just something beautiful that happened somewhere far away, and I don't want to be the only one who's aware it existed."

"Okay," Jane said, unsure of what else to say.

Billy smiled at her, and she couldn't tell if the water around his eyes was just from the rain, or something else.

"Okay," he said back.

"Let's go home, Billy Case."

"Yeah," he said, his voice soft. "Home."

CHAPTER 65:
A DIFFERENT FUTURE

On a bridge, in the City, Keaton Bohr looked out over the water and felt his life's work slipping away from him.

He had such great hopes. Such great plans. I wanted to change the world, he thought. Wanted to make it a better place. And no one will ever listen.

The university hierarchy had listened, a bit, but funding became scarce, and nobody welcomed new ideas anymore, not the radical kind, not the type that caused trouble. The Institute had challenged his theories, had placed him in an intellectual battle with his peers and superiors, and they eventually had him banished.

He ventured into the corporate world, but his ideas were not in a category that usually generated cash. His were designed to ease the pain of the planet, to give the future a better chance at surviving, but there were few on Wall Street who were interested in paying for preventative maintenance.

They'd stolen his ideas, though. His intellectual property. Locked them away. They all had. The school, the institute, the corporation, everyone managed to take pieces of his theories for their own benefit, most were willing to suck a drop of his blood, but no one wanted to imagine the bigger picture.

He just needed someone to project these ideas on a broader canvas, to envision things on a larger scale.

"You look like a guy with a lot on his mind," a stranger said to him, stopping to join Bohr on the bridge. He had a cane, and, judging from his gait, Bohr figured this man relied on it heavily to walk. It wasn't simply for show.

"I'm not interested in talking to anyone right now," Bohr said.

"Really?" the stranger said. "I think you need just the opposite."

"Now is not a good time," Bohr said.

"I think it's just the right moment," a second man said. Reed-thin with a perfectly groomed silver mustache, he wore a fedora and a weathered overcoat.

"Is this a mugging?" Bohr asked. "I swear, I've got nothing."

"You've got quite a bit to offer, but we're not here to rob you," the first man said. "We want to offer you a job."

"Now you're teasing me," Bohr said. "It's a prank. Who sent you?"

"The future sent us," the mustached man said.

"What my associate means is, we'd like to enlist your services for future projects," the first man said. "My name is Henry Winter, and I'm the head of the Department of What. That grim little fellow is Agent Sam Barren."

"The Department of What?" Bohr said.

"That's us," Winter said. "And we're hoping you might like to come work in our think tank. I understand you've got some interesting theories on renewable energy."

"And if I say no?" Bohr said.

"You're not going to say no," Sam said.

"And how can you be so sure?" Bohr said.

"Because," Winter said. "You recognize an opportunity when you see one."

CHAPTER 66: LEGACY

A girl sat in the corner booth of a coffee shop, drawing charcoal sketches of strangers on thick white paper. She had a gift, an ability to capture faces she only just saw. This was how she interacted with the world.

A man wearing a long black coat and red-lensed glasses walked in. She took to sketching him immediately, curious what those red lenses meant, wondering why anyone would wear such an ugly threadbare coat. Tattoos crept out from beneath the cuffs of his sleeves, just barely hidden by the Henley tee shirt he wore. He sported a goatee. It looked almost blue in this light.

Perhaps he was from the circus.

He bought a coffee. The girl expected him to leave, though she hoped he'd sit a while. She wanted a bit more time to be able to draw his face.

Instead of leaving, he sat down next to her.

"Hello, Sasha," he said.

Well, I've never had a stalker before, the girl thought. This should be horrific.

"It's extremely creepy that you know my name," she said.

"I know. There were better ways I could have done this," the man said. "But it's been a very difficult week, and it couldn't wait any longer. I've learned a few things."

"Like how to find peoples' private information on the Internet?"

"I knew your father, Sasha," the man said. "He was my friend."

"I don't think my father really had any friends," the girl said. "I'm sorry."

"No, I'm sorry," the man said. "I knew him for years, but I only just recently learned his real name. I only just discovered some important things about him. He was a hero, you know. But he never told anyone about himself. He was a good man."

"My father was a hero," Sasha said. "Were you?"

The man smiled into his coffee.

"I try," Doc said. "You live long enough, it's hard to tell. But I try."

"What are you doing here?" the girl said.

"The White Shadow taught me a lot of things. How to investigate a crime scene. How to read expressions and body language. He was quite the detective, in his own way," the man said. "But he never asked for anything in return. And when he stopped... doing what we do, none of us knew how to find him. We were never sure. Did he get sick? Did one of his enemies get him? Did he simply retire? We hoped it was the latter. We thought, well, if something really terrible had happened, we would have heard about it. He would have ended up in an emergency room somewhere. Or something like that."

"Nothing like that happened," the girl said.

She found herself wanting to trust this weird man, despite the glasses, despite knowing her name. He reminded her, just a little bit, of her father. There is a stillness to men and women who have saved a life. It's like for every terrible thing they've experienced, they weigh a little bit more. Gravity pushes down on them. Her father moved very slowly in his later years. He seemed to carry the weight of the world on his back.

"Sasha, we all owed your father a debt," the man said. "Not a repayment, not a bargain. We simply owed him the honor of looking after the people he loved when he couldn't any longer. And we weren't there. Now I'm really the only one left who can. And I wanted to make sure you were okay."

The girl set aside her pencil, took a sip of coffee. She looked at this strange man in his ugly coat and ridiculous glasses. Yeah, she thought. This is the type of person who truly could be my father's friend.

"He kept you all at a distance on purpose," she said, at last. "It wasn't because he didn't trust you. He just desired... another life. A safe place. And safety for us. He needed a barrier between what he did and who he was. It's why he wore that mask. A mask with nothing on it."

"A blank slate," the man said.

"Yes," she said.

"And what are your plans?" the man said. "Will you follow in his footsteps? Planning on taking over the family business?"

The girl stifled a laugh. "If he were alive that would certainly break his heart," the girl said.

The man raised an eyebrow.

"How so?"

"One of the last things he said to me," the girl said. She felt a twinge in the back of her throat. It had been a long time since she'd spoken of her father. Certainly longer since she'd discussed anything at all about his secret life. "He said to me, I've spent my whole life trying to make this world a better place, and I haven't. Not through my actions. But I made you, and that's enough."

"He died happy," the man said.

"As happy as he could be," she said. "He missed my mother. He thought I'd be lonely. But he was at peace."

"You're an artist," the man said.

"As much as anyone is," the girl said.

"You'll pursue it? Your art?"

"My father tried to make the world a more beautiful place with his fists," the girl said. "I'd like to give it a go with my pencils. Maybe we're both wrong. But it's worth a shot."

The man rubbed his eyes under his glasses.

"That's a good goal," he said, standing up slowly, adjusting the wrinkles in his coat. "If you ever need anything. Ever. Just ask," he said.

"And if not? Will I ever see you again?" the girl said.

"Only if you want to. Or if you look up into the sky," the man said.

The girl bit her lip. "There aren't too many people I can talk to about my father," she said. "If you ever . . ."

"Any time."

"I'm here a lot," she said.

"I'll find you," he said. "I'm sorry for your loss."

"Thank you," she said.

"He was a great man," the man said.

"The best," the girl said.

The man in red glasses tipped his chin to her, picked up his coffee, and walked away.

She looked down at the sketchpad, flipped the page. And she began to draw her father from memory. It was something she hadn't done in a long, long time.

CHAPTER 67:
AND NOTHING WAS EVER THE SAME

The Tower felt cold and sterile after their days hiding in abandoned buildings. Jane wandered the halls at night. Sometimes she'd find Emily playing video games or reading comics by lamplight. Occasionally she'd stop to talk with her. Other times, they would not even acknowledge the other's presence, letting their fellow insomniac find her own solitary method of passing the time.

Titus and Kate paced in the night, as well, though rarely together, and always with an almost supernatural ability to avoid Jane's path. She knew it wasn't meant to be hurtful. The werewolf and the Dancer had always flourished in isolation. They needed those lone hours in the dark to sort things out.

Billy slept like a baby at night, or so it seemed, curled up with his dog, glowing softly in the dark. But he spent a lot of time on his own in the daylight, patrolling the skies, a bullet of white light traveling—seemingly with the absence of a pattern—above the City and beyond.

A few days later, Annie called them all together to say she was leaving.

"It's been long enough," she told them in the large conference room.

"You can go back to the moment we left," Emily said. "There's no such thing as long enough."

"That period of time missing matters to me," Annie said. "It throws my internal clock off. I can sense the hours running by. I need to go."

Kate, hanging in reserve at the back of the room as she always did, then chimed in.

"You took us on this expedition to teach us something, didn't you?" she said.

"I did this to save a world," Annie said. She took a breath and pushed her red sunglasses up onto her forehead, nestling them in her pink and silver hair.

Kate held up her hand. "I'm not belittling that," she said. "But you brought us there for another reason, too. You wanted to show us how bad things could really get, if we let them."

"I could have picked a thousand futures to show you that," Annie said. "I just needed your help."

Titus and Kate exchanged a look, then Titus shook his head.

Kate shot a dark expression towards him but let the conversation drop.

"You'll come back though, yeah?" Emily said. "Because you're the closest thing to Doc who I'm ever going to meet. I do not like the idea of being abandoned."

"I'll try," Annie said.

Emily popped up out of her chair, walked up to Annie, unwound her long, multi-colored scarf and draped it around her neck. "It's dangerous to travel alone. Take this," she said.

"Only Emily can figure out a way to work a Nintendo reference into an otherwise sentimental goodbye," Billy said, sitting with Watson perched on his lap. The dog appeared to agree with his assessment.

"I'm serious. Take the scarf," Emily said.

"You sure? This is your favorite thing," Annie said.

"I can make a new one. It's okay," she said.

Annie wound the scarf around her neck and shrugged a bit. "Couldn't clash any worse with my hair, could it?" she said.

"Neon pink and manic tartan look great together," Emily said. "Live long and prosper, lady."

Annie offered the traditional Vulcan salute, fingers split.

Emily threw her arms up in apparent victory.

"Stay safe, you," Annie said.

"Try not to end up in a future where the apes take over," Emily said.

"I don't like that one much," she said.

Doc walked up, kissed Annie on the cheek, and placed his hand on her shoulder. "Don't stay away so long this time," he said. "We miss you when you're gone."

"I know," Annie said, smiling wryly. "Look after them. And don't disappear into another dimension while I'm away."

She stepped back, closed her eyes, and put her arms to her sides, palms facing downwards and parallel to the floor. Annie looked at each one of the Indestructibles once again, and then faded away.

"Can I propose we stick to saving our own timeline from now on?" Emily said. "I don't think I can do that on the regular."

Jane leaned back in her seat, exhaled a long sigh, and closed her eyes. "I kind of think that was the point after all," she said.

CHAPTER 68: NORTH COUNTRY

Titus and Kate left on a Friday morning. She argued they could take a shuttle from the Tower's bay, but Titus insisted on the long route and bus tickets, departing from the City's central terminal. They rode north, passing through suburbs, crossing state borders, finally leaving the streets behind to travel on foot.

At some point, they crossed international borders as well, the way forest creatures do, without care for the laws of man.

The journey this time was not nearly as difficult as the last trek Titus undertook northward. This was a good thing. While the creature within was a hunter of the wild, he remained city born and bred, a predator of the city, and his companion had never been anything but a being of the urban jungle. An unnatural journey for the both of them, Titus worried that while he knew Kate could handle anything the world threw at her, she would be utterly miserable after the first few days passed.

Kate handled it all with the same stoic strength she faced all tasks with and he knew he should not have been surprised.

They followed runes carved into tree trunks and hidden messages in stone. Titus transformed when no one was around in hopes of catching faint scents in the wind. Eventually he discovered what they had been looking for in a small off the path cabin, covered in dried pine needles and memories, a dwelling that didn't seem to be in use anymore.

Titus approached slowly, Kate stood guard on his flank. He let their footsteps fall loudly, hoping to warn whoever might hear them of their presence. Finally, someone spoke.

"You'll come no further," the man said.

Titus recognized the voice. Younger, but belonging to one of the werewolves he'd met in the future. One of the men who died during the final battle with the hunters.

"You leave him be, lad," a truly familiar voice said. "That's Titus Whispering. He's one of ours."

"He has a human with him," the younger werewolf said. Both men emerged from the woods like ghosts to cross in front of Titus' path.

"There he is," Finnigan said. Younger, and whole, more red in his hair than the last time Titus saw him. "I never thought I'd see you again this soon. Come on in. Bring your friend."

Finnigan led them to the camp itself. Signs of a half-dozen werewolves were scattered around, bedrolls, weapons, shirts abandoned while they hunted in the forest. Gabriel, the lanky, long-haired werewolf who had helped train Titus when he first found the rest of the pack, sat by the fire, sharpening a long knife.

Leto, as she always did, seemed to materialize from nowhere, gliding in to join them.

"You're the Dancer," she said, looking at Kate.

She nodded.

"You're a long way from your hunting grounds," Leto said.

"I've come to ask a favor," Kate said.

Finnigan and Gabriel exchanged an odd look.

Titus laughed, hard.

"What?" Finnigan said.

"Just missed the both of you, that's all," Titus said.

"So what's this favor?" Finnigan said.

"We were wondering," Titus said, joining Gabriel by the fire. "If you knew anything about teaching someone the art of blind-fighting."

"You came all the way up here to ask to learn something you could pick up in a dojo in your city?" Finnigan said.

Titus threw a fistful of dirt at him. "I came up here to see you madmen," Titus said. "Because . . ."

"Because something has changed," Leto said. "And you know more than you did when you left."

"A lot more," Titus said.

"And because Titus doesn't trust anyone to teach us as much as he trusts you," Kate said.

"Do you not trust us?" Gabriel asked her in his deep, quiet voice.

"I don't trust anyone," Kate said.

Finnigan roared. He pointed his crooked finger at her, then at Titus. "That's an excellent place to start," Finnigan said.

Gabriel stood up and began rummaging through a bag of gear. He threw Kate a long black scarf. "Blind-fighting is something you'll never regret learning," he said.

"C'mon, Gabe, let them have dinner first," Finnigan said.

"What are you having?" Titus said. "Venison?"

Finnigan belly-laughed again. "Pizza," he said, grinning impishly. "We knew you were coming two days ago. Figured we'd use your city girl's visit to let us remind ourselves we're human too sometimes."

CHAPTER 69:
THE PATH TAKEN

oc Silence found the Lady Natasha Grey, the one from his own timeline, in a very different castle. An old stone structure on the coast of Spain, which she had rented with real money, the sort mortals use. How she came to possess it, and whether that money would eventually evaporate in the pockets of those she gave it to, remained a matter of conjecture, but this certainly was no castle in the sky. Filled with life, the sun lit the place and the soft caressing echoes of the ocean's waves could be heard if you only just stopped a few moments to listen.

He knocked.

A moment later, the Lady answered the door herself.

"Got bored babysitting your wards?" Natasha said. "Hoping to find another adult to talk to?"

"Can I come in?" Doc said.

She led him into a small parlor. The entire place decorated with a strange blend of modern and archaic. The Lady had taken an active hand here, changing things with magic, giving it her brand, making it more like her own. He knew the building was bigger on the inside. That was probably the first step she took after moving in.

"So," the Lady said. "What mysteries would you like me to unravel for you?"

Doc rubbed his eyes beneath his red-lensed glasses.

"If someone came to you," Doc said. "If someone approached you and asked you to kill me, would you do it?"

The Lady let loose a short, sharp laugh. "If someone tried to hire me to assassinate you?" she asked.

"This is what I'm asking."

"If someone came and asked me to derail you, or put you off balance, or to distract you while they tried to commit the crime of the century, I hope you won't be offended if I tell you I'd do it if the offer had an element to it that benefited me," she said.

"That's not what I asked," Doc said.

"I know," the Lady said.

"Well?"

"Darling, if someone asked me to murder you I would wipe their very existence from this planet," she said. "I would burn them from the multiverse. I'm able to do that, you know."

"I'm well aware, Natasha," Doc said. "I just didn't know what your response would be to the request."

The Lady raised an eyebrow at him. "I'm vaguely insulted," she said.

"We've been on opposite sides for such a long time," Doc said. "I was just curious."

The Lady ran a hand through her hair, smoothing it back.

Doc found himself almost amused by how human she'd dressed today, a white cotton shirt, khaki shorts, slip-on sandals. An ordinary, if well-to-do woman on vacation. Not quite in disguise, but abandoning her role or roles. Not looking like someone with the power to do almost anything she wanted.

"Doctor, I have almost everything I could ever need, and I can get anything I don't already have," she said. "But the one thing I *am* in very short supply of is friends. And, no matter how much we clash, I know I have a place in your heart. You might very well be the only one in this reality I can still say that about. Why would I ever destroy something so unique, so precious?"

"What if they offered you something better?" Doc said.

"There's nothing better than to be loved, Doctor Silence," the Lady Natasha Grey said. "Even monsters like me know that there's nothing whatsoever in all the worlds, above and below, that's more valuable."

Doc smiled.

"I'm... remarkably relieved to hear you say that," Doc said.

"Well then," the Lady said. "Now that you've insulted my honor and questioned my loyalty, can I offer you a drink?"

"I should get back," Doc said. "Strange things have happened lately."

"You smell like time travel," the Lady said. "You should try to get that fixed."

"I'm trying," Doc said. "Soon. I'll come by again soon."

"Good," the Lady said. "You spend too much time with those little minions of yours. The sunsets here are glorious."

She showed Doc to the door, and watched him take flight, curious why he chose to simply fly away instead of moving through space by employing proper magic. Needs time to himself, she thought. The twisted hint of another timeline on him. No good has ever come from time travel. No one ever returns the same way they left.

And when he was gone, Natasha went to a room that never existed before she bought this castle, and drew back a thick ruby curtain. Behind it, a sculpture of a woman stood waiting. This clay woman was ordinary, though not without charm, smaller than Natasha herself, in a neutral pose. Natasha picked up a molding tool and finished a few more small arcane marks pressed into the clay, some on the woman's inner wrist, some on her lower back, a tiny emblem behind her ear.

And then she was ready.

The Lady Natasha Grey leaned in and whispered in the statue's ear.

"Lady Dreamless, Queen of the Dreamless Lands, your vessel is ready," Natasha said. "My debt is paid. You are welcome here."

The clay woman opened her eyes, her skin warming from gray to pale, pale white.

And she smiled.

EPILOGUE:
IT FELL FROM THE STARS

Jane, Billy, and Emily sat on the roof of the Tower, watching the sun set over the City; clouds drifted by lazily. Emily, as always, let her feet dangle over the edge. Billy was half-tempted to nudge her off just to watch her freak out for the half-second she always forgot she could fly.

These are the moments I wonder why I chose you, Dude said.

Come on, Billy thought. I'm the best partner you've ever had.

There is so much more time to find an improvement, Dude said.

"Anybody else feeling really not indestructible right now?" Emily said. "I mean, I feel so destructible I'm thinking about petitioning for a name change."

"We made it home, Em," Jane said. "That's all that matters."

Billy noticed Jane had been quieter than ever since they had returned and hadn't known quite how to behave around her. Nothing felt appropriate. "I don't think it's all that matters," Billy said.

"I know," Jane said. "I guess what I'm trying to say is that we have to try to remember that this is our world. This is where we belong."

"Have you talked to Broadstreet since we got back?" Billy said.

She sighed heavily. "Yeah, that was more than a little bit awkward," Jane said.

"Did you tell him what happened?" Billy asked.

"Absolutely not," she said. "Look at how it's affected the three of us! And we're used to confronting this weird stuff. I wouldn't put that burden on a regular person."

"Were you at least a little bit nicer to him?" Emily said.

"I was," Jane said. "It's pretty hard to be mean to someone who you know was a hero in a different timeline."

"Yeah, about that," Billy said. "Winter recruited Bohr for the Department."

"Can't kill him for what he did in a different timeline," Jane said.

"It worked in the *Terminator*," Emily said.

"It did not work in the *Terminator*," Billy said. "That's why there were about twenty-five sequels. It kept not working!"

"Anyway," Jane said. "It's a way to keep an eye on him. Maybe help him do better this time around."

They sat in silence for a few minutes. The sun crept toward the horizon, turning the sky from gold to violet.

Emily pretended to spit over the edge of the Tower—sound effects and all.

Jane nudged her to cut it out.

Emily rolled her eyes.

"You know, I wish we just traveled to outer space instead," Emily said. "That would have been so much less depressing than a horrible post-apocalyptic future."

"You say these things," Billy said. "But it's not like something absolutely horrible can't like, attack the Earth or whatever this very moment."

"I'm just saying, in the overall scheme of things, space adventures fun, time travel adventures depressing," Emily said. "A time-honored tradition."

"I'm going to push you off the edge again," Billy said.

"Try it, Glow Worm," Emily said.

Jane jumped to her feet.

Billy did the same, automatically, with absolutely no idea why.

Emily stayed sitting. "What?" she said.

"What's that?" Jane said pointing in the distance.

Just above the horizon, a bright streak of blue-white light fell from the sky, flaring as it burned through the atmosphere.

"I don't have a clue," Billy said.

Go, Dude said.

"What?" Billy said.

"I didn't say anything," Emily said.

Go to it. Find where it lands. Now, Dude said.

Billy launched into the air. "We gotta get there," he said.

"I'm coming," Jane said.

"I can't keep up!" Emily yelled.

"Meet us," Billy said. "We need to get there now!"

He thrust both arms forward, rocketing across the evening sky. Jane kept pace, though not as easily as she once had prior to Billy getting his unexpected power-boost during their trip to the future. The two lanced through the air, a streak of blue-white and one of red-gold, following the trajectory of the falling star. They watched the impact, saw a flash of light and heard a sonic boom. The duo flew faster. They located the crash site a few miles outside the City, a crater in the middle of a national park, just a few feet away from a small lake. The ground inside the hole was burned a grizzled black.

And a living creature lay in there on its back.

Shaped like a human, it had two arms, two legs, and a head. The similarities to the human species started to diverge there, with the appearance of large, luminous green eyes, a slit-like mouth, and reptilian skin. The creature wore a uniform of sorts, dark blue with white piping, though much of it was burned or ripped away. Raw wounds, some almost healed, marred the being's scaled skin. Then it started to speak in a language neither of them understood.

"Dude, can you translate?"

I know this language, Dude said. *Let him talk.*

Emily arrived then, cursing loudly, complaining about the inequities of second-rate travel.

"Every time," she said. "You have the warp drives and I'm puttering behind you like a 1920's biplane. I'm tired of it."

"Em, hush," Billy said.

He climbed into the crater and lifted the alien gently so that it could sit up.

Dude performed translator duties for both of them.

"They are coming," the creature said. "The enemy. They are

coming for your world."

"What enemy?" Billy said. "Who's coming?"

"You need to be ready, you should prepare . . ."

"Prepare for what?" Billy said.

"This sounds as terrible as it could possibly be," Jane said.

"Dude, I need some help here," Billy said.

Remember, when we first met, I told you that you had a nemesis, and you had no idea who it was? Dude said.

Billy felt a sinking feeling in the pit of his stomach. "Oh, boy," he said.

Your nemesis is coming, Dude said. *This being is another of us, a Luminae and a host. And they have traveled to warn us. The nemesis is on the way to Earth.*

"And they're from outer space?" Billy said.

Unfortunately, Dude said.

"Emily!" Billy yelled. "You had to make that joke about traveling to outer space, didn't you?"

"Let's pretend I didn't," Emily said. "What do we do now?"

"We get ready," Billy said.

A Brief Interview with Author Matthew Phillion

When you write about superheroes, it pretty much goes without saying that you eventually need to address time travel.

Matthew Phillion: Time travel, alternate timelines, and superheroes are inherently linked together. Whether you're talking straight up time travel like "Days of Future Past" or "Elseworlds" style stories like "The Nail" or "Red Son," some of the most powerful and important superhero stories directly talk about other futures, or other presents.

Did you think you'd get there this soon in *the Indestructibles* series?

MP: I knew the first few story arcs for *the Indestructibles* before I even sat down to write Book 1, to be honest. I debated quite a bit between time travel and another time-honored superhero story tradition as the follow up for *Breakout*, but taking the kids into the future just felt right for Book 3.

Did you know exactly how time travel would work in *the Indestructibles* universe?

MP: There was a balance between needing to make things up as I went along and actual time travel theory (I love that there is legitimate time travel theory out there to read). To tell you the truth I didn't want to make too many hard rules too soon. Time travel is so big, and has the potential to be so complicated, I didn't want to tie my hands for future stories.

You take the team to some dark places in the third book. What was the reasoning behind that?

MP: Any series about young heroes is also about growing up. A story about time travel allows for some really interesting questions to be asked—what if you don't like what you've become as an adult? What if this future version of you has made decisions you don't agree with? And if you don't like the future you see in this grown-up version of yourself, what can you do to build a better future for yourself?

The characters say several times that you can't change the past, you can only make things different. Will *the Indestructibles* walk away from Book 3 different?

MP: One of the things about Jane, Billy, Titus, Kate, and Emily that I truly love is that they grow and change with each new book in ways I never expected when I set out to create them. The things they experience in this alternate timeline will have a lasting impact on how they view the world, and especially how they view their own actions. They've always wanted to make a better world—with *The Entropy of Everything,* they realize they can also strive to make a better future as well.

Also by Matthew Phillion

Novels in the Indestructibles Series – in print and e-book formats

The Indestructibles (Book 1)
The Indestructibles: Breakout (Book 2)
The Entropy of Everything (the Indestructibles Book 3)
Like a Comet (the Indestructibles Book 4)

Tales from the Indestructiverse

Echo and the Sea

The Indestructibles One-Shots (digital shorts)

The Soloist
Gifted
Blood & Bone
The Monsters We Make
Krampus in the City
Roll for Initiative (an Indestructibles Story) – also available in print

The Dungeon Crawlers Novella Series

The Player's Guide to Dungeon Crawling (The Dungeon Crawlers Book 1)
The Dungeoneer's Bestiary (The Dungeon Crawlers Book 2)
The Ghoul Slayer's Guidebook (The Dungeon Crawlers Book 3)

www.ingramcontent.com/pod-product-compliance
Lightning Source LLC
Chambersburg PA
CBHW030414180626
46812CB00005B/2006